RASPUTIN'S NEPHEW
A PSI-FI THRILLER
Marc J. Seifer

Rudy Styne Quadrilogy
Book I

Lynn Sevigny

Doorway Press
Box 32, Kingston, RI 02881

RASPUTIN'S NEPHEW
Rudy Styne Quadrilogy Book I
Copyright © 2019 Marc J. Seifer

ISBN: 978-1-931261-21-0

Library of Congress Control Number: 2016903714

Published by **Doorway Press Box 32, Kingston, RI 02881, USA.**

Printed on acid-free paper.

The characters and events in this book are fictitious. Any similarity to real persons, living or dead, is coincidental and equivocally intended by the author.

Doorway Press
2019

First Edition

Cover art & Tarot Cards: *Lynne Sevigny*
Cover design: Devin Keithley

mseifer@verizon.net
MarcSeifer.com

A Doorway Press Edition

Also by MARC SEIFER

Non-fiction
Wizard: The Life & Times of Nikola Tesla
The Definitive Book of Handwriting Analysis
Framed! Murder, Corruption & A Death Sentence In Florida
(with Stephen Rosati)
Transcending the Speed of Light: Quantum Physics & Consciousness
Nikola Tesla: The Man Who Harnessed Niagara Falls
Where Does Mind End?

Editor-in-chief
MetaScience: A New Age Journal on Consciousness, Vol's 1-3
Journal of American Society of Professional Graphologists, Vol's 1-5

Screenplays
Tesla: The Lost Wizard (Tim Eaton, co-author)
Hail to the Chief

Fiction
The Rudy Styne Quadrilogy:
I Rasputin's Nephew
II Doppelgänger
III Crystal Night
IV Fate Line

PRAISE FOR MARC SEIFER'S BOOKS

DOPPELGÄNGER & CRYSTAL NIGHT

Dr. Seifer's novels **DOPPELGÄNGER & CRYSTAL NIGHT** contained some fascinating and well-researched details about World Wars I & II that added richness to the narrative. He displays admirable ambition and he crosses genres ably in his quest to tell a large-scale story in the second two novels of his **QUADRILOGY**. Using an impressive amount of research, the author paints a wide panorama which includes an inside look at Nazi Germany as a Jewish family struggles to maintain their small prestigious airline in an anti-Semitic environment. But these two books are not just rooted in the past. There is also a modern story, a search by the protagonist, news reporter Rudy Styne, to uncover a master hacker who is attempting to take over the internet as he is also moved to discover who is German double is and who his biological parents really are. Yes, there are a number of diverse paths in this complex tale, but Seifer deftly brings all threads together in a satisfying way that enriches, because the reader, not only gets to learn a lot about real history, namely how both world wars were conducted from the German perspective, but also experiences the complex emotional strain of a family doing their best to maintain their assets and survive in a hostile environment. Given the novel's breadth, the pace is quick, particularly considering the myriad topics covered and the large cast of characters. Overall, this is an imaginative, worthy and ambitious work.

Compilation of comments from New York City Editors.

RASPUTIN'S NEPHEW

An espionage thriller, (a la Tom Clancy).... You write with great intelligence and authority. *Nicolette Phillips, New Vision.*

This is a terrifically original book, with elements of satire as well.
Dr. Stanley Krippner, author of *Song of the Siren*

As one who believes that good science fiction writers are the precursors of things to come, your novel's early pages are causing me the first symptoms of Future Shock...Your writing about the psychic world seems so precise that it seems more real time than a work of fiction. Can I assume you are writing fiction or are your fictionalizing real historical events? *Al Perry*

Like a journey through the Major Arcana [of the Tarot], *Rasputin's Nephew* takes the reader into the bizarre and mind-boggling world of the paranormal. I enjoyed Marc Seifer's book thoroughly.

Uri Geller, Paranormalist Extraordinaire

DOPPELGÄNGER

In *Doppelgänger,* Marc Seifer runs a story of the 20th century through German eyes together with a contemporary U.S. murder mystery set in the cyber-world. He masterfully ties the two stories together through Abe Maxwell (b. 1906) who is about 98 years old in the contemporary story. Seifer tied Abe to both Rudy Styne, the hero, from the U.S. to Rolf Linzman, Rudy's sometimes protagonist, of Germany.

Richard Vangermeersch, Professor Emeritus University of Rhode Island

CRYSTAL NIGHT

I had to tell you how much I am enthralled with *Crystal Night!* You are an incredible chronicler your knowledge is vast! You have woven such minute detail into the tapestry or rather web of the novel. It lives for me, that is the [Germany] and times I remember.

I rush through supper to get comfortable on the sofa with The Book. I just can't put it down.

Gloria McMurrough, Admissions Office, Roger Williams University

The overall presentation of the trials that faced a Jewish-German family, during the rise of Anti-Semitism after World War I, is stirring on how the triumph of faith and spirit, can overcome the suffering of a strong, resilient people during one of the darkest periods in modern history.

Edith Moraglia

FRAMED! MURDER, CORRUPTION &
A DEATH SENTENCE IN FLORIDA
with Stephen Rosati

A story that must be told!

Robert Leuci, "Prince of the City"

A fascinating and exceptionally documented case study that reads like a best-seller.

Midwest Book Review

Amazingly readable book - a true page-turner that had my complete attention from the first page to the last!

5 Star review Amazon.com

WIZARD: THE LIFE & TIMES OF NIKOLA TESLA
BIOGRAPHY OF A GENIUS

Seifer's vivid, revelatory, exhaustively researched biography rescues pioneer inventor Nikola Tesla from cult status and restores him to his rightful place as a principal architect of the modern age.... Seifer provides the fullest account yet of Tesla as an entrepreneur, experimental physicist and inventor.

Boxed & Starred, Publisher's Weekly

Seifer's biography rescues [Tesla] from oblivion, bringing back to life the amazingly creative intellect that gave us fluorescent lighting, wireless communication, cheap electrical power and the remote control. But Seifer also resurrects the wounded, self-destructive personality who never recovered from the loss of a favored older brother and who spiraled into weird obsessions, mental collapse and poverty as he watched other men use his inventions to win fame and riches. Seifer does an admirable job of explaining his subject's technical feats and analyzing his psychological idiosyncrasies. Tinged with pathos, this meticulously researched biography deserves attention from all who would understand the human tragedies played out in the shadows of our neon culture.

Bryce Christianson, Booklist

Marc Seifer is an excellent writer and scholar, who has produced a wonderfully readable and illuminating biography of one of the most intriguing men of this century.... mak[ing] us understand not only the man, but also the times in which he lived.... [a] masterpiece.

Nelson DeMille, New York Times best-selling author

Seifer paints a picture of Tesla that anyone familiar with the life of someone such as Orson Welles will recognize. Here was a man who peaked early, traveled in famous company.... and started believing his own press hype. That made him spend the rest of his life trying to score another universe-changing coup..... *Wizard* does a pretty good job of placing Tesla within the firmament of inventors, thinkers and futurists. With Seifer's scholarship to build on, anyone reconstructing those dizzy years of invention and litigation at the turn of the century would be foolish to try and leave out Nikola Tesla.

Winston-Salem NC Journal

Underneath the layers ... the core of Seifer's book is a serious piece of scholarship.

Scientific American

I highly recommend this biography of a great technologist.

A.A. Mullin, US Army Space & Strategic Defense Command.

THE DEFINITIVE BOOK OF HANDWRITING ANALYSIS

Altogether this book rises like a lighthouse out of the morass of the other graphology publications in the USA. The author presents a great array of American handwritings on astoundingly high level. Although the author only had access to English sources, in spite of this, it is amazingly comprehensive. Maybe this book gets into the hands of one or another university professors and if so, it may help to break up his/her prejudices and this could lead to a raise in standards of academic psychology in the America.

Helmut Ploog, Ph.D., Editor-in-Chief of the German handwriting journal
Angewandte Graphologie und Personlichkeits Diagnostik.

TRANSCENDING THE SPEED OF LIGHT
Consciousness, Quantum Physics & the Fifth Dimension

I highly recommend this book to any and all readers who are seriously interested in the puzzling problem of the nature of mind and consciousness.... Marc's epochal achievement will offer thoughts and areas of new thought to the reader for many decades to come.

Col. Tom Bearden (retired) Author of Excalibur Briefing

How is it possible for consciousness to exist in the physical universe? This is the classic mind-body problem that has eluded philosophers for many generations. Now, it appears that answers are within reach -- provided that one is willing to explore unorthodox approaches. This is exactly what author Marc Seifer has done. The depth of his scholarship and the clarity of his thinking make this book a worthwhile read for anyone interested in the frontiers of consciousness research.

Jeffrey Mishlove, Ph.D., Dean of Consciousness Studies, University of
Philosophical Research

Happy is the man that hearkeneth to me,
Watching daily at my gates,
Waiting at the posts of my doors.
For whoso findeth me findeth life

PROVERBS 8:34

* * *

For Lois, Uri & Robert

* * *

RASPUTIN'S NEPHEW
A PSI-FI THRILLER

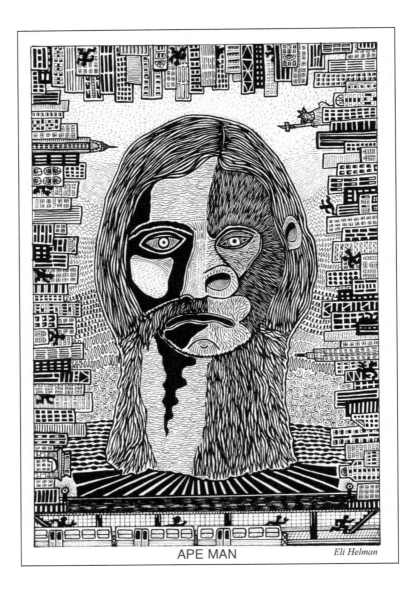

APE MAN

Eli Helman

PROLOGUE

It was that brief period after the collapse of the Soviet Union, before Google was Google, ebooks and smartphones and before the Internet was truly ubiquitous. Right-wing extremist Petar Bonzovalivitch had waited his entire life for an opportunity like this. Although Mother Russia had now annexed Crimea, Eastern Ukraine, Belarus and Estonia, the new empire was in turmoil, having, once again overextended, and the time was right for Bonzovalivitch to make his move. With the West propelling towards alternative energies such as wind, solar and geothermal, and worse, plug-in cars, the New Russia had seen it's massive oil-based revenues go into free fall. With the reputation of the brazen sitting premier in the crapper, corruption at an all time high and the stock market at an all time low, the world community had finally had its fill. How many more dead journalists would there have to be before critical mass would overturn the ruling power? The cold-hearted total since 1993 was over 200, and still counting.

The first major attack occurred during the siege of Ostankino Television Center, *Igor Belozyorov and five other TV cameramen and reporters all shot or killed in one day. Thus began an unprecedented vendetta against the press which included the assassination of Sergey Bogdanovsky, another TV newscaster in Moscow, Marina Iskanderova, the TV journalist, slain in her home in Nadym, Igor Domnikov, investigative reporter, beaten to death with a hammer in Moscow, Iskandar Khatloni, reporter for* Radio Free Europe, *bludgeoned to death with an axe in his apartment in Moscow, Aleksei Sidorov, newspaper editor of* The Independent Daily, *stabbed to death by two assailants along the River Volga, 800 kilometers from Moscow, Uri Shchekochikhin, deputy editor of* Novaya Gazeta, *poisoned to death in Moscow, Dmitry Shvets, of* TV-21, *shot to death in Murmansk, Ilyas Shurpayev of* Channel One, *strangled to death in Moscow, Nadezhda Chaikova, newspaper reporter, executed with a shot to the back of the head in the Chechen village of Geikhi and Magomed Yevloyev, website designer critical of the Kremlin, killed in police custody in Ingushetia, a Russian republic.*

This string of executions was followed by two more killings that were so dastardly as to make international headlines: Anna Politkovskaya, the highly popular newspaper reporter, with a book published by Random House exposing Russian corruption, who had already eschewed numerous death threats, brazenly shot in an elevator in her apartment building in Moscow, and the in-your-face, I dare you to do anything about it *assassination of Lieutenant Colonel Alexander Litvinenko, ex-KGB officer turned author, taking on the Russian high command, poisoned to death with a miniscule amount of a rare radio-active isotope in Great Britain. Litvinenko's rapid demise was covered in the world press, a bald-headed impending corpse staring tellingly into a camera, accusing the former KGB high command, wiped from the realm of the living within days.*

And that was just the journalists. Hit men had been hired to also knock off leading billionaires, bankers, corporate magnates, heads of unions and vice-governors. Anyone opposed to the prevailing government or with strong ties to the West was a potential target. But it seemed the West had had enough. Litvenko's death had been the high-water mark of brazen-sanctioned annihilation. Perhaps if the world economy had been on an uptick, the Russian premier may have been able to ride out the storm, but financial markets were in ruins, flurries of factory closings, fires in Moscow and a record heat with few air conditioners available were further crippling the economy and continuing bad publicity had taken its toll.

To maintain power, a new more clandestine measure had to be taken. Now was the time to institute a covert assassination team that would be virtually untraceable, the latest weapon: psionic warfare. Timing was everything, so Petar Bonzovalivitch sent in a proposal and set up a top secret meeting with the High Command. Accompanied by his little army of neuroscientists and psionic soldiers, Bonzo the Pipe Dreamer, as he was affectionately known, was able to demonstrate psychokinetic feats, such as using mental energy to levitate small objects, hypnotize subjects, blank out smart phones and erase computer hard drives, and thus he was able to convince the great power that this virgin method of brain manipulation would be more effective with little chance of backlash. Added to the list of targets would be neuroscientists and psychophysicists from the West, any researcher who had a chance of discovering the technique that would reorient the balance of power back to where it belonged.

MODERN TIMES

NEW YORK CITY: CUSP OF THE NEW AGE

The rhythmic clang thwacked his slumbering brain, jostling the man into a semi-awakened state. Groping the darkness, beyond the alarm clock, his hand settled on the telephone, which rattled in its cradle until he fumbled it to his ear.

"Rudy, are you OK?" A voice sounded uneasy on the other side of the line.

He blinked at the red clock numbers as they came into focus: 5:42. "Chess, is that you?" Stunned, he sat there trying to clear the cobwebs. "One second, babe, give me one second." *Why had his girlfriend called at such an ungodly hour?*

"I'm so glad you're there. I just had this terrible dream that you were run down by a creepy grocery van. I'm so relieved you're all right. It seemed so real.... Is Vermont still on for the weekend?"

"Are you kidding, absolutely not. Our relationship is over."

"Great, it will be good to get away. Be careful today, hon." Chessie hung up the phone with a smile. She was looking forward to their getaway.

Rolling out of bed, waking man stumbled into the bathroom to adjust the shower. It was another work day, a Tuesday to be exact. As he waited for the dribbling water to slowly warm, he listened to the occasional truck clatter over a patch of cobblestone which lay at the base of his building. Gazing up, the 34-year-old man stared at yet another irrepressible roach scamper along the top of the tile, a quarter inch from the ceiling. "Jeeze," he mumbled, as he grabbed the back end of a razor, and stood upon the toilet seat to crush the bastard vermin. Disgusted, he reached for a Kleenex to scoop up the slimy mess and flush it down. He pushed aside the plastic curtain to step gingerly into the still cool spray. God, he hated the plumbing in this place, he thought, as he washed away the night and thought about Chessie's odd call.

Grabbing yesterday's towel, Rudy turned the radio on to listen to the news. Something about jazz and an Alaskan airplane crash and two dead congressmen. He heard no more, as he stopped quickly to fix some stale toast and reheated coffee as still in a daze he gazed drearily into the murky gray which clung like a cape over the predawn skyline; and before he knew it, the metropolitan reporter was down the stairs and outside, dodging a yellow cab to cross the street to catch the downtown local. Rudy waved hello to Carl, the grocery man's son, who was just emerging from his bright white delivery truck, when suddenly the rattle of dull green-paneled van could be gleaned screaming dizzily down the shiny cobblestones. Rudy caught Carl's eye turn to horror. Brakes jammed as the delinquent van skidded before impact. Carl's body lay smashed, sandwiched between the two now silent vehicles, his package of groceries scattered, the dreams of his father shattered.

TAJIKISTAN

TWO YEARS AGO

High in the Hindu Kush, along the Baroghil Pass, Chi Jhenghis enjoyed milking his father's shaggy yak herd in 50° below zero weather. Even as a small child he had loved the extreme cold, the smell of frozen shrubs, the crisp lingering echoes and stinging shivers of chilled winds. Alone in the frozen crystal barn, the Tajik youth rhythmically tugged on the animal's firm pink teats as whitish gray fluid squirted into his rusted metal pail. Concentrating on his job, Chi did not hear the snow-crunching footsteps approach until his eye caught the long shadow growing under the barn's wooden saloon doors. They swung open as he heard his grandfather's voice.

"Chi," grandpa said, "hurry up, or you'll miss your mother's blood pudding!" The old farmer's head remained in shadow as the backlit sun cast yellow shafts through his rugged woolen-hooded parker. He smiled deeply, his 80-year-old eyelashes glistening with melted snowflakes in the dawn light; the breath of each word hovered in misty rainbows as grandpa moved forward in a steady bowlegged flow.

Eeeeeeeeeeeeeeeeeeee. Both men froze as the shrieking scream of a lone timber wolf pierced the air. There had been reports of six villagers missing within the last three weeks. Many of the old women blamed it on animal spirits; but the old man sensed a different presence. A descendant of Genghis Khan, who ruled the region in the 13th century, the elderly Mongolian could smell the evil of deeper danger, *human head hunters,* modern technological warriors who had overrun his country these past score years.

"Chi," he said, his manner changing as swiftly as the wind, "prepare for the shadow of our Great One. Hurry along before your pudding turns to ice." He grabbed the youngster by the protective collar and huddled him back to the house.

Chi's mother, father, two brothers and four sisters had already started nibbling dried strips of squirrel meat as he and grandpa entered the warm kitchen. Father added more coal to the cast iron stove.

"Burrr," Mother Jhenghis said. "Close that door and bring yak's milk here. You must have our cool blood pudding son, before hot potato soup. We don't want your teeth to cold crack from the bite of winter's chill." She smiled broadly revealing a full set of saw-toothed incisors. The children giggled gleefully.

Mother Jhenghis reached into their live food cage and grabbed a squirming squirrel firmly by the scruff of its neck. As she held the chubby rodent over the milk pail with her left hand, her right clasped their sacred dinner knife. Plunging the blade in under the chin, she slit through to the pulsing aorta and heart. Bleeding red juices drained into the sloshing milk, as one of the sisters stirred the now pink coagulation with a brown wooden spoon. This was the family's favorite breakfast, a rare treat for midwinter.

Bang! A shot exploded, splintering open the front door as four armed Ukrainian soldiers smashed their way in, and forced the family against the back wall. Still holding their food bowls, three of the four sisters shook in unison by the clan's live food cage as the remaining squirrels tore around it in a maddened pace. Father and Grandpa Jhenghis turned squarely to face their enemy.

"Come here," one of the soldiers motioned to Chi and his two brothers. The trooper whipped his rifle across their behinds as he separated the boys and started them for the door. "Recruits," he mumbled, pointing his weapon at Mr. Jhenghis' face, which scowled grimly in return. Grandpa reached for the sacred knife. Ukrainian weapons spit forth, disgorging the old man with six lead slugs. Red gobs sputtered from the heart wounds as grandpa shuddered briefly.

Avoiding the eyes of the family, the commander threw back the youngest son, handcuffed the older two and marched them out onto the cold tundra. A transport vehicle rolled into sight as black army boots kicked the brothers on board. Chi Jhenghis tried fruitlessly to get one last look at his home, but he would never see his family again.

* * *

...the Knicks out at the Utah Jazz, and in the news, two congressmen are dead in a plane crash in Alaska. Details after the weather.

Hadn't he just heard that bit of information in a dream, Rudy thought, as he slammed his hand on the radio timer to get his extra ten minutes. But he knew it was too late. He was awake. He tumbled off the mattress and staggered into the shower and adjusted the knob as he tried to rectify the moment. Warm trickles of refreshing water soothed the effects of a troubled sleep.

Grabbing a towel and lathering his face, he ran a razor blade over it, as he stared at the eyes in the bathroom mirror shaking his head in disbelief. A timeless moment of self-reflection, and then out the door and down the stairs. He disliked the elevator in the morning.

Entering the morning air he said, "Hi," to Carl, who stood at the grocery stand, as he paused to purchase the *Trib.* A yellow cab zipped past as his mind suddenly flashed back to Chessie's odd call, and the feeling that he had experienced aspects of this very street scene in a dream just a little while ago. Slapping some coins on the counter and nodding good-bye to the boy, he stuffed the daily into a big coat pocket, and followed the commuting hoards down the cold clammy subway stairway, past a fresh pool of urine, and over to a comfortable spot by the slick steel tracks. An express train shrieked by: *WHHHHaaaaa, ch, ch, ch, ch, ch.* A few minutes later the local arrived, and with a flowing push the sardine subway car filled rapidly to capacity. *Chug...Chug...Chug...* flickering fluorescent platforms, multicolored movie posters, magazine and trashy doughnut stands checkered by.

The seasoned journalist perused the notes on his laptop, a story about Nielson ratings and the impact the new use of frontal nudity had on TV. He began to punch in a few ideas as the train halted at his stop, and he emerged as one from a school of spawning salmon to begin the new workday. By 10:15 coffee break, the dream about Carl's death and Chessie's call was just another anecdote to tell his co-workers.

MORNING IN CHICAGO

Craning his neck to watch the stacked planes circle from his tourist seat window, Chi Jhenghis fantasized about nothing. After his craft touched down at O'Hare, he grabbed his carry-on along with the hordes, deplaned, and breezed through the airport. With his fur toque and long herringbone coat, he could almost pass for anyone else.

Not even taking a moment to brace himself before he stepped into blustery winds, Chi began his trek through the parking lot to make his way to the waiting car. He glanced at the snow piled around him and became faintly aware of an old memory trace, his father's wooden barn encased in diamond-like ice. It had been two years since Chi was taken from his Tajik home. Now he was a soldier, thirty pounds heavier, much stronger.

Saddled with high heels, three bags and a bulky faux fur coat, an inexperienced traveler slipped on ice and careened into Chi, bags flying in all directions. "I'm sorry," she tried to say, half expecting the big man to help her retrieve her things, but Chi marched on, unfazed.

The bald Ukrainian greeted Chi with a firm stare as he reached above the back of the soldier's neck to apply steady Pavlovian pressure. Dr. Alexi Patrenko was proud of his work. He pressed another button and Chi took his seat on the passenger side. Traffic was miserable. As Dr. Patrenko fought the weather and wind to lurch out of the parking lot, he steered onto the boulevard to make his way past the city to the Loop, and thought about his fat partner, Vladimir Kopensky, now, too afraid to leave his safe haven in St. Petersburg. Chi sat motionless as his driver motored along Lake Michigan, turned up the midway and onto the campus of the University of Chicago.

Guiding the car under the elevated railway, Dr. Patrenko spoke in Uzbek as he circled the site to find a place to park his car. "After this run, you will be on your own, Chi Jhenghis," the doctor said. "You have to be in New York this afternoon." Finding a spot, Patrenko parked catty corner from the library. "Remove your hat."

Chi took it off, revealing his plasticized forehead. The doctor reached to the top of the soldier's partially removed skull, checked the computer chip in the cerebellum, and adjusted the wires and dials. As the Tajik placed the toque back on his head, the Ukrainian parapsychologist reached inside a black briefcase and removed a small control panel, which resembled a miniaturized pocket calculator. "Chi," Patrenko said, "you know what to do."

The Tajik stepped from the car, crossed the street, walked up the stairs and entered the library. Monitoring the man's robotic-like brain-waves on his portable oscilloscope, Alexi Patrenko subconsciously caressed his bare skull with his free left hand, triggering tingles.

Mechanically, Chi stepped up to the computer bay, logged on and punched in for a search of the field of parapsychology. Dutifully, he wrote down the call slip for Gregory Hereward's book *Eurasian Parapsychology* and then by touching the screen, sent a cybernetic jolt which effectively erased all mention of the topic on the library's hard drive.

Something in his manner attracted the attention of Miss Elderberry, a librarian who had worked the stacks for half a century. Perched behind the rungs of a nearby stairway, like an egret tracking a water snake, she followed Chi about the corridors pretending to dust the shelves as he roamed for the text he was looking for. She watched the man find his prize. Deftly, he plucked it from a shelf and marched himself back to the entrance. Waiting for his turn quietly, he handed the book to a waiting attendant.

"I'll take this one," the old biddy said, as she scooted in front of the trainee and eyed Chi's library card warily.

"Of course, Miss Elderberry, if you insist," the attendant responded testily. Chi moved to pick the book back up.

"I'm sorry," the librarian declared, "this is a reference work and cannot be removed from the building." Snatching it back before he could respond, Miss Elderberry stood on her small haunches and glared. Having not been programmed for this contingency, bewilderment and then rage erupted in Chi's preternatural brain.

Back at the car, Patrenko watched with great concern his soldier's brain-waves change radically and he knew there was trouble. Adjusting two dials to *increase* Chi's telekinetic capabilities before he jumped out, Patrenko moved swiftly towards the library, just as his soldier emerged in triumph, a cold smirk on his lips. Chi handed the book to the scientist as they made their way back to the car.

As library computers crashed and nearby cellular phones blanked, Miss Elderberry was rushed to the emergency room, having suffered a massive stroke. Two nurses stood beside her waiting for the doctor to arrive to read her chart.

Dressed in usual white lab coat attire, stethoscope around his neck, clipboard in hand, the doctor looked down at the old lady. Enunciating each word carefully, he spoke in non-committal fashion. "You should be able to walk again within six weeks," he said matter-of-factly. Slowly, Miss Elderberry's head lifted towards the doctor, fearful sadness expressed in her remaining good eye.

REALITY, MR. STYNE?

During the surprisingly heated discussion, the coffee-break had stretched to twenty-five minutes. Sally-Ann insisted that Rudy was telepathic, but he doubted it. ESP was too much hogwash. It was just an unusual coincidence. Most everyone agreed.

"I'm telling you Rudy," Sally-Ann's round breasts bounced with each emphasized syllable, "you're psychic. These things happen to me all the time." She became suddenly quiet, afraid that she'd said too much.

"They do?" Rudy asked.

"They do?" Bill and Mary chimed in. "Like when?"

"Well," Sally-Ann paused. "I dream things before they happen. I do it all the time. Like this Alaskan plane crash--two nights ago I dreamt that Arnold Johnson and Jesse Patterson, you know, the two dead congressmen, were buried in an igloo!" Sally lowered her eyes.

"I think it means you've eaten too many Eskimo pies." Mort pinched the slight fold in her middle, and she slapped his hand away. She disliked Mort's constant touching, but aside from that, everyone got along quite well at the office. With all the kidding, everyone knew Sally-Ann had almost as many political contacts as John Hirshon, head of *The York Tribune.*

Mort feigned great hurt, as Bill and Mary cackled, yet Rudy remembered another detail of his dream about the radio announcement. He smiled at his coworkers, but this incident concerned him. "Prevision is not possible," he mumbled.

Talk finally meandered to the layout for this week's magazine, and the workers returned to their respective cubicles.

Rudy finished typing his outline. He had Nielsen ratings from the last two years, statistics on trends in TV viewing, and some spicy information about major shakeups at Transworld Communications. He was looking forward to seeing Captain Dean Whitmore, editor-in-chief of *Modern Times Magazine.* He approached the chief's door.

"Come in Rudolf," Captain Whitmore said dismally. He was staring absentmindedly at a framed picture of Mark Twain he had on the wall with an original signature attached expertly beneath. The captain wore his usual black bow tie, dark blue pinstriped suit, orange-and-white striped suspenders and brass-linked watch, yet something seemed out of place. He was usually chipper on Monday mornings, twenty-six sit-ups every day. At sixty-three, the editor-in-chief was a healthy specimen, swimming three times a week, thirty pushups on the other mornings. Although his fingernails were always clean and polished, he appeared to be a man who lived a rugged life. Whitmore turned to face Rudy. His sky-blue eyes seemed wistful. "Let's see, son, what have you got?" He managed to lift an eyebrow.

"What's wrong, captain?" Rudy asked.

"I saw a chap die this morning. It was my grocery boy--smashed by a gad-blasted delivery truck--green...splattered in red. Charlie was leaving for college next week. I've known him his whole life." Pausing to reflect, the captain added, "He was smiling at me right before he...was snuffed." The captain removed Twain's portrait, traced his fingers longingly along its frame, and then resolutely placed it in his drawer. "Let's see what you've got, son."

Rudy's eyes widened, his forehead furrowed. This was one too many coincidences for his liking.

"I'll be all right, Rudolf. I just liked the boy, and it was just so damn sudden. Yet when I think about it, it looked like it happened in slow motion. Now, let's see that Nielson article."

"Captain Whitmore," Rudy spoke before thinking, "I've been meaning to do a report on ESP in American society." It was almost as if he were watching someone else speak. "Can't you let Bill or Cal finish Nielson?"

"No, Styne, you finish it. Then talk to me about ESP." Captain's voice was stern, his sorrowful mood suddenly curbed.

An image of Buddha flashed through Rudy's mind. He could see the robed being glowing high on a mountain top. Rudy blinked, trying to pay attention, as Whitmore spoke again, "Sure, I guess you can do something on ESP when you finish this TV piece. Maybe you could link it to the new interest in Buddhism and gurus. It could be interesting."

Rudy had been out of therapy for over a year and a half now. Confused and somewhat troubled, he decided to call his psychiatrist, Ann Kaufmann. She had helped him sort out his false fears from his real ones, and except for that one moment of passion between them....No, he didn't really need her anymore, but he did miss discussing his dreams and revelations.

"Ann, this is Rudy Styne. Could we meet?"

"You're giving me your last name?"

"Well, I, er, it's been awhile."

"Is this a dinner proposal?"

"No, professionally."

"Oh, professionally. So, let's hear it."

"I have some dreams and things to talk over with you. I've had some, well...some, some...."

"Some what?"

"Psychic experiences," he blurted.

"I'm sorry, Rudy," she said, "That's a fucking can of worms. Call me when you need me; when you have real problems."

He had trouble understanding her callous response, and the use of profanity. Shouldn't she have realized that he had called her for a reason? She gave him pause, the anger in her voice, particularly when she heard what it was about. But, what could he do? He sloughed it off, and crossed her off his list.

Tall, slim and cheerful, Chessie had sparkled in their fresh romance. But as with most recent divorcees, he realized, that although the love was there, she was not ready to get serious. They had met by accident at a local coffee shop, having seen each other in the street for close to a year before smiles were converted into hello. Downtown, there are hundred of faces you see every day. No one says hello, there are too many faces. If she hadn't spilled coffee on his shirt sleeve, they probably would never have met. On their first magical date, he remembered how she nestled her head into his lap and hugged him tightly around the waist. "It's been too long," she whispered. In the midst of their passion there was a reverence that sealed their silent contract...only three months ago--it seemed like eons.

Anticipating Friday and their date to the hills of Vermont, Rudy tried with great effort to get this morning's events out of his mind. ESP, telepathy, the similarity between his dream and Chessie's, the psychiatrist's strange resistance to it. *Just a coincidence*, he told himself. *I'm thirty-four and never had an experience like this one,* he reasoned. *So naturally statistics predict that once every thirty-four years or so a strange occurrence will take place. Chance, that's settled.*

Rudy started for the library to research TV trends and censorship--some good photos of husbands and wives in separate beds, erotic Pepsi-cola ads...the whole story was written in his mind. It was just a three-block stroll.

Fifth Avenue bubbled with the fall styles: hip models with their long strides, iridescent body suits and black leather portfolios, chartreuse pimps in soft hats and velveteen pant-suits, old and young messengers weathered in blue jeans clutching paper brown packages, purplish gray-haired widows delicately dressed in white fox and mink, cyberpunk yuppies with their labret pins and cellular head-sets, double-breasted businessmen, hard-luck bums, DINKS, busses, cabs, stretchhh limos, luncheonettes, galleries, sidewalk newspaper and magazine stands and designer label boutiques. As he passed the shoeshine stands on 42nd and Fifth, a newspaper heading caught his eye:

TWO CONGRESSMEN DEAD
ESKIMOS AID IN SEARCH FOR BODIES

Three at a time Rudy scaled the marble steps of the library and took the elevator to the main reading room on the third floor. He passed the primitive art exhibit rather rapidly, a slight sense of compulsion to his gait. Walking to the information desk, he waited in line until a tall, big-boned woman with long sinewy forearms nodded him over. She peered over half-moon glasses that hung in suspension at the tip of her nose.

"Do you have any books on ESP?"

"Have you tried the computer," she said in a haughty Austrian accent.

Rudy pointed to the notice posted above the terminals. "The sign says they're having trouble picking up words that start with the letter E."

"Then try psionics," the lady huffed.

Rudy just stared. He did not understand. Intimidated, he did not want to inquire further. She smiled, pretending to be genuine.

"Psionics, as in parapsychology or the study of extrasensory perception. There are a number of researchers in Europe and even some here who are active in the field." She spoke offhandedly, yet he was visibly taken aback. As far as he could remember he had never heard the word psionic, and felt a little embarrassed.

"The P's are out, too, mam," said another attendant. "Seems like the whole interlibrary net is folding."

"Humph!" the librarian proclaimed. She stepped from behind the oak counter, glared down at Rudy, and led the way through a catacomb of back passageways, to a basement stairway, where he was told the antiquated card catalogue system was stored. He felt as if he were back in grade school, her large hips and long stride magnifying the effect, as he followed her down. She did not look back as she descended, merely assuming he would follow. An annoying Prussian power play, he thought, as he followed her into a large cellar crypt.

Extending her arms to indicate the entire old wooden catalogue, which to his great surprise was still intact, she led him to the aisle which had the p's. Pulling out a drawer that read *Penguin--Pygmy* she handed it over, wheeled and disappeared down a dark corridor, nowhere near the stairway they had just come down.

It struck Rudy as odd that the stack opened immediately to Psionic. There seemed to be a gap within the files. About four or five broken ringlets from the torn out cards still attached to the metal runner caught his eye. The first book he noticed was titled simply *Thought Transference* by Alfred Archer, MD., F.A.S., D.D., P.P., 1892, Appleton & Co., Boston. He wrote the call number. There was also a note to see *Mysticism, Parapsychology* and *Occultism*. He walked over to the appropriate cases. Under *Parapsychology* there were more cards ripped out and *Mysticism* also had blank spaces. Frustrated, Rudy finally turned to *Occultism*. These files looked intact. There were journals, pamphlets, and texts from nations as far away as Eastern Europe, South Africa, Iceland and Australia, and there were also a number of American sources. *Eurasian Parapsychology: Psionic Research Above the*

Khyber Pass by Gregory Hereward caught his eye. He wrote the call number, noting that chapters included research from former Soviet satellite countries like the Ukraine, Uzbekistan and Moldova as well as the Russian cities of Moscow, St. Petersburg and Vladivostok.

As he continued taking down all the titles and call numbers, Rudy heard a heavy wheezing behind him. It came from a tall Oriental man wearing an oversized herringbone coat and fur hat that covered his entire head. A small open area exposed an intense space for the eyes, nose, mouth and chin. Back and forth, back and forth he paced, the man occasionally brushing Rudy's coat with a swinging arm, as he pounded his fist into his other open hand...heavy breathing, back and forth. It seemed obvious that the man wanted this file rack.

The journalist wrote as fast as he could. Not wanting a confrontation, he turned to say, "I'll be just another minute." The thin slitted eyes did not focus directly into Rudy's, but seemed to look through and beyond him in a peculiar far-off stare.

The man continued to pound his fist. He had that vacant look that seemed to permeate so many of the more hardened New Yorkers. Rudy thought it best to move on. He picked up his call slips, and retraced his steps back to the request counter, as the Asian descended swiftly upon the rack. It struck the reporter as odd that with the library so warm, one should wear such a heavy fur hat.

Allowed only three books, Rudy handed the requests to the young fellow behind the counter for Archer's *Thought Transference, Eurasian Parapsychology* by Gregory Hereward, and one by a name he somehow vaguely recognized, B.K. Pine. Deftly, the attendant grabbed the sheet and placed it into a vacuum tube, which led directly to the stacks. "Here." He handed Rudy a call slip. "You're #192," he said, as he pointed. "Turn left at the hall."

Entering a huge Gothic room, Rudy was humbled by its size. He looked over seventy-five yards of heavy wooden tables and chairs, lights by each seat, 18th and 19th century texts around the walls, and in front, a huge electric board with numbers that lit up in red when the books arrived. He sat at the waiting bench...183, 191, 194, 178. His mind wandered.

There's something mythologically enjoyable about the New York Public Library, Rudy thought, *a certain timeless quality about its people.* Sitting by a golden lamp an elderly gentleman with a magnifying glass peered through endless stacks of ancient manuscripts. To his right...two pig-tailed girls chatted, a wrinkled lady furiously wrote, an Asian couple whispered in a strange language. Yes, there was a certain pleasure here for him; a free place quite close to an ideal. It was good that books could not be withdrawn from the library. One could only read them in this huge reading room, and its identical twin at the other side of the hall. The numbers lit up again rapidly, mostly in sequence: 189, 190, 192, 197, 186.

Rudy walked to the desk to pick up *Thought Transference* by Archer. The book was written in 1892. He noticed the address of the publisher, 192 Beacon Street, Boston, the same number as his call slip. *So what,* he thought.

Taking a seat close by, so as to quickly retrieve the other books as they arrived, he began to read through the section on controlled experiments in thought transference, which were conducted by such prominent members of the Royal Academy of Sciences as Lord Alfred Tennyson, Alfred Russell Wallace and Sir Oliver Lodge. Why hadn't he learned of these tests while studying in school?

192. Walking to the front, Rudy picked up the Pine book which dated from the 1950's, and also a yellow slip with scrawled handwriting: *Eurasian Parapsychology* by Gregory Hereward--MISSING. Disappointed that the only modern text he had called for was unavailable, he went back to his seat to read:

Introduction to Parapsychology
B.K. Pine
1937, DeBuke University Press
South Carolina

Meandering through the pages, he came across an unusual word: Psychokinesis or PK. He looked it up in the back dictionary of terms:
PSYCHOKINESIS: A mind over matter effect whereby an individual can influence an object without touching it, that is by *will power* alone. Synonym: **TELEKINESIS**

To Rudy's astonishment, the parapsychologist stated that he was able to train subjects to influence the outcome of a dice roll even when the subjects did not physically touch the dice. Pine had constructed a machine that performed the operation automatically. Here was clear-cut evidence that the mind, without the body, could influence matter, and the proof could be calculated through simple statistical means. Pine concluded by quoting the great turn-of-the-century scientist and psychic researcher Sir William Crookes, who once said, "I never said it was possible; I only said it was true."

Rudy looked down at his notes. *Could man really be psychic?* he asked himself. *Could I be?*

Why yes, of course! he tried.

This answer had a telling affect upon his world view. He stared at a pencil lying on the table, and considered the possibility of moving it by thought power alone. His eyes explored its beveled cylindrical shape, and he thought, *How could I go through thirty-four years, a human of the Earth, study journalism at Columbia, interview some of the great leaders in America and Europe, and not know that psychic ability had been studied and achieved in laboratory experiments countless times over the last 100 odd years. Something is amiss.* Styne reasoned this way for timeless moments of self-reflection, all the while trying mentally to move that pencil. The more he thought about the actuality of man's supersenses, the more the pencil refused to roll. His ego began to dissolve and a giant chasm appeared in its stead.

What kind of a world are we in? Waves of self-doubt began to overtake him. He felt for a moment as if he might crumble. He did not know what he was. As in a dream, he began to view the faceless crowds as reflections of his own ignorance. *What is man?* he asked. *What is this man? Who* am *I?*

Not only had well-known scientists established that thought transference was a fairly easy ability to muster up, but some important laws concerning its *modus operandi* had also been uncovered. He felt betrayed by a lopsided society, a world that had somehow kept this information from him for all the years of his life. His self-concept began to dissolve.

The loudspeaker blared: *Five Minutes, Please Return All Books To The Counter.* Rushing past the guard, Rudy ran down the stairs that led to the Occult card rack to take down the names of all the books he had missed. His purposeful movements blinded him from the exiting people. He opened the rack with anticipation.

The entire Occult section was gone!

A guard took the rack and nudged him to a hallway. It all happened before he had time to comprehend. He felt dizzy as he tried to talk to the emotionless man-machine. "I'm sorry, sir," the guard said, guiding Rudy all the way to the elevator. "You come back tomorrow." Rudy picked up his jacket at the coatroom, and accidentally walked out with the Archer book. The night air and unexpected darkness made Rudy feel alone. He was dizzy from the entire episode and mentally exhausted from all the reading. He latched on to the bus-stop sign for support, regaining some semblance of stability as the vehicle arrived. Climbing aboard, he grabbed the first available seat, and then noticed the book he had forgotten to return, was still in his hand. He began to read the section titled *Levels of Mind*: "What one man thinks, all men think at deeper levels. The fact is, we are at one with the Universal Mind."

Contemplating these words, he stepped off the bus at 14th Street just as his girlfriend appeared from the subway exit. Chessie's green eyes seemed to radiate from her brisk walk up the subway steps. Her light brown hair was tied in a sparkling red bandanna, fur lined boots and suede coat accenting her assured stride. Without breaking rhythm, she draped her arm around Rudy's waist as if it was the most natural thing in the world to do.

"Chess, do you think that the mind of man is telepathic?"

"Of course we're telepathic. How do you think Jean Dixon predicted John Kennedy's assassination?"

"You don't believe that *Public Enquirer* garbage, do you?" He turned to face her, and she twirled to respond, but kept walking.

"Well, some of it must be true," she said walking backwards then twirling forwards. "How else can you explain how we found each other! Just like Bogey and Bacall!"

"Lunt and Fontaine."

"Moe and Larry."

"Abbot and Curley."

"All right, all right," Chessie said, as they climbed the three steps to the front door of her building and entered. "Now you're getting silly." Fishing for her keys from her low-slung fabric bag, she opened the large wooden front door.

"Silly? Moe and Larry! You think I didn't get that? But I want to change the subject."

"To Harpo and Zeppo?" She raised her eyebrows.

He followed her up a flight of stairs to her apartment. Her eyes flicked to his as she turned the key.

"No, to this morning. I think I had a telepathic dream with you," he said seriously.

"An astral traveling Peeping Tom?" she teased. Chessie placed her things on a front counter, and led Rudy down the short hallway which led to her modest brownstone flat.

"No, really."

"Sure, sure."

"You called me this morning at 5 AM to see if I was OK. Why did you do that?"

"More like quarter to six."

"More like middle of the frigging night."

"Well, at least you didn't say *fucking*," Chessie chastised sarcastically. "Because I was worried about you." She reached over and pinched Rudy's cheek as if he were a little boy.

"I'm serious," he said. "My editor saw a kid he knew get run over by a van today."

"Just like my dream! Only it was you that was run over."

"And you mentioned a van, didn't you?"

"Yes."

"And what color was it?"

"Green."

"I knew it! The same color as the one that killed that kid. You think that could be a coincidence! And, furthermore, not that I'm complaining, but you have never called me before at that time."

"Maybe we both saw the same TV show last night."

"Captain Whitmore saw his grocery boy get hit by a green delivery truck this morning." Rudy paused to let it sink in. "He's dead, Chess, just like in our dream. The boy's dead."

"My god!" Chessie spun away, and shook her head from side to side. Turning back she said, "Then why," she began firmly, "did you get run over in one dream, and the grocery kid got it in the other?" Her voice rose at the end of the sentence, as she realized that the incidents were remarkably similar.

"It's OK when it happens to Jean Dixon," she continued, "but it's kinda scary when...Rudy, do you really think it could be telepathy?"

"I don't know, Chess, I just don't know."

Nudging him to the kitchen, for she had a night class to attend, Chessie had Rudy wash the spinach while she pulled out a large wooden bowl and meticulously prepared mushroom salad. Adding olives, cherry tomatoes and the spinach Rudy had washed, she placed the salad on an old oak table that had come with the apartment. Opening cupboards that reminded her of Cape Cod windows, she gathered the plates, her grandmother's, the ones with the little purple flowers along the rim, wine glasses and silverware and neatly set the table. "May I?" She poured the wine, and used two large wooden tongs to place a sizeable helping onto his plate.

Rudy doused his dish with salad dressing, grabbed a fork and began to eat.

"Why don't you just get a shovel?"

"OK, OK, I'll try to eat more slowly."

"That's not the point, Rudy."

"Well then, what is the point?" He stabbed a tomato from her salad bowl.

"To taste it," she said, as she grabbed the tomato from his fork and stuffed it in his mouth. His tongue searched her fingers as their eyes met. Her cheeks flushed. She reached over and gave him a kiss, her lips lingering softly, and then she turned to check the clock.

With Chessie's pottery class at 8:00, Rudy saw it as a good time to go over to the 23rd Street Library, a branch he knew had late hours. There, he could return the Archer book, and also maybe locate a copy of Hereward's Eurasian text. They kissed and parted at the front door.

"Half a buck for a guzzler, brother?" A dirty bearded bum with bulging bloodshot eyes stepped out to block him, grabbing his cuff with a trembling grey hand. Rudy cut left and kept moving. Trying to avoid eye-contact, he could not help but notice lime green slime oozing from the drunkard's forehead and tear ducts. Armed with crumpled bag and menacing gait, the vagabond followed yelling after him, "Fifty cents for a lousy beer, you fucking bastard...Cheap bastard." Rudy picked up his pace, half running to his destination. Sometimes he hated this city. He wondered how the elderly survived.

Turning into the library, he dropped the book in the proper chute, and continued on to the index section. The terminals were still down. He walked over to the card catalogue. Under Parapsychology he saw only one card which read: "See *Occultism, Mysticism, Psionics & Pseudoscience.*" There was no slip for *Eurasian Parapsychology,* although again Rudy noticed that cards had been ripped out. He inquired at the desk. The girl was young, had to be over 18, looked to be 12.

"Miss, do librarians often tear out cards from the catalogue racks?" He showed the stubs to her.

"Odd," she pondered. "Perhaps, when they are redoing the files, but I've never seen it."

"Do you have *Eurasian Parapsychology* by Gregory Hereward?"

"Wow," she said, her eyebrows raising. "I remember only this afternoon another gentleman came looking for the same book, peculiar accent, funny fur hat." As she spoke, she typed the name of the book into her fire-wall protected computer. "Yes, here it is," she spoke with satisfaction. "Look at this! It's that wacky professor from NYU," she was now talking more to herself than to Rudy. "Humph! Five months overdue." She wrote the name down on a card, and Rudy acted quickly, trying to read it upside down. As she looked up, Rudy raised his eyes to hers.

"And the professor's name?"

"I'm not at liberty to say," she said with a smile. "I've been waiting my whole life to say that."

"It's Ketchembach, isn't it?" Rudy bluffed.

"How'd you know!" she said with a furled lip, her hand subconsciously covering over the card she had written.

"How many wacky professor's are there from NYU," he quipped. She conceded a smile as he turned to depart, pulling his cellular out when he hit the streets. Using information, he dialed NYU.

"I'm sorry," the school operator said. "You'll have to call back during office hours."

As Rudy thanked the voice on the phone, it occurred to him that the professor could have gotten the book from his own school. He called NYU back and asked for the library.

"Reference desk."

"Do you have *Eurasian Parapsychology,* by Gregory Hereward?"

"One moment, I'll check...I'm sorry, its been missing for six months and is on reorder. We should get the updated edition in a few weeks."

Rudy clicked off. Now he wanted to see Hereward's book more than ever. Stepping into the night air, he walked towards Greenwich Village determined to scour every book shop until he found a copy.

THE MAN IN THE HERRINGBONE COAT

From 14th Street at Eighth Avenue all the way to the heart of Greenwich Village there are quite a number of well-stocked used and up-to-date book stores. Rudy intended to hit every one of them. He found out rather quickly that all books related to parapsychology could be found in the Occult section. Thumbing through works on psychic healing, astral projection, Atlantis and the like, Rudy was getting exasperated. He walked almost in a half run to get to the next store, rummaged through the stacks, and kept moving. Finally, he entered Sam Weiser's, a large metaphysical bookshop near the end of Park Avenue. "Do you have the book *Eurasian Parapsychology* by Hereward?" he inquired.

"Why yes," the lady behind the counter said. "We just got a whole shipment in this afternoon. Just go down the main aisle and turn right."

Rudy thanked the lady and moved swiftly down the aisle. As he turned right, *Smash!* a steel forearm flattened him, sending a book sailing to the ground. It landed with a thud at his side. As he looked up from the floor, Rudy's eyes met the other's in undaunted recognition. It was the Asian from the library, still dressed in herringbone coat and large fur hat. A hardcover edition of *Eurasian Parapsychology* lay beside the fallen reporter! As the man stared down, cold darts of energy seemed to stream from his eyes. The man leaned down, grabbing the text and offering the same arm to Rudy, this time as an aid. With a seemingly effortless upward pull, Styne was standing back on his feet. He could feel the surging energy of the fellow but could not quite place the face. It was not Japanese, nor Chinese. Mongolian seemed to ring true. Before the words "Thank you" were completed, the man was already on his way to the check-out counter.

Turning once again to the far wall, Rudy faced a giant pyramid stack of the book he had searched so hard to obtain. There in front of him in bright yellow and black was a large display with over 100 copies of *Eurasian Parapsychology*. Above the bold title were the following words: 4th Printing. And on the back: *New York Times*: THE MOST IMPORTANT WORK IN THE FIELD SINCE B.K. PINE! He grabbed a copy and happily walked back to the counter. And then it struck him as the Asian was leaving the register: they were different editions. The other book was hard-covered, while his was paperback.

Slapping a twenty on the table, Rudy cautiously followed the fur hat down the street. His heart beat louder as they ambled towards the Lower East Side. He knew it was rash to follow a man this way, but he also knew he wanted a first edition copy of that book. Following this fellow seemed to him the best way. Trailing slowly behind, Rudy would allow his mark to get about half a block ahead, and then he would gallop to the corner whenever a block was turned. As the streets passed, the man picked up his pace and turned another corner. He had circled back up towards Third Avenue again. Once more, Styne ran rapidly to the turn, pasting himself against the building's edge, as he peeked around the other side, pulling his head back before it was too late. The man was standing no more than twenty feet away at a bus stop. Rudy closed his eyes for a moment, and tried to quiet his gasping for air, lest he reveal his position. The Asian's package seemed to be missing. Rudy waited impatiently for the bus, and as the foreigner stepped aboard, he peeked once more and confirmed it. There was no Weiser bag.

What had the bastard done with it? Rudy thought. As Chi Jhenghis walked to the back of the bus, his slanted dark animal eyes darted a glance in Rudy's direction.

THE RASPUTIN LEGACY

Eerie shivers rippled up Rudy's spine. He pulled back once more as the bus sped away, an unfamiliar feeling of anxiety dwelling deep in his lungs. Turning, he walked slowly back towards Park Avenue, as he began to think. The book was no longer with the man. Now he was sure of it.

Retracing each block in his mind, Rudy was able to narrow the drop-off point to only one corner. He hurried back there and looked about. There were the usual number of apartments and small shops. A line of garbage cans caught his attention, and one by one he opened each and peered in. The smells of the city had never pleased him, but the added odor of putrefying food triggered a sense of nausea.

"Hey, get away from there!" someone yelled. He looked up to see a lady with a neat row of rollers in her hair shouting to him through a nearby window. Ignoring her, he continued opening each can lid by lid. She tapped the pane vigorously, causing it to vibrate in an arrhythmic patter. People on the street began to look about, but Rudy paid them no mind.

He almost passed it by, but there was the Weiser bag settled in a heap of broken eggshells. Slightly covered with goo and slime, he carefully found a clean part of the bag to grab with pincer fingers. Neatly, he removed the book from inside. Covering the lid, he turned with a wave-off gesture to dismiss the lady, and triumphantly walked back to Chessie's apartment, now the proud owner of a first *and* fourth edition of *Eurasian Parapsychology*. Chess was not back yet, so Rudy found a comfortable spot on the sofa and spread the two books before him.

He had the first edition hardcover, March 2002, and the fourth printing, a paperback, January 2004. On a hunch, he turned to the back of each and began cross-referencing the name index. Two names appeared missing in the newer book: Vladimir Kopensky and Alexi Patrenko; whereas there were four names added: R.M. Inovitch, Hugo Kolikowski, Dimitri Lamonov and Boris Lettlin. He thumbed through the paperback first. Inovitch and Lettlin were two scientists involved with teaching the blind to see with their fingertips, and Kolikowski and Lamonov were doctors studying the effects of sound and color on newborns. Rudy was about to turn to the first edition when the front lock rattled and the door opened.

Chessie walked in, dabs of clay still smudged on her cheek and forehead. "How 'djado?" she said, reaching over with earthen hands to place a fresh teapot on Rudy's lap. Its glaze was marbled in blues, greens and yellows. Eyeing the books, she asked, "Getting into redundancy, Rude?"

"Um hum."

"Different editions?"

"Very good, Watson."

"Have you cross-checked the indexes to see if there are any changes?" Before he could react, she snatched each one, and turned them to their backs to begin comparing.

"I already did that, Watson. There are four names added to the new addition and two names missing which appear in the older one."

"Three," she declared, as she began to read something to herself from the weathered hardcover copy. Delicate eyelids lowered in concentration, as she sat herself by the kitchen table, and rested her chin upon the crook of her thumb and forefinger.

"Two. This coffeepot is beautiful. Is it for me?"

"Wanna bet, Mr. 'olmes?" Chessie's eyes never left the page.

"OK, Dr. Watson. Dinner at the Greek Room."

"With dessert at Mama Pazzie's, and the DVD of my choice next week."

"Your choice! Hah! Chess, I counted four times. There are only two scientists' names that are missing."

"So now it's scientists. We agreed on names, Mr. 'olmes, not scientists." Chessie looked up slyly, as she began to read from the hardcover book:

> Dressed in pleated black robes, he appeared suddenly one afternoon in Moscow in 1903, a tall, mysterious, large-boned peasant with protruding forehead, long oily black hair, flared nostrils, broad sensual lips, primitive stance, massive shoulders and hands, and gnarled trunklike fingers. His gaze was unforgettable, penetrating, imposing, soul shattering, for he was more than a holy man, he was a Staretz. It was said that women fainted with one glace from Rasputin.
>
> This Siberian monk, who made his way into the Russian aristocracy, captured the mind of the Tzarina and imagination of the Tzar as he cured their hemophiliac son, and mesmerized the men and women of the court....
>
> However, according to his enemies, this dangerous and powerful creature, despicable charlatan, Holy Devil and debaucher, was traitor to Russia and to its people.

"Chess, I read that. You know that doesn't count. He's been dead for a hundred years. And that's a lot of crap anyway. I'm only interested in today, not 1903."

"Are you saying that you're going to welsh on the bet?"

"Well, er, no. I guess not. It just has nothing to do with anything. It's a fun story from the old days when people believed in that sort of thing."

"And I suppose you read the passage that followed?" Chessie said innocently.

"Gimme that book," Rudy said as he swiped for it.

Chessie pulled back. "Hush Mr. 'olmes. I believe that you have just been demoted to a Mrs. Hudson." She returned to the text:

Rasputin's hold upon the Russian aristocracy extended well beyond his role as a healer of the Tzarevitch Alexis. The Staretz was known to influence the policies of the Tzar and Tzarina and also a significant number of members of the ruling party. At the height of his power, he could raise a brawny arm and declare, *I hold the Russian empire in that hand.*

Chessie was standing now, having grabbed the teapot back from Rudy. She held it high to accentuate the end of the quotation, then paused for dramatic effect and continued:

It is rumored that a blood relative of Rasputin, a tall and mysterious Ukrainian, carries on the mystic's legacy in a secret organization tied to right-wing extremist Petar Bonzovalvitch. This nephew, it is said, is a conglomeration of hypnotist, healer, parapsychologist and spymaster.

One of his greatest accomplishments to date appears to be the uncanny success of the Ukrainian sorceress Deus Maxima, a self-proclaimed messiah, who has the capability to mesmerize tens of thousands of the masses.

She finished with a flare and dramatically dropped the text back into Rudy's lap.

"Mama Pazzie's, here I come," she said as she exited for the shower.

"Chess, I'm gonna be up half the night with this, so don't wait. And give me a kiss." She returned, gave Rudy a peck on the cheek, and departed.

Looking at his lap, he noticed that the hardcover had fallen opened to page 192, and there he saw reference to one of the scientists whose name was missing from the newer paperback, Vladimir Kopensky. *This is a giant trick,* Rudy noted, 192, *this is a giant trick.* There were only two lines for Kopensky:

Vladimir Kopensky, and six other scientists, were at the hotel when we arrived. Kopensky discussed telepathy, PK and vector states, brain-waves, microwaves and the EEG.

That was it! He flipped to the index to find the other missing scientist, Alexi Patrenko, listed on page 291. Refusing to acknowledge the reversal of the numbers, Rudy thought for one fleeting instant that this too was a dream, that he hadn't yet awakened from the morning:

A robust gentleman who prefers his head shaved, Dr. Alexi Patrenko had written his doctoral thesis on antimatter and relativity. After a brief discussion about mind/brain interactions, PK and hyperspace, Dr. Patrenko then displayed a laser-like apparatus which he used to shoot, and apparently dematerialize three flies which were on the wall! Needless to say, the experiment was effective, and of course, quite startling, although none of us knew the exact nature of the technology involved.

Although nothing else was written on Dr. Patrenko, a few paragraphs later Hereward mentioned after-image effects and dull headaches experienced by some of the scientists and by himself, following the dematerialization episode.

Rudy was beginning to wonder just who this Hereward fellow was, and why that NYU professor would want a book on ESP. Could he be a parapsychologist too? What other credible psychic researchers could there be out there? His mind began to race wildly. Why were Kopensky's and Patrenko's names missing in the later editions? Why were the hardcovers missing from the libraries? And who was that fur-capped Asian fellow? After fifteen hours of study, Rudy was already considering himself to be a well-versed *aficionado* in the field. He decided to meet with Captain Whitmore and ask for a full time go-ahead on this project. The first plan would be to see how many libraries had missing first edition copies of *Eurasian Parapsychology*.

Chessie's nightlight was still on. He decided to investigate.

INCREDIBLE FANDANGOS

Cheerios and milk, a vitamin C and off to work.... Morning had come and gone. Rudy was excited about his parapsychological discoveries. Full of himself and imbued with the vibe of the percolating metropolis, Rudy entered *Modern Times* and briskly walked into Captain Whitmore's office. It was an occasionally acceptable practice, if done with the right timing.

Unexpectedly, John Hirshon, editor-in-chief of *The York Tribune* was there. He and the captain were golfing buddies, but they rarely spent time in each other's offices. They were discussing one of the Congressmen who had died in the Alaskan crash. Well-placed rumors had spread to say that Arnold Johnson had been gay, but he was also married. Hirshon spoke, acknowledging Rudy's presence, apparently aware of who he was. It was a subtle compliment.

"We're pretty sure that Johnson was sexually involved with two male U. N. translators in an unusual ménage a trios, and our sources tell us that *Drudge.com* is going to unload the story on page one. It was our story fourteen months ago and we killed it. I just don't think those bastards should do it. The man's just died, and he has a family."

Captain nodded, and they pondered the problem during an unusually long silence.

"Leak the details to *Public Enquirer*. That will surely kill their credibility," Rudy said, quite pleased with himself. All three laughed.

"Hirsh, this is Rudolf Styne. You know his writing. Here's your chance to combine his face with his work."

Hirshon gave the appearance of a man who had not changed in forty years. He turned to Rudolf, "Damn it, young man! I think I'll do just that!" Hirshon slapped his thigh, and was about to storm out, when he stopped and spoke to the young reporter once more. "You wrote on capitalism and bribery. Excellent point-- profit and loss replacing moral decisions."

Rudy beamed. He couldn't believe that John Hirshon had actually read his article. Everyone knew Hirsh, his face had been on the cover of nearly every major magazine, and he had a Sunday night talk show on cable and internet video. Rudy was glowing with pride. He felt flattered. Perhaps all the coincidences had climaxed for this moment. He seriously pondered this possibility.

"Rudy wants to do a report on ESP," Whitmore said.

"Garbage," Hirshon shot back, as he paused before exiting, his manner suddenly quite stern. "What slice of that ESP crap-pie are you interested in, Styne? Astrology, parapsychology, palmistry or spiritualism?" His sense of purpose demanded a succinct answer.

"Parapsychology," Rudy said. He had to keep it short. "I read some of the laboratory reports," he added timidly.

"God, don't get caught in that shit." Hirsh turned away shaking his head. "We did a piece three months ago on that phony Egyptian psychic Abdullah Manu. It's all bullshit, Mr. Styne.... Look, thirty years ago Garner did a whole exposé on the statistical manipulations performed by B.K. Pine. Pine was disgraced. His so-called ESP cards were transparent when held up to the light, and score sheets were discovered with blanks every so often, just enough to make a random run not random, that is, statistically significant. Hey, I've stayed long enough." He nodded to the captain and to Rudy.

Rudy couldn't stop himself. "Who is Abdullah Manu? How do you know he's a fake?" The name was not totally unfamiliar. Hadn't he seen the fellow on the Dolly Carson show, fixing watches or something? It took balls to stop Hirshon, but he spoke before he thought.

The editor of *The York Tribune* glared back at Rudy with an air of annoyance, but then glanced at his colleague with a knowing smile as if to imply that he would help the captain by saving Rudy for something important.

"This Manu fellow claims he can levitate small objects and bend metal, Hirshon laughed. And so our roving reporter, Charles Koswell, invites him over. We're skeptical, but what the hell. He had been successfully tested at Oak Ridge. We decided to invite the magician, the Incredible Fandango as a witness as well, and we also brought in Judge Peterson. Fandango's introduced to Manu as a physicist," Hirshon smiled to himself, "Peterson as Peterson."

Hirshon paused a beat, then continued, "Manu was all over the place, a bundle of nerves and energy. Could not sit still for three minutes. He is a striking man though--beautiful jet-black hair and burning black eyes. 'Can you fix a watch?' I asked. He takes the watch, I know it hasn't run in seven years, I even wound and shook it that morning to no avail. So, I thought I had him for sure. But Manu seemed genuinely happy to *fix* something. He held it tightly in his palm while he paced and answered questions.

"Judge Peterson asked where his powers came from and he said. 'Higher intelligences beyond man.' 'You mean UFO's?' Koswell asked. 'That is your term,' Manu said.

"He placed the watch suddenly on the desk and squeezed his fist in a churning motion over it. 'Work, Work,' he commented, and the watch began to tick! I picked it up and checked my markings. It was definitely my watch. When I put the watch down the hands of the face had warped! Right under the glass crystal! Needless to say, we were stunned.

"Manu then asked for a key and gently rubbed his hand over it. 'Sometimes it doesn't work,' he said. Then, he paused and stared down at the key. 'Why do you fail me now?' he began and then suddenly I blurted out, *'It's lifting.'* I thought I saw a beam of light shoot from Manu's forehead, and then the key floated up towards the ceiling!"

The editor looked down at the floor for a moment and shook his head. "We were all mesmerized. I can't explain the feeling--almost as if we had entered some primeval ritual."

Hirshon paused again, his eyes were staring deeply out the window...then he snapped back to the conversation. "In fact, I have it here." He produced a heavy key with a 70° kink in it. Each man took the key and held it curiously. It was a normal brass key with a distinct bend to it. Hirsh paused once more, as all three peered at the warped metal.

"I don't know why I keep the damn thing with me. It was bent when it floated gently back to the desk," he continued almost in a whisper. "Damn it, the lad seemed so straightforward and sincere. He guessed a number I was thinking of and departed with a warm, sincere handshake. When he left the room, I heard a distinct 'ping' come from the window and another 'ping' from the key. I was speechless." He paused again. "We all were, even Fandango. For one brief moment, I thought I just witnessed one of God's special children."

Hirshon stared at Rudy and Captain Whitmore in a peculiar questioning look. Then he snapped back and continued. "However, two minutes later Fandango was laughing almost uncontrollably. I was quite perturbed, but his mirth was so contagious, that we all began to smile. He produced lit candles from each of our pockets, and then floated a key in front of us. It too bent before our eyes...or so it seemed. Then he produced a watch and asked me to start it. I shook it, wound it, and shook it again and Fandango just smiled, grabbed it, and paced back and forth holding it tightly in his hands as he spoke. 'Why, I believe in Martians and life after death and telepathy. There is a card in my left shoe; tell me what it is.' I said, 'King of Hearts' and he produced it! He levitated another key supplied by Judge Peterson, and told us that he had been following this Manu fellow for six months and had thereby learned his best secrets. 'The key bit is just a slight of hand, an invisible thread, but the watch thing is a bit more clever.'

"'How does he do it?' we asked. Fandango paused and produced a xerox of a one-page article from a magazine called *The Rationalist*. Two well-known experimenters collected one-hundred so-called broken watches and tested them. Seven percent started with just winding, four percent by shaking after five to ten minutes. It seems that the heat of the hand causes the oil to warm up and so loosen the gears. The watch is thus greased in this manner. Seventy-nine percent of the watches started. The Incredible Fandango has performed this trick forty times, and he's failed only with seven watches. It's all chicanery. Manu's tests have had poor controls, repeatability is virtually nonexistent, and no reputable scientists that I know of, have spent any time with him. You know, parapsychology as a supposed science is over one-hundred years old. If there was something to it, you would think it would have surfaced by now. The Incredible Fandango had a great laugh on us." Hirshon mumbled the word turkey to the captain, and they chuckled, as Hirsh winked at Rudy on his way out.

Although embarrassed, Rudy was somehow relieved. So Pine was a crock. *Of course. Jeeze, I almost got sidetracked into a stupid superstition,* he thought to himself. *Telepathy, levitation, life after death, psychokinesis.* "Gad, who could believe that stuff!" he said to the captain as he walked out.

Rudy called CBS for interviews and worked with the photo-editor on sexual repression on TV. His feeling of loss of identity had completely dissolved. It felt good to get back into the old grind.

MASS MEDIA

After lunch, Rudy reached the TV network, scheduled to see old video clips of *Father Knows Best, Charlie's Angels, Santa Barbara, Sex In Suburbia, Baywatch, Another World* and two dozen other shows from the last fifty years. Upon finding his way to the screening room, he met a slinky girl named Greta who had picked out various segments to show him. Dressed in a canary yellow jump suit that clung to her every fold, her two perky nipples seemed to pop through the fabric in order to obtain a better look at him. She offered a limp handshake. "I hope you like my selection." She tilted her head in planned self-assurance, as a heatwave began to transfer between them.

"I'm sure I will," he said. She twirled, and led them to their seats. The chairs were lush. They sank in.

"Now, please keep in mind, these cuts are only from commercial TV." She tapped his thigh as if to emphasize the point.

"Thanks," he said, "and I appreciate your realization of what I want to achieve."

"You're welcome." She stared back, and flicked the remote.

Resisting the pressure, Rudy moved his eyes to the screen where he was bombarded with a tapestry of exotic images covering five decades of movies on mainstream TV. The clips began with a knockout shot of Jane Mansfield waddling down an urban street in a tight sweater with her bra stuffed with what looked like two cantaloupes, and ended with a tight-bunned shot of Demi Moore in a thong outfit from the film *Striptease*.

As the pictures flashed before them, Greta casually removed one of her shoes and breathed that she had a cramp in her toe, and would he mind massaging it. Everything happened so quickly with her foot suddenly on his knee that he found it awkward to resist. "Oh, yes, that's it! Thanks," she squeaked. "This always seems to happen."

His face became flushed. Realizing the moment, she smiled as she clasped both hands behind her head, and stared down at his thighs. His extremities began to quiver. "Should we go on to cable or just get right into the internet?"

Rudy's heart thumped. Her lips seemed to pout through her soft tight pants. A moment in time, he used her foot to straighten himself and stood. "Thanks," he mumbled, and left.

The energy had been too great, her pull magnetic. He thought back twenty years to the last time his heart pounded like that. It was when he had felt up Arlene, his sister's best friend, one delicious Saturday morning. The family was asleep. She had come over early, and he was still in his pajamas. As she reached...Rudy walked into the office.

"What *are* you dreaming about?" Sally teased. "You're red as a beet."

A SPOKESMAN FOR THE AMERICAN
PARAPSYCHOLOGY ESTABLISHMENT

Thursday, Rudy performed the automatic rituals of life totally unaware of his I-ness. He was caught up in the mechanical grind of the eight-hour day. Time passed quickly, and by Friday, he began once again to question the psychic data he had studied a few day before. After reading the various parapsychology books, he found himself reexamining the data, reconsidering the real possibility that humans were telepathic. How else could he explain those van accident dreams. Plagued by his vacillating opinion, he still questioned why this information had never been taught to him in school. *What is going on?* he kept asking himself. Surely, some of the research has validity, but certainly Hirshon's skepticism was worthy of notice too. Nevertheless, the melted hands on Hirshon's watch remained a mystery. Fandango hadn't done that one.

Abdullah Manu, what a phony sounding name. On impulse, Rudy skirted the office, and headed downtown to New York University to try and meet up with the parapsychologist who had removed *Eurasian Parapsychology* from the 23rd Street Library. The professor's name was Jay Ketchembach, Department of Physics.

Rudy was becoming mentally tormented. The mechanical crowds flowing through the Manhattan madness only confirmed his intuitions that something was being overlooked. Philosophical questions he thought he had left behind his sophomore year in college raged back into his psyche. Passing a building marked Psychology, he decided to forego the Physics Building, at least for now. Why not question an expert from psychology about it first before going to a physicist? Rudy passed a long hallway with signed photos of famous psychologists such as Freud, Floria, James, Skinner, Jung, Sherrington, Lashley, Luria, Maslow.... The chairman's door was open.

Sitting by a desk was a lanky man intently writing some notes. Rudy could not help but notice the myriad and almost bedraggled clumps of black hair that dotted his balding cranium. "Dr. Beaman, do you have a moment?"

'I'm not going to change your grade," the professor shot back.

"I'm not here because of a grade, professor."

"Well, finally, a real student. What can I do for you?"

"May I ask you a question?" Beaman nodded. "Do you know anything about ESP.... You know, parapsychology?"

"Freud considered it," Beaman's bushy eyebrows knit into Rudy as he spoke rapidly. "Old Sigmund felt that telepathy may have been the mechanism by which thought is transferred from the unconscious to the conscious. Rudy had to strain to understand. The man talked so quickly that one word became almost indistinguishable from the next.

"And then of course," he went on, "there was Carl Jung's hypothesis of a collective psyche, that is, a mental structure common to all humans." As he spoke, he periodically ran his fingers over his lips, further obscuring his words. Rudy wanted to interrupt him, have him speak more slowly, but he could not get a word in to slow the professor down.

"Personally, I rather doubt telepathy exists, for in forty years of teaching psychology I have never witnessed it." Beaman's eyes followed the border of the ceiling as he waited for Rudy to speak. But Rudy couldn't react quickly enough, and Beaman went on. "There was one incident...No, but that was a coincidence. No, I rather doubt it." He dropped his gaze conclusively, and then turned to stare at Rudy.

"Could you relate that incident?"

"About eight years ago I had a patient for psychotherapy. She was only nineteen. Her name was Martha, beautiful girl, suffering from depression and severe migraines. She had a schizophrenic father who was an alcoholic, and an introverted and rather fickle mother. I'll skip the details. Anyhow, one night she had a dream about a man who wore a woman's gold-speckled glasses, circa 1958, you know, with the pointy rims?" Rudy nodded. "Well, the night she dreamt that, my wife had actually put a pair of those funky gold-speckled sunglasses on my own head as a goof. She had found them in the attic. I was initially astounded, and even read a bit about telepathy. But after thinking about it, I realized how ridiculous. It was simply a coincidence. That's what a coincidence is!"

"Possibly," Rudy wondered out loud. "But wouldn't telepathy be a more logical explanation for the girl's dream?"

"Sure, if in the forty years I have studied the mind, I had seen similar events happen more regularly. But, in all that time, in all that time, one insignificant incident about sunglasses. No, I'm sorry, just a coincidence, just a coincidence. Calling it telepathy is really pushing it a might."

Rudy remained unconvinced, but decided not to battle it out with the man. "One more question, Dr. Beaman: what do you think of B.K. Pine's laboratory studies in parapsychological investigations?"

"Sloppy, very sloppy controls. Have you ever read Garner's 1934 study? Classic. Pine was disgraced, caught faking the statistical data. No, I'm afraid I just can't buy it...Wait a second," Dr. Beaman reached into a stack of papers and letters on his desk. "Why just today I received a copy of an article on this very subject. Odd, isn't it." Dr. Beaman handed him a magazine. "Here, I think you will find this revealing. This is *The Rationalist*. It'll set you straight." Rudy took the magazine and thanked the professor as he departed.

"And Styne," the professor called out as Rudy departed, "bring it to class when you've finished reading it."

"I'll do that sir," Rudy responded automatically, before the sense of surprise hit him. Shaking his head from side to side, he exited the building.

Taking a bus uptown so as to have time to read the articles, Rudy began at the bottom of the inside cover where it read: *Rationalist: An Affiliation of the Foundation for Humanity.* Beneath were the following words: Dedicated to Objective Appraisal of All Border Areas of Science. The lead article was by

Hanley Kranz. Rudy recognized the name from some of the parapsychology journals he had rifled through at the 23rd Street Library. He began reading about various well-controlled studies in precognition and telepathy using simple ESP cards.

In many instances, the sender was not even in the same room as the receiver. In some cases, the sender was in another country, and in one illustrious case, he was on the moon! There seems to be no attenuation of ESP ability with distance. Kranz concluded, "Telepathy has been produced endless times in many different parapsychology laboratories across the globe. Much to the dismay of the skeptics, parapsychologists do not spend their time exclusively Abdul Manu glaring, because we deal with common folk as well."

The rebuttal article was by Eugene Hobson, editor from the *Rationalist,* and psychology professor from the University of Colorado. He started the article by citing the earlier Garner studies which claimed that Pine had faked his results, and then proceeded to discuss Abdullah Manu at length, noting that parapsychologists did indeed Manu glare.

In 1986, Hobson wrote that after Manu was discovered by Egyptian parapsychologist Gabal Imhotep, "pseudoscientists" as he called them, "from every corner of the Earth flocked to Egypt" to witness the boy's supposed ability to levitate small objects.

Hobson thus observed, "Now, if that is not 'Manu glaring,' I don't know what is. Further, one of their own parapsychologists who was present at the performance, Dr. Kimono, remained skeptical during, and well after the event, never committing himself to the irrational thinking that so plagues most people in that field." Hobson then commended Dr. Kimono "for having commissioned the Incredible Fandango to attempt to replicate Manu's feats by the normal use of magicians' tricks," and then let Dr. Kimono speak for himself, by quoting his article which appeared in *Natural Science:*

> On one occasion Fandango made a paintbrush float towards the ceiling. To duplicate the bolt of lightning, he blew orange, red and yellow foot-long flames from his mouth! I remain skeptical and feel that Manu's abilities are still unproven.

Rudy checked the blocks. He had six to go, so he read rapidly so as to finish the piece. It ended with Hobson's closing:

> I am informed that 100 million Americans believe in ESP. Are these the same 100 million who believe in flying saucers and astrology? Our society is crazed with wonder at some trivial magic act or other illusory fantasy.... So quickly do they set aside the teachings of philosophy, science and common sense and face destiny

with a lie. Never do they wonder at the magnificence of the laws of nature or the mysteries of modern science. Instead they guffaw with delight at the mindless ESP card games of a third rate experimentalist and the charismatic hand passes of an Egyptian Houdini!

Rudy arrived back at *Modern Times,* about to enter the elevator.

"Hey, Mr. Styne." It was that red-headed janitor whose name he could never remember.

"How 'bout those Yankees!" Rudy said, exchanging the thumb's up sign, as he stepped into the elevator.

The janitor responded with his customary, "You're the man," as the doors closed.

Styne entered the office. Looking at the clock, he could see that he had the time to input his corrections and hand in the Sex in TV manuscript before the captain left for the day. A crisp cover story, it would run 3,500 words. With visuals, it promised to be quite a feather in his cap. Influenced by the Hobson article, he decided once again to forego the parapsychology piece. He was getting sidetracked by fantastic garbage about lightning bolts emanating from a man's forehead and levitating objects. Hobson was right. The gullible American people have lost their common sense. Styne continued to think to himself that the editor of *The York Tribune*, a top university psychiatrist and a number of scientific magazines had uncovered fraud, trickery and sloppy thinking in parapsychology. *Who am I to question them?* he reasoned. *I never believed in that crap anyway.*

True, he felt he had been sucked in for a while, but now all he wanted was to get his article published and take off with Chessie for the hills of Vermont.

Marc J. Seifer

LONDON

TWO YEARS EARLIER

It was Gregory Hereward's 70th birthday and the British Psychical Society had outdone themselves to honor him. Invitations had reached as far away as Japan and Australia, with representatives attending from most European countries, the Asian Commonwealth of Independent States, Canada, Brazil and the USA. For Dr. Hereward had been a creative leader in parapsychology for almost 50 years. Even the so-named Father of Parapsychology was there, B.K. Pine, himself well into his eighties.

Theoretical physicist/neuroscientist Dr. Jay Ketchembach of New York University was answering questions being asked by journalist Irving Moth of the *San Francisco Chronicle,* as others on the podium congratulated Dr. Hereward for his latest work.

"Well, I guess that's it," Moth said. He scribbled a few final thoughts, took off a pair of glasses and began to clean them with his tie. "Gift from my former wife."

"Ahh," Ketchembach nodded knowingly.

"I've already got Hereward's statements, so if I skedaddle in a minute or two, I've got a good chance to make my plane."

"Where you off to?"

"Tashkent," Moth hedged.

"To see Raudow?"

"How did you know?"

"If you're covering ESP, he's the man in Asia to see."

"But his lab is in St. Petersburg," the reporter said, "so how'd you know he'd be in Tashkent?"

"Well, let me see," Ketchembach teased. "I had a precognitive vision."

"I'm impressed. I would have guessed email."

"You got me, Moth. Good luck with the trip." The two shook hands and Moth departed.

Ketchembach was a Nobel Prize contender and a former protégé of Albert Einstein's at Princeton. The pride of the parapsychological community, the professor watched Moth disappear around a corner, and then he stepped up to the podium to introduce the honored author. Having just finished a delicious roast partridge dinner, Dr. Hereward smiled proudly to himself as he sipped a cup of coffee and prepared himself for the accolades.

"I have known Dr. Hereward for thirty-five years." Ketchembach began, turning to face the good doctor. "And having just completed reading his newest work *Eurasian Parapsychology,* I can only say, bravo, fine job indeed."

Beneath the applause, the two scientists from the Ukraine fidgeted nervously in their chairs. Obtaining exit visas for the affair had been one thing, but this was something entirely different. Sweat dripped profusely from the portly one,

Vladimir Kopensky, who dabbed his forehead with a wrinkled handkerchief. He turned to his colleague. "Alexi, let's leave while we can."

With fierce determination his bald companion responded coldly, "It is too late." As he spoke, he used his fingers of his right hand to press along the pulsing veins that protruded from his sleek cranium, as with the other hand, he pulled out a small microwave resonant amplifier that was built to resemble a pager. With an assured sweep of his brawny fingers, Alexi Patrenko aimed the antenna at the Guest of Honor, and turned the switch to a red-colored zone.

Gregory Hereward dropped his cup of coffee. Tumbling from the podium, his head fell like a lead weight, face down into the dessert cakes. A lady screamed.

On November 15th, at the dawn of what had been promised to be a new era in international cooperation in the study of psi phenomena, Dr. Gregory Hereward, parapsychologist extraordinaire, died of a malfunctioning heart pacer. What a shame, someone said. He looked so young for his age.

ÖZ BEG

Sitting comfortably in his first class seat, Irving Moth read about Hereward's death on his laptop. "Jesus H. Christ," he murmured, as he read through the report, and then shifted to a search to read up on the history of the region he was entering. While he was at it, he also punched in Boris Raudow's name. There wasn't much. Raudow had been editor of an international journal in parapsychology, he had spoken at conferences in Scandinavia and America in the 1980's, and over a decade ago, he had published a series of papers on the neurophysiology of telepathy.

The plane touched down at Tashkent airport. Moth deplaned, and went through customs. Grabbing a cab, he began composing his story, as the hack took him through the heart of the city en route to the Sarmoung Palace Hotel.

"Tracing their roots back to the Mongol Empire, the Uzbek people were named for Khan Öz Beg who ruled the region from 1313-1340," Moth typed. "Now, in modern times, with oil, gas and sulfur reserves, and maize and cotton as their main crops, this was a land blessed. With sixty different ethnic groups, one could still see in Tashkent wispy bearded men in turbans on camels packing muskets and herding sheep to the ancient marketplace, or downtown in the high-rise section, honking automobiles, hi-fashion suits, Rebok sneakers and the finest (Soviet-built) subway system in the whole of Eurasia...."

Mama Bern had been a happy Uzbek grandmother these past seven years. Walking past a foreigner in a cab stopped at a light, their eyes met for the briefest of seconds. He seemed to smile at her before putting his gaze back down to what she guessed was his laptop, as she continued her walk by the rug merchants, and made her way to her husband's fruit stand. Just back from the fertile Fergana basin, Papa Bern had stocked his shelves with his usual assortment of exotic fruits and vegetables. Looking much younger than his actual age of 68, he tore apart an orange and handed his wife a few sections. As she chomped into the sweet pulp, Mama picked through potatoes, beans and apples before stopping in front of another fruit. "Pomegranate," she said in astonishment.

"They're early this year," he said with pride. "Take only one."

"I know," she replied, "You have to," and then she paused so that they could say it in unison, *"Make some money this week!"* They laughed, as she adjusted her husband's red fez before she headed back home to prepare an early dinner. They were planning on going down to the track with their son Imo, to watch their other son, Heinreich, practice his high jumping. Six years her husband's junior, Mama Bern spent most of her time taking care of Heinreich's children, the young man's wife having died at the birth of the second child.

Heinreich was more than just another athlete, he was an icon, the pride not only of the family, but of the whole of Tashkent. Having traveled to almost every major city in the world, Heinreich had represented the former Soviet Union in various Olympic and world meets, and now competed for the Commonwealth. Tall and graceful, unlike his modest-sized sibling, Heinreich was a natural athlete. He had originally played with the Soviet basketball team. However, he was never much of a team player, and so switched to high jumping.

There was always an imperceptible distance from his parents and brother, particularly as his fame grew, but the love was there. Everyone, even the neighbors, celebrated and benefited from the connection to their Olympic hero.

Mr. and Mrs. Bern's most fulfilling experience as parents was perhaps when their son won the silver metal in high jumping at the 1988 Olympics. This event served not only to launch Heinreich into the ranks of a national hero, it also bumped the stature of his parents as well.

Imo, the younger son, was scientifically inclined. At only twenty-five, he was working for a medical degree. He had been fortunate to work for the famous neurophysiologist, Alexandr Floria, in Tashkent, and had written two credible papers on higher states of consciousness. His study on EEG detection of hemispheric differences during dream states was the catapult that paved his way to his interest in parapsychology, and eventually to a secret laboratory in central Siberia.

"Professor," Imo said.

"What can I do for you?" Floria had taken to Imo, had told him stories of his work with Pavlov from the 1930's, and of some of his experiences with brain-injured soldiers during WWII. Imo had no idea that the man was so close to death, his speech and actions had been so vital and self-assured.

"I wanted to ask you about telepathy."

"Don't you have to leave early to see your brother at the track?"

"You remembered. I've got a few minutes and, well, Boris Raudow is in town."

"And you are going to ask me about his work in telepathy?"

"How did you know?"

Floria smiled as he waited for the joke to kick in.

"Is there any truth to his work?"

"The real problem, Imo…." Floria looked at his watch. "Are you sure you have time for this?"

"Yes. No, not really. But he may be at the meet."

"Oh, I see. He's a friend of Heinreich's?"

"They met in Athens some years ago."

"That's when Raudow was in the government's good graces."

"But about his work?"

"It's true," Professor Floria confided, "Thought transference can take place, but, [and he emphasized the but], it is so rare a phenomenon that it is quite useless for practical considerations. Raudow seems to be in it more for the glory, and that's what irks the powers above that be. You'd be better off, my boy, to deal with what we can see about the brain, such as localization of functions, rather than worry about what we cannot see. There are too many blind spots as it is. Now, get going, and go cheer on your brother." Floria feigned swatting Imo on the rear end.

The young intern exited the building, unlocked his bicycle and peddled down to the local stadium, just six kilometers away. Grabbing the cellular his brother had lent him, he dialed home and apologized for missing dinner.

"Where are you, Imo?" Mama Bern inquired. "Your food is getting cold."

Imo swerved around a man on a donkey and scooted down a brick alley, which cut through towards a back entrance to Öz Bek Stadium. "I'll eat it when I get home," he warbled as he struggled to control the bike with just a single hand. "Maybe Heinreich will join us!"

"He'd better join us. Your father and I will find you at the stadium."

Imo parked his bike, chained it to a fence, and walked into the arena. This was only an exhibition, really a practice run for an upcoming international event which was being held in Madrid, so crowds remained sparse. Only the sprinters and the jumpers, high, pole and long, were there.

Heinreich waved to his brother and called him over. Imo saw him speaking to a man he recognized by a photo he had seen. The bushy black shocks of hair above the man's ears were unmistakable. He scooted across a track and walked over to a waiting area where some of the athletes were doing stretching exercises and warming up.

"Imo, this is Boris Raudow, the great neuroscientist."

"Heinreich, you're too much," Raudow said, extending a hand which Imo happily shook. "Good to meet you."

Imo beheld a stocky man, balding at the top of his head, with unruly tufts of hair not only above his ears, but also for eye-brows, as a moustache, and even as tufts which could be seen below his neckline sprouting from his chest. His bearing was that of a man with a sense of success about him.

"Heinreich tells me that you plan to be a doctor. I'm jealous. I only have a graduate degree in psychology."

"I thought you were a doctor," Imo responded.

"You know of my work?"

"Of course. You study telepathy. Is that not true?"

"Yes. And even though they won't let me talk about it here, I've got a reporter from America who will print anything I say."

"Irving Moth, from *The San Francisco Chronicle,*" Heinreich interjected. "Don't tell anybody, but I helped set that up."

"You know everybody. Don't you?" Imo said, his chest bursting with pride for his beloved brother.

"Hey, I'll let you two get acquainted." Heinreich reached down to tousle his brother's hair, as he always did, before loping off to the high jump area. "I think that's Moth down there." He pointed to a concession stand before making his way to the inside of the arena.

"He's the best there is," Imo said proudly. "And not just because he's my brother."

"You'll get no argument from me." Raudow's gaze shifted to where Heinreich had said. "I'm going to have to check this man out by myself, Imo. So now we've met. Don't be shy. Look me up. I'll be here for a couple of weeks. I'm at the University. Don't be a stranger." He shook Imo's hand again and departed.

Imo watched as Raudow walked over and greeted the foreigner. Moth leaned on a rail by the stand, as Raudow leisurely handed him a large manila envelope which had been casually rolled up in such a way that it had stuck out of his coat pocket. Imo found himself also scouring the seating areas, trying to find his father and mother, as his eyes kept returning to Raudow and the other man.

"Hey, what the heck," someone in the stands shouted at a man dressed in a trench coat who ran down the wooden seats, scattering people as he did so. He was heading for the very concession stand where Raudow and Moth were talking. The commotion caused a pole vaulter to miss his cue, and he let out a scream, his shoulder apparently dislocated. Two other men from two other directions, also dressed in trench coats waving what appeared to be guns, also closed in. Boris Raudow took off for an exit but the man he was talking to, the American reporter, stood fast.

Imo watched one of the assailants grab the paper from Moth's hands, throw it to the ground, spin him around and cuff him with his wrists behind. The others gained on Raudow. It was pretty clear to all that could see, it was just a matter of time.

CZAR EYES

Three weeks later Dr. Floria was dead. He passed away quietly in his sleep. The old legion had disappeared and over two-hundred scientists attended the funeral. Many came from Europe, the Americas, and even Japan, for Professor Floria was unmatched as a pioneer in delineating the superstructure of the higher cortical functions. A letter from Premier Polekov was read at the services, and then a long procession of limousines drove the mourners out of the city to the stark somber cemetery on the outskirts of Tashkent. Imo sat with Vladimir Kopensky and two other scientists whom he did not know.

Dr Kopensky was a flabby fat fellow, the kind of man who continually wore yesterday's brown suit, and yesterday's almost white shirt. His face was pudgy and sweaty, his hairdo, the type that attempted to camouflage his baldness. Strands of brownish-gray about eleven inches in length greasily straddled the girth of his fleshy cognitive dome.

"Imo," Kopensky said, reaching into his coat pocket for half a wrapped fish sandwich, "I want you to stop by my laboratory." This was not idle invitation. The doctor chomped into the bread, causing a red splash of herring juice to ooze out over his mandible. As he continued to espouse, the fish oil began to etch its trail around Kopensky's first chin and rolled on towards the second. "We are doing exciting experiments with brain-waves and neurosurgery." He belched. "I'm sure we can integrate your work with RNA/protein memory construction into our program."

"And dream creation?"

"Certainly."

"Thank you," Imo replied. Sad over the death of his mentor, he still had to smile about Kopensky. The man was a compulsive eater. When Imo next looked up the sauce was gone.

The sunlight was very piercing that day at the cemetery. An iridescent green dragon-fly lighted momentarily upon the coffin as it was lowered. A few people from the immediate family cried softly, as well as one American, the scientist Dr. P. Karl who reached over and comforted Floria's wife. Imo could sense the oddness of jealousy among some of the Russian scientists at this time. But, Dr. Karl had grown close to the Florias these past fourteen years, having set up numerous speaking engagements in America for Dr. Floria, having been a kind host, and most importantly, having been responsible for translating into English most of the doctor's encyclopedic writings on the brain. In broken Russian, Dr. Karl offered his sympathies to Mrs. Floria, his alcoholic breath soothing them both. "Come back to the house and sit awhile," she said. Mrs. Floria had deep feelings for the man who had brought her husband's books to the West.

Dr. Karl was himself immortalized for his work with schizophrenia in monkeys in Wisconsin. His face cast the perceptible appearance of confidence and self-assurance, even though his eyes were saddened with the Russian scientist's death, and his nose reddened from years of drink.

It was at the house that Imo met Dr. P. Karl. Their discussion centered around some American dream telepathy studies and Imo's work on the EEG and dream states. Imo liked Dr. Karl from the start, and was pleased to see some of the other scientists say hello. Karl seemed distant to most, but was certainly concerned and interested in Dr. Bern's work. "Death is a strange phenomena, Dr. Bern," he said to Imo. His voice was matter of fact, but also troubled underneath. "I deal with death every day." Dr. Karl belted down another vodka. "Monkeys," he added, and waited for Imo's response.

As Imo was about to introduce Dr. Karl to Dr. Kopensky, instead Vladimir ducked out of the house. It seemed that he had deliberately avoided Dr. Karl, but Imo could think of no possible reason why.

Another well-known figure conspicuous by his absence was Boris Raudow, the man everyone there knew had been arrested just a few weeks before. Raudow had organized two Soviet/American parapsychology meetings in the late 1980's, and then, as Imo found out from Dr. Kopensky, had been hassled by the Uzbek Secret Police, charged for, of all things, teaching parapsychology without a Ph.D. Raudow had edited articles for a prestigious Norwegian journal on consciousness, and had lectured throughout Europe. But when he combined his prominence with unhushed statements regarding the Jewish problem, he became a liability. His cavalier nature had gained him an international reputation; it was also his undoing. He had gone to Tashkent ostensibly to open a dialogue with the neuroscience department at the University and maybe gain himself more credibility in a more conventional arena, but it was at that time that he was arrested for passing state secrets to the American news correspondent, Irving Moth.

Where Moth was held in jail for about a week, due to pressure from the American embassy and the world press, he was finally released, but Raudow was nowhere to be seen. Rumors had it that he had been given shock treatments and sent to a prison in Siberia.

With Dr. Karl's presence, Raudow's plight became even more of an embarrassment. And it was for that reason that few Eurasian scientists had the courage to approach the great American colleague.

"They've broken him," Kopensky whispered to Imo, referring to Raudow. Our work, unfortunately, is not for American eyes." But, Imo was not American. He moved to St. Petersburg, and began to work for Vladimir Kopensky shortly after the funeral.

THE LAB

A FEW MONTHS LATER

Dr. Kopensky's lab was two stories below the St. Petersburg University Hospital's main floor. Much of it lay beneath a small terraced patio used for luncheons and sun basking. Imo had performed uncountable numbers of rat experiments there, and even some feline studies, but he privately drew the line before canines. He had tacitly abhorred the mutilation of animals, but knew animal experimentation was a necessity. However, as with most medical students, after the initial shock, he became accustomed to autopsies, and even enjoyed the dissection of the innards of the skull, in his quest for scientific knowledge. Working with deceased persons was quite different than killing living animals.

One of Imo's pet projects was the anatomical structure of the pineal gland, an organ from the center of the brain. Known as the third eye, as Kopensky referred to it, the pineal gland in humans controlled the wake/sleep cycle and contained a neurotransmitter biochemically compatible with psychedelic drugs such a LSD. Imo was working on the hypothesis that the pineal also controlled other states of consciousness, all of which, he theorized, were monitored by different atomic structures.

Imo reflected back to his first day on the job when Dr. Kopensky greeted him in the main lobby of the hospital. They obtained security clearance and entered the elevator. The young intern felt the lift quiver under Kopensky's massive weight. Perspiring profusely, the corpulent doctor's body exuded oppressive odors from two-day-old sweat that lingered like a smog about his general vicinity. Imo thought he might pass out from the smell, Kopensky practically smothering him in the small compartment.

The young doctor tried to hold his breath, or breathe lightly. "I never realized that there were floors below the hospital," he managed. "What's on the first lower level?"

"I'll show you." Dr Kopensky pressed button A with a chubby forefinger, as he dabbed the sweat of his ample brow with the palm of his other hand. The elevator dropped beneath the cellar and opened up to cages of rats and cats lining both sides of the main hall. Acrid fumes from animal litter boxes, nitric acid bottles and other chemical and hospital paraphernalia bit into Imo's nostrils. He felt woozy, but suppressed it as best he could. Kopensky swaggered down the passageway, swinging his full weight from side to side, as he passed a large gruff-looking woman dressed in a white lab coat. She was holding a young Bonobo who had a small knapsacked-looking device sewn directly into his shoulder. Two-thirds of the right side of the ape's head and face was completely removed and replaced by a plastic skull cap with a number of color-coded outlets and protruding electrodes laced with wires and cathode ray tubes. This cybernetic gear was connected to an attaché case, which the woman held in her other hand.

The monkey looked towards Imo. Their eyes met.

Holding Imo's attention in silent communication, the ape lifted a pleading eyebrow as if to say *Please kill me.*

The woman grinned. "Hello, Vladimir." Kopensky nodded in return.

Imo felt his soul shudder, and his stomach drop to the floor. The monkey had clearly spoken to him, although not with words. Kopensky grinned back, "Madam Grotchka! This is our new laboratory assistant, Dr. Imo Bern." Grotchka's mouth turned up at the corners, as she whisked the monkey away. Kopensky and Imo walked on.

"In these rooms we have primates with various diseases such as cancer, schizophrenia and epilepsy.... This room has rats and mice, over here, cats.... In behind that steel door are the dogs. They make such a racket that we built sound proof enclosures."

At the end of the hall was a room with a water cooler, coffee machine and pool table. They had a drink and shot a few games of eight-ball. Dr. Kopensky spoke, as he lined the cue stick up between the white ball and his sagging jowls. "Most of the hardware is on the floor below this one. Also, computer terminals, Kirlian photography equipment, MRI, EEG and other bio-feedback machines, our molecular biology lab, and most importantly, my private library is there."

With all he had seen, Imo had difficulty concentrating. He also knew Kopensky did not want to lose, so he flubbed a few shots and was beaten handily.

"Come," Kopensky announced, happy with himself for the way he had played. He led the way to yet another stairway. "It's time to read your brain."

They descended to Level B where Kopensky guided Imo into a room filled with all types of fancy machinery. He huffed slightly as he peeled his shirt away from his sweaty chest.

"I've got to get back in shape," he smiled, patting his belly affectionately. A machine with red lights beeped and bleeped as the doctor spoke again. "Let me hook you up."

Sitting Imo down, Kopensky rubbed alcohol on the youngster's forehead and behind each ear, and taped four electrodes to these areas of the skull. The brain-wave machine was showing a rapid up and down movement, telling them that Imo was in beta, a state of alert awareness.

"Try and relax."

As Dr. Kopensky stated the word *relax,* the EEG instantaneously shifted to the regular and slower alpha rhythm. Afterwards, the EEG bounced right back to beta. Imo looked at Vladimir. They both recognized that the mere suggestion of relaxation caused an instantaneous response.

"Pavlov would be proud of you," Dr. Kopensky joked. "Now, try and regulate your own brain-waves."

Dr. Bern closed his eyes and tried to calm himself. Slowly, he opened them. The EEG had slowed down, and through intuition and meditative techniques, Imo was soon able to produce a continuous output of alpha.

Working part-time in the lab as partial requirements for his internship, he became entranced with the work in the molecular biology lab with their research on neurogenesis, that is, creating certain proteins and enzymes that could enhance brain growth. The possibilities for the future astounded and exhausted him. As long as he avoided emotional consideration about the experimental animals on Level A (and Madam Grotchka's pet monkey) he was all right. However, Level A was an everyday aspect of his duties, thus he forced himself to create a suitable framework that would alleviate pangs of conscience. Without trying to think too deeply, he put to sleep the cat he was experimenting on. *Better animals than humans* became his mantra, so with each passing day he winced less. He tried to think about his brother high jumping at the Olympics, as he sliced open the central part of the feline's face and removed the still warm brain.

Dr. Kopensky was a jovial sort of man, yet a disciplined teacher. Contradictory at times, he nevertheless raised his voice on occasion. Sometimes, he became morose. Although he constantly talked about dieting, he seemed always to have a sandwich in one hand, oftentimes while operating on an experimental animal with the other. Periodically, Dr. Kopensky would miss appointments with Imo. But as they got to know each other, this practice came to be expected. Sometimes he was away from the lab for a week at a time, and Madam Grotchka took command. She was an unpleasant woman and Imo dreaded these longer absences.

Although Vladimir Kopensky's work in biofeedback and states of consciousness was well-known throughout Russia, he never published theoretical papers. Therefore his work was virtually unknown to the West. However, Imo occasionally proofread some of Kopensky's private notes, and it was during one of these readings that his destiny changed irreversibly.

Grotchka rang Imo unexpectedly one Tuesday morning while Kopensky was gone. She was sitting beneath a prominent jar of human brain soaking in formaldehyde. "Imo, bring the microscope and Kirlian photography machine to A-4." A shiver went up Imo's spine, for that was the wired ape's room. As he wheeled the equipment down the corridor, he reflected back to the day when Madam Grotchka had gone to Moscow. He had heard the whimpering from Grotchka's laboratory and went in to investigate. The ape was wailing in deep soulful sobs, and had reached out with both hands for his compassionate friend. Imo and the Bonobo held hands for well over an hour that afternoon, the animal not allowing him to leave.

Somehow, even in that condition, the ape was able to retain an emotional connection to himself and his tragic predicament. Imo's heart had broken that night. He felt it snap deep within his chest cavity, and he cried for hours before falling asleep.

The following day the Bonobo bit off Madam Grotchka's pinky above the second phalange. It was a swift move which took her by surprise. He held it in his mouth triumphantly, the woman too startled to respond. She ran to a medic, who sutured the bleeding end. When she returned, the top part of the finger lay spit out on the floor. Imo had avoided A-4 ever since.

Nevertheless, Dr. Bern would inevitably run into Madam carrying the Bonobo on one hip, black-dialed attaché case in her free hand, as she brought the animal from one experiment to another. Often the ape would cry out for Imo, but Grotchka would just walk more swiftly.

Grotchka had written four papers on the neuroelectric states of the chimpanzee. Her specialization was the instincts MRI brain imaging and EEGs. In point of fact, her work on the sexual arousal system of primates was unprecedented research. With electrodes dropped into the thalamus, amygdala, hippocampus, hypothalamus, cerebellum and cerebral cortex, she could make the Bonobo hungry, aggressive, calm, excited, loving, maternal, sexy or depressive--all by merely switching a dial on that case. And that's before she injected cerebro-specific proteins to enhance neuronal growth in the various lobes she was interested in.

Stepping onto the elevator, Imo dreaded his upcoming encounter with his poor primate friend. He thought back to a few nights before, when his brother Heinreich had rung his apartment unexpectedly.

* * *

"Imo, it's Heinreich. Can I come up?" The brothers hugged affectionately before Heinreich spoke. "There was a fire at a hotel downtown, and all the Eurasian athletes were kicked out of where we were to allow American travelers places to sleep!"

"So, this is the only way I get to see you!" Imo jested, a bit of truth to his barb.

"I'm afraid so," Heinreich said, somewhat apologetically. "Let's get some sleep and tomorrow I can take you to the tourist section." He smiled and flashed a stack of American money.

"Where'd you get that!"

"Friends."

"Heinreich, suppose someone will see us?" Citizens of The Commonwealth were dissuaded from purchasing items at American tourist traps.

"Imo, don't worry. Everything is cool."

"Cool?" Imo inquired as he thumbed through the strange green bills.

Excited about spending quality time alone with his famous athletic brother, Imo had difficulty falling asleep that night. "I can only get off for a couple of hours," he said to Heinreich, who was by now snoozing on the living room couch. "I've got to be back to the hospital by two."

"Um hummm."

Imo paced the floor that night, and watched the full moon cast its eerie glow through the bedroom window. He approached the glass pane and stared down at the empty street below, listening to the sound of rhythmic footsteps: *Drumpp...Drumpp...Drumpp...* A platoon of armed soldiers goose-stepped by. Imo could see their right arms bent in front of them as their left arms swung free, as they disappeared into the predawn hours. It was a typical 4:30 AM in downtown St. Petersburg.

During lunch, Imo was able to meet Heinreich in the tourist section. His brother brought him fresh fruit and vegetables, meats and pastries. It seemed odd that locals had to pay so much for items that foreigners could purchase so cheaply. It was as though nothing had changed since the days of the old Soviet state. "I'll drop these off for you in your apartment," Heinreich said, having spent about $65 American. See you soon.

"Good luck with your next track meet, old man," Imo joked.

"Thanks, doctor."

That night, Imo returned home and found a pair of bright new blue jeans lying on the sofa. As he wheeled the EEG machine to A-4 the following day, he suddenly remembered that he had forgotten to try them on. He had simply folded them neatly into a bottom drawer.

* * *

Imo entered A-4 and gasped, fumbling to keep the microscope from falling to the floor. The Bonobo had a full erection, which looked to be about five inches long. Madam smoothly stroked the animal with her four-and-one-half fingers, as she adjusted dials with her other hand so as to inject neuro-specific proteins to enhance the sexual arousal system of the ape's brain. "Place the Kirlian device between his legs and attach the electrode here." She pointed to the top of the penis. As she spoke, the primate ejaculated, his fluid landing on her shoulder, cheek, and black attaché case.

Wiping her face with one hand, she marked the EEG graph paper that was monitoring the ape's brain-waves, and placed the ape's specimen on a slide. "Imo," Grotchka said, never altering the cadence in her voice, "take Kirlian microscopic photos every hour for the next twenty-four." She handed him the slide. Before marching out of the room she switched a dial, and the Bonobo slumped into unconsciousness.

"Up her fucking ass," Imo cursed under his breath, as he wheeled the apparatus into a darkroom and attached an electrode to the sperm. Deep waves of self-hate began to overtake him. He felt trapped with Dr. Kopensky gone. Fortunately, a timing device would allow photos to be taken automatically hour by hour, but still he had to come down occasionally to make sure everything was running smoothly.

Rumbling sounds from the lab caused Imo to stop and listen. There was a crashing sound coming from A-4. Rushing in, he saw the monkey gyrating furiously in an epileptic seizure. Arrhythmically rocking its chair back and forth and drooling profusely, the Bonobo pounded its placticized skull into the back of his harness. Dashing down the stairs, two at a time to Grotchka's booth, he blurted,

"The ape is...is...is...." Imo was panicking, unable to express himself quickly. "Hurry," he blurted out, as he rushed back upstairs.

Damn it. She was writing notes. Deliberately, but somewhat slowly considering the circumstances, she moved up to A-4, her big hips swinging in tandem to her football shoulders. Imo noticed her yellow stained armpits, as she removed a vial from the nearby cupboard. Moving back to the vibrating animal, she gripped the monkey's jaw tightly, and opened up a plastic screw-cap near the motor cortex. His eyes rattled madly as foam bubbled down his chin. Deftly, she emptied the small flask into the appropriate channel.

All movement ceased.

"Melatonin," she said in a deprecating voice.

As Madam Grotchka walked back to her booth still wearing a splash of primate sperm on her lab coat, Imo pilfered one of the vials.

APE MAN

The work began to pile up on Vladimir Kopensky, and then of course, his health was becoming a factor. The clandestine bimonthly trips to the heart of Siberia were getting to be burdensome, yet there was so much to do in St. Petersburg. But Kopensky was committed to the necessity for human experimentation, and Yakutski Science City was the only place where it could be safely carried out. Unlike his colleague, Alexi Patrenko, he secretly abhorred using psychic energy as a weapon of war. Paradoxically he liked people, and he liked Americans. Vladimir was good-natured at heart. It was just that the pervasive paranoia from the Secret Police prayed upon his psyche like a relentless parasite. Alexi, on the other hand, appeared so confident when he talked of Eurasia's role in the destiny of humankind. Vladimir wasn't so sure. Nevertheless, he was committed to their ideals and knew that the linkage of his work with the military would give him the stature and financial support that was essential for success; and so, with mixed emotions, he still looked forward to seeing Comrade Patrenko and Yakutski Science City.

As he changed planes at Yakutski airport for the sea plane to fly up river, Kopensky began to realize the necessity for another lab technician there, one that had brains as well as abilities to carry out orders. His eyes searched the barren Siberian landscape, as he reflected upon his work with the famous psychic Nubea Lanilov back in St. Petersburg.

Their studies had reached a standstill but the world had heard of her. A brief positive report of her psychokinetic abilities had appeared in *The Commonwealth Daily,* and so the appropriations continued. But without further experimentation, he knew he would stay at an impasse.

In recording Nubea's brain-waves he did, in fact, discover a high frequency harmonic off of the theta range which occurred whenever she levitated objects, but in Nubea's case, the placement of computer chips was unthinkable, and Kopensky had only partial success in duplicating similar brain-wave states with two young gifted Russian students. Until he experimented with the sinking of depth electrodes into the interior of the human cerebral cortex and enhancing PK specific areas with neurogenic injections, he feared he would never be able to uncover the exact formula for discrete psychokinetic states. Equally as important, he might lose prestige and funding. This was why Yakutski was so vital. The pilot announced over the crackling intercom that the farm was in sight as the aircraft skimmed the choppy river waters, coasting to a halt by a solid wooden dock.

As he deplaned, Kopensky watched his longtime associate, Alexi Patrenko, burst through a small flock of Canada geese in order to reach the dock.

"Welcome to Yakutski Science City, comrade!" A taut muscular hand gripped Vladimir's flabby arm and guided him off the bobbing pontoons. Alexi's shaved head glistened in the bright Siberian sun. He reached over to slap the fat man's belly. "Vladimir, you look troubled? You've got to lose some weight."

Colleagues for over twenty years, there was some warmth between these two scientists, but they had never crossed that invisible line to become real friends. They were business partners, associate explorers into the secrets of man's neurophysiology.

"Come," Patrenko said, as he took Kopensky off the dock to an asphalt path which led to a camouflaged entrance to the underground city.

"It's not that, Alexi. I'm just over-burdened. I want the Bern boy here. Imo's a good worker and we need more theoretical input. Our experiments progress, but our *ideas* are stagnant. Imo's very creative and certainly more intelligent than some of the automatons you've sent to Siberia." They had a good laugh, for in this case going to Siberia was an honor.

"Vladimir, did you see this article out from China?" Handing him a computerized translation, Kopensky read the headlines: *Russian Interest in Parapsychology Links Trends Towards Irrational Thinking & Pagan Beliefs.* "Paganism! Did you read that!"

Still chuckling, Patrenko avoided the main gate as they walked along the hillside to aid in their covert status and then skirted through a side entrance that led to another subterranean passageway. Marching past an airplane hangar, the barracks and a commissary, they walked over to an elevator which took them to the fourth underground level where their laboratory was located. Filing by white-coated scientists and numerous military personnel, they pushed through a FORBIDDEN sign, then turned to face each other.

Patrenko spoke, "The Secret Police do not trust Dr. Bern. I don't think I can put this any more bluntly. It's not Imo, of course, but his globe-trotting brother Heinreich. He may be an Olympic hero to our people, but he is a threat to our national security. He has been linked with defectors on more than one occasion, and his contrary ways have been blue-penciled since the first time he won a silver medal over a decade ago."

"And what athlete has not been in contact with defectors?" Vladimir questioned. He wiped his nose with the back of his hand, in a vain attempt to remove the endless nasal drip he inevitably acquired each time he returned to the Siberian sanctorum.

As they continued their conversation, they approached a sector that resembled a hospital setting with beds for two patients. Mechanically, Patrenko removed a blood-stained sheet from a prone figure. Underneath, lay a young male Tajik who had wires jutting from a series of plastic covered openings lining his partially removed cranium. Blood dripped slowly from one of the valves. It had trickled down past his left ear lobe and had coagulated in a small red pool by the side of his neck. The boy was monitored for Stage IV, delta sleep. Strapped securely to the bed, his neurological headgear resembled a bowling ball-shaped hat complete with shiny black ear flaps.

Patrenko pressed a button to bring the youth to a seated position. "But I think we can talk to them. Is the Bern boy really worth it?" The doctor wiped up some blood off the boy's neck, and sutured a small wound.

"Alexi, I think you take the Secret Police too seriously. Our work is paramount. Bern's input could be crucial here."

"Dr. Kopensky," Patrenko responded, dropping his tone of informality, "we will not discuss old disagreements again. You are like the girl who thinks she is a little pregnant."

Kopensky reached nervously into his pocket for a small box of doughnuts, but Patrenko threw the box down and crushed it with his foot.

"Why must you be so cruel?" Kopensky said as he looked down longingly.

"This isn't a goddamn dining room, Vladimir. It's a laboratory." Patrenko stared at his colleague waiting, and Kopensky, as he usually did, gave way.

"You're right, Alexi," Kopensky said. "Have you gotten the tape recorder ready?" He changed the subject back to the task at hand.

"Yes, I put it on as we entered."

"I hadn't noticed."

"That's because you were too busy eating the goddamn doughnuts."

Kopensky bumped past his colleague on his way to the recorder and rewound it to PLAY: "...It's not Imo,...but his globe-trotting brother Heinreich..." the tape spouted back.

As the recorder continued to play, Patrenko adjusted the dials on a black attaché case.

"Looks like a new model."

"It's a 685."

"We've only got the 485," Kopensky said.

"I'll put a requisition in for Madame Grotchka."

"She'll be pleased."

"I know," Alexi said in a self-congratulatory tone.

Hooked up at one terminal to the brain of the subject, the case was connected with another terminal to an EEG/brain imaging machine that was situated on the other side of the bed. They watched a color-coded computer generated image of the boy's brain as his brain-waves continued to sputter a simple deep-sleep pattern.

Patrenko nodded to Kopensky who pressed the On button, and the subject shook his head and awoke. His sad eyes peered out indifferently at the antiseptic landscape. Patrenko then held up a photograph of an EEG brain-wave pattern, injected neurogenic proteins into the cerebral cortex and ordered the youth to duplicate the pattern. The boy's eyes clicked to attention, and the machine beeped.

"It's a hit!" Vladimir exclaimed. The Tajik was producing an identical brain-wave to the one desired and PK specific dendritic growth was thereby inaugurated. Key areas of his frontal lobes, motor cortex, thalamus and amygdala lit up on the screen. He was on target: *beep...beep...beep.* As the boy's brain continued to produce a psychokinetic pulse, Alexi plotted the cerebral cortex and midbrain wave fronts.

The machine continued to beep again and again, as Vladimir intuitively regulated some of the dials to alter slightly various neurochemical balances. The boy began to jerk and then passed out, yet the beeping continued. Vladimir smiled to Alexi as they approached the tape recorder and played it back.

"Dut   grubrich   thknutum..."   The   recording   was   now   completely incomprehensible.

"When can you get Imo here?" Alexi said, covering the youth with a thin blanket and throwing the dirty blood-stained sheet into a hamper. "Better yet, first introduce him to the psychokinetic experiments. We must proceed slowly. Has he seen the Nubea film?"

"Not yet," Dr. Kopensky replied. He inoculated the sleeping youth with a vile of soybean and carrot extract, and then, they left for dinner.

Vladimir piled his plate high with two extra helpings of powdered mashed potatoes, found Alexi at one of the tables, sat, and continued the conversation. Suddenly the room felt still. Clanking silverware and clattering chatter ceased.

A shadowy figure stood in the doorway and then moved forward. Vladimir did not dare look up, as a tall, big-boned man in a black leather overcoat reached down. Large, thick fingers grazed Vladimir's forehead as they continued over to Alexi's shoulder. As if in trance, Alexi rose, and the two figures departed from the room. Talk in the room did not resume. Vladimir had trouble keeping his hand from shaking. He returned to his meal, but his appetite had disappeared. He pushed the potatoes to the end of the plate and buried his fork.

Kopensky waited nervously for Patrenko's return. Holding back feelings of nausea, he finally felt the tension dissipate when he saw his colleague re-enter the room. "I've got to get back to St. Petersburg," Vladimir said apologetically.

Patrenko just stared and handed him an American parapsychology journal. Penciled in red was an article by Dr. J. Ketchembach entitled *PK Effects on Magnetic Tapes With Abdul Manu as Agent*. The article contained a long section on Manu's ability to alter digital recording devices and influence computer storage banks. There was some preliminary EEG work, but as with most American studies, very little was conclusive in a theoretical sense. Within eleven hours, Kopensky was back in St. Petersburg.

* * *

Imo was looking forward to getting to work. He felt certain that Dr. Kopensky would be back from wherever he had gone. Peddling his bike past the Hermitage Museum and the Cathedral of Mother of God, he turned into the Technical University and coasted past the west wing of Kazan Hospital to the Neuroscience Center.

Dr. Kopensky was waiting for him. "I want you to spend more time studying parapsychology," the doctor said. "I want you to become an expert in all phases of psychic phenomena. You will be reading text..." As Kopensky spoke, one of the younger female students ran into the laboratory, tears streaming down her face.

"Orie is gone!" she cried.

"Lima, I want you to calm down. Have you checked all the lab rooms, the cages and the kitchen?" Kopensky spoke with a sense of care to his voice.

"I saw him not more than seventeen minutes ago walking towards the elevator," Imo said. "He told me he was going on a picnic, and I told him not to eat too much."

"Dr. Bern, do you think..." she began, and Imo interrupted.

"Did you not tell your orangutan that he was going on a picnic? Lima? All of his hand signals were quite lucid."

"Yes," Lima responded, "but I thought I'd wait a few more days," she rationalized. "I've had much homework to do."

"You cannot lie to that animal, Miss," Dr. Kopensky said. "You should know that. Let us try the park. He knows the way. Hopefully he'll not stray too far."

Imo and Lima ran for the stairs, while Dr. Kopensky chose the elevator.

By now a small crowd had surrounded the laboratory primate. High in a tree not far from the hospital, Orie sat placidly. Like a wise old man, he gazed contentedly down at the group as he relished three bananas. A policeman had removed a long rifle from his vehicle and had taken aim, hoping the ape would stay in place. With his free hand, and walkie talkie out, the policeman was about to call in back-up just as Dr. Bern and Lima arrived.

"What will we do?" Lima cried, tears beginning to cascade from her eyes. "Orie will never come down from that tree." Turning towards him, she cried, "Orie, please, please come down. Orie!" He sat ignoring her.

"Be quiet," Orie finally said with hand signals as he chomped down the last banana.

"Let me handle this."

"Yes, Dr. Bern," she replied tearfully.

Orie looked peacefully over the handful of onlookers below him. His vocabulary was over 240 words. Confident that he could handle a day by himself in the park, Orie was reminded of his early youth in Borneo, before he was caught by natives and shipped to St. Petersburg. "You lied to me, girl," he signaled to the student with his hand language.

"She bad. She sorry," Imo signaled back. "Apologize to him," he commanded to Lima under his breath.

Sweating and wheezing louder the more he tried to calm down, Kopensky had finally arrived. Onlookers parted around the wake of his trail. "Dr. Bern," he said, his body exuding, "go get the tranquilizer gun. We've got 485,000 rubles tied up in that primate! I'll handle the policeman."

"It's all right," Imo reassured him. "Orie is a good person. He will come down as soon as our young lady apologizes."

Some of the onlookers snickered, and Kopensky moved to scatter them. He whispered to the policeman to reassure him that the animal was completely harmless, and that Premier Polekov had had lunch with him only last week. The man took his finger off the trigger. Then Kopensky announced to the throng in as serious a tone as he could muster, "This is a very dangerous animal comrades. Officer, have them stand back!"

The girl held her hands up ashamedly and motioned to the orang. "Orie," she signaled, "I apologize. Me bad. Orie."

"Me want 5 bananas. Picnic. Tomorrow." The ape signaled back.

"Yes," the girl said. "Come down. Please."

The pedestrians looked on in amazement as the ape scratched his head to consider the proposal. He looked out over the St. Petersburg skyline, sighed briefly and then descended the tree, moving from his perch to the branch below with a graceful swing of his arm. He grabbed the girl's hand and together they lumbered back towards the hospital. She appearing more like his daughter than his trainer.

"She wrong," he signaled Imo, then, "Me love Lima." The orangutan smiled wisely at the small group of humans and some of them began to applaud. Doctors Bern and Kopensky followed the odd couple back to the laboratory.

"Come, Imo. I'll show you the Nubea film." Kopensky brought Imo up to the hospital auditorium. He showed the youth how to work the movie projector, his chubby hands threading the film at an impatient pace. "Here, you do it!" he said in frustration. The flickering light cast an eerie brightness upon the scientist's portly face, the angle of the glow emphasizing his corpulent cheeks and the knotty imperfections on his skin. "Hand me a review by tomorrow afternoon." Kopensky sounded moody as he exited the room.

The crude black-and-white film began with the face of an overly-large farm woman. She was sitting by a long wooden table concentrating intently, apparently in some sort of trance. One of the scenes showed her rubbing her hands rapidly together and then pressing them over cigarettes, forks and ping-pong balls. Many of the objects jumped about like Mexican beans. Some would even float above the table, though she appeared not to be touching them. Her fleshy round face and bulging eyes strained mightily with each pass of her hand. Imo watched the Nubea movie three times, and wondered if he should broach the subject of inputting the film into digital media.

Returning to the lab he said excitedly, "Dr. Kopensky, I can not believe my eyes! How does she lift those objects? Trick photography?"

Kopensky reached over to a stack of books and proceeded to hand over four American volumes on parapsychology, all translated into Russian, and also five xeroxed articles from Germany and three old Soviet texts.

"Read these and summarize all chapters referring to psychokinesis. Have that report by this time next month. You need not come to the lab until then...except to finish any pet projects."

"Thank you," Imo said. He sat down to look through the books. "Dr. Kopensky."

"Yes."

"Why not put the film on DVD?"

"What film?" Kopensky looked at him.

Imo realized it would be prudent not to respond.

"Take those books home and read them under better light," Kopensky continued, his voice trailing off as he left the room.

"Thank you, doctor," Imo called out. "I'll do that as soon as I finish this chapter."

Waiting an hour, pretending to read, Imo furtively turned to Kopensky's desk and cautiously removed a master key. Having prepared to enter the supply room where all the drugs were kept, he crept out of the office and moved swiftly down the corridor. Normally permission was required, but Imo wanted no log of this visit. He was obsessed with ending the life of Madam Grotchka's Bonobo and had conceived a plan that would minimize the chances of his being blamed.

Slipping by Grotchka's laboratory, he darted around the corner. A lab technician nodded hello as Imo walked by. After the man passed, Imo doubled back. Placing the key in the lock to the storeroom, he clicked it open, and entered. Silently securing the door behind him, Imo waited for his eyes to adjust to the dim light, as he maneuvered to a back cupboard. Finally, when he could see, he carefully thumbed his way past bottles of chloroform, Prozac and hydrochloric acid, before finding the proper remedy. Swiping a vial of curare, Imo turned back towards the door. Madam Grotchka's silhouette could be gleaned through the frosted glass. He watched in shock as her manly hand reached for the handle. Placing her key in the lock, she turned the knob.

AUTUMN IN VERMONT

The city was finally quiet, Chessie fast asleep. Rolling over to an emptiness, she awoke with a start. "Rudy, where are you? Come back to bed." She found it disconcerting to be in bed alone, when he was there. "What time is it?"

"4:30." The voice came from the living room.

"My God, get back to bed; we've got a big day ahead of us."

As Chessie returned to oblivion, Rudy paced the kitchen floor. Three hours to morning, he thought. Only three fucking hours. A large truck grumbled by. *Those bastards can drive all night,* he thought, as he walked over to the living room sofa and sat....

Chessie stretched her arms to welcome morning. She whispered Rudy's name, but he was still missing from her side. Peeking into the living room, she found him asleep in a sitting position on the big brown single sofa. She smiled wistfully at this new complex man of hers, while she prepared the picnic lunches and read over her neatly printed list for their Vermont weekend: flashlight, camera, undies, sweater...each word adjoined by a neat checkmark. Taking out the map, she calculated the mileage and then approached her lover.

"What day is it? What time is it? Who am I?" Rudy awoke with these strange words. He looked around at the unfamiliar resting place, taking a few moments to reorient. "Chessie, did I say something?"

"Yes, you said, 'what day is it; what time is it; who am I'." They looked at each other in silence. "Rudy, this is our chance for an emotional break. From the old grind."

"Did I really say that?"

"No, I said it! You're locked in so deep with one stupid assignment after another that...well, that at times you're not really alive. Are you with me?"

"I'm looking forward to this trip, Chess."

"So am I. It's time for us to be alone for awhile, away from New York--to get close." She reached out and kissed him on the lips.

At times Rudy groaned about the exorbitant monthly charge for garaging a car he hardly ever used, but the feeling of freedom he and Chessie had as they drove out of the city Saturday morning made it worth it in spades. "Vermont, here we come," Chessie shouted as they crossed the Triborough Bridge, catching one last glance at the dull gray skyline.

Rudy was dressed in new denim jeans, a blue flannel shirt, riding gloves and his favorite leather vest. He loved driving his little Hybrid Gazelle in those neat leather gloves. They made him feel as if he were on the Grand Prix in Italy or Monte Carlo. Priding herself in being one step ahead of Bloomingdales, Chessie wore a khaki skort and fur-lined boots, white-laced tunic and paperboy chapeau. She reached her hands up, pulling her head and chest out of the car window and gingerly grasped the roof, turning her face to the wind. "*Eeeeeee,*" she screamed in delight.

"Hey, get back in here. You could fall out!"

Chessie would not listen, but squiggled further out, finally sitting on the window sill. Feet loosely planted on the passenger seat, she nudged Rudy's knee with her left toe and mushed her face into the windshield. Alarmed, Rudy pulled the car over and brought it to a halt.

"Why'd you stop, Rude?" she pouted.

"Hey, what's with you? Don't you want to go to Vermont with me?"

"Oh, Rudy, let me drive and you sit here like the punching bag."

"How 'bout later. I feel so jazzed behind the wheel."

She gave him an expression of acquiescence, and returned to her seat. "Just trying to make a point."

"Uh huh," he said.

As they left behind the gray-worn tenements of the Bronx and pushed for the New England Throughway, Rudy grew pensive. Two hours passed in silence.

Chessie reflected about this new fella, how he was so different from Hank, and yet how much all men are the same. She could hear her mother's tirades, how her father, Chas Barnsworth, retired at age 50, seemed to spend more time on the golf course than he did at home. With her mother dead, galloping leukemia, gone in two weeks, all dad now ever thought about, or so it seemed, was the next foursome, and whether he could do eighteen or twenty-seven holes that day.

"Did you hear the latest rumor?" she tried to break the ice.

"No, love, tell me." Rudy's eyes stayed glued to the road.

"Bob and Phil are planning on investing in a chicken farm. They figure on raising 450,000 chickens and clearing $0.37 cents a piece."

"Come on, where? Phil? Are you sure?"

"That's what I heard. In New Jersey. Can you imagine--a chicken farm?"

Rudy groped for something to say. "I like your new cap."

"You already said that, Rudy. What's going on?"

"I'm thinking--I mean, I'm trying to push it so we can get there," he rectified. "Chicken farm, eh?"

"Yep." Chessie reached for her hat and flung it out the window. It sailed across the highway. Rudy began to break in order to retrieve it.

"Don't stop," she said.

"But Chess."

"Don't stop, don't! I tell you, we've got to get there."

"Chess, what's gotten into you?"

"'What day is it, what time is it, who am I!' You said it Rudy. We're here. This is it, buster."

"What's that supposed to mean?"

"It's you, Rudy. You haven't left New York for two minutes since we started this trip. Let's get away. Let's really get away. I need to be free as much as thee, dear sir, but you won't let it be."

"That's not true, Chess."

"You're lying, Rudy. You're still in metropoland rewriting some boring article. It's me, here, lover. Me! Me!" Chessie grabbed at the keys and removed them from the ignition as Rudy jammed the brakes and turned the wheel onto a flat grassy embankment. The car skidded to a dead halt. She got out, keys in hand, and disappeared swiftly into the lush autumn trees that lined the sides of the road. Brittle leaves crackled under her feet. Rudy waited by the car, but he knew he would have to relent.

"You're right." He shouted into the greens, reds, browns and yellows. "Chess, you're right, where are you?"

Chessie had come upon a warm oak tree. There was something friendly about it, the felt-like texture of its bark, the natural feathery green grass that lay below it, the way its long gnarled limbs seemed to twist out gently in order to let sun-light in as it established its quiet assured presence. She removed her white-laced tunic, bra and khaki skort, and hung them from a low hanging limb. Tossing fallen leaves up as if they were confetti, she spun delighting in the mellow October sun.

Rudy trampled into the sparse woods talking loudly as he progressed. "I'm here now, Chess. You're right. I've left my work behind. Your web is warm enough for me."

"Well then, pull you pants down and prove it to me!" she exclaimed, jumping from behind the oak. Her eyes sparkled with enlightened boldness. Rudy parted Chessie's lips with an agile kiss as she wiggled gleefully. A nuthatch, a downy woodpecker and two juncos flitted by.

"You drive," he said upon their return to the car.

She shifted gears deftly and broke into song, as they churned northward. Three hours later Chessie pulled the speeding machine off the sleek highway, exiting at the familiar crumbling cemetery, as Rudy lay sleeping. "You've finally let it be," she whispered.

"Where are we?" he said awakening as the car slowed.

"White River Junction." She smiled, down-shifted and turned onto the narrow one-lane thoroughfare that ran along the waterway. "You've been sleeping for two-and-a-half hours."

The vehicle motored through mountain passes bursting with autumn colors, rock-lined valleys carved by streams, and old villages with churches and graveyards and manicured houses with bright picket fences, and farmlands with rows of dried cornstalks, acres dotted with grazing cows, apple orchids and fields scattered with pumpkins with their spiffy roadside stands.

Finally, they came upon Al's place, a turn-of-the-century three-story dwelling adorned with fancy shutters and old New England parapets. Tucked in, near the river, the building lay high on a hill peering down upon the winding path that led to its door.

Overshadowing the entire north side above dingy blackened shutters stood a mighty four-hundred-year-old beech tree, it's height, breadth and girth overpowering the 18th century tavern. Snake-like roots rippled through the lawn in giant undulations, as hulking dank branches hung ominously. Although the north side stood in dreary darkness, the side facing south beckoned, with its bright clapboard siding and lofty panorama of sun-lit windows.

Rudy and Chess walked hand in hand up the path. They saw Al waiting on the landing. Tall and prematurely balding, Al was dressed in suspendered blue jeans, blue-checked lumbershirt and a pair of sneakers that gave off sparks of light as he walked.

"Funky," Chess said, referring to the sneakers. She reached out to give Al a hug.

"You know me. Always ahead of the curve." He leaned his head back to give Chessie a better look. "So this is the new beau you've been yapping about." He reached over and shook Rudy's hand.

"You had your chance in high school," Rudy countered.

"Yeah, yeah, so I blew it. What else is new?"

"I wouldn't say you blew it, Al. You own this place."

"Yeah, Chess," he said, feigning agreement. "Ahh, it's so great to see you. Only next time, come alone! Only kidding, Rudy. Chess knows she's welcome any time. You still got the key?"

"Of course. I keep it in my purse."

"Nice to meet you, pal. I hear you're a reporter for *Modern Times*?"

"Yes."

"But we're not going talking shop today," Chess interrupted. "Now that you're retired. How do you do it?"

"What?"

"Keep your sanity."

"Because I'm not on Madison Avenue anymore?"

"Well, yes," Chessie said. "But more than that. You live in such great isolation."

"It's not as hard as it looks, and this place isn't as dead as you think. I can still do work right here with the computer scanner and skype. Your priorities shift. That's all."

"You can print and do layouts?" Chessie asked.

"Of course. Don't even need a darkroom anymore. You can put a slide or a negative right onto the computer."

Rudy stared up at the gargantuan beech tree and simply cut into their conversation. "Gad, Al, why don't you saw a bit of that monstrosity off? The north side of your house looks colder than the dark side of the moon."

"Rudee!" Chessie spoke sharply, "What the heck kind of greeting is that?" Two plump ravens swooped, lighting in tandem upon a great low branch which clung to the roof like an octopus to a clam. The back-lit sun enhanced their blackness.

"It's eerie. That's all." Rudy continued. "Jeeze, Al knows I'm just giving him constructive criticism."

"Actually, I started to once." Al smiled casually. "But when I hooked up my electric chain-saw to that big sucker," he pointed to the branch where the birds were, "every fuse in the whole blinking house blew. Aunti Velma wasn't too happy about it."

"Aunti Velma?" Chessie and Rudy repeated in unison.

Al changed his voice to a more sober tone. "You won't believe this, and Chess, I know you'll be mad because I kept it from you, I mean when you were here before, but I share the house with a spirit. Younno, a ghost."

"No!" Chess said indignantly.

"I didn't want to scare you. She's harmless. Sometimes you can hear her, open'en and closen doors and going up the stairs....So, to get back to the tree, I thought she was warning me off. What can I say. I was afraid to continue with the saw. You think I'm nuts, but...."

Al paused. "Ah, forget it. Let's go in." He turned towards the door.

Chess gave Al the look. So did Rudy.

"All right. You asked. But I'm not crazy. I was afraid of the electricity, and younno, chain-saws, they're fuck'n dangerous. Excuse my French. So I went for an axe." He motioned to a large pile of split logs which lay neatly stacked by a self-standing garage. The amount of lumber spoke for itself.

"I got a ladder. Lashed it to the trunk and gave a few practice swings to get the angle right. Then slammed the sucker into that branch, the very one you were talking about, but as I hit it, the blade just shattered. I was freaked. That's hard-tempered steel, younno. Come on, I'll show ya."

Al brought them into the living room and pointed. There, framed behind a former window pane were fifteen, or so, broken pieces of metal glued together into the crude shape of an axe blade.

"As I struck the tree," he repeated, "I heart a loud ping, and whammo, just like that, pieces all over the place!" He paused and stared at the rug. They looked on in silent wonderment. "Velma's never been unkind, though," he added. "Just don't mess with her tree!" He grinned, his eyes fused with permanent lines of smile wrinkles.

"You're not serious?" Chessie gasped as her eyes subconsciously searched the house. "You must have hit a nail or something."

"The axe *shattered*, Chess," Al almost shouted. "It's a fuck'n, excuse my French, miracle, that I didn't lose an eye."

Rudy's readings in parapsychology had prepared him somewhat for this peculiar event. Thoughtfully, he began, "I've read about this, Al. You're not kidding, I can see that. It sounds like spontaneous psychokinetic phenomena. Who was she?"

"Spontaneous psycho-what?" Al interrupted.

"Poltergeist phenomena," Chessie butted in.

"Oh, poltergeists. Sure. Why didn't you just say so?"

"Well, that's what the scientists call it. A form of mind-over-matter effect," Rudy said. "Did she die in the house?"

"Yeah. Velma moved in with her new husband in 1897 and lived here until her death in 1965. Died in the kitchen while cooking a vegetable stew. Old Yeager, the farmer down the road, found her slumped on the floor with the ladle still in her hand, the stew frozen solid. She was well-liked, guys. They say over 200 people attended the funeral."

"Have you seen her?" Chessie asked incredulously.

"Sure, on three, possibly four occasions. But I hear her all the time." Al paused for a moment, and after seeing that he had an accepting audience went on. "For awhile I attributed the noise to the shifting of the house, or to squirrels in the attic or whatever....the cold spots to drafts....Younno. But all these things were subtle, so they were easy to explain away. Then one night I had a dream about a little old lady...."

"So it *was* a dream." Chessie's tone was now one of relief and self-satisfaction.

"Let me finish. Early that morning, before dusk, a chill came over me. It felt like a wave of cold air--not a breeze, but a wave. There's a distinct difference. My hair seemed 'lectrified and I felt paralyzed. Yet my eyes were wide open. And there she was, hovering by the bed." Al made a sweeping gesture with his hand. "She smiled at me and then disappeared into a mist."

Rudy was staring at Al thinking beyond the story. His interest in the mystery of the missing Eurasian text, in parapsychology in general, and the psychic Abdullah Manu had reignited, but he didn't have to be psychic to see that Chessie was not too happy about it.

"We're taking a walk," she said changing the subject. "This is too spooky for me." Grabbing Al's arm with her left hand and Rudy's with her right, she marched them out of the house and into the sun-lit woods. With Autumn in full swing, the trees had already shed a blanket of yellow, maroon and sienna petals onto the cool dank ground. Chess suddenly broke into a run, Al chasing after. They left Rudy in his pensive state, as they scampered towards their favorite stream.

Quietly, Rudy paused and listened to the silence of the forest. He felt as if he could almost hear the trees think. Carefully, he reached down and plucked a bright red oak leaf, its veins etched in aquamarine. It seemed to whisper to him, "Life is a gift; do not remove its mystery." Sitting on a stump, he stared at the tiny cells ingrained in the leaf, and remembered his days as a child, when he had burned holes in similar flora with a shiny new magnifying glass his Uncle Abe had given him. As he reflected, a translucent aphid crawled onto the stem, and continued its trek up his thumb. Stopping at the fingertip, it turned and glared at him, its clear eyes bulging.

"Rudy, Rudy, come on!" The voice was far away. He shook the insect off and jogged up the tree-lined path to a bend on the hill, then shot down the other side. Al and Chessie were stooping by a brook, floating a series of odd-shaped mushrooms down a steep rock-lined channel.

Misty diagonal shafts of sunlight illuminated the canopy of transparent leaves as if they were stained-glass, while shimmering waters reflected these colors back onto the faces of the two crouched figures. Rudy came over and put his arms around them both, kissing Chessie lightly on the cheek. She turned to him and smiled. The moment was still.

Saturday night at the house, they lit a fire and shared stories of New York City, recent movies and general gossip; Chess repeated the chicken farm tale. Al took out his most recent water colors and some old favorites and played a montage of classic albums: Dylan, Glenn Miller, the Beatles' White album, Joni Mitchell, Io and the Asteroids....The stars and two planets were visible through the upper windows. Chessie had her arm around Rudy. He whispered. "Shush. Shush. I can feel the Earth turning. Do you *feel* it?"

They nodded in understanding as a tear ran from the corner of his eye. He felt as though he had touched the very wheelwork of the universe, and he began to sob, the others just quietly sitting. Chessie rubbed his back as he wept, purging himself of all the aching urban parasites.

"I can't stop," he whimpered between deep heaves and embarrassed laughs. It had been years since he had cried. "I'm not even sure why....It feels good to be alive!" Aunti Velma hovered near the ceiling. She too was crying, but no one heard. She missed Vermont and her house. Velma did not want to leave this Earth and solar system. Life had been beautiful for her here. She especially loved Autumn.

As the fire burned down, Al said good-night and retired to his chamber. Chessie and Rudy climbed the stairs to their room, a soft bed and newly washed sheets awaiting their arrival. Swiftly, they sank into deep dreams, the down mattress dissolving their gritty city souls.

About four hours later Chessie felt a chill overtake her. She snuggled into Rudy's warmth, but he too was aware of the cold. Between rapidly moving thunder clouds, the moon had traveled to their window, lighting up the room in an eerie yellow glow. She whispered, "I love you, Rudy." He kissed her gently and cupped her breast in his hand.

Whoosh! The door opened and closed. In glided Aunti Velma. There was no fear in the air, only wonderment. She wore a full-length nightgown with semi-transparent bed jacket, and her aura was visible, a luminescent amber, tinged with flecks of red and lavender. Her long gray mousy hair hung to her waist, having been released for the night from its day-tight bun. Without a word, she smiled at the couple, as she bent over to straighten their rumpled blankets as if to tuck them in. Rudy noticed tears streaming down her cheeks. They glistened in the lunar light.

Good bye, White River. Then slowly at first, the apparition started whirling. The room grew chilly as purplish-white static charges started jumping from the curtains and wallpaper, until finally the spiral shrank into a tiny dot. It disappeared, *plunk*, and that was that, leaving the couple in a state of befuddled amazement. They smiled oddly, and then returned their souls to the night.

Crack! The room erupted with a flash, as a thunderbolt detonated above their heads. Lightning jumped from the window to the doorknob as every girder in the house rocked. A wind from the east drove the torrent past them as again the moon could be gleaned, appearing and disappearing behind the fleeing clouds. *Crack!* Lightning struck to the east as the rumbling continued, fading out, as the flickering storm zipped past.

Sunday morning, Chessie awoke to the noise of a flying squirrel scampering across the sun-drenched roof. Following the sound to the edge, she watched it glide past the window, the flight blurred by the 19th century window-pane imperfections. "It's gone!" she exclaimed.

Al was in the kitchen preparing breakfast: bacon and eggs, homefries and onions, the tasty smell of food permeating Rudy's hypnogogia. "What's gone?" he retorted.

Chessie shouted as she darted down the stairs and out the front door. "That crazy branch."

Rudy and Al followed. "It's gone!" they too, exclaimed. "It's gone."

"Look," Chessie said, her breath visible in the morning mist. She pointed to the juncture where Al tried to cut the limb. Hit by lightning, the branch had been neatly severed. It lay at the base of the tree, a charred shadow of its former size.

The house appeared almost naked as it stood for the first time unprotected, leaving the trio standing dumbfounded, their cloudy breaths lingering. Soon the chill began to bite through their no-longer warm pajamas, so they returned to the house's warmth and fed their empty bellies.

As if life were of human design Al finally concluded, "I musta sawed more than I thought. It's too unbelievable. I must have. Younno."

"No, Al, we don't know," Chessie responded.

And then all three became quiet, each person searching for a rational explanation. There simply was none. They ate in silence. Al finally spoke again as he cleared the table. "I'll have to get back to the city and see you guys."

"I thought you were retired," Chessie said.

"Yeah, well, younno. Semi-retired. Anyhoo, I probably won't be back for a week or two. Come up whenever. Younno....it gets kinda lonesome especially during the skiing season."

They ate doughnuts and drank coffee in the amber living room, and then packed their Gazelle ninety minutes before the sun crossed the mid-heaven.

"We want to hit some antique stores on the way down," Chessie said. Their host nodded. There was nothing else to say. She kissed her high-school steady on the cheek. Al and Rudy shook hands.

NUBEA

Imo ducked under a rickety pile of spare metal desks, and hid in the darkest corner. He watched in fearful wonderment as the burly Madam Grotchka stomped around the supply room, rearranging boxes and taking inventory of the various cases of drugs she was interested in. With each step, she shook the floor and rattled the walls, coming closer to his thin hideout.

How long can she stay? Imo thought to himself. Becoming more and more horrified with the thought of being discovered, he tucked himself into a fetal position and closed his eyes. She would have no reason to look under here, he reassured himself, crouching deep in the shadows. He opened one eye and stared oddly at one of Grotchka's rolled up stockings.

And then, as swiftly as she had entered, she was gone.

Imo sat upon the floor and sighed. It was close to 7 P.M. She should have left the building by now. *I've got to get out of here before the night janitor arrives,* he concluded.

Shoving desks aside, twisting with his back to the entrance, he reached a metal shelf with his left hand and hoisted himself to his feet, his noise drowning out the click of the door opening again.

"Dr. Bern, is that you?"

Imo wheeled to face the night janitor.

"I didn't know anyone was in here," the janitor continued.

"Petar," the doctor said boldly, "I want you to take these desks into the back closet and create more space for our new inventory." He nodded to the man and walked out.

"Yes, comrade," the janitor called after, "but my name is Edgar."

Bern stopped at the door and turned. "I'd like you to do it anyway."

Down the dim-lit corridors he marched, back to Grotchka's laboratory, using the master key once more to enter. The room was eerie and quiet. He moved quickly and strode over to the monkey's chamber. The ape seemed to recognize Imo's footsteps in his sleep, and drowsily opened one eye. The young doctor approached the drug cabinet and removed a vial of melatonin. Tipping a drop of curare inside it, he carefully placed the lethal container back onto the front row of the appropriate rack, closed the glass door and walked over to the ape. Removing A-4's muzzle, Imo stroked the monkey silently on the face, turned and walked out.

During the next convulsion, Madam Grotchka would reach for the medicine, and Bonobo A-4 would sink benignly into death-sleep. His lungs would silently collapse, cutting off all oxygen to his broken heart and torn brain.

Imo practically skipped out of the hospital that night. The ape should be dead days after he left, and at least a week before he returned. They would never discover his deed, for the dosage of poison was less than five millionths of a gram. It was, he felt, the perfect crime.

* * *

The first article Dr. Bern read was on poltergeist phenomena (translated into *noisy spirits*). It seems that occasionally an adolescent becomes the focus of a series of paranormal events whereby objects spontaneously crack, explode, or levitate. Pools of water can appear from nowhere, strange lights may also be seen, and rapping noises often resound from the walls. The article went on to state that the situation usually parallels a stressful time in the life of the subject. Interestingly, sometimes the subject remains unaware that he is the source of the disturbance.

Imo read about PK experiments involving psychics who could create temperature differentials in a thermometer from across a room, move a pendulum sealed in a closed glass case, change the direction of a compass, interfere with electrical equipment, and even materialize and dematerialize small objects. The young doctor read about the history of psychic research from Europe, America and the former Soviet Union, present-day neurological and quantum physical theories, animal and spontaneous PK tests, attempts at creating machines run by psychic power, and autobiographical statements concerning 20th century psychics. The sheer volume of the data overwhelmed him, especially in lieu of the initial disbelief he had when viewing the Nubea film. When he sat down to write, he organized his study into four parts:

1 - The history of research into psychokinesis.
2 - Current evidence for mind over matter effects.
3 - Neurophysiological brain imaging correlations.
4 - Quantum physical and other theoretical speculations.

The paper ran sixty pages. He kept it conservative, but at the end of the history section, Bern did make mention of such silly topics as table tipping, Ouija boards, psychic surgery and dematerialization. Some of the readings were so bizarre that he felt like a fool writing about them. Nevertheless, he reasoned, if any one of these occurrences were valid, then why not any other? Did the mind's ability to influence the weight at the end of a pendulum differ qualitatively from the ability to levitate it? Imo planned to ask Dr. Kopensky for a meeting with Nubea Lanilov, which was of course, exactly what Kopensky had wanted.

As Imo boarded a train for Nubea's home, Madam Grotchka stuffed her Bonobo into a trash can. She had suspected the Bern boy, but this was due more to her nature than to logical deduction. She was too overwrought with depressive temper to think clearly. It would take over twenty months to train another monkey able to reach the neurophysiological capabilities of Bonobo A-4.

"Kopensky," she demanded, her face twisted in repressed rage, "give me clearance for Yakutski. It will take me two years to catch up to my research with this death, whereas there I can train human subjects in three weeks."

Kopensky smacked her hard across the mouth. A statement like that could be heard, even recorded by anyone. As far as his staff knew, human experimentation was taboo. Drawing himself to his full height he said, "Madam, you are to take full charge of our operation. Imo and I are leaving for Siberia in a month. All workers are to report to you. You know how to reach me."

Grotchka huddled in a chair, her lip already swollen and tender. She spoke quietly and very slowly. "Get me that male orangutan your students are working with." She cared little that she would destroy someone else's research, or that the orangutan was a favorite.

"Impossible," Kopensky replied. "Good day."

Grotchka placed a hand on her swollen face and looked at Vladimir with vengeful darts of hate. "Get me the orangutan," she repeated, as she spit some blood out onto one of Kopensky's reports. He should never have hit her, and he knew why.

"You're joking," he whispered.

"I never joke, Vladimir. You know me by now."

"But...Orie's almost human. He's like one of us."

"Exactly, doctor. Exactly."

Madam Grotchka stood her ground and stared at Kopensky fiercely. It was clear that she was walking a tightrope now, utilizing her brute strength to suppress a sinister force that Kopensky could not chance to have unleashed. He simply had to relent or risk the integrity of the scientific edifice he had created here in St. Petersburg. Without the aid of this woman, not only would his trips to Siberia cease, but he would have to explain this to Alexi; and if she became crazy, Bonzo the Nut might review the matter. "Yes," he said quietly.

"I did not hear you!" she taunted.

"Get out."

As Grotchka left the room, she dumped a stack of Kopensky's papers on the floor with the sweep of her brawny forearm.

Imo traveled to Nubea's small farm house, realizing what a rare treat it was to take a train ride out of the city, especially on a week day. Excited and hopeful, he stammered in his mind as he rehearsed the questions he was going to ask her. Hailing a cab from the sparse wooden train station, the young doctor was driven past deep fields of rich green potato plants before the car approached the quiet country abode. A horse, two cows, a few sheep and some goats were corralled to his right. The horse and one cow looked up at him casually as he knocked boldly at the front entrance.

The door opened slowly, revealing a round and husky farm woman. Crinkling pouches around soft ping-pong ball eyes smiled sagely at him. Her short-sleeved dress revealed fleshy, yet muscular arms. "Come, come, she motioned. It is time."

The interior of her warm house revealed simple living: floors and shelves, benches and walls all of wood. They entered a living room adorned with plants hanging in radiant window sills, two large potted vases to his left, a spinning wheel by the opposite wall and in the center, surrounded by six thick chairs, a big oak dining room table, the one Imo had seen in the film. "Sit," she said. "Talk. This is your time."

Imo wanted desperately to see a paranormal demonstration, but he feared putting Nubea out. Meekly, he handed her a wooden box of matches and cigarette lighter, and asked her if she would move them psychokinetically. Nubea smiled.

Suddenly this middle-aged farm lady transformed. She began to gleam. Grabbing the lighter confidently, she hid it in the palm of her hand as she paraded around the room, her mind now focused very far away. "Must feel vibration....Get in tune with them." She spoke as almost to herself, but definitely for Imo's benefit.

Dr. Bern deliberated, not at all happy that she was controlling all of the variables, but he was willing to sacrifice scientific rigor lest he embarrass Nubea and stop her performance. She wheeled and plumped down at the head of the table bringing the lighter by her forehead. Rubbing it rapidly between her hands, stopping occasionally to blow on them, she placed it forcibly down on the table only to see it accelerate away from her chest as if a large magnet were repelling a tiny one. It jumped three feet and skimmed a few more. Imo ran to it, scooped it from the floor, and placed it in front of Nubea. Again, it skipped across the table.

He began to get up to fetch it. "Stop." Nubea said, and he froze. She began to hum loudly and sway as she stared at the small device, her melody beginning to radiate from her vast chest cavity throughout the walls of the farm house. She swayed gently back and forth and the whole room seemed to electrify. Imo felt the hair stand up on his arms and thought he could see a beam of light extend from Nubea's forehead. The lighter oscillated as it gently *lifted* off the floor and slowly rose to the height of the table. Then, like a flash, it ascended at a rapid speed and careened off of the ceiling, off two walls and bounced onto the table. Blacking out momentarily, Nubea soon regained composure, her forehead covered with beads of perspiration, and her armpits soaked.

After tea and light conversation, Imo caught a late night train back to St. Petersburg. He had no words for what he had seen, and had said simply before he left, "Thank you, Madam Nubea." Her sunboiled eyes smiled.

Although disappointed about the lack of scientific controls, he felt elated. For the first time in his life he understood the term *walking on air*. He felt in the presence of higher knowledge and meticulously wrote out his notes on the train. He was in deep concentration when it hit him. "Man is blind," he wrote. *So very small,* he thought. Why, if Nubea could do all that, what other secrets lie within our psyche?

The following morning Imo awoke to the ring of the telephone. It was Dr. Kopensky. This was a first. "Imo, Vladimir here. How'd it go?"

"Amazing, Dr. Kopensky, I cannot tell you. She levitated my lighter and sailed it across a table, bounced it around the walls....Fantastic, fantastic."

"Did you check for tricks?"

Imo paused. "No, I uh..."

"That's all right, Imo. There were none. See me at the hospital at 9:30." Kopensky hung up before even saying good-bye.

Imo decided to call home. "Mama."

"Imo, is that you?" Mrs. Bern sounded surprised and pleased. How's everything?

"Mama, I saw Nubea Lanilov, the great Ukrainian psychic. She levitated my cigarette lighter. I saw it with my own eyes."

"Son, are you studying your school work? You mustn't get sidetracked. You seem overtaxed. You mustn't let Madam Nubea take you away from yourself. Heinreich will be home for your Papa's birthday. Perhaps you will make it also?"

Imo began to realize that he could share this experience with very few people. His friend Paige would not believe him, nor could his intern colleagues. Two hours later when Kopensky offered him a position in Siberia to work with psychokinesis and neuro-biological states, Imo was even relieved. So few people could really understand his brilliance. Saying good-bye to Madam Grotchka pleased him enormously, but he pretended to be unhappy to leave.

"Good-bye, Madam. I will be leaving the hospital and wanted to thank you for your guidance," he lied, trying not to stare at a boil which had recently erupted on the side of her nose.

"Have you returned all equipment and chemicals?" Grotchka was writing notes and did not look up to acknowledge his effort at parting on good terms. Somehow she knew his secret, but had not quite realized it, and somehow Imo knew that she didn't know that she knew.

"Watch him carefully," she cautioned Kopensky in Imo's presence. "He's squeamish and vacillating. And then she turned, faced Imo squarely and said, "Before you go, Dr. Bern, bring me up the microscope and working slides from A-4." Her cold stare could not quite hide envious hatred. Imo took the elevator up to Level A. As he approached the 4th room a cold shiver overtook him. He went back to the lift and left the building. He could not face the orangutan.

SIBERIA

Imo wrestled with sleep, the Siberian air cold and stale. Corkscrew portals of different shades of beige and obscured worlds disturbed his dreams. A deep thrumming resounded within. After just weeks underground at Yakutski Science City, it felt like years. Imo had hardened to the idea of wiring the brains of the numerous gorillas and orangutans that were being used in neuroelectric mapping experiments. There was just no other way to get information on the internal organs of the cerebral cortex. Nevertheless, he still preferred to read the research rather than get involved with primate experimentation, and so most of his lab time was spent working on dream telepathy tests with human subjects, or in the library. He also experimented with PK dice-throwing tests, MRI and brain-wave studies.

As the dread of winter approached, Imo longed for the summer Uzbek sun. Siberia was too harsh to enjoy a walk out on the tundra, and also, walks by oneself were tacitly frowned upon. So instead, he day-dreamed. While sitting in the library he mentally drifted back a year and a half...to his family and their last reunion: his father's birthday.

At that time Imo had just begun his research in parapsychology, having returned from Nubea's farmhouse only twenty-five days before that. Now, his memory was fuzzy. Ironically, although he dealt with PK and telepathy on a daily basis, he simply had not witnessed as dramatic an example of gross effects since that one and only time. The Tajik subjects could not *move* objects, they *influenced* the outcome of random number generators. Imo constantly relived the Nubea episode because it was such a mystery. He had the paradoxical experience of knowing the scientific reality of psychokinesis, having witnessed it, but he had trouble in total recall of the sequence of events, and therefore doubted his perceptions. Did the lighter hit the ceiling and *then* the wall, or did it bounce off the wall *first*?

It was details such as these that plagued him. The past seemed like a dream. Even when he related the incident to his family just a few weeks after it took place, somehow the story lacked that ring of surety. Imo even questioned his own handwritten notes; he would read over and over such sentences as: "The lighter flew from her chest as if repelled like a magnet." At Papa's party, Heinreich dissected the account with unrelenting skepticism, and Papa kept one eyebrow permanently raised. Mama, however, was more concerned that the family was together than in the validity of Imo's story.

Papa said, "You sound like your Jewish grandmother... always with the fortune cards, reading the future, making the wishes." It was rare that they talked of religion, let alone their Jewish heritage, for they feared reprisals from the officials. The Jews were still a sore spot in governmental policy. It had been just two months prior to Imo's family visit that two Jewish refusniks had been tried for treason and sent to the Gulag. If it were openly publicized that Heinreich was 1/4 Jewish, it might be difficult for him to travel abroad. Papa's remark brought silence; Heinreich's children were led from the table.

Heinreich leaned his chair way back, placed his long lanky ankles on the corner of the table and spoke as Mama returned, "The West also has their so-called psychics. I saw the Egyptian Abdul Manu on the Dolly Carson show the last time I was in America. Just as Nubea, *he* levitated objects and shot light from his forehead." Heinreich paused dramatically, adeptly tipping his chair farther as he continued, "but the next guest was a magician with the strange name of the Incredible Fandango. This fellow not only duplicated Manu's tricks, but he spouted green flames from his two nostrils!"

Heinreich positioned two fingers from his nose to mimic the fiery illusion, and with his other hand between his legs, he flipped himself back over the chair, stood tall and held it high as a prize. Papa broke into deep belches of laughter. Mother Bern tittered in spite of herself, and even Imo began to smile. Soon the house was one of merriment again and the children were called back for dessert.

During their stay at home, Heinreich took Imo for an important walk. They strolled through the concrete playground they had spent their youth in. "Imo," he said, while tightrope walking a four-foot high rail fence, "I know you are serious about Nubea, and I have heard that both the CIA and our own Secret Police have been involved in the use of microwaves in subtle biological warfare--it's been in the Western papers for years." He leaped to the ground. "So be careful. Make sure you know who you work with. Some are former KGB. We have them even among the athletes."

They climbed atop a concrete barrel and sat there with arms around their knees. As the last 15 years of their life evaporated, the brothers peered down the favorite alley way to watch through the kitchen window of their home the silhouette of Mother Bern washing dishes. "If you ever need me, leave a message with Yon Dubinoff."

"Dubie the sports reporter?"

"Yes, Yon lives in Suchan, not far from Vladivostok. He will know where I am."

Reliving eternal squabbles, the siblings shoved each other off their respective perches, wrestled, hugged and scooted back through the alley to their home.

"Imo, I want you to have this." Heinrich opened up a dark black pouch and handed Imo a digital camera.

Imo looked it over. "Fifteen megapixals," he exclaimed. "Hein, I can't."

"Sure, you can. I can always get another, and this way you could take pictures and email them to Ma and Pa, or to me, when I'm on the road." They talked until two in the morning and then both crashed in their beds.

By 10:00 A.M. the following day, Imo was back in St. Petersburg--a few weeks later, Yakutski Science City.

Flying in a sea plane up the Lena River from the town of Yakutski had been exciting, and Imo fantasized hidden dangers. From the air, nothing could be seen except grazing cows and huge hills of low growing shrubs. He had had no idea how well his government could camouflage an entire metropolis. Kopensky met him at the pier.

"Dr. Bern, this is Dr. Alexi Patrenko, director of the laboratory." Kopensky hugged Imo as they walked from the dock, and a moment later, Imo shook hands with a well-built man dressed in the classic white lab coat, reading glasses dangling from a black neck strap, and a shaven sagittal crest. His deep-set blue eyes receded so far into his cranium that they seemed to peer out of shallow caves. He had thick muscular biceps and Neanderthal bone structure. Patrenko's bow-tie added an abstract component to this vigorous appearance.

"Come, Dr. Bern," Patrenko sounded dramatic, "Let us show you around."

For effect, he avoided the side gateway he and Kopensky always took, and led the way, instead, to the main camouflaged portal. It looked like a plain old hill covered with brittle green shrubs. However, as they got close, Imo could see the plants were all plastic.

As if Imo's life were a dream, thick seventy-five-foot high mottled brown and lime colored curtains parted...and a large aeroplane hangar was revealed. Imo was astounded by the success of the illusion, for during the flight in, although he had noticed the protruding mound, he had not seen the entrance, nor guessed its actual intention.

Inside, on the right was a small fleet of tanks, a few helicopters and three jet planes, one of which had the cockpit removed. Along the back wall, five rows of shiny sleek white warheads were stacked sixty feet to the ceiling.

"Nuclear," Patrenko mumbled.

People were moving across the expansive surface on roller-skates and bicycles, and a small train carried packages from one end of the hangar to the other. Quiet echoes rebounded.

Imo was taken by the jets, two of which had their wings swept forwards instead of backwards. "What are those?" he asked.

A handsome man in a flight suit approached and greeted Patrenko. "Those," the man said, "are our new Sukhoi-67s."

"Colonel Kandinsky, I would like you to meet our latest addition to the city, Dr. Imo Bern. Dr. Bern, Colonel Kandinsky."

They shook hands. "Any relation to Heinreich Bern?" Kandinsky inquired.

"He's my brother," Imo said proudly.

"Well, imagine that. Good to meet you."

Imo watched as the unusual looking cockpit was being lowered into the second Sukhoi-67.

"This is our latest design," Kandinsky puffed. "It's a next-generation supersonic two-seater which we developed at the Sukhoi Flight Test Center.

"Near Vladivostok?" Imo inquired.

"Yes," Kandinsky said.

Petrenko became intrigued. "What's so special about it, Colonel?"

"The forward wing design, for one."

"And?" Patrenko prodded.

"Alexi, there are only four of these two-seaters in existence, and two of them are right here. Dr. Bash's orders."

"Yes," Patrenko agreed. "But you suggest other reasons."

"Ah, yes," Kandinsky acquiesced. "The cockpit. We call it the *Zeus ex machina*. It's a fully self-contained ejection compartment that has retractable wings."

"You mean, it can fly, if ejected?" Imo asked, excitedly.

"That's what they tell me. You need two passengers for stability for the two-seaters. There's no engine in the ejection compartment, of course, but those bulges you see around the seat...."

"Yes," Patrenko cut back in.

"Those are the retractable wings. They should spring open after ejection and then the thing flies like a glider. We also have a fleet of one-seaters, but they mainly stay on the Gudunov," Russia's state of the art air-craft carrier.

As Kandinsky continued talking, he was interrupted by another pilot carrying a walkie-talkie. "I'm sorry, men, I've got to take this call." Kandinsky placed his hand over the speaker to say goodbye. "Dr. Bern, perhaps if you get to the coast, I can tell you more." Kandinsky waved them off, and turned away.

Continuing on their tour, Patrenko led the way between two of the tanks to an elevator. "The entire complex lies in four floors below the gateway level," he said. "There is no need to reiterate the high priority of this village, comrade. You may tell no one about it. No one--especially your family." Alexi paused to let his remark sink in, cocked his head and stared deliberately into Imo's eyes. Seconds passed before he continued, "All letters will bear the postmark Vladivostok, and you will be flown there periodically to acquaint yourself with the hospital and surrounding landscape."

"With Colonel Kandinsky?"

"No doubt, but mostly with Dr. Bash."

"Oh?" Imo said, questioningly.

"Any break in security, any breach at all, will be considered an act of treason." Spotlights from the ceiling reflected off Patrenko's forehead as he pounded point after point.

"This is the first floor." The elevator silently opened to a long hall with glass partitions on both sides. "We keep all computer hard and software here, although there are terminals on all five underground floors. We also have a secure-line digital phone-linked terminal interconnecting Yakutski to Vladivostok, Tashkent, St. Petersburg and Moscow. In this way, while you are on the East coast, or Kopensky is in St. Petersburg, you can both work on your programs together. Of course, there are also terminals in your bedrooms and digital cameras in all rooms.

"And, just to reiterate, this is a secure circuit completely independent of the Internet. These terminals can never be used to access the web. Do you understand?"

"Yes, sir," Imo responded.

"Good. If you want to go on line, we have separate machines for that." They walked on. "The military keeps control of the right half of this hall," Patrenko paused to slap the wall. "It bisects the underground complex. Their section is off limits. In case of nuclear war there is enough food for 2.4 years, seeds for every type of fruit and vegetable, and a 175-cubic-foot dehumidifier that can condense water directly from the atmosphere. The barn you flew over doubles as a green house; the roof is paneled with photovoltaic cells. Naturally, it is disguised to look like regular shingle. At the far end of this hall are the administrative bureaus, post office and grocery store. The game room is to your left."

They turned down a staircase to Level 2. A thick steel door marked FORBIDDEN lay to the right. "Radioactive equipment," Patrenko explained. "Links to rooms in the military wing." They passed the animal experimentation laboratory on their left. Imo ignored the horrible sounds and smells. He was not going to get emotionally involved again. Damn it, he had his professional career to think about. He was no longer a boy.

Down at the far end was another big door and Alexi pushed it open. The clanging lock-click echoed down the hall. Imo was taken aback. They had entered a theatre during the middle of a lecture.

Before them, on stage, stood what could only be described as a goliath. Dressed in a heavy leather flight jacket, brown Lenin peasant cap, faded blue-jeans and cumbersome riding boots, the man seemed to emanate a sinister glow which was amplified by his big bushy eyebrows that tailed away from his forehead like feathered wings. Easily 6'5", with long oily black hair that straggled from beneath his cap and a large broad nose, his face was further adorned with flaring nostrils, and a tufted moustache that drooped and bobbed in precise staccato with each syllable that he spoke. Imo sensed Vladimir and Alexi tremble. The smell of fear pervaded the place.

The giant faced a semicircular arena that contained an audience of about 200. Below them, seated comfortably in a center box, was the great politician Petar Bonzovalivitch. The giant nodded to the politician, who in turn, nodded back, as Patrenko whispered from the side of his mouth, his eyes glued forward. "You are wondering why Bonzovalivitch is here?"

"Yes," Imo responded in kind.

"A good bit of our funding comes from revenues diverted by him," Kopensky chirped.

"But all he talks about is invading Alaska and dropping A-bombs on the Chinese," Imo found himself blurting.

Patrenko semi-turned and shot Imo a stare, as his face swung back to face the stage. "You underestimate him, Doctor Bern."

"Shush!" one of the scientists a few rows away reprimanded.

All eyes turned. The three did their best to avoid the stares. "His name is Dr. Georgi Bash," Kopensky finally managed after the curiosity of the group seemed to be mollified.

"Doctor?" Imo questioned, staring at the fearsome figure. Patrenko silently bobbed his head.

"A great hero from the Ural uprising. He's from the Ukraine," Kopensky added.

Stretched before the lecturer between two 4-foot slabs of granite, and supported by just her ankles and neck, Imo was surprised to see the Ukrainian sorceress Deus Maxima. Just five-feet tall and draped in her customary jasmine robes, Deus spanned the two supports while immobilized.

Dr. Bash paused in his demonstration until Imo finished his survey. Four Ukrainian soldiers were posted at each corner of the auditorium with hand-held weapons that appeared to the young doctor to be laser guns. Six overhead cameras panned the gallery and stage. A peculiar shudder tingled down Imo's back as he looked on in awe. For he could feel the waiting silence and now realized that the magi had paused for him.

A deft performer, Bash guided the emotions of his audience. Lumbering swiftly to the end of the stage, he nodded to Patrenko and another scientist, and then he whirled and returned to his starting place. The two arose as one, stepped up onto the stage, and walked over to a third block of granite which was much thinner than the ones being used to prop Deus up. About the size of a thin tombstone, Imo estimated its weight to be a hundred pounds. In unison they lifted, and struggled to bring the slab to the suspended Deus. Bash nodded again. Each man used an inside knee to help with the leverage. Smoothly and cautiously they hoisted the block onto the self-proclaimed messiah's stomach and chest, then let it rest. Imo gasped. Deus didn't budge.

Silently, Bash surveyed the room and carefully climbed upon the block supporting Deus' head. Testing the granite slab delicately with his foot, he found the point of balance, and pressed down. Deus held firm, her body rigid as a steel girder. Like a circus performer alighting a tightrope, he shifted his weight, lifted his other foot and stepped aboard.

"Psychokinetic states," he boomed, "are inherent in all levels of animal matter." Pointing with fingers outstretched to the crowd, he began to chant, leading the audience with his mantra. *"Ommm, Ommm, Ommm."* Lifting both hands, and bringing the hymn to a vibrating crescendo, Bash then leapt from the slab like an overgrown cougar, landing on the stage with a dull thud. Placing a single hand on the woman's forehead, he shouted, "Up!" And with that, the sorceress thrust her hands forward, and heaved the slab some fifteen feet to the rear of the stage!

Crashing through the wooden floor, it sent splinters into the air and a shock wave throughout the complex.

Directing the chanting to a soft hum, Bash began to pass his fingers over Deus' body, delicately stroking what looked to Imo to be her aura. Appearing almost as a musician, the hypnotist began to strum this strange bioplasmic zitar. Deus seemed to glow as her body began to pulsate, the chant mellowing into silence as the vibratory effect petered away.

Bowing his head to the house, Bash lifted the rigid body from the stone posts that had supported her, and held it in his arms out symbolically, as if it were an offering. Grinning broadly, his lips pulled tight and eyebrows preened, he flipped his subject up as he snapped his fingers, quickly catching the body on its downward flight. It collapsed limply into his massive forearms.

Gently, almost fatherly, the mesmerist stood Deus Maxima back to her feet and took her out of trance. She turned to her audience and spoke. "The Holy Spirit has guided me," she intoned, "to reveal to you the great powers I enfold. With Dr. Bash's guidance and the help of the great visionary Petar Bonzovalivitch, we can see a day when our empire shall reclaim the mighty sphere of influence it once held."

Bash's glancing hypnotic eyes flashed like a beacon across a sea of heads, piercing Imo's when they passed. The young scientist felt his soul flutter, as some other victims fainted in their seats.

THE OCCULT LIBRARY

SUB-BASEMENT THREE. Kopensky spoke first as they descended to Level 3, his stomach bouncing rhythmically with each downward step. "Bash has gotten her to levitate objects. We've seen the video." He nodded to a camera overhead. "But the damn resolution's so poor....He claims when the moon is right and her 'horoscope' is in proper alignment, her powers increase proportionally."

"Is that really possible?" Imo asked Kopensky. Patrenko answered instead.

"Come, friend," he said, putting an arm around Imo's shoulder, "to my library and then, tonight, we have dinner with Bonzovalivitch!"

Passing a large number of marked and unmarked laboratories and classrooms, Patrenko turned into a chamber which glowed a deep cherry red.

"Lasarium," he said. They walked through to a hallway that led to a back door marked PRIVATE. Alexi took out a key and opened it. Tweaking his bow-tie, and letting Imo and Vladimir enter before him, he marched them down rows and rows of hardbound books, touching many with an affectionate hand.

"This is my private library. I have spent many hours studying the lives and powers of the most spectacular occultists of the past 5,000 years: Moses, Jesus, Merlin, Paracelsus, Mesmer...." He seemed to address each tome with a different intonation. "People think everything is on the Internet, but I tell you true, it is here." Patrenko glowed. Removing a particular text, he handed it to Imo. "This is Anton Mesmer's doctoral thesis, with an original comment by Levi."

Imo looked at the title: *A Physico-Medical Inquiry Concerning the Influence of the Planets on the Human Body.* Taking the book back, Patrenko read the foreward out loud:

> Mesmer's purpose is to show that the planets not only affect other planets, but also biological life here on the Earth. In this tradition, Mesmer will discuss such events as the Moon's effects on the tides and the weather, how planets stay in their orbits, and how light affects living organisms. Mesmer shall also reveal what he has discovered about a subtle energy which he calls animal gravity, a force which he says, has the properties of cohesion, elasticity, irritability, magnetism and electricity.

Placing the book down, Patrenko continued excitedly, "Besides being a hypnotist," he began with dramatic emphasis, "Mesmer was a healer. He worked with biomagnetic forces not only to affect the behavior of his subjects, but also to control their subconscious minds. Mesmer believed that his powers were enhanced by magnets, which in turn derived their powers from the planets. He healed his patients not only by suggestion, but also by having them ingest magnetized water. We have done only preliminary studies, but have found a tendency which does suggest beneficial effects with the use of magnets." Patrenko closed the book and placed it back into its slot on the shelf.

"Come," he said, leading Imo and Kopensky to another book-stacked corridor. Once again his face lit up as he selected another book. "This is a personal account of human levitation of the psychic D.D. Home, an outspoken superpsychic who toured the United States and Europe during the late 1800s. Many numbers of witnesses have testified to his abilities. The British scientist Sir William Crookes said after many controlled studies, 'The evidence in favor of it is stronger than the evidence in favor of almost any natural phenomena the British Association could investigate.'

"His extensive investigations of Home appeared in the *British Society of Psychical Research,*" Kopensky added as Alexi handed Imo a copy where Imo read:

> On three separate occasions have I seen Home raised completely from the floor of the room....On such an occasion I have got down and seen and felt that all four legs were off the ground at the same time, Home's feet being on the chair. Less frequently the levitating power was extended to those sitting next to him. Once my wife was thus raised off the ground in her chair.

"Imo, I am giving you a copy of the key to my library. No book may leave this room."

"I understand."

"And, what is this?" Patrenko held up a black pouch, and dangled it in front of Imo.

"A digital camera, sir."

"Vladimir should have told you. We do not allow any electronic processing of the events which take place in this compound. And, of course, emailing from here is *verboten*." He used the German word.

"Well, then, I won't use it."

"It is not as simple as that. You cannot keep it, and in fact, the camera will have to be destroyed."

"But what about my single lens reflex camera?"

"That's another story entirely. We would want you to keep it."

"I don't understand the difference."

"Are you aware of Echelon?"

"No."

"It is an omni-present eye that the American's have. Their defense department, as I'm sure you know, erected the first platform, which is the underlying superstructure of the World Wide Web. The sad truth is, they have, at least in theory, the ability to read any email sent anywhere at any time throughout the globe. And they always did."

"I wasn't aware of that."

"So, that is why we do not allow the emailing of sensitive material. Hard copy whenever possible is mailed, so your single lens reflex camera is good. We also use our own satellite system for secured wireless communications. But, as you know, even those could be intercepted. With encryption, we feel pretty safe about it, but the mail system is really the best way. So, I am going to have to confiscate this camera, and just so you know, it will be destroyed as soon as I leave you."

"Am I allowed to take notes here?"

"Yes. And you also may occasionally photostat a page here and there. I prefer you mainly take notes in pencil. But, keep your camera in working order. We might make use of that as well. In the mean time, I want you to report on levitation and psychokinesis in hypnotic experiments. Eventually you will link your findings to neurological data and states of consciousness." They left Imo in the room with a pile of rare manuscripts. He poured over works from every country and every age from the Renaissance to the present, falling asleep with his head resting quietly on Alister Crowley's treatise on alchemy.

* * *

The dining room was transformed, as if by magic, into a banquet hall. All of the plastic tables and chairs and even the lunchroom counters had been removed. Placed in their stead was a long, T-shaped table with the horizontal dais raised two feet above the vertical. Tall maroon-colored curtains surrounded the walls.

Sitting next to Vladimir and about two-dozen scientists, Imo looked up from his salad plate as Bonzovalivitch drifted in, arm and arm with the lovely Miss Maxima. They were accompanied by a small entourage that included Alexi Patrenko.

"Where is Dr. Bash?" Imo inquired.

"I've no idea," came Kopensky's reply.

As if on command, the scientists stood and gave the regal couple an ovation.

Dressed in a long flowing robe of yellows, pinks and oranges, Deus seemed to float as she drifted to her seat and waited for Bonzovalivitch to fix her chair.

Curiously, with all eyes upon him, he ignored the lady's request, and walked over to the pulpit. There, he stood and waited as the applause built up once again. Bonzovalivitch continued to wait for long strained moments, until Patrenko gathered the presence of mind to pull back Deus' seat and help her get settled in. An awkward silence permeated the room.

"Sit, sit," Bonzo declared, motioning with his hands. Adjusting his microphone, he continued. "She may be Deus Maxima to you, the 'Spiritual God-Mother' and self-proclaimed messiah, but to me she is just Koltrena Zbjovi, a subject of the state, and former mistress of the late charlatan Chanook Vrhynnahov.

"I remember when Koltrena was dancing in a tawdry vaudeville act in Sevastopole on weekends, and holding rigged séances in gullible people's houses during the day."

The shock of Bonzo's speech took Deus by surprise, and when she finally realized what he was saying, she began to get up to leave.

"Oh, just keep your place, Koltrena. You are in the middle of Siberia. There is nowhere you can go. I do not doubt that you have some psychic abilities, or Dr. Bash would not have taken you under his wing, but let us not keep up this messiah charade, here in this great secret science environment.

"We are involved in the serious business of harnessing the human mind for one purpose only," Bonzovalivitch continued, "and that is to recapture the Empire that was once Russia."

Raising his hands to stifle applause, Bonzovalivitch went on. "My task, and yours," he said, "is to raise our country from its knees. We shall not let any other nation offend us anymore. Premier Gorbachev was a pussy-man, who allowed our nation to crumble into fifteen separate pieces, and it is my task to reassemble them, and extend our predestined borders south through Afghanistan and Pakistan to the Arabian Sea, west through the Balkan Peninsula to the Adriatic and Mediterranean Sea, and east through Alaska.

"This can be done through armed conflict and nuclear war if necessary, or it can be achieved by more clever means--through hypnosis and the threat of mass suicide led by our own lady queen." He gestured to Koltrena who was sulking in her seat. "Or, my friends, triumph can be achieved by implementation of psychic cybervision and our Nimrod Contingency."

Behind Bonzovalivitch, a curtain parted and Dr. Georgi Bash entered, accompanied by a Tajik youth whose head was adorned with a woolen toque. The room seemed charged with an electric force field. Two scientists fainted, and Deus Maxima collapsed at her place.

Perhaps it was an optical illusion, but Deus seemed to float up under the guidance of Dr. Bash, who raised her as if he was a puppet master and she was attached to his fingertips by marionette strings.

Imo sat with the rest of the scientists in awe as the robed figure floated out of the room with Bash and the youth by her side.

"Eat, eat," Bonzovalivitch said.

RAISING THE ANTI-MATTER

After just a few weeks of research in Dr. Patrenko's private library, Imo approached his overseer. "Doctor, I've read about your work in anti-matter and dematerialization. How far along the road of repeatability are we in controlling this form of psychokinesis?"

"Where did you read about me?" Patrenko sounded conversational.

"In the English text *Eurasian Parapsychology* by Gregory Hereward. It's in your library."

"Yes, well, we're working on that," Patrenko said in a seeming non-sequitur.

"On what?"

"I'm sorry. What were we talking about?"

"Your PK work involving the decay rate of radioactive material versus experiments using dice."

"And?"

"Well, in the decay rate instance, the mind would have to interfere with the interior of the nucleus of the atom."

"And in the other instance?"

"I don't know. It's a more gross effect," Imo hedged. "It's just that it's different."

"Well, good! Now you have a starting point."

Imo still wasn't sure where Dr. Patrenko was headed.

"The four known physical forces of the universe."

"Of course." Imo suddenly realized.

"Now, if we describe them, we will see that the mind is interfering with at least three." Patrenko dramatically wrote out the name of each force with a magic marker on a dry whiteboard

"According to traditional physics, these four forces account for all known processes in the physical world," Patrenko spit out his words as if he were a drillmaster. "As you can see, we are talking about binding forces. The Strong Nuclear Force binds the nucleus together, the Weak Nuclear Force binds the neutron together, Electromagnetism binds molecules together and Gravity binds stars and planets together. Levitation, of course, interferes with the force of gravity. Metal bending, with the electromagnetic force. The decay rate of radioactive material involves the weak nuclear force. And dematerialization and rematerialization, ultimately involves the transmutation of the nucleus."

"The Strong Nuclear Force," Imo said, more as a reflection than a question.

"Yes."

Kopensky waddled into the room and joined the conversation. "Physicists all over the world dematerialize electrons and protons every day of the week. The event is called pairing phenomena. By stepping electrical frequencies above the million volt range," Kopensky continued, "pairing phenomena can begin to take place."

"Naturally, we have been attempting to duplicate these phenomena with psychics in the lab," Patrenko explained. "Through biofeedback we have been able to cause the minds of our human subjects to attain altered states of consciousness which are harmonically related to these precise physical negative energy states."

"You mean having their brains replicate the extremely high frequencies created by particle accelerators?"

"Exactly, Dr. Bern. If we can get them to step up their frequencies, their brains can generate anti-particles."

"Theories like those of Einstein only apply to existence *within* space/time," Kopensky pointed out, as he wrote out Einstein's famous equation on the whiteboard. "But the mental domain, the very concept of consciousness, as a separate force different from the other four which would exist in inner space, doesn't really fit into existing theories."

"Mind is not equivalent to mass," Patrenko cut back in, "and therefore, it need not be bound by the speed of light. It exists in a tachyonic dimension which is faster than the speed of light."

"In some derivative sense," Kopensky added, "it is apparently also linked to the concept of antimatter."

"Wait a second," Imo said. "I've been reading Ouspensky's ideas about the role of spin and the squaring of one dimension to get to the next dimension."

"You mean, if A is a line, to get to the next dimension, A^2, we turn 90° for a length of A to get the plane...." Kopensky began.

"Yes, and spin the plane up 90° for a length of the plane to get a cube, A^3," Imo cut back in. "We could do the same thing with the limiting factor of the speed of light." Imo requested the magic marker from Patrenko and rearranged Einstein's equation.

$$E = MC^2$$

"You see, it is very simple. All we do is solve for C." He wrote:

$$E/M = C^2$$

"I see that." Patrenko said. "But what does it mean?"

"E, or energy, would correspond to mind. And M, or mass, would correspond to matter. That old adage for psychokinesis, mind over matter, would now equal the speed of light squared. Just as we change physical dimensions by orthorotating and squaring, from A to A^2 to A^3...." Imo began.

"From line to plane to cube," Kopensky interjected.

"Yes. We do the same thing for changing from the physical dimension, C to get to the mental domain, C^2." Imo stood back proudly, both hands on his hips.

"A mental world square to the physical," Patrenko considered.

"And tachyonic, to boot," Imo added.

"I like the geometry of it," Kopensky concluded.

PROFESSOR KETCHEMBACH

First thing Monday morning Rudy dialed New York University and asked to speak to Professor Jay Ketchembach.

"Professor, my name is Rudy Styne. I am a reporter for *Modern Times* and hear that you are involved in parapsychological research. May I come over and chat?"

"Sure, son. Be here at a quarter after eleven. I can show you the lab, take you on a few errands?"

"OK."

"Good."

Styne ducked underground. It was 11:04. He paced the bleak platform, another nameless face awaiting a speedy train. The subway felt cold, as the stale damp air bit into his clothing. Two travelers went upstairs, leaving the staging more desolate. And then a few more people trickled down.

A crumpled bum with hostile eyes and mysterious brown paper wrappings, paced in the distance near a far exit that had been padlocked shut. Pounding his fist in haphazard fits, the vagabond drifted closer, his purple pants permanently stained with dark black blotches. Not about to bluff indifference, Rudy moved away. The man seemed crazy enough, there was no point in proving it. And then the bum disappeared.

A few minutes later the air seemed to change. Milling metropolytes parted instinctively as the tramp reappeared once more, pounding and cursing, another fluorescent-lit schizophrenic about to explode.

When the train arrived, Styne made sure to sit in a far-away car, choosing a seat by a 260-pound athlete and his family. The enormous father wrapped huge NFL arms around his sensitive wife and dark-eyed child. As Rudy looked on, the youngster stared up noticing yellow and lavender luminescence surrounding the reporter's head. Clattering tracks chugged past.

Rudy smiled at the family, feeling safe...until the paper-bag bum crashed through the sliding doors and rocked past. He seemed to "humph" at Rudy as he swung around an empty pole and smashed his fist violently into one of the closed subway doors. No eyes budged. Someone turned a page. The train rattled on.

Rudy was late, which was evident by the professor's expression. "I have a lot to do before class," Professor Ketchembach said. This physicist had long gray hair and the wild'n-free look of success. He looked to be a young 68 years. "Come," he said, before Rudy had time to even sit.

The professor led the reporter down a cold linoleum stairway to a hygienically smelling laboratory. In one room an assistant was injecting the arm of a man who had a severe case of Parkinson's disease, and in another room another assistant was sitting with two paralyzed individuals and monitoring an EEG machine.

"Hey Jackie, Bobbie," the Professor said, as both of the subjects smiled and nodded hello back at him.

Rudy watched as each subject, in turn, moved a robotic arm which was able to lift objects and also direct a remote controlled vehicle which sped around the room.

"Sarah, why don't you tell Mr. Styne what's going on here. He's a reporter for Modern Times."

"Yes, professor," the lab assistant said. She then explained that Jackie and Bobby, who were both paraplegics, had learned to generate specific brainwave patterns that a computer could translate into commands which where then transferred to, in the first instance, a robotic arm, and in the other case, to a toy car which received remote signals to direct it around the room or through a maze.

"I don't see any head gear," Rudy said.

"And you won't," Professor Ketchembach replied. "We have performed minor brain surgery on our willing victims to sink in small electrodes which can be read by this computer."

"So, we are victims," Bobby cracked.

"Of course. Do you think anybody with any intelligence would have allowed us to tamper with their brains," the professor shot back.

This cracked everybody up, and the professor took that as the cue to move on.

In a third room was another lab assistant who was monitoring a somewhat different type of EEG machine. Sitting beside her, a cosmetically enhanced woman in orange terrycloth pants, off-white silk blouse and matching orange turban whispered, "Jay." Upon each sleek pink hand, she wore rainbow reflecting titanium nail polish, and a number of gaudy rings. Her face was radiant, her lipstick, pasty-magenta.

"Tanya, this is Rudy Styne, a reporter for *Modern Times*."

Rudy and Tanya exchanged hellos. Her look was sensual, penetrating. Rudy felt a stirring.

"As you can see, we've got her hooked to an EEG neuro-mapping machine." The professor pointed out the various electrodes that were pasted to her scalp which were hooked up to a computer screen that displayed a map of a virtual brain that pulsated with different intensities of color in various regions as Tanya's mind shifted focus.

"No depth electrodes?" Rudy asked.

"Heaven forbid!" the professor shot back. "Tanya's a Stradivarius. One of the most important psychics of the last fifty years!"

Peering back through false eyelashes, and pretending embarrassment at the accolade, Tanya interrupted. "Professor," she said as she twisted a tiger-eye pinky ring, "I had a dream about you last night." Tongue to her tooth, she drifted to the professor's frequency, "...dreamt that many American parapsychologists were visiting you in a church. You were seated on your motorbike on the pulpit and on its side the following letters could be discerned:

U-S-R-R

"Your wife was sitting in the front row and was wearing a diamond teardrop locket." Tanya elevated her eyebrows, creating two furls which etched themselves deeply into the gentle undulations of the other wrinkles of her pulsing forehead. "Are you planning a trip?"

"Yes, but not by railroad. And it won't be in the U.S. There's a psychotronic conference in Florence in a few months, and my wife has been upset about me going without her." The pupils of their eyes intermingled. "Tanya," he said, the way he would say *thank you.*

He turned to Rudy as they drifted from earshot, "She's one of the most thoroughly tested psychics of the last decade. At this very moment, we are correlating her brain-waves with another psychic in Chicago, trying to see if any resonance can be discerned during successful telepathic interchanges.

"Haven't neuroscientists linked particular brain-wave patterns to spoken words?" Rudy asked.

"Yes," the professor said, "and with reverse engineering, to movie trailers, face recognition and even deeply buried memory traces."

"Reverse engineering?"

"Yes. Say experimenters play three different trailers, for instance, one for the movie *Gladiator*, one for *Pretty Woman....*"

"You mean the one with Julia Roberts?"

"Yes, and say one of the original *Star Wars* movies."

"OK," Rudy said, following so far.

"Each film is going to generate a different generic brain-wave pattern in the subjects being neuro-mapped. And this principle can be extended to face recognition, sentences read, memory traces and so on."

"So, if an experimenter sees a particular brainwave pattern...." Rudy began.

"A computer can punch out a precise image, with a statistical certainty, give or take, of what the person is seeing. We aren't exactly 'seeing' what the person's brain sees, but it's damn close."

"Let me see if I understand what you are saying," Rudy said.

The professor cut it. "Say, you show ten people a photograph of John Kennedy or Jackie Kennedy. You get a brain scan when they view those images and they become like a voiceprint."

"You mean, if another person produces that pattern...."

"Within a statistical range of certainty," the professor added.

"Then you would know that the person is thinking of John or Jackie Kennedy?"

"Exactly, Mr. Styne, exactly! And the more brain prints we catalog, the greater our certainty. For instance, you can do the same for emotions. You can imagine the possibilities. Privacy is dead. Just consider the use of such equipment by law enforcement officials who are questioning suspects."

You mean they could even pick out the killer by reading his brain-waves?"

"Well, there's a real chance for error, but yes."

"Error?"

"What do you do with someone who has a vivid imagination, or worse, and here's where we come in, how about a case of telepathic transfer. Even as far back as the 1960's and 70's, the old Soviet Union had great success in being able to tell when a telepathic message is sent because of an idiosyncratic brain-wave pattern that they identified. Of course, there are many false positives, but this kind of research is where it's at."

"You mean like reading Morse code?"

"I think voice recognition software is a better analogy."

"And, what's with the guy with Parkinson's?"

"Oh, that," the professor began. "That is linked to our work in neurogenesis."

"Neurogenesis?" Rudy asked.

"The enhancement or transfer of genes and growth of neurons in specific areas of the brain to repair damaged parts or enhance latent abilities."

"You mean, get the guy to stop shaking?"

"Exactly, and we do the same for cases of Alzheimer's."

"I don't follow," Rudy said.

"What we have found, is that there are deficits or malfunctions in specific areas of the brain that cause these specific diseases. For instance, in the case of Alzheimer's, the hippocampus, which processes memories, isn't working well, which means that that brain area is no longer synthesizing the correct proteins in the proper amounts. In actuality, in most of the cases of neurodegenerative diseases, there's too much protein. The shut-off valve isn't working and this process becomes toxic and spreads to neighboring areas, thereby destroying them. For Parkinson's, it is the substantia nigra."

"Is that a part of the brain?"

"It's in the brainstem."

"And what does that have to do with telepathy?"

"No easy answer. We're thinking that psi-enhancing protein synthesis is occurring in the frontal lobes, the limbic system, because emotions are involved, and maybe the pons which controls REM and other deep brain functions."

"So, how are the two linked?" Rudy asked.

"What we are trying to do is understand how toxic proteins propagate, but use that technique in a positive way. That's where neurogenesis comes in."

"You find the good proteins that make a person telepathic...." Rudy began.

"Or psychokinetic...." the professor prompted Rudy to continue.

"And then you propagate these proteins?"

"Exactly, to enhance those areas of the brain that are responsible for telepathic or psychokinetic abilities."

Rudy got what he saw as dynamite stuff and shifted gears. "By the way," he said, "when are you going to return Hereward's book *Eurasian Parapsychology* to the library? That's how I got your name in the first place."

"It's very odd, but only last week I was copying notes from it on the desk and now it's gone. I'll have to purchase another to replace it."

"But professor," the lab assistant offered from across the room, "another teacher borrowed it. He told me you said it was OK."

"Who? What department?"

"Electrical engineering. He said he knew you quite well -- called you Jason. I think he was Korean -- spoke with a heavy accent. I figured you had to know him.... He was so deliberate, so firm."

"Shit, Harve, have you ever heard anyone call me Jason! I'd appreciate it, if you would keep people that you don't know out of my office. Is that asking for too much?"

Harve gave him a look and stormed out.

"Why would anyone steal a library book that is so readily available?"

"I think I know the answer," Rudy responded.

The professor motioned with his head to the various people wandering around the lab. "Let's discuss it later in my private office. First, I'm gonna test you, and then maybe take you on a quick tour of the city?"

"Sure."

"OK," Ketchembach smiled as he guided Rudy to another room where a wire mesh tumbler containing three pairs of dice stood upon a solitary white metal table. A row of silent computer terminals stood along a rear wall poised as if ready to take immediate commands. "What's your favorite number from one to six?" Ketchembach asked.

"Five."

"Really?"

"Yeah."

"OK. Let's see what you can do. Try to will a specific number to come up."

"What do you mean *will*?"

"Will power. You know, wish. You can do it. Just concentrate on your fives when I roll the tumbler and let's see what happens."

The professor turned the switch on and the tumbler began to rotate. When the dice rolled to a stop each man looked at the upturned faces. Four of them had fives turned up. The others had a two and three showing.

"Very impressive," Ketchembach remarked.

They proceeded to do a run of 100 with six die being rolled each time. Rudy got a score of 144 fives.

"That's amazingly good, son. Since, in total, we did 600 actual runs, and since there is a 1/6th chance of getting any one number to come up, statistics predicts that you should only get 100 fives, 1/6th of 600, if it is chance. But, you got 44 hits above chance. That is statistically significant. I would say that you have PK ability. But let's do another test."

Rudy was led to a row of lights arranged in a circle like numbers going around a clock. The professor turned a switch and the top light became illuminated. "I want you to try to will these bulbs to light in a clockwise manner. They are hooked up to a random number generator. Here, I'll show you." The professor clenched his fists and began to concentrate, but the lights would only move in a counterclockwise manner. "Hmmm, negative psi," he mumbled.

"Negative what?"

"Psi. It's another name for ESP. Sometimes a subject gets an opposite reaction to what is expected. This is called negative ESP or negative psi. Somehow a person's beliefs influence the outcome. If a person is pessimistic and thinks he can't affect the dice, he may achieve an outcome less than chance would predict. From a statistical standpoint, this is just as relevant as a score above chance, and thus a negative form of ESP."

"You mean the person does so bad that that is also statistically significant?"

"Now you got it."

"So why did you just get negative psi? Didn't you think you would influence the lights in a positive way?" Rudy asked.

"Yeah, I did. It's just one of those things. Maybe it was because I was thinking about that stolen book."

"Or going to Italy without your wife?" Rudy teased.

"She's got this wedding. Yeah, that's gotta be it. Here, you try it."

Rudy began to concentrate. Sometimes the lights would light clockwise, and then counterclockwise giving an overall random motion. Then suddenly, there was a burst of clockwise movement and then another burst and then another.

"Very good, son. Excellent," the professor exclaimed. "This is one of the most important experiments in parapsychology."

"This row of lights? Why? From what I have read, psychokinesis has been established for over half a century."

"That's true, Mr. Styne. However, this is a more modern study, because this chance number generator, controlling the lights, is being triggered by the random decay of radioactive material." The professor turned on a Geiger counter and moved it to the source. It began to click rapidly. "Inside is a gram of low grade uranium," the professor said. "If left to its own, these bulbs would light in an aimless fashion because radioactive material decays at a random rate. This is the whole underlying premise of quantum theory. If, however, one were to alter the cadence of the decay rate, it would establish that the human mind *can* interfere with the atomic structure of matter. And *that* has serious implications."

The professor paused to let his remarks sink in. "You, son, have influenced the way the lights illuminate. You have imposed order on its randomness just by thinking about it. Clearly, you can see that the human mind *can* interact with the elementary particles in very specific ways. This is why we quantum physicists are so excited about psychokinesis. Somehow, the very structure of atoms allows human information systems access to its Gestalt patterns.

"By synching the MRI with EEG readings during PK tests, we hope to find the proper state of consciousness conducive to PK manifestations. Through biofeedback and brain imaging, we should be able to generate PK in a more elegant fashion by isolating the specific regions of the brain that are involved when our psychics are successful in their PK experiments."

They walked back to the professor's office. Rudy glanced up at the wall. There, tacked up and scattered about, were articles and photos of the professor covering a lifetime of achievement. There he was with Albert Einstein, on the front page of *The New York Times*... "Another time," the professor said, referring to the walls.

"Sure," Rudy replied.

Once seated, Ketchembach spoke again. "A few of us in the West are close to controlling PK through brain-wave monitoring. And, it seems, the Eurasians have done the same thing. That is why Hereward went there in the first place--to get more information relevant to his own research. One of the biggest problems is getting EEG patterns from the deeper layers of the brain. We know what is happening on the outside layers, but the mid-brain activities remain a mystery. We can't very well sink electrodes into Tayna's brain."

"I see," Rudy said.

"So, obviously, human experimentation remains off limits. However, and this is a big however, we have Dr. P. Karl at Wisconsin and a Ukrainian experimenter, M. Grotchka, both working with chimpanzees, Bonobos and orangutans, and, independently, they are obtaining important information that does have profound implications for this research.

"Naturally, the biggest problem is to find an ape who has PK ability." They both laughed. "We have enough trouble finding human subjects. All we can do is simulate similar brain-wave states and extrapolate from there.

"Hey, enough of this for awhile. Would you care to join me on some errands? You'll enjoy the ride. And then we can come back here if you want to, and finish up any other questions."

"Sure," Rudy said. "What the heck."

The professor grabbed a shopping bag and led Rudy out the door, and down an alley-way which led to a parking lot where an old German motorbike was chained. "Hold these." Ketchembach pointed to the bag which contained two prints.

"May I?" Rudy asked, as he reached in to look the prints over.

"Go right ahead," the professor said as he helped fish them out. "This one is a modern and the other--here, I'll show you--comes from the early 1800s."

"Neat," Rudy said.

"It's called Jesus in the Synagogue." The professor held the older piece respectfully as he turned it towards Rudy.

The picture depicted a youth standing in trance amidst four wise rabbis, and a fifth, who stood off in a corner with a look of consternation and betrayal. A cross-shaped aura surrounded the child's head as he stared into space, his right forefinger pointing to passages in an open bible.

"You can see why I want it framed."

"Yes, I can. It's truly wonderful. And what about this one?"

"Oh, that. It's a gift from one of my students. It's not on the same level, but, what the heck, I figured I was doing one, why not do'em both. It's just a motorcyclist jumping a skyline. But I like the shot of the setting sun beaming light through the spokes of the front wheel."

"Yeah, it's nice," Rudy agreed.

Unlocking the bike, Ketchembach handed Rudy a jet-black helmet which he put on. Sitting behind the professor on the extended seat, Rudy grabbed the bag with one hand, and wrapped his other around Ketchembach's waist.

Having never been on a motorbike in the city before, the experience took the reporter by surprise. Before he knew it they were down on Second Avenue. The Lower East Side bristled with hippies, yuppies, roller-bladers, college kids, groups of ladies with baby carriages, nouveau artistes and delivery men.

Ketchembach scooted along the walk-way up a short wrong-way side street.

Rudy took this relatively quiet moment to shout a question. "How did you get interested in parapsychology?"

"It was 1951 when I had my first telepathic experience." Ketchembach barked back as they drove. "I knew that my uncle had passed on....Didn't think it, just knew it. There is a real difference between the two." They turned up 9th Street.

"What happened?" Rudy vociferated, as they overtook a police car slowly cruising.

"He appeared in my room and said good-bye."

The bike swerved to a curb and was parked. Rudy followed Ketchembach into a mat-cutting store.

"Professor, what have you got today?" An unshaven man in his mid-40s with a spare tire of complacency around his middle accepted the pictures, and they discussed different frames and mats. "I'll have them back to you by Friday?" He seemed pleased with the professor's taste in art.

"It was an apparition, so it was more than just telepathy," Ketchembach continued, as if there had never been a break in the conversation. "No one believed my story, but there was never a question in my mind. He was in the room like I am here with you....kind of misty, but it was definitely him."

They were walking rapidly, talking. The professor turned into a brightly colored archway. As the door opened, pungent fumes of incense blasted vast recesses of Rudy's smell center. Boxes of pink and green, yellow, white and orange from places like Singapore, Turkey, India, Sumatra, Taiwan and Hong Kong decorated the multi-leveled interior. "Aroma therapy," the professor quipped to Rudy as he picked out eight different fragrances and two candle holders. "Feizel," he said, "any new imports?"

"Just dees." The plump Arab stepped from behind a stack of wicker and leather thongs. Adorned with a bulbous red proboscis which seemed to absorb the nuance of every weird scent in the store, Feizel grinned as he carefully presented the professor a statue of a four-armed elephant god, whose rippling fingers echoed the snakelike shape of the sinewy trunk on its face.

"How much?"

"Nantee-fi dollarr; but for'd yuuu," the olfactory merchant breathed yet another sensuous sniff deep into his rhinencephalon, "$78.50."

"I'll take it." And Ketchembach bought it, peeling out four twenties from a sizeable roll. "Keep the change."

Rudy could not know that it was a sought-after piece which completed a set of Tibetan gods the professor had collected over many years.

"Some schnoz on that guy, hey?"

"Yeah," Rudy grinned as they returned to the street.

They stepped into a bank. Ketchembach handed Rudy the statue, and then took his place in line. Styne could feel the weight and vibration of the mysterious piece, its four arms frozen in the middle of a rhythmic motion. Made of bronze, it looked to be over one hundred years old.

Rudy stared at the icon as he awaited the professor's return. Its visage seemed to change again and again, triggering a series of archaic mental images in his mind. For an instant, Rudy felt himself enter a timeless dream-like state as the bustling city disappeared from his consciousness.

"I know this sounds crazy, but the statue's face transformed when I looked at it." Rudy continued the conversation as they strolled unconsciously past the motorbike. "Perhaps it was just my imagination, but I saw a slanty-eyed face appear where the elephant's is. It was a real mirage. I could see the eyebrows, golden and orange colors, an aura....It was....I don't know. I never really saw something that wasn't there, before now." Rudy considered the incident in Vermont with Aunti Velma, but chose to remain silent about it. He glanced up in time to glimpse the head of an Asian man who quickly turned away. His fur toque struck a chord.

"That phenomena is called transfiguration."

"You mean there is a name for it!"

"Of course," the professor said. "It's well known in some religious practices. Signifies an entrance into the Mysteries--the deeper levels of mind. It is said that Great Masters have the ability to appear one way to some of their adepts and at the very same time, quite another way to neophytes." The professor leaned down and picked up a dead bumble bee. "Some people just see a statue. You saw something else."

They had walked half way through Washington Square, and Rudy had not even noticed. It was a typical morning in Greenwich Village, the park alive with its mixture of foreign visitors and city slickers. Gaggles of giggling children unleashed bursts of soapy bubbles into the breeze, as frisbees floated by like a fleet of miniature extraterrestrial aircraft.

Selecting an appropriate spot to rest, the professor held the well-preserved insect up to the sun, its wings tucked as if it were praying. "We pass the Great Mysteries all the time, but never recognize," he said reflectively.

"So, did I actually see a god?"

"Well, there are some theories that say you had simply released an archetype from your collective unconscious. The statue triggered the memory stored in your primate brain-slash-mind so that you did not see a conscious entity per se. It was an image from man's collective past....buried in your own unconscious."

"What exactly is an archetype?"

"A mental structure or formative pattern that exists in the psyche of all humans....a predisposition for the creation of primordial images."

"And what do *you* think, I mean, personally?"

"It's hard to say. There are other theories that suggest that you actually contacted a member of the intelligence hierarchy, a dweller beyond the threshold...., ET's, angels or saints in your language. The 19th century psychic Madam Blavatsky called these gods the Masters of Wisdom. Alice Bailey, another occult writer, referred to them as the Great White Brotherhood. These are spiritual entities that live in a realm beyond the Earth dimension--a higher step up on the astral plane. In this case, the magical statue would have acted like a trigger tripping your mind to the correct frequency--an access code, if you will, to that dimension."

The professor held the icon up and rotated it. "Somewhat like a tuning device."

"Is there any hard evidence for the existence of the White Brotherhood?" Rudy had begun to take notes.

"Well son, that's a tough one."

They had settled on a park bench next to a French gentleman dressed in a crisp chapeau, tailored coat and shiny patten-black shoes. The grey-haired man nodded hello at them as he leafed through a neat leather-bound satchel containing 8 X 10 glossy photos which he displayed to other elderly gentlemen. Rudy and the professor looked over to see 1960s style pictures of scantily clad showgirls that the man had obviously dated or met personally fifty odd years ago. Each photo was addressed "Dear Rudy."

In one picture "Rudy" had his arms around one topless gal, and in another he had *his* shirt off. The old Casanova smiled graciously to any newcomer in his continuing attempts to widen the circle of onlookers, a crowd of gentlemen laughing and smiling, momentarily living in the amorous residue of another's bygone adventures.

When the professor noticed the similarity in names, he looked at Rudy and asked, "Any relation?" They began to laugh, the Frenchman smiling in return.

Across the way, along the low cement wall, a nine-year-old magician captured a crowd of about thirty-five. Dressed in a tuxedo and penciled-in moustache, the polished prestidigitator performed fabulous miracles. With his younger brother as an aid, scarves disappeared, rabbits emerged and torn newspapers were made whole. Myriad quarters kept the boy's top hat solidly weighted on the asphalt stage before him.

With their eyes to the right, Rudy and the professor could see three different musical groups, each with varying amounts of onlookers. Under the Washington Arch, a hippie, dressed like Uncle Sam, complete with long gray goatee, red suspenders, pin-striped blue and white pants and stove-pipe hat, belted out original hits on a make-shift honky-tonk keyboard, his syncopated melody resonating under Stanford White's architectural legacy.

A frisbee overshot its mark, Rudy tossed it back. The professor began to speak. "Hard evidence is a difficult term to deal with, m'boy. There are psychic photographs of the Count St. Germain, Coot Humi, and Jesus of Nazareth, but would that be considered hard evidence?"

It was apparent to Rudy that the professor was not seeking answers necessarily, just pointing out some of the difficulties in proving the reality of the mysterious world of the psyche.

"The hierarchical structure of the Masters of Wisdom is alluded to in the Twelve Apostles, and in the continuing discussion of the archangels in both the *Old* and *New Testaments*. We start with the One, and Lucifer sits to God's left, Michael to his right...."

"Good and evil," Rudy added.

"No," the professor was quite serious. "Yin and yang, conscious and unconscious, material and non-material, male and female. Evil is not a necessity, and Lucifer is not the Devil. Evil is of human creation."

"How can that be? Look at the world. There is so much that is wrong and immoral--murder, ripoffs, pornography, wars, that horrible take-down of the twin towers just a few blocks from here."

"All human creation," the professor replied.

"Nearly 3,500 innocent died."

"Doesn't change a thing. Look at Hitler. Look at Stalin."

"OK, Dr. Ketchembach, if evil is man's doing, how do you explain the appearance of the Devil in the Bible?"

"That's a mistranslation of the original writings. The Bible talks about a tempter or deceiver, not an inherently evil force. That's a very different thing. But the problem is that the work was always translated at the level of understanding of the translator." Professor Ketchembach paused to let the information sink in. "It is clear," he continued, "that when you go back to the original sources, this entity in its original meaning, was not intrinsically bad, but rather, sly. That's a horse of a different color, but it is easy to see how the translator got it wrong.... So in the case of Lucifer or Satan, originally these entities were meant to be cunning forces, now they are seen as evil."

"But, Lucifer is always depicted as evil," Rudy protested.

"Not at all. Look at the very word Lucifer. Do you know what it means?"

"Can't say I really ever thought about it."

"Lucifer is the light-giver. The occult or hidden meaning for Lucifer or 'lucid' is related to the snake in Genesis, chi energy in Kundalini Yoga and to what Carl Jung called the shadow, the animal nature in man -- his libido. Evil is the misuse of this energy. The correct use wins ball games, invents wireless television, makes babies. The Devil on earth is created by human mistreatment of the power source."

"That makes some sense," Rudy agreed, "but it still seems to derive from a power that seems awfully ruthless."

"Nevertheless, humans need not kill in order to survive. That is our choice.

"According to Sufi philosophy, we are born incomplete and must evolve during the course of life on earth, to, as the alchemists tell us, turn our base nature, Lucifer, into a golden one, Michael. Our creativity and our evil derive from the same wellspring." The professor took out the elephant icon and stared at it again. "Occasionally when *homo sapiens* sink too far into the muck, a Master of Wisdom descends to the earth incarnating into a body of a human. This person is called an avatar."

"Would this Abdul Manu be an avatar?"

"I suspect he is rather an emissary. Sri Nilaya Baba in Bhutan is a living avatar. He is a Being of Light taking the form of a human." The professor leaned back and watched a cascade of bubbles drift by.

"How do you know this Baba fellow is an avatar?"

"Number one, because he says so. Number two, because he has a huge religious following. And number three, because he can prove it. This man can materialize golden objects with the turn of his hand. He has been studied by parapsychologists from all over the world, including myself."

"You've tested him?"

"No. He will not allow himself to be tested in controlled experiments, because he feels we must cultivate faith. Proof of this power will not give us faith, he says."

"Do you really believe this?"

"I have seen."

"Is that proof?"

"For me."

"But doesn't materialization violate natural laws of physics?"

"No," the professor said. "Psychic phenomena is as magic to us as an airplane is magic to a savage. However, before we discuss such bizarre forms of psi phenomena as materialization or psychokinesis, we should begin with discussing the little experiment we just did with the dice. Come, let's go back to the lab. And if you've got any more questions, we can take care of them there."

As they got up to go, the elderly Frenchman caught Rudy's eye. Flashing a picture circa late 1950s of a tall blonde girl in pasties and a G-string, bending over a dresser in a most compromising position, he said, "Oui, oui," with a broad smile. There he was in the photo, several generations younger, but definitely the same face grinning as a reflection in the bureau mirror. He was dressed in a tuxedo. "Oui, oui," he said once more, lighting his eyes up as Styne and the professor departed.

"I think I'll walk," Rudy said. "It'll give me a little more time to reflect."

"Sure," the professor nodded. "See you in 11.5 minutes."

"Look out, mister! Duck!"

Instinctively, Rudy dropped to the ground as a yellow frisbee silently zipped past his ear. As he began to rise, his eye caught sight of a familiar fur cap and herringbone coat flowing rapidly along the periphery of the park. The Asian paused and proceeded to lift a long tubular-shaped device. He was aiming it directly at Professor Ketchembach, who had stopped near the Arch to speak to some friends. In blind fury, Rudy bolted forward.

NEGATIVE ESP

Washington Square Park bustled in weekend rhythms as Professor Ketchembach continued to chat, oblivious to his surroundings.

Pumping his arms like a freight train, Rudy raced headlong. Chi Jhenghis, lost in thought, did not notice. Carefully, he monitored his long cylindrical instrument, aiming it at the professor as Rudy grabbed a child's croquette mallet and hurled it in whipping fashion. Spinning parallel with the ground, the wooden hammer struck the fur-capped infiltrator on the left chinbone, slamming him backwards in shock and pain.

Socked, the man rolled to his feet, felt for his jaw, and scampered up towards Sixth Avenue, disappearing amidst the endless flow of the overpopulated metropolis.

On the ground lay the strange device Jhenghis had been using. Along side was the croquette mallet--split neatly in two.

Professor Ketchembach came running towards the huffing reporter. "I know him," Styne gasped. As he spoke, Ketchembach picked up the tubular machine and dangled it incredulously as he stared at Rudy.

"What the hell was that all about! Who the hell *are* you?" As they argued, a small crowd began rapidly gathering.

"Who the hell am I? The bastard was tailing you! I thought this was a rifle."

Already busy unscrewing the back, Ketchembach changed his manner. "Come," he said, the anger having subsided. Gently he guided Rudy's elbow as their eyes met again and they knew they were still friends. "It's a microphone--foreign service." The professor spoke under his breath so on-lookers could not hear. "I apologize for the outburst."

"That's OK," Rudy replied as they filed through a throng whose attention span had already begun to dissipate. "I went crazy. That guy's been ripping off parapsychology books from the New York Public Library system, and who knows where else. He looks like he's from Korea or Tibet."

Tucking the instrument under his jacket, the professor motioned, "Let's get back to the lab." Threading their way to where the bike was parked, they got on and Ketchembach gunned it. Rudy held tightly as they scooted through Little Italy, Chinatown, SoHo, and made their way back to NYU.

At the office, the professor lay the tube on the table and closed the door. He rummaged through his drawers until he found a screwdriver. "Is there something I should know about?" He talked as he carefully began dismantling it. "That guy was monitoring our conversation! If I'm not mistaken, this is surveillance equipment that can pick up voices at distances of 150 yards."

"I think this is linked to Dr. Hereward's book, and my guess is that his life may be in danger."

"You're a little late, son. He's already dead. Two years ago of a heart attack at a dinner in his honor. I was there, up on the podium, announcing him right before he kicked the bucket. Head splattered in the dessert cakes. It was a mess, particularly awkward because so many parapsychologists from all over the world were attending."

Reflecting, the professor continued. "Why would anyone want to steal a text that has close to a million copies in print?"

"Because," Rudy revealed, "there is different information in the first edition as compared to the others. They only printed up a relatively few number of hardcovers, and my bet is that the first edition is the only accurate one concerning the experiments of two Ukrainian parapsychologists. I even have their names." Rudy reached into his pocket and produced a Xerox of the paragraphs on Alexi Patrenko and Vladimir Kopensky.

"Patrenko...Patrenko...I think I met him at that very dinner--bald guy, muscular, with deep set beady eyes." Jay reflected. "Yes, yes, wore a bow tie. Now I remember. Definitely a weird SOB. Let me see those...." Ketchembach reached for the papers and began to read:

> Kopensky discussed telepathy, PK and electromagnetic states, brain-waves and the EEG.

"Not much on Kopensky, although he's working along the same lines as myself. Hmmm. I wonder if he was with Patrenko at Hereward's dinner. I don't think I have ever come across his work before." He read on:

> Patrenko, leading physicist...filmed the great psychic Nubea Lanilov.... He had written his doctoral thesis on anti-matter and relativity..... "Mass exists in present time, which occultists tell us is multidimensional. With mass/energy transformations, pairing phenomena and resonance effects, high energy particles can be converted from one dimension to another...." Patrenko then took a laser-like apparatus and proceeded to instantaneously melt a golf ball before our eyes!

"This is heady stuff. May I keep this?"

"Sure."

Ketchembach placed the pages into the top right drawer. "Thank you." Under his breath he mumbled, "Malfunctioning pacemaker."

"What?"

"Nothing."

"Professor, have you ever worked with the government in this capacity?"

"Well, it's very interesting here." The professor continued talking, but his mind strayed. "Basically, the American people are blind to the progress and potential of parapsychology. They think it is all fiction like in the movies. Twenty-five years ago I went before Congress to try and get money appropriations.

"Hell, parapsy grants are today under a mill-five per year, whereas the Eurasians are spending sixty times that. But, no one believes our test results--not one congressman of any consequence, that is. And these are simple studies like card reading and dice throwing. Their consensus realities just can't accept the evidence.

"Now when this fellow Abdul Manu came to the USA just four years ago, he was immediately tested at Oak Ridge. Brought him there myself. This guy not only levitated objects and performed like a charm on the ESP tests, but he also knocked out the computer center--distorted and erased hard and zip drives kept in the computer library, even altered a stack of DVDs. It was a total mess! Took 'em fourteen months to reconstruct all the lost data and programs. Backup systems were toasted as well.

"Son, I'll tell you, it was a real jolt to the national security people. They were freaked, and who could blame 'em? Now Oak Ridge keeps all backup programs on CD's, not tapes, and on punched out IBM scrolls, like the ones we used in the early 60's. The new whiz kids think they're crazy. DVDs are fine with them, but the old guard is not talking, 'cause no one would believe them. It's crazy.

"And the rest of the security community won't listen either, and everything stays electromagnetically coded. I'm telling you, the Y2K mess was chicken-feed compared to this. I testified in Washington, told 'em the Ruskies had a way of knocking out our satellite systems with PK, but it was like talking to the snails on the sidewalk. I said, remember in '99 when every pager in the country went out? They remembered, but insisted it was a computer glitch. Had some guy from Motorola giving them the so-called 'scientific' bullshit explanation, but I know it was PK. Those guys got ways of wiring brains, generating coupling effects and so on. And there are ways we can combat it, but we gotta start by recognizing that telekinesis is a reality.

"But the guys who should be doing this just aren't listening....and the CIA keeps their ruse going. Since Manu's a foreigner, the CIA does a check on him and instigates the whole 'Incredible Fandango' episode. They get the magicians interested, tell the world Manu's a fake. It's all a trick. Then they create an anti-parapsychology backlash by pumping money into the skeptics' coffers--just another typical disinformation operation. It's almost laughable. They support an entire nay-sayer publishing arm out of the University of Buffalo.

"In any event, the magicians get to invent new tricks because of Manu, levitate objects, bend keys and so on, Oak Ridge gains plausible deniability about their real link to the psionic research, and the CIA buys more time to investigate. But they alienated some of our top scientists in the process.

"So, to answer your question, the CIA and FBI have used psychics to track down moles and to second guess the enemy, the cops use psychics occasionally to look for murderers and lost bodies, there has been a bit of dabbling in remote viewing of Eurasian military installations -- but in truth, its penny ante stuff. Not one government agency officially studies PK. Why? Because they think it's a hoax! They can't explain the Oak Ridge computer tape erasure incident, because they now believe the Fandango ruse that they themselves created!

"So, for us in the know, we don't even try to change public opinion anymore. Frankly, we're beyond it. We simply do our thing. My colleagues and I are close to uncovering the quantum physical laws involved. That's what's important. In fact, in a few weeks at the upcoming Psychotronic Conference, I am going to present a paper on this subject. You should come. It will be on the tachyon."

"The what?"

"Tachyon, a theoretical particle that travels faster than lightspeed. As I'm sure you know, Einstein proved that nothing physical can travel as fast as the speed of light or it would attain infinite mass. So this theory speculates that there are already particles that operate in tachyonic realms, and this gets us around the Einstein limitation."

"You mean like precognition?"

"Yeah, precognition. In order to get information from the future, a supposed carrier frequency from this tachyonic realm travels back in time to the present, thereby announcing the upcoming event."

"Wouldn't this be predetermination?"

"Not exactly."

"But, it would involve another dimension?"

"Yes."

"And there is proof that this other dimension exists?"

"Tons. Physicists call it hyperspace, parapsychologists call it inner space. Either way, just as there are three outer dimensions for space, namely height, width and depth, there should also be a structure for inner space as well. You can call it virtual space if you like. Whatever you call it, instead of things going outward, things go inward. This realm would not only house the mind, but also a fourth physical dimension."

"So the future would actually exist there?"

"In a sense," Ketchembach replied. "The future really exists in terms of probabilities, that is, one of a number of likely possibilities. It is our theory that this extra dimension, which we can also call hyperspace, would contain the seeds of tomorrow. Information packets, that is, the tachyons, could then travel back from this space to our physical dimension with solid clues as to a number of probable events that might take place in the future."

"You mean they already exist in hyperspace."

"Yes, they play out there. But again, only as possibilities, or probabilities, if you like. What a good psychic does is read these, mix in a little intuition and bango, he's got a picture of what will probably happen. Ultimately, it is our goal to manifest this realm by studying how the psychic accesses it."

The professor rearranged some papers on his desk as if to help gather his thoughts, and then continued. "So now, what I am involved with is to try and find the states of consciousness and brain-wave patterns associated with either generating this particle or receiving it. We are in the beginning stages, but already have interesting research and potential equations."

"Dr. Ketchembach, this is most fascinating. Would you consider stopping by my office, say tomorrow morning, so that you could speak to my editor about your work and about the importance of the missing names in the Russian book? With your support, I know the captain, er, I mean my editor, will give me the time and expense account I need to pursue this story." Rudy reached into his wallet and gave the professor his business card.

"Splendid. Tomorrow. I'll just finish up a few things in the office and scoot uptown by eleven o'clock. Okay?" The professor placed Rudy's card on a filing cabinet.

"Fine." Rudy shook hands and departed.

Elated, Rudy decided to forego the subway so he could return to Washington Square Park where he could sit down and complete his notes. He passed the Frenchman again, still seated at his favorite bench. This time, the fellow was engaged in cordial conversation with a stout woman who perched herself on the seat like an embalmed sparrow. Robotically, she nodded at every dramatic pause. Glancing over at Rudy, the Frenchman smiled, as he leisurely caressed his sleek black leather satchel, which rested closed on his knees.

Trying to contain a broad grin, Rudy turned his attention back to his notes. He sprawled some papers on the bench, and began to jot down the day's events. Pausing long enough to gaze at a stylishly-cropped miniature poodle crap into his master's pooper-scooper, Rudy recounted the day.

THE RED BUG

Having almost been caught by the Americans, Chi Jhenghis knew he had to contact Dr. Bash immediately. Hurrying back to his West End apartment, the Tajik paramilitary operative removed a false panel in his bedroom floorboards and resurrected his Ukrainian designed intercontinental surveillance equipment.

Placing an ice pack on his swollen mandible, Jhenghis released a pain killing neurotransmitter directly into his thalamic pathway by way of a cybernetic valve near his premotor cortex. A bloody and broken tooth lay by the multifaceted instrument panel.

Hooked to a network of sophisticated Eurasian microwave communication satellites, one of which was over North America at that very moment, Jhenghis cranked open the door to the roof of his apartment, and aimed his transmitter to a pre-arranged point in space. Via a computer tracking encryption system, Chi Jhenghis relayed Styne's and Ketchembach's entire office conversation to his home base in Yakutski, as it occurred:

"....packets, that is, the tachyons, would then travel from this realm back to our physical dimension with solid clues as to a number of probable events...."

"Would you consider stopping by my office tomorrow?"

* * *

Dr.'s Alexi Patrenko and Georgi Bash sat securely in their underground Siberian laboratory and monitored the American conversation.

"Patrenko." Bash stared deeply at the bald man and spoke not another word. Alexi knew that the day he had shown Hereward and the Americans the anti-matter resonator, his ego had transcended his common sense, and Ketchembach's conversation with Rudy vividly drove the point home. But even Bash had allowed the demonstrations to go on, so long as the real activators of the machine were kept secret.

Beneath the laboratory had been six Eurasian cyborgs, their brains interconnected with depth electrodes, a bio-feedback EEG machine allowing them to self-regulate the proper PK states until all were producing the same wavelength. Arranged in a hexagon, the Tajiks, in turn, were linked to a laser-like transmitter which could beam the tachyonic anti-matter frequencies they were producing.

Smuggling these subjects to Moscow had been no easy feat, but the thought of fooling the Americans had been too much even for Bash. For one moment in their relationship, Alexi and Georgi had enjoyed a tearful laugh together. This moment had created an emotional bond between them until *Eurasian Parapsychology* had been printed. Murdering the author Gregory Hereward at a convention in his honor, and changing the second edition printing plates, was the only thing that saved Patrenko's neck in the eyes of his overseer. Now, this

Ketchembach matter might cost Patrenko his position or even his life. It would certainly curtail his access not only to the West, but maybe even to Moscow. Bonzo the Alaskan Pipe Dreamer had enough criticisms concerning his support for the work in psionics. He would not tolerate mistakes of this magnitude.

Bash approached. Raising both palms, fingers outspread, the sorcerer displayed the full force of his magnetic powers by thrusting his hands forward, gripping the underling by his heart and head chakras. "Sleep," he commanded.

Patrenko dropped to the floor like a stone.

Bash looked down with a bemused smile. Stepping forward, he placed each Frankenstein-sized boot by the sides of Patrenko's sagittal crest and said, "Alexi."

"Yes," came the reply in trance.

"Awaken."

Patrenko's eyes slowly opened. Frozen, he gazed up in horror.

"We must keep Bonzovalivitch at bay. Do not tell Kopensky," Bash spat. "The fat man is getting soft. I am going to New York to correct your errors." Sneering through his long drooping moustache, Bash squatted and placed his lips by Alexi's ear. "You are in charge."

Within hours, Bash was on the Orient Express flying to New York. Perhaps he had mixed feelings about murder, but there was no doubt, he loved the hunt.

* * *

Rudy returned to *Modern Times* and spoke to the captain. "May I come in?"

"Sure. Fine job on the Sex & TV piece. Fine job." As usual, Captain Whitmore monopolized the conversation. "I want you to follow up with a Sex In The Printed Media story. The point is that you will not use girlie magazines, just *Time, Newsweek, People, Glamour.* Get as many racy pictures as you can. We want to point out that in their own way they may be more guilty even than *Playboy, Pussycat,* and any other sleazebo periodicals. They pretend to be non-sexual, yet in fact, are very sexy."

"Sleazebo?"

"Well, I guess *Playboy* has good articles. I wouldn't know, of course. I only look at the pictures." Whitmore waited for the obligatory laugh before continuing. "By playing with the very instincts they purport to suppress, the so-called conservative periodicals create an unusual psychoanalytic bind for the reader."

"Excellent, captain," Rudy said boldly. "You have so much insight into the idea, I think *you* should tackle it."

"Rudy...."

"I'm serious. When was the last time you wrote a piece?"

The captain thought back to his heavy writing days, his numerous articles for the *Sunday Magazine* of *The New York Times,* his columns in the *Saturday Evening Post* and *The New Republic....* "Nice try, Rudy. You almost had me. Now get out of here and get on it!"

"One favor, Cap'n; I have been talking with a psychic researcher--really, a physics professor from NYU, and well...well, I think between the two of us, we have discovered some espionage by a Eurasian psychic cabal."

"Styne."

"Mr. Whitmore, the CIA has used superpsychics for years in remote viewing and mind control. A parapsychologist told me..."

"Enough. Hirshon already took you to task about the ESP hoaxes with B.K. Pine and that charlatan Manu. We don't want sensationalism for sensationalism's sake. But, I don't want to totally cut you off. If you find some credible, and I emphasize academic, down-to-earth scientific experimentation going on...."

"There is. And he is right here in the city."

"Oh?"

"His name is Professor Ketchembach. I've been trying to tell you. I've taken the liberty of inviting him here tomorrow. He made his mark in the field of quantum physics, but now he's involved in brain science, neurogenesis as a potential cure for such diseases as Parkinson's and Alzheimer's and also he studies parapsychology."

Captain raised one eyebrow.

"He worked with Einstein at Princeton when he was in grad school. And some top secret stuff with the neutron bomb about the same time. Now, he's publishing articles on potential cures for various brain disorders and more recently, he's gone back to quantum physics to expand upon the Kaluza-Klein hyperspace quark compilations."

Rudy handed the captain a new *Physics Review* and also an old Princeton catalogue paper-clipped open to a photograph of the physics department. Next to the scraggly white-haired wizard in his later years stood a young man with an arrow ball-pointing to his head. In the caption, the names of Einstein and Ketchembach were juxtaposed. The captain stared at it, pondering.

"Einstein, huh? Is there really something to this field?"

"Yes, there is, captain."

"I want that sex article. We need the publicity." They both realized that Whitmore was caught in a contradiction, but of course, the exploitation of sex, the way he had planned it, was a clever idea. "Styne," he added, "we can't strain our credibility. You understand." He didn't say it as a question.

"Yes."

"You say he'll stop by tomorrow? What time?"

"11 AM sharp."

"All right. I'll see him, but none of this spy crap. We are finally at peace with the Ruskies."

Rudy walked back into his office. Cal and Bill were chuckling by the water cooler, Mort was catching up on phone calls, and Sally-Ann was busy inputting an interview she had with Senator Highland. Nobody knew how she did it, but somehow she was able to set up more political appointments than Hillary. As he walked past, Cal sprayed Bill with the nozzle of the cooler. "You two should open a comedy act," Rudy smiled.

Sally-Ann looked up. "How was Vermont? Did you go to a funeral or something there?"

"Thanks a lot," Rudy said, and then he remembered the bedroom incident and the whole thing with the beech tree. "No," he said, "but I did see a ghost." He added these statements reluctantly. "Chessie saw her too--and Al, the guy who owns the house, he admitted the place was haunted."

Rudy watched himself as he talked. He felt almost as if he were separate from his body looking down on the conversation, realizing that he probably sounded crazy to them. But he persisted to complete the description. "She was an old lady that had lived in the house. Floated into our bedroom and tucked us in late at night." Rudy looked down, wishing he had never begun the tale. "I know, it sounds crazy."

Cal came over as Mort followed. "You're not serious, Styne?"

"Yeah, I am. I'd like to say that I was kidding or that, no, I didn't see anything, but I did."

"It wasn't a dream?" Cal asked.

"If it was just me, maybe, but there were two of us.... and Al described the very same ghost. She died in the house thirty years ago. We all saw her. That's all there is to it."

Cal changed the cadence of the conversation. "Yeah, I know it's true. My uncle and aunt live in a haunted house. They say they have seen this young girl on a number of occasions, and I've...I've heard footsteps there....Why half of the castles in England are haunted." He looked over and shrugged apologetically to his buddy.

"Come on," Mort could not accept it, but without Cal's support he was unable to hold up the skeptic's point of view.

"No, Mort," Cal said. "I feel like Rudy. I'd like to say I made up this story, but ever since I can remember, we knew that the house was haunted. We even checked into the history and found out that 18 years before they bought it, a small girl had died there of scarlet fever. In fact, her grave is nearby down a path in the woods."

"You guys are giving me the willies. Really...." Sally-Ann said. "However, I'm glad it was something, Rudy. I really had a bad feeling that someone died that was close to you."

The messenger boy walked by. Mort swiped the bag he was holding.

"Hey," the boy protested, but Mort dumped the contents, Cal's lunch, onto a desk, punched two holes in the bag and swiftly placed it over the boy's head.

Privy to Mort's shenanigans for a long time, the kid got into character. Waving his arms and shouting, *"Oooo, Oooo,"* he began to chase Mort around the desk, and then swiftly removed the bag, timing a dead-pan face, right before

Captain Whitmore opened the door to his office. The captain just barely missed the entire episode.

"Cal," the captain said. "Get that law piece to me by 5:30 tonight. Stay till six if you have to. Sal, finish up the Highland interview and try to get an interview with his opponent what's-his-name." The mood had reverted back to business. "Mort," Captain Dean Whitmore looked squarely at him. "Go fuck around by the water cooler."

ABDULLAH MANU

Rudy would be alone that night. Chessie had a date with one of her male friends. He didn't like the idea of her going out, but she was not yet ready for total commitment. Or, maybe she was, and he just had to get used to the idea that she could have a social life separate from him. When five o'clock rolled around he covered his laptop, shoved some holographic memory cartridges into his desk, and walked out of the office. With nothing to do that night, he found himself out the door, meandering down the Fifth Avenue window-shopping, watching his own reflection flicker on the storefront panes. It was rush hour.

Rhythmic human streams poured from building entryways in seemingly endless flowing waves. Styne walked against the tide. Preoccupied with various showcases that the city had to offer, he inadvertently bumped into someone. Jesus, it was one of the local street schizophrenics.

"Sorry," he mumbled.

The only reply was the woman's schizo eyes. Dressed in a weathered dress and gray shawl, she huddled up to her favorite concrete sanctorium and rocked, her grit-flecked heels bulging from the back of someone's discarded caved-in tennis sneakers. This one always looked frightened, shifting her weight from foot to foot, her long, mousy hair swaying to the movement of the hustling city fleet.

Rudy did something he had never done before. He looked straight into her seedy eyes and said, "Hello." Yes, she recognized him. He had passed her daily for over three years, but she did not respond. She never lost a beat. A beggar pushed his way into Rudy's view and asked for a quarter. The reporter found a 50¢ piece in his pocket, one he had kept there for weeks, but he handed it to the bum anyway, having created a tinge of jealousy in the wiry old bitch. How serious is life? he thought. And what about all this parapsycho jumbo--how much of it was pure bull? If humans are telepathic, let alone psychokinetic, what does it mean? Surely there must be writers and gurus who understand this dormant superbeing. Could he meet Sri Baba? actually travel to Bhutan? Abdullah Manu seemed a more reasonable goal since he lived right there in the city. Shangri-la too much a dream, the reporter decided to try and meet the Egyptian Manu as soon as possible.

He stared at the boring walls of his apartment for what seemed to be endless oppressive hours. It was 7:15, the time of night he called the dead zone, in between the news and a potential movie. Another of those idiotic game shows on TV nearly caused him to go berserk, to throw an unopened can of cold beer through Alex Barker's polka-dotted cravat. Why was he so close to the edge? He had to call Abdullah Manu immediately and seek an interview. The operator said, "I am sorry, sir, but this number right here is unlisted. I am so sorry."

Rudy scanned his memory banks for a lead and narrowed down possibilities to Sally-Ann. He dialed. "Sal, Rudy here. I'm trying to get that psychic Abdullah Manu's phone number. Can you get me on track?"

"Abdul? Sure, Rudy. In fact, I was just thinking of you." Sally-Ann was nude, sitting in front of her bureau mirror admiring her ample physique, beginning to swoon as she continued. "I'll try a few people and call you back, Mr. Styne."

Rudy attempted to sit still, but found himself pacing the room. He even did twenty pushups. The phone rang; he caught it immediately. "Sal?"

"Yes." She sounded breathy. He felt himself sweat. "I've got it: 555-7037. Are you going to call him tonight?" There was genuine enthusiasm in her voice. "Boy, I'd sure give anything to meet him. He's supposedly a channel for the Masters of Wisdom, you know...Well, see ya tomorrow."

Rudy dialed. Strangely, his hand trembled. Hell, he had spoken to top movie stars, Jesse Jackson, Henry Kissinger, Vice President Harrswell and many others, but had never been this jittery. It rang.

"Hello."

"Yes, hello. Is Abdullah there?"

"I am he." The voice had an unusual accent.

"Hi, my name is Rudy Styne. I'm a reporter for *Modern Times*."

"The magazine?"

"Yes."

"I know of it. What can I do for you?"

"I'd like to meet you sometime. In the near future. So I could interview you for an article. On parapsychology."

"Who sent you?" Manu sounded friendly, but cautious.

"Well, no one really. Just this morning I was with Professor Ketchembach and your name came up. I've started reading about parapsychology, and... well, I wanted to meet a genuine psychic."

"Hah. How you know I'm genuine? I got to tell you, you were lucky to find me in. Tomorrow I leave for Belgium. Perhaps you call later."

"Abdul," Rudy paused and seriously collected himself, "I won't be able to sleep tonight thinking how I missed a chance to meet you. Could we just..."

Abdullah interrupted. "I have small dinner party here. You come after--say nineish--bring date."

"Thanks. I appreciate it. See you then." Rudy hung up, then quickly redialed. "I forgot to ask for your address."

"457 East 56th Street, apartment 12H."

Sally was lying upon her couch. With one leg languidly slung over the back of the sofa, she leisurely caressed her rib-cage with long fingernails. The record player spun hazy music. The phone rang. She placed it on her belly and picked up the receiver and breathed, "Hello."

"Sal," Rudy began, "I'm going to Abdul's apartment around 9. Would you like to join me? I can pick you up for a drink before hand."

"Why bother with a drink. I've got something here. Come on over."

Sally entered the bathroom and let steamy water run into her tub. She dropped in her favorite oils, removed her only bar of soap, placed it in the kitchen, opened the lock on the front door, and returned to test the temperature with her big toe. As her body slowly adapted to the heat, she slid down the squeaky porcelain, submerging her lithe torso and pink extremities. Lying with her head underneath the water, she listened to the sounds of her heartbeat. Rudy knocked a few minutes later.

"Come on in," she shouted. "I'm in the tub."

Rudy entered and put his coat down.

"Can you get me the soap. It's in the kitchen."

"Sure. Take your time," he called back. "We don't have to be there for an hour."

An hour later they were headed for a cab, and by 8:48 they were on East 56th Street. During the elevator trip the couple stared separately at two different spots on the floor rug. Rudy broke the silence. "Nice boobies, Sal."

"Yeah, I know. You creep."

They exited at 12.

Abdul, himself, answered the door. He was a tall handsome Egyptian with jet black hair and dark black eyes. Dressed in tailored pants and a red silk shirt open to the navel, Manu glued penetrating eyes upon the two friendly guests. Around his neck hung a solid gold pyramid. It was a scale model of the one at Giza, an image of a sphinx stamped into each side. "Rudy Styne?" he asked.

"Yes."

"Very good to meet you," Abdul said. They shook hands.

"This is my associate Sally-Ann Karpana."

Abdul nodded and ushered them into a bare hallway which led to a large dining room/living room. Rudy guessed two bedrooms in the back. On the wall were dozens of framed magazine covers from all over the world with Abdul Manu pictures on them: *Parade, Life, TV Guide, Discover, GQ, Cairo Times, Deutschland.* To the right was a rack of men's magazines, and by the dining room and kitchen were two laptops, some office space, and shelves containing a large library of books on parapsychology. Most of the titles were either about Manu or contained references to him.

The host left them alone for a moment, so Rudy leisurely thumbed through *The Manu Documents,* as Sally read over his shoulder. The cover leaf claimed the book was the definitive work on the psychic's abilities. Edited by the famous science writer Dr. Alton Tokler, the work comprised research reports from seventeen university and science labs from around the world ranging from controlled studies in simple telepathy tests, to Kirlian photographs of energy emanating from Manu's finger-tips, metal bending and time sequence photo documentation of levitation of objects, to experiments displaying his ability to move a glassed-in pendulum by thought power alone. Other important textbooks on the shelves included Manu's memoirs and a biography by an Egyptian university teacher, Professor Valequez, M.D. Rudy noticed that Valequez had set up most of the laboratory experiments that were mentioned in *The Manu Documents.*

"Thank you for having us on such short notice," Rudy said when Abdullah returned. He was followed by another young man and two women, all of whom had been in a back room with Manu.

"The pleasure is mine," Manu smiled. "Let me introduce you to my spiritual brother, Ron Valequez, professor's son, and these lovely ladies are Rita Chevelier and Monique Baltano." Manu led the way to the living room where everyone found places to sit. Rudy would have trouble later remembering what Monique looked like. She was pretty, with auburn hair. He did remember that. But because of what was to follow, he certainly would remember Rita. A striking black-haired girl of Lebanese descent, Rita had deep brown eyes, large supple breasts amplified by a lavender cashmere sweater, and a waist so tiny, he felt he could encompass it with the thumbs and first fingers of his hands.

They all appeared so youthful and naïve to Rudy. His gaze, however, quickly returned to the charismatic Abdullah. As Rudy's pupils adjusted to the light, he continued to study this so-called superpsychic from Egypt. An intense energy field became apparent about Manu's head. It seemed as though he were bathed in light, as though he were wearing a translucent helmet made of golden threads. Rudy saw motion and rainbows in this aura and also several symbols near the regions of the temporal and frontal lobes.

"A halo! You have a halo!" Sally-Ann exclaimed.

Like the rings of Saturn, a circular glow encompassed Manu's cranium.

Excited by the newcomers' presence, Abdul began to strut about the living room. "Let me show you some things," he said as he reached for a shiny black leather box and gleefully opened it. Inside were a stack of news clippings and photos of Manu with the U.N. Secretary General Jurgen Olaf, rock stars David Bowie and Michael Jackson, sports giants Sammy Sousa and Brian Boitano, Canadian Prime Minister Henri Bordeau, parapsychologist B.K. Pine, Steven Spielberg, Elliott Harrison, Senator Edward Bennisy, Vice President George Harrswell, David Letterman, Penelope Cruz, Cambridge Sunveil and also NASA astronaut Peter Whiting.

Manu moved so quickly that he knocked a *Playboy* to the floor. It opened to a naked girl, lathered in soap, kneeling in a bathtub. Sally-Ann blushed. Abdul apologized and began to straighten up various trinkets that lay on a shelf above the girlie rack. With his nervousness approaching the overbearing stage, Rudy asked if he might levitate something. "Maybe just to 'diffuse' you a little," he softly jested.

"OK," Abdul said, almost relieved. "But remember, this does not always happen." The Egyptian went into a period of meditation, and placed his hands over a coffee table that lay before him. Rudy took out his keys and some change and placed them with the other objects on the table. Manu began to hum and ask for

Osiris to give him the power. As he concentrated and chanted, a bluish-violet hue began swirling in his aura.

"This is awesome," Rudy whispered under his breath in rhythm to the chant.

Yo He Vo He Yo He Vo He
YO HE VO HE YO HE VO HE
h h h h H H HHHEEE E E E E M M M M

As Abdul brought the last *mmm* to a loud crescendo, his hands began to tremble at a fantastic rate, the air electrified in anticipation. "No, not going to happen." Manu sank back into his chair.

"Wait!" Sally-Ann blurted. "I think something is happening! The keys look like they are suspended." And then barely discernable, they lifted 1/4 inch and began to oscillate.

"Yes, there it is." Abdul brought his hands above them again and up they rose. A dime and a quarter also began to ascend, the objects hovering as if on an invisible sea of surface tension. Four of the books on the shelves about seven feet away, and two of the framed pictures, also began lifting.

Abdul rose. Standing above Rita, he passed his hands over her forehead. This mysterious man from Cairo stopped time, his face transcending, transforming again and again into hundreds of other faces, some quite primitive, others far out, Martian-like, futuristic. Cosmic symbols sparkled in his eyes, as Rita slumped unconsciously onto the couch. Now in deep sleep, Ron and Monique helped stretch her out into a prone position.

The psychic placed his hands above her shoulders and smoothed her aura down from the top of her head to beyond her soles. He seemed to extend the length of her body, so that she now appeared taut. Placing one hand on her solar plexus and the other underneath her coccyx, he held her and meditated. Cleanly, she lifted along a seemingly visible sea of surface tension, and with a gentle push, he floated her smoothly towards the far end of the room. And then, when she got there, her body rotated, and she rebounded slowly back.

Rudy could swear she looked naked. Her face transformed into that of an Egyptian princess and a golden pyramid appeared to encase her aura. Rita began to speak, "Man's soul is eternal." The voice seemed to come from her stomach. "He is at one with the Universal Mind. His actions create reactions." The aura became more substantial as glittering letters emanated from the region of her solar plexus: **MANU BEWARE.**

The message coalesced and transformed into that of a sphinx and then a jet plane. As it faded, Rita slowly sunk to the floor. It seemed as though her triangulated aura was somehow responsible. Rudy could see hieroglyphics, Chinese and Hebrew letters rapidly circling the pyramid as it vanished. The coins, keys and books dropped with a plunk. Rita woke slowly, her mind just a haze.

Manu was exhausted, now a soggy ball of sweat. "Excuse--must shower," he said breathlessly, and then he staggered from the room.

The guests sat in silence as the moment evaporated.

"How long has Abdul manifested these powers?" Rudy inquired of Ron, his voice quivering.

"It began when he was three. One night in a dream his father was called before the Holy Sphinx. He was told to carry his son on the Nile and have him baptized at the next full moon. The dream was so real that father Manu decided to consult the priests. They told him that this may be a great sign and they went to the Great Pyramid to pray. A full moon appeared over the Sphinx beside another which was a three-quarter moon. That was enough proof for them, and seven days later they anointed Abdullah. He lived a fairly normal childhood. Except for a few telepathic episodes and some minor poltergeist activity, very little happened. But the priests continued to teach him the secrets of the dead and of Osiris, and slowly Abdul developed his powers."

After not too long a delay, Manu returned. "I have to tell you," he began, his glow subdued, "I started levitating everything I could as child. I lost many friends because they thought I weird, so from 1967-71, I did little, although priests' teachings continued. I joined soccer team in high school, and became captain sophomore year. Scored 45 goals. When Arab-Israeli war of '73 broke, I almost lose life. Two nights before attack on our airports, vision appear in room and these came flying through window." Abdul reached under a sofa and brought out a large conch shell with the Ten Commandments carved out in Hebrew. The lettering was fine and tiny. On the back Manu translated: 'There is only one God. We all One.'

"I brought conch to priests, and they in turn called president Sedat, our leader. Sedat himself came to temple and saw the shell. Spoke to me night before Israelis attacked and destroyed our airport. When atmosphere cool down, I arrested for treason. One priest and Professor Valequez wrote Sedat pleading, how you say, my behalf."

"On my behalf," Sally-Ann corrected.

"Yes. They told him that I warn them, not reverse, and that I not controller of powers that be. It was Bellarosa, a truly holy man, who finally persuaded Sedat to let me go, but as payment I forced to leave country. Not official exile, for I return many times, but my family felt it unwise for me to reside there permanently."

Ron looked at his watch. "Abdul, we have a plane to catch."

"It's late," Rudy said.

"My God, it's nearly midnight," Sally-Ann said. The duo edged towards their coats.

"Ciao." Abdul said.

"Ciao," Sally-Ann echoed, as she took the psychic's hand with both her own. "Thank you for everything."

Rudy also shook hands, first with Ron, and then with Abdul. "Thank you for your hospitality. I can't thank you enough." He nodded to the ladies. "Have a fruitful trip."

"Call me next month." Abdul said sincerely. "Better yet give me number. Maybe I call you." They shook hands again.

Abdul returned to the couch and stared at it.

"Why do you think Osiris told us to beware?" Ron asked, waiting patiently for a response.

"I not know. I only channel."

DR. GEORGI BASH

Rudy was dreaming of pyramids, spaceships and planets in their orbits, when the rings of Saturn faded into the sounds of his alarm clock radio. The warm shower cascaded tiny wet explosions onto his sleep-worn brain.

The phone rang. It was Chessie. She felt culpable due to the intimacy of the night before with a man that was not Rudy. She hoped he wouldn't hear it in her voice. "Rudy, how about going out to the Hamptons with me today? My boss has OK'd the time off. It's already October, so let's get in a swim while the water's still swimmable."

"Great idea, but I can't today. I have to see Dr. Ketchembach with Captain Whitmore at eleven. Let's go Friday or Saturday."

Strips of yellow police tape barred his subway entrance, so he decided to go overland. Grabbing a newspaper from Carl, he ambled over to the crowded bus stop, just as one of the smoking monsters screeched to a halt.

The bus lurched forward. Rudy grabbed an overhead rail before falling, and waited unsuccessfully for a seat. The hues of New York City flowed past the windows as he drifted uptown, still in a bit of a daze from the events of the night before. Getting out at 45th Street, he walked briskly cross town to Fifth Avenue, crossed to the entrance of his building, a third of the way towards Sixth Avenue, and strolled into the office at 9:17. Sally-Ann looked up from her desk at him briefly through long eyelashes. Their energy was too intense. He tried to return his mind to Chessie.

Burying his head in the keyboard, he began his report on parapsychology. Fuck sex and the media. Fuck the captain. This thing was too important.

```
Man is telepathic…
```

He pounded at the electronic keys. Every word and nuance seemed so incredibly important, as they spontaneously appeared up on the chartreuse LCD screen.

```
       Perhaps in and of itself this is not too earth
    shattering, but the fact that as a news reporter I
    did not know this fact only two weeks ago does not
    cease  to  amaze  me.  Now,  let's  be  fair  with
    ourselves. How many of you readers know for a fact
    that telepathy is an actual ability in humans?
```

Agile fingers easily transformed each thought to electronic words on his virtual page.

```
         There  will  turn  out  to  be  three  general
    groupings to your answers. My guess, given my own
    experience,  is that most of you do not know that
    ESP is  fairly  commonplace. Psychic  abilities  such
```

as telepathy, psychokinesis and precognition are
well-known and proven factual events replicated
daily in card reading studies and parlor games,
more rigorously in scientific laboratory
experiments and off the cuff, at crap tables and
gambling casinos from Las Vegas to Monaco. Granted,
the phenomena are elusive and to some extent
arbitrary, but they occur.

To me, what is more astounding than these
particular human abilities is the overriding
resistance by the news and scientific community to
recognize a few simple truths. In the short time I
have studied the field, I have come across over 100
years of organized research documenting various ESP
events. I have even experienced dream telepathy
myself. If scientists refuse to recognize the
phenomena, how can they ever begin to grasp its
theoretical implications?

Rudy looked up at the clock. Ketchembach would be there in twenty-five minutes. He checked on the captain to make sure he would be in.

The professor left NYU at 10:20, fifteen minutes earlier than he had originally planned, because he was excited. He unlocked his motor scooter and hopped upon it at about the same time Georgi Bash dropped into the city from the heliport atop the great building that sat above Grand Central Station, the TriStar Oracle, at 45th Street and Park. Against the cries of a panicky public who could never get over the nine-eleven Twin Towers attack, the owners of the TriStar Oracle had resurrected the helipad which hadn't been in operation since Pan Am owned the building in the 1970s.

Bash had been flying non-stop from the cold depths of Siberia to the modern North American city in three planes and a helicopter for the better part of eleven hours. He figured if he could get to NYU by 10:30 he'd be safe, but it was already 10:24 as he stepped out onto the street. He would have to put his contingency plan into action.

The gangly spymaster loped across Park Avenue to attach a small microwave-tracking camera to one of the panels of the solarium of the Chemical Bank Building which sat diagonally across from the TriStar Oracle. Aiming it at the uptown traffic which poured from the overland Park Avenue tunnel, the scope was set to relay a continuing picture and a "beep" at any two-wheeled vehicle that came through. Stepping into the onrush, he hailed a cab.

Bash always felt uncomfortable in three-piece suits. He kept adjusting the fit of the vest and playing with his food-encrusted moustache as a yellow hack pulled over. The sorcerer reached deftly into the driver side window and placed his hand onto the young Puerto Rican's forehead. The boy slumped, and Bash got in.

Shoving the driver with his foot to the passenger side, and placing the company cap on his own head, Bash drove north to 52nd Street and then east to Third Avenue.

Waiting impatiently, the hunter kept one eye on the video camera which covered Park, and the other eye on Third Avenue. No sign of Ketchembach. Cursing Chi Jhenghis for putting a GPS system on the wrong motor bike, he looked south in a view that stretched six blocks, and waited. At precisely 10:39, he gunned the cab madly cross town. Careening around pedestrians at Lexington and 53rd, he swiveled his way to Madison Avenue.

The professor was just passing a bus on the right side as Bash smashed him broadside, plowing the front grille of the cab into both the motor scooter and suitcase compartment of the larger vehicle. Gobs of red blood splattered. As the bus screamed to a halt, the Ukrainian flung the cabby's hat to the floor, jumped out of the car, and lost himself in the crowd.

Professor Ketchembach rose above his body and watched the macabre agent cross Fifth Avenue, to thread his way past the library into Bryant Park. As the dark sorcerer stepped around pigeon droppings and dog shit, Ketchembach spiraled upwards, through astral planes. Met by Johannes Kepler and Ernst Mach, Ketchembach's sandwiched physical body became a crumpled and useless shell. Fortunately, the head remained unscarred so the family could see Jay's face one last time at the morgue.

At precisely 10:51, Mrs. Ketchembach reached for her heart to rub away a distinct pang that had pierced it, as Rita slumped to the living room rug of Abdullah's apartment and Manu sliced himself while shaving. At the same instant, Rudy's watchband snapped, its crystal cracking on the floor. Embarrassed, he waited as Captain Whitmore became more and more disgusted.

"I don't like a man who can't keep appointments," the captain said as he paced around the room squeezing a black-handled hand-gripper.

"Something has happened to him, Cap'n. I can feel it." Looking at his cracked Timex, Rudy's head kept spinning. Soon after, both men heard the news on the radio's noontime report:

> A well-dressed man with long gray hair was crushed between a yellow cab and commuter bus on 53rd Street while riding his motorbike uptown along Madison Avenue. The cabby, Juan DeSouza, a former resident of San Juan, told the police that he has been drugged and does not remember a thing.

Rudy called one of his contacts at the 44th Street Precinct and confirmed his suspicion. Dean Whitmore approached, but Rudy couldn't think. Running from the room, he was just about out of the office when Whitmore called after. "I'm sorry, Rudy" he shouted. "You know how I get. I thought he was late." But Styne did not hear.

Leaving the building, and catching a train, he surfaced at Cooper Union. Running headlong towards the university, Rudy entered the physics building, went up the stairs and over to the professor's office. The door was unlocked. He went in.

There the professor was, smiling with his family, neatly framed on the wall, amidst other photos and news clippings covering a half-century of work. Pasted on walls and thumb-tacked on bulletin boards in haphazard fashion, were articles from science journals, tear sheets from books, and other photos, such as a recent one of the professor in a laboratory with Abdullah Manu hooked up to an EEG Machine, and older ones from the 50s and 60s. There he was, in a heated conversation with Robert Oppenheimer, head of the Manhattan Project, shaking hands with President John Kennedy, and in a classic action shot with Niels Bohr and Albert Einstein, all grinning on a bicycle built for three, Einstein in the middle with both hands off the handlebars.

The reporter began opening the drawers looking for the xeroxes of the cross-referenced indexes he had given the professor. Not to his surprise, they were nowhere to be found.

He pulled the chair out and looked under the desk, and then his eye caught sight of a tiny yellow wire. Crawling under, he followed the line to see it attached to a small circular object that was taped to the underside of the support, which housed the middle drawer. A listening device!

Rudy shuddered. His voice was on tape. Had they located who he was? Where could he go? In a panic, he ripped out the bug and then dialed Chessie's number. "I can't talk now. I'm headed where you suggested this morning. I'll call you," and he hung up. His eyes were glazed and he found his mind spinning.

Rudy hailed a cab back for his apartment, using the time during the ride to plan. Retrieving his car, he drove downtown to avoid expressway traffic. The little Gazelle zoomed at 65 mph swerving through other speeding vehicles, as he weaved his way to the Manhattan Bridge. Catching a gap, he banked right towards Sheepshead Bay and then turned east onto the Southern State.

By 3:05, he had sped through Nassau County and most of Suffolk, now a hundred miles from the city, past Jones Beach, Fire Island, East Moriches, and on into the Hamptons.

Parking the car by his favorite beach, he tore for the ocean, shedding his clothes in a trail. Not breaking stride, he dove into the cold sea, its clear freshness jolting and then quieting his aching psyche. With the water as flat as a still lake, and the surf essentially non-existent, he swam for endless seconds totally submerged, his eyes open. Surfacing twenty yards away, he swam until exhausted. Flipping onto his back, Rudy watched one interference pattern after another circle his toes and stomach as they radiated out in ever widening circles, the crisp ocean water soothing his overwrought soul. He must think carefully.

Bobbing like a partially submerged submarine, Rudy reflected back to the madness of what had occurred. He found himself praying for guidance and for shelter, and then emerged to crash by his clothes in the sand.

The sky was a rich and pure powder blue, the wind still, the sun penetrating. The youthful man slept in a fetal position throughout the afternoon.

Awakening with an autumn shudder, his head felt different. He wondered for a moment where he was. The shadow of a sleek figure stretched over him. He opened one eye cautiously. Chessie was cradling his head in her lap. "How did you get here? Did anyone follow you?"

"I took the train and a cab from the station. And yes."

"Yes?"

"I made sure I was followed."

His inability to smile at her joke got to her. "Rudy, what's wrong? You sounded so dreadful on the phone."

"Ketchembach's dead." His brain still cloudy, Rudy closed his eyes once more and nuzzled his head into her soft thighs. "Thank you for this moment, God." Silently he prayed.

They walked back to the car slowly, and drove to an obscure motel. Got a room under Chessie's name. After showering, Rudy stopped by the mirror to stare at his naked body. "Chess, I don't know what I should tell you," he called into the bedroom. "I think the Eurasians killed him." He looked into his own eyes trying desperately to see beyond the mask of superficial day-to-day existence.

He left the bathroom to sit beside Chess on the bed. "We went over those scientists' names in the original copy of *Eurasian Parapsychology* in his office. There was a listening device. They have my name, and by now, most likely, my identity. I don't want to drag you into this. We have not known each other long enough for you to risk...shit, it's not worth it. I want you to return to the city and date other people. Let it be known that we were only casual associates and that you have not seen me in over a month."

"You think it's that serious?"

He nodded.

"Oh Rudy, I miss you already." Tears began to stream down her cheeks. "Are you sure?"

An ambulance wailed in the background.

"Beside that bug, we caught an Asian spying on us with a tape recorder in the park. Clearly, something big is underfoot. Maybe even Manu is in danger." He decided against telling of the details of his meeting with Manu. He could not afford straining his credibility at this moment. There would be plenty of time for relaying *that* bizarre episode.

"I can stay the night, can't I?" Chessie's eyes looked desperate. She held her face close to his chest.

"Of course," he said, and kissed her forehead. Chessie disrobed and jumped into the shower as Rudy dialed Abdullah. There was no answer. Then he called Whitmore at his home.

"Dean, Rudy."

"Rudy, glad you called. I tried to stop you today. It was terrible, the accident, I mean. How tragic. I'm sorry."

"Captain, that was no accident, and I think I'm next on the list."

"Rudy, don't you think you're carrying this conspiracy thing a bit too far? These things happen."

"No. These things don't just happen. You got a pencil?"

"What do you take me for?"

"I'm sorry, Dean, but I'm frightened. The first edition of *Eurasian Parapsychology* by Gregory Hereward has been stolen from many libraries. The reason is that there are two names in it that are missing from the next four editions, Alexi Patrenko and Vladimir Kopensky. I think they are involved in top-secret Eurasian experiments and anyone who realizes this is in danger. Therefore, you may be in danger by me telling you this. Clearly, the best way to reduce the possibility of more killings is to publish what I'm telling you in the next edition of *Modern Times.* Meanwhile, I am going to have to take an extended leave, at least until the article appears. Can you do that Cap'n?"

"Rudy, if the story holds up, we'll print it. But, frankly, I am going to have to consider you for dismissal."

"Dismissal?!"

"You're in the big leagues, son. I can't let you start that kind of precedent. So when you come back to your senses, come back and see me, and we can discuss rehiring you."

"If you feel that way, why are you printing the story?"

"Because, if it is true, and you can be sure we will check it out, then it's news."

"Cap'n, one more thing. I suggest you put the piece in last minute. They know who I am, and they could have listening devices anywhere. I don't want to put *your* life in jeopardy, or anyone else's for that matter."

"The guy was on a motorbike in the heart of the city in the heat of the day. A cab hit him. He hit a bus. You're losing it, kid."

"Better safe, Mr. Whitmore. If you run the article, mum's the word. I'll fax the details to your private office in the morning."

"Yeah, whatever."

"What does that mean?"

"Two names are missing from a book. You know I'll have to double check this."

"But you'll miss deadline. That will delay this another whole week. I could be dead by then."

"Styne, you're a reporter. And this is the big leagues. I said I'd put it in, but this isn't exactly a press stopper. We'll carry it ASAP. That's the deal."

Rudy hung up the phone disgusted. The captain was delaying simply because he didn't want to acquiesce to an underling's demands. He knew how the captain's mind worked. But time was crucial. He considered calling back, but knew it would be fruitless.

Rudy and Chessie spent the evening in the motel room eating pizza, drinking beer. Cuddled in the big double bed with new clean sheets, they propped themselves up with their pillows to vegetate in front of the tube. The 11 o'clock news mentioned briefly that a professor of physics, Dr. Jay Ketchembach of NYU, had died in a motor scooter accident on Madison Avenue. The funeral would be held Wednesday at 11:00 AM at St. Matthew's Church. They showed the famous bicycle-built-for-three photo with Bohr, Einstein and Ketchembach, only Bohr was cropped out. Physicists from all over the country were expected to attend, as Ketchembach had been one of the few living scientists left who had worked with Einstein.

Next morning, Rudy drove Chess back towards the city. "From now on, if I call you or write, I will sign it Chuck. Understand?"

"Yes, Chuck." She saluted and kissed him gently.

"Also, I will be mailing you a safety deposit key. Keep it for me and if I should get killed, give its contents to the captain or Hirshon of *The York Trib.*"

After faxing the details to the captain from a nearby copy center, Rudy took Chessie to the local railroad station, where he left his car in a long-term lot. They rode the train together and parted with another kiss.

Styne continued on to his apartment. With slight hesitation he ran up familiar steps, trotted down his hallway and opened his door.

The entire room was overturned.

Beads of sweat suddenly flowed from his forehead, chest and armpits. Rapidly, he rifled through his underwear drawer, and retrieved his bankbook and passport. The two copies of *Eurasian Parapsychology,* were nowhere to be found, his two couches ripped to shreds. The air was oppressive. He could stay no longer.

As he started toward the elevator, Rudy heard the rapid sequence of pounding steps. Half turning, he noticed a big-boned man with a long moustache, fiery eyebrows and black leather coat rushing toward him. The man's teeth were bared. His hands stretched out in a grasping motion.

Rudy darted down the hall heading for the staircase when his neighbor, Mrs. Brown, opened her door. Bursting blindly in, he shoved the woman inadvertently to the floor, closed and locked the metal barrier, apologized and dialed security.

"There's a murderer on our floor," he screamed into the phone, "a tall man with leather jacked and drooping moustache. Call the police, hurry! He's breaking down the door!"

The molding around the entranceway cracked with each earsplitting kick. "Hurry!"

Frantically, Styne scooted around the apartment, too frightened to think. He stupidly began to open and close the closet doors, as the big-boned man continued to burst his way through the bolted entrance.

Finally, Rudy ran to the bedroom and began to struggle with the rear window. Making his way onto the steel-framed fire escape, he grabbed the rail with both hands and clambered down. With the gigantic hunter just a few flights above, the reporter faced a twelve-foot drop to the bottom.

Swinging down with primate certainty, Rudy leaped to the pavement and rolled back to his feet. Two Asian men came running towards him from different directions. Both wore fur hats.

"Get him!" The man boomed in Russian out Mrs. Brown's window.

Rudy grabbed a bottle from an open garbage can and flung it at the soldier to his right. It smashed on a fire hydrant sending shattered splinters in all directions. The assailant ducked, as the reporter turned to the street, and rushed into oncoming traffic.

Cars lurched to avoid him, Rudy veered right. A cab screeched to a halt, as he continued to pick his way across the busy road.

Bash was on the ground by now, galloping like a camel. With long bony fingers, he directed his warriors to close in on their prey.

Sprinting at full speed now, Rudy barged through crowds blindly dashing onward, his heart pounding like an overheated steam engine. Finally, a subway entrance. He ducked downstairs, pushed through a line and vaulted over the tollbooth, only to run back and forth to wait hopelessly for a train that never came.

Scowling faces of waiting passengers steered clear, as a fearsome clatter thundered down the cement steps behind him.

MADAM GROTCHKA

Madam Grotchka began to tire of the routine job in St. Petersburg. She had felt a sense of triumph after seizing the talking orangutan, for now there was a chance to experiment with a brain that could communicate on a more human level. But after infesting Orie's skull with cybernetic paraphernalia, she became *persona non grata* among the students, especially Orie's former trainer. Although Lima never said a word, the girl's daily hateful stares were too much even for Madam Grotchka. Her confidence shaken, the capacious woman transferred the girl to an obscure old-age clinic in Turkmenistan.

Madam was tired of St. Petersburg. She wanted to return to Yakutski to continue her original experiments on humans, research she was forced to relinquish too long ago. When her former lover, Vladimir, returned to the hospital, Madam told him she was unhappy. She wanted to go to Siberia. "And what is that little prick Imo up to?" she inquired.

Dr. Kopensky looked drawn. Deep folds of sadness were beginning to develop under his eyes. "Dr. Bern is correlating psychokinetic states with brain-wave patterns. We find that he is quite adept at synthesizing the Russian and American data. He has also created a number of new lines of research."

Kopensky tugged nervously at his jowls, unsure of his colleague's exact motives.

"Does he work with the animals or the humans?" She was testing Kopensky, but also Madam Grotchka was curious as to just how much Imo knew...and how much he did not know.

"It is true that Dr. Bern is squeamish with the physiological experimentation, so we thought it best to let him work where he feels most comfortable. In fact, his naiveté has become a useful asset for international conferences, such as the December one coming up in psychotronics in Italy. Dr. Patrenko is also attending. Dr. Bern will be discussing some of his experiments with dream telepathy and EEG states. It's good press and keeps the West guessing. Officially, of course, he is from Vladivostok." Kopensky turned directly to face her. "Don't ever forget that."

"That girly two-shoes momma's boy! Hah! Bring the little twang back here and let me go to Siberia. I miss working with the Tajik subjects....Vladimir," she attempted a sincere tone. "I'm close to completing a neuro-map for five different feedback circuits in the mid-brain and cerebellum." She was obviously jealous of Imo, but she was telling Kopensky the truth and he knew it. One human subject could speed up her research a hundred-fold.

"Madam Grotchka, I thought we came to an understanding. Your refusal to integrate parapsychological findings into your work and the need for a strong experimenter here in St. Petersburg precipitated our decision. You should be honored, as you are in charge of a highly respected laboratory, even if you *have* destroyed the years of work we did on that orangutan. Question me no further. Both Alexi Patrenko and myself are in agreement."

"Dr. Kopensky," she snapped, her voice now irritatingly haughty, "Professors Slomov and Chezinko were here last week. As you know, the Academy of Pedagogical Sciences is quite unhappy with the spiritualistic overtones of your work. The meetings with the West by Patrenko and the others has not helped. Unless a physical basis for telepathy is discovered, the Academy may have the impetus to close you down like they did Raudow. Three years in a labor camp changes a man."

If only she knew, he thought to himself.

"Some even die of the shock." She jabbed each point vindictively. "Without a doctorate and with his alliance with the refusniks, he didn't stand a chance....Vladimir, there is so much to do in brain research. Why deal in so obscure an area? So what if humans are telepathic."

"Don't you know what we have accomplished, Madam? We have Deus Maxima on our side and the backing of Petar Bonzovalivitch. I can say no more. If you refuse to read the literature you will never replace Dr. Bern."

"Comrade Kopensky, I entertain absolutely no interest in your work or in replacing, as you say, the Bern boy. If you do not give me leave to Yakutski, I may be forced to side with Slomov and Chezinko. Your mother has been trying to emigrate to Israel for the past six years, has she not?"

"That's a lie...." He shifted the focus rapidly, "Bash will be interested in your affiliations."

"Bash!" she whispered, her eyes drawn back in horror. "Don't, Vladimir. The students vilify me here. I'm desperate. I need human subjects. These first-order primates don't have the cerebral complexity. Vladimir...."

She reached to his thigh and began to rub the bulge in his pants. "I'm desperate; I'm bored ...." She began to unbutton his trousers. "My work is as important as the other....We could have times like before. Send me to Siberia."

Nausea rising from his stomach, Kopensky slammed her across the face, the blow impressing the fleshy part of her right cheek with the imprint of his knuckles.

Madam dropped her head in pain and shame as she considered. Counterpoised with calculating audacity, she reached inside her jacket for a small scalpel. Swiftly, she stabbed the fat man above the right scapula, twisting the blade as it entered, leaving it imbedded, as she threw her hip into his anguished face and turned to depart.

With cries of pain, Kopensky reached for the metallic thorn, pulled it from his shoulder, and whipped it towards the retreating beast. He wanted to kill her, to slice out her concretized heart and feed it to the laboratory rats, he thought as the scalpel landed point first in the back side of her upper neck. Dropping from the shock, Madam Grotchka searched for the weapon with her opposite hand as blood spewed from the wound in rhythmic spurts. He had nicked an artery.

"Medic!" he screamed into the telephone, running over to plug the small hole with the first three fingers of his right hand, holding his own wound with his left. Within minutes, attendants were there. Both Kopensky and Grotchka were wheeled to respective emergency rooms. Madam had lost much blood and was weak. Kopensky's wound was not serious, but he knew imprisonment could follow their rash acts of violence.

SUBWAY SUBTERFUGE

Stranded on a subterranean concrete island with three assassins in pursuit, Rudy had no choice. Down into dank, smelly tracks, he jumped and hurdled over to the opposite side. Above, waiting faces silently watched, almost pretending it wasn't happening.

Everything seemed to be occurring in slow motion. Surely, they all thought he was insane--all those uncaring eyes. *No-one* jumped into the pits, he thought, as he vaulted up the opposite side, hopefully to catch a different oncoming line.

Bash burst through the exit gate in front of him. Back down he sunk. The bastard had anticipated his move, and by now, the two Tajiks had reached the pit themselves and cascaded in. Rudy let out a curdling scream as he dashed furiously down the railway blindly into darkness, Bash and the two soldiers following.

"EEEEeeeeeee."

Rudy glanced back. One of the Eurasians had stepped onto the third rail. Electric shocks issued from his hair and hands, his cybernetic existence instantly snuffed. The American was picking up speed, but he felt Bash gaining.

Chock. Chock. Chock. Chock.

The train was coming. Rudy had no choice and continued running, running towards the growing light at the end of the bend. Pumping his arms in accelerating rhythm, sweat continued to pour down. The gangly hunter was gaining.

Impending mass-transit, Styne plastered himself into a moss-stained alcove as the train screamed by. "Oh shit, God. Oh shit. Oh shit."

WHOOSH!!!!!!!!!!!......

Just as the iron horse screamed by, Rudy tore out again taking three railroad tiers at a time. His clothes stuck to his thighs and chest, his heart pounding painfully. The smell and putrification burned his lungs. His mouth became acid dry, yet onwards through the slimy green/black muck he pushed, the next stop less than 200 yards away.

By now, Bash was only about fifteen feet behind him. Rudy managed another burst. With a leap, the spry journalist was up again crashing through the waiting crowds.

Plummeting out the grilled exit door he careened up the stairs, throwing people down to block his path as he ascended. Surfacing, he saw a businessman step into a cab. Completely crazed, Styne barreled in, heaving the man to the other side.

"Step on it or I'll blow his head off! Step on it!"

The cabbie gunned it.

"Turn here!" He was screaming, but the cab was caught in traffic.

Rudy pushed the door open, darted to the sidewalk and skidded down the nearest subway stairs. Arriving on the platform as a train was about to pull away, he slithered between the sliding doors as they closed shut--another anonymous entity rattling on.

Switching lines and cars too many times to count, Rudy ended up near the Bowery, surfacing like some primitive cave dweller, his clothes pasted to every crease of his body. He tried to slow his pace when he walked into one of his branch banks and wrote out a withdrawal slip for $3200. That would leave him with only pocket change in the account, but "Fuck it," he thought.

Still sweating profusely, he walked up to the teller. She looked back at him warily. "Can you put that into travelers' checks?" he asked, his voice quivering in spite of every try to appear calm.

"You are aware, you will only have $23 in your account?" the teller requested an ID.

Although a wreck, his wallet proved his identity. She handed him the cash. He took out a safety deposit box and sat in a small wooden booth long enough to write a brief account of the entire episode, pausing once to shudder.

His mind laced with animal fear, Rudy did everything he could to prevent himself from shitting his pants. Stumbling into a men's room, he exploded into a toilet, washed his face and stopped at a clothing store to grab underwear, and a change of clothes. And then he turned into the nearest hotel. Paying cash, he signed the register William Gatekeeper.

Entering pristine sleeping quarters, Rudy found himself draped over the toilet, puking. Spitting up bile, he retched dismally into the bowl. Finally after a shower, some sanity began to return.

Grasping the safety deposit key, he addressed an envelope to Chessie in care of Al in Vermont. He sealed the small package and handed it to the desk clerk on his way out. "Could you do me a favor," he handed the boy a twenty-dollar bill. "Mail this out in about ten days. It is very important."

The clerk smiled and nodded assurance.

Rudy made his way uptown to attend the professor's funeral. On the way, he stopped at various stores where he bought a cane, orange-checkered suit and matching hat, dark glasses, cigars and a rather large pocketknife. Stuffing his other jacket into his undershirt to change the shape of his torso, combing his hair straight down over his forehead, and sticking one of the Dutch Masters into his craw, Rudy played the distant uncle no one would want to draw attention to. Cautiously, he entered St. Matthew's Church.

The sermon had already ended and people were milling about, mostly near the coffin. It sat center stage between two pulpits adorned with cascades of white and purple flowers. Ketchembach's eldest daughter was crying hysterically. "He's not in that body!" she wailed, "He's not in that body."

Replicating the walk of the nerdy uncle, shoulders back, stomach out, Rudy followed a group out towards the waiting cars. As he crossed under the balcony, his heart began to pound, for he could see the very monster who had chased him through the subway, descending a staircase near the pulpit. The Eurasian's face was twisted in subdued rage, as he made small talk with a man in a three-piece-suit. Ducking outside, Rudy slipped into the first available car in the motorcade. The Eurasian had not seen him. *God, he looks evil,* Rudy thought.

"Do you mind if I join you?" There were two men in the front seat and two in the back. It was a large black Oldsmobile.

"It's a little crowded," one of them said bluntly. "That's some get-up. I don't think I saw you at the service. My name is Professor Jorn--Physics, Samford University."

Did he say Samford? Rudy thought.

The other man nodded. Dressed in a pinstriped suit, crisp, manicured moustache, he looked oddly familiar to the reporter.

"I'm sorry I missed the service," Rudy apologized as the car pulled into traffic behind the others in the procession. "But that man over there was trying to kill me. I think he murdered Professor Ketchembach."

All four of them, including the driver, turned back to look at Bash who was socializing on the church steps. "Professor Boshtov?" Jorn asked.

No answer was necessary once Bash saw them. Staring right through Rudy, the Ukrainian walked deliberately to the street where he proceeded to hail a cab, a horrible smirk adorning his face.

Suddenly nauseous, Rudy had difficulty holding himself back from throwing up on the man next to him. "God, that was dumb. I'm sorry."

"Stop!" He then yelled, as the next corner was turned. Shedding the coat and placing the hat on Jorn's head, he jumped from the car, and motioned it to keep going. The moustachioed man on the other side of Jorn exited as well, and together they ran into a coffee shop. Waiting near the window with one hand on his pocketknife, all the while shaking, Rudy watched Bash's car glide by, its headlights eerily lit in honor of the dead victim.

"That fucking bastard. And who the hell are you?" he was almost screamed in a hoarse whisper.

"You're Rudolf Styne, aren't you? I saw you interviewed on *MNBC* after that capitalism and bribery piece you did for *Modern Times*. My name is Irving Moth, *San Francisco Chronicle*."

"Moth. Yeah, I know you." As he reached out to shake hands, he began to shake violently, so much so, that he started to whimper, half from nervousness and half from embarrassment. "Weren't you picked up on spy charges in Russia a few years back?" he managed. "That was national news."

"Yeah, that was me, all right, but it was in Uzbekistan, although it might as well have been in Russia. The spy charges were national news, but the real reason I was picked up was hardly mentioned." Moth pulled out a gold watch from his vest pocket and eyed it, apparently as a way of focusing back to the events he was relating.

"Wasn't it something to do with state secrets?"

"If you call ESP a state secret."

"That's unbelievable! We've got to talk...but can we get out of here before that madman doubles back?"

"Sure. I've got time. Let's grab a cab." They walked through the back of the building and out to another street. "I was picked up for my interest in Eurasian studies in psi phenomena. Most of the media reported only the spy charges. Except for *The York Tribune* and a few of the progressive radio stations, the real issue was never released."

"Cover up?"

They walked back to Fifth Avenue and hailed a taxi as Moth continued, "I was interviewing a psychic researcher in Tashkent. Guy named Raudow. Unfortunately for both of us, he was also a refusenik. He was telling me about the bioplasmic energy which surrounds all living beings, and about the mind control experiments Bonzovalivitch was sponsoring in Siberia when we were arrested."

"He's that powerful? I thought Bonzo was a clown." Rudy said.

"He's not as crazy as he looks. It's all an act calculated to keep himself in the public eye. And, frankly, it works. All that hype about taking back Alaska and pushing Russian borders to the Mediterranean and Indian Ocean makes good press. And it's not all bluff. It's my belief that Bonzo is funding experiments involving mass hypnosis, neurosurgery and the transmitting of diseases through microwave radiation.

"That's how I got into all of this in the first place. Originally, I wasn't interested in parapsychology beyond it being just another story. It all started when I was on assignment in Mongolia, doing an article on the history of the horse. Someone hands me a leaflet about a Slavic sorceress, Koltrena Zbjovi."

"That nutcase from Uzbekistan?"

"Deus Maxima, she called herself."

"The female messiah. *US News* did a skinny on her so *Modern Times* wouldn't touch it. But we all read it. She definitely had her fifteen minutes. I remember Jay Leno did a bit. Her father was a virgin even though her mother had a burning bush."

"Yeah," Moth laughed. "Five thousand miles away and five years later, we can laugh about it, but if you saw what I saw, you wouldn't think it was that funny. In fact, it was the first time I saw that Rasputin guy."

"You mean...that large creep that almost killed me? In Mongolia?"

"Actually, it was across the border in a river town called Kachug."

"You mean in Siberia?"

"Yeah. Believe it or not, it's quite a modern little metropolis. There must have been 5,000 people in an open stadium. Koltrena seemed to float in a trance. I'm telling you, it was a real trip. She was dressed in flowing purple robes. And, she was with her control, a tall, primitively handsome fellow, but really a con-artist whose name was Chanook Vrhynnhov. He spoke first. I taped it and got it translated."

"Video?"

"No. Unfortunately, just audio."

"So, what happened?"

"She hypnotized 5,000 people. No lie. It was fuck'n incredible. Told them that they had to relinquish their Earth parents to take *her* as Deus Maximus, their spiritual god mother. And they all converted, right then and there, to her emerging religion. Twenty three million members worldwide, last time I counted."

"And that was it?"

"No. I thought it was going to be it. Believe me, that was enough. But then this Rasputin character comes on stage, the guy you said killed Ketchembach, and there was a pushing match with Chanook. It was freaky. Chanook stormed off, and this Frankensteinian behemoth puts Koltrena into another trance. Stretched her between two seats, and fucking stood on her chest. It was, my God, just fuck'n amazing. And then, it seemed like he floated her right over the audience! They must have used guide wires, because I can't explain it any other way, but it was very impressive.

"I wrote the whole thing up. But, you know what happens. It got cut, abstracted and morphed. Would have died altogether if they hadn't found this Chanook guy dead -- sexual asphyxiation in a whorehouse in Minsk just a week after I handed the piece in. He had been threatening the higher ups of the Commonwealth with outbreaks of mass suicides if Deus Maximus' church would not be officially recognized.

"It seemed flaky to me, but I got hooked on reading about hypnosis, and that's what got me into this ESP thing. Even interviewed Gregory Hereward."

"You mean, the author of *Eurasian Parapsychology*?"

"Yeah. And as it turns out, that was the last interview he ever did, because he died that night at a dinner in his honor. Ketchembach was there. That's were I met the professor. The next day, I was in Tashkent interviewing Raudow when I hear that Hereward died not more than a half hour after I left. And the next thing I know, I get arrested."

"You couldn't have been too happy about it."

"I thought I was a goner for sure. If my own paper and the *Tribune* hadn't supported me, I think I might still be in Tajikistan pounding stones with a sledge hammer. And don't think the Iron Curtain doesn't still exist. Cutting Russia out of America's resurrected interest in Star Wars weaponry does not play well in the old Soviet Bloc. Many of those guys are still young men." Moth looked intently at his palms as he talked. He casually looked up when finished.

Rudy spoke, "You know, I think *Modern Times* covered that story too, because I remember when you got arrested, we talked about it in the office. That was big. But I just don't remember parapsychology being mentioned at all. I mean, I think I would have remembered that....Jesus, I can't stop shaking."

"*Modern Times, Newsweek, Time.com, The Post, ENBC.* They all covered the story, yet each and every one of them obliterated any mention of the contents of the science report I had obtained. It was fuck'n amazing. My own colleagues hiding the story. And of course they don't believe a word about Bonzovalivitch either."

"How can that be? Censorship by our own media? I don't get it."

"After thinking about it for the last few years," Moth said, "I've realized a simple conclusion. Underneath it all, they think it's all bullshit. It's as simple as that."

"But what about all the experiments. A hundred years of research?"

"It's all explained away. Like TWA flight 800, Senator Wellstone's death, the AIDS bio-warfare thing and JFK.

"Amazingly enough," Moth went on, "some of the reason that parapsychology gets such bad press has to do with a magician by the name of the Incredible Fandango. After Fandango supposedly proved that the psychic Abdullah Manu was a charlatan, *Time* and *Newsweek* followed suit. And the rest of the news establishment, like sheep, just went along.

"Even when it slaps them in the face, as with my own incident with the Eurasian Secret Police, the powers that be, Bryan Williams and all that jazz, they simply refuse to publish anything even close to being accurate about ESP.

"Of course to some extent I can understand their position. The field is a quagmire: crop circles, UFO's, Bigfoot, Lochness Monster, exorcisms, crying statues, miracle cures. It's all lumped together, as if each has equal weight. *Scientific American's* the worst. And then, there's the military. With one hand, they're using psychics in remote viewing experiments and studies in PK. And with the other hand, they fund the skeptics."

"You mean, they give the skeptics money?"

"Of course. They practically support an entire publishing house in Buffalo."

"I don't get it," Rudy said.

"It gives them plausible deniability. Rudy, I think we Americans may be more of an enemy to psychic research than the Eurasians."

"We don't commit murder, do we?"

"Well, it depends on who you are talking about. Colby, head of the CIA disappears in the swamp, Ron Brown, that's Clinton's guy, dies in a plane crash. That Enron VP, and now, you think Boshtov whacked Ketchembach? How's a guy like that get into this country so easily?"

"Good point. After Hereward, Ketchembach would be second on their list. I was almost their third. That giant bastard chased me through the stinking subway tunnels not twenty-four hours ago. Look at this shit in my shoes, the fear in my eyes."

"For what reason?" Moth asked.

Rudy related the entire story.

"You have a hot item, Rudy. But there has to be more to it than just two names. Perhaps the Eurasians have discovered something important, such as a sure-fire way to harness PK with brain-wave biofeedback. If they've really tapped a neural psychokinetic center, their powers could be limitless. But, if Whitmore prints your article, that should put you out of danger."

"Yeah, two weeks from now. I could be fertilizer by then. You still got contacts in Tashkent? Can you find where Patrenko and Kopensky are? What they are up to?"

Moth replied, "I'll try. I'll get the name discrepancy in *The Chronicle* immediately. If that's all right with you."

"Damn straight it's all right."

"That should rub salt in their eyes, and it will be echoed by your magazine the following week. Meantime, I'll run a check on our Rasputin character. Jorn, knew who he was, there must be tons of stuff on him. I know he's behind Deus Maxima."

The conversation ended as their cab approached Rudy's hotel. They parted with a firm handshake.

That night, in his rented room, Rudy was agitated. He desperately wanted to sleep, but could not slow down his mind until nearly dawn. Finally, sleep overtook him. He got a full three hours before the phone rang. It was Moth at 7 AM.

"Hey, you see this morning's *Chronicle?*"

"You're kidding?"

"Did I get you up?" Moth said. "I emailed the story in last night. Also got a make on Rasputin. His name is Boshtov. Also goes by the name of Bash. First name, Georgi. He runs a secret unit for Bonzo the Nut in Vladivostok. It's believed he has trained the Red Chinese in brain-washing techniques during the Khrushchev/Kennedy years. It's also believed that some of his soldiers, often Tajiks, are in hypnotic trances, and thus they are impossible to interrogate if captured. There is more on Boshtov, but my contact would not go into it. The FBI has as search out for him because of my call. He does have diplomatic immunity, however, but can be pressured to leave the country if they find him."

It was as if a great weight had been lifted from Rudy's brain. Although unshaven and still washed out, he returned to his office with the morning edition of the *San Francisco Chronicle* tucked securely under his arm.

Before entering the building, Rudy watched the main entrance from across the street for a full forty minutes. Finally he sauntered up and walked in.

"Styne, get your ass in here!" the captain roared. Sally-Ann, having just left his office, was afraid to even look at Rudy with the editor-in-chief in such a state. "You bastard. You give me this crap about Eurasian intrigue..." Rudy tried to interrupt. "Don't say a word...and then you ask as a favor, as a favor mind you, to print this *Eurasian Parapsychology* discrepancy," he was slapping his own copy of a *San Francisco Chronicle* with the back of his hand, "and you have the goddamn balls to give the story to Moth?

"Who in the hell do you think you are? I was running it as a small second page story under the News and Views column. And then this morning--I'm feeling sorry for my harshness with you from yesterday--Sally comes in and tells me the most amazing bullshit about an Egyptian prestidigitator--levitating books and coins and floating a girl across a room.... I explained very clearly to her what a magician does for living. She seemed to understand, even though she's a woman. But you?-- a top science and news reporter! Styne, you're fired. Get out." He crumpled up the *Chronicle* and threw it across the desk in disgust.

By the time Rudy reached the elevator, he found himself unsuccessful in swallowing his tears. So, he took the stairs instead. When he got to the street, he used his cell phone to call Moth at his hotel. The clerk said Moth had checked out, but he had left Styne a message:

BOSHTOV HAS TAKEN A EUROPEAN FLIGHT.

Relieved, Rudy found himself walking the thirty-five blocks back to his apartment. Slowly, but with perseverance, he put all his clothes back in his drawers, straightened out his papers, picked up all the books and furniture, and even sewed some of the ripped sofa pillows. Bash had done more than look for those two texts. He had virtually destroyed Rudy's haven. Attempting to reclaim composure, and on his reporter's instincts, he began compulsively looking for bugging equipment. He called up the phone company and told them to install a separate, unlisted line. He searched the area by the phone, under the desk, beneath the refrigerator, along the tops and bottoms of the moldings on the walls, behind the pictures....Finally, on the back of a parody lithograph of a Dali entitled *Melted Watch at Monument Valley,* he located a wire running the perimeter of the frame. It was attached to a tiny black receiver. He took the device, picture, frame and all, wrapped it in brown paper and addressed it to Dean Whitmore, Editor-in-chief, *Modern Times.* Inside he put this note:

> Dear Captain:
>   I'm sorry for all the grief I have given you, and for giving the story to the *Chronicle* when it was already slotted for M.T., but time was of the essence. My life was in danger. I offer this painting as a token of all that you have done for me through the years. Please hang it on the wall of your office so that instead of being beaten to the punch by a San Francisco daily, you'll be scooped by The *Siberian Sentinel*. The picture is from my apartment.
>
> *Rudolf Styne*
>
> P.S. Do not look carefully at the back.

Then he stopped by Chessie's office at Tailor & Tailor Auction House. The place looked like a museum, only the inventory changed every month. Rudy walked by a series of Egyptian statues, a sculpture of a nude woman by Rodin, and several brightly colored prints of birds by Audubon. He knocked at her door and entered. The clarity of her expression and youthful beauty brought a smile to his heart. "Hi Chuck," she said, her eyes glistening. She gave him a big hug. Her energy said it all.

Rudy gave the *Chronicle* article to Chess, told her about Moth and Boshtov, and told her how Captain Whitmore had fired him.

"Want to go to the Caribbean with me?"

"You know I can't, Rudy, "Chessie said despondently. "I've got a dozen Picassos and all these Dadaists to catalog, and the auction is less than a week away."

"I just have to go," Rudy said.

"So, go, and I'll see you when you get back," Chess said testily.

"You know I can't go without a kiss."

Reluctantly, Chessie offered him a cheek. Rudy knew he had blown it somehow, but he just couldn't stay, and from his point of view, it was just too bad, if she couldn't come.

Reading his mind, Chessie retorted, "You know, kiddo, I've got my own responsibilities too."

"I know," Rudy said, "but I gotta get out of here." The vibe sucked, but what could he do? "I'll see you when I get back."

Chessie didn't respond, but instead, returned to her cataloging. He felt sometimes, she could be awfully mean. He went back to his apartment, packed a suitcase and inside of seven hours was walking off a plane in Antigua.

ELUSIVE OR ILLUSION?

The damp thick heat startled Rudy as he descended from the plane to a brightly flowered customs gate at the Antigua airport. His body may have been on a tropic island, but his mind remained tuned to the curse of Bash's mad plan, peppered with his argument with Chessie and the unfortunate demise of poor Professor Ketchembach. Rudy watched the gaily-adorned tourists bicker with the uniformed officials in an out-of-body like state, his mind still on the City.

After checking into the hotel, the lost reporter stepped out onto the hot sandy beach. The lure of the green sea drew him deeper within himself. He walked along the water's edge, his spinning psyche pressing his mind further into the psychological maze he had entered. *What is the point?* he thought. *How can I appreciate this tropical fantasy? How stupid of me to have come...to have run. I am deeply troubled...and yet there must be a reason why I am here. Was it a whim, a lark, or an irrational urge to flee...or something else?*

Rudy continued to reflect on his situation, the psychic events, the race through the subway, Bash's Eurasian goon squad. He pondered about the lightning bolt in Vermont and the appearance and disappearance of the ghostly Velma, as a school of fleeting minnows darted between his city-slicker toes.

Somehow Styne's retreat to the Caribbean made him more anxious, not less. And, so utterly alone. He began to reflect once again about the whole of parapsychology. It was too ridiculous--too absurd. Watching the primordial tide splash its preverbal message upon the beaten shore, he considered Abdul Manu and the levitation episode. He thought about PK machines, the parapsychological literature he had read so carefully...the Garner exposé which allegedly proved that Pine was a fraud...the talks with Ketchembach in the park, with Hirshon and with NYU psychology professor Berman. The skeptics all gave such rational explanations for these bizarre occurrences. Their impeccable logic seemed to remove all of the mystery, yet doubt began to disturb him once again.

He decided he would meet the Incredible Fandango. Perhaps *he* could settle the issue once and for all. Or maybe he should see Pine or Jorn or Hereward, the author of *Eurasian Parapsychology*. But he was dead, so was Ketchembach. Still in a muddle, he moped back to his hotel.

The day disappeared.

He lay awake at night in the hot room with open eyes staring into blackness. He missed his girlfriend, but more than that, he missed the security he had once felt as a reporter and someone who understood his own life. Now he understood nothing. What was reality? How could so many fantastic experiences have evaded his consciousness for thirty-four years? Something was wrong. Were there two worlds out there--the real world and a separate reality? Why was this other world elusive, sporadic and so...well so unbelievable? And Ketchembach--Rudy felt responsible for the professor's death. If he had not told him about the books, he thought, he'd still be alive today.

Styne suspected the professor was being followed before he called on him. But either way, his inquiry could have been the spark that did the professor in. Still bewildered the following morning, he decided to dress for the beach. The tropic sun, palm trees, fallen coconuts and limon water gave him spiritual comfort, but still he felt confused. At the edge.

Deep philosophical questions continued to gnaw at him: What was the meaning of life? What was the purpose of being? Who am I? What is a human? How come these so-called psychic abilities are so rare? Why do they exist at all? Rudy felt he could never go back to that world he had lived in virtually his whole life. He wanted a more meaningful existence, but was completely lost as to where to turn.

"Ey mon, give me a hund!" An old, jet-black fisherman called out, motioning Rudy to help push his skiff off shore. Complying, he walked ankle deep into the water and grabbed the hull with both hands. He looked up at two white sails and pushed the vessel toward the oncoming surf.

"Do you mind if I come along? I've no place to go," he shouted as he leaped aboard.

"Sure mon, but we may be out all de day." The fellow had deep brown friendly eyes, gray hair and weathered skin wrinkled and scarred from battles recent and past. As the fisherman steered past the reefs, Rudy hung his head overboard and watched various schools of colorful fish meander through spattered turquoise seas. Suddenly a stingray appeared. Banking to its left, it disappeared from sight.

The two spoke without language, their minds gliding smoothly with the sailing ship. About an hour went by before the boatman broke the silence. "Ow long you down for?"

"Don't know, I've lost my way."

"We all do, mon. All do. You city peoples lose sight of your maker, de great Cosmo God." The man pointed to the sky. His gnarled hands on the rudder, the sun beaming off his eyeballs, the old fisherman gleamed a wisdom Rudy had never realized before. His being spoke truth.

Off to the right Rudy could see a school of dolphins moving towards them. The old man motioned to the sleek mammals. "De Mexicanoes and Panamanians hunt dese people. Day pay in next life." Again the fisherman pointed to the sky. The boat had picked up sail and leaned into the sea, the dolphins riding the wake and leaping through the surf in alternating rhythms of syncopated feats. Many of them skipped completely out of the water, horizontal to the surf, twisting a full 360° before diving back in, their corkscrew pattern piercing Styne's urban-programmed psyche.

Turning his skiff into the wind, the sailor tilted his head back and laughed, exposing fourteen ivory white teeth. Dropping sail, he threw the anchor overboard and jumped in....Surfacing and grinning, and reaching back into the boat for a facemask and snorkel, this great grandson of African herdsmen began to swim and romp with the aquarians.

"I know dese people, mon," the old native shouted amidst his dives. "Dis big one here is Kondu and dat pretty one, is his wife, Lavora."

As if she understood her introduction, Lavora came to the edge of the boat. Sticking her bottled nose up towards Rudy's hand, she cackled. "Come on in and play," she said. Rudy reached down for another diving mask. Flinging off his sneakers and shirt, he rolled into the sea.

Rudy had known great fear in his life, now he knew instinctive security. There was no doubt, these natives were friendly. The female by the boat had told him--had spoken directly to his soul.

As he entered the clear crisp water, he continued to swim totally submerged, Lavora circling his body. He reached out gently and held her tail with both hands. Pulling him at great speed around the boat, she played with him for timeless moments as the old man stayed with Kondu.

Rudy was filled with reverence for Nature's creation. He lie on his back. A baby bottle-nose approached, and nestled on his stomach. He wanted to die right then.

He was so peaceful.

Their chatter and songs continued to keep beat with the lapping of the waves on the side of the ship....

* * *

The next day, Rudy awoke in the old man's bed. Lying in a beach shack made out of strips of corrugated metal and planks of driftwood, he looked out through a paneless window beyond bright scarlet leaves of a poinsettia tree. A lone wind surfer was making his way across a placid aquamarine lagoon. The fisherman was gone.

Next to Rudy were his sneakers, and strung to one of the shoelaces was a little porpoise carved out of coral. He turned over and went back to sleep.

Later, he dialed his girlfriend.

"Rudy," Chessie said. Her voice seemed close. "Captain Whitmore gave you your job back! He even said he was sorry...and asked you to call him as soon as possible.

"Rudy," she sounded inside him, "I'm sorry."

"Me too," was all he said as tears began to flow. "Gotta go."

"OK."

He dialed *Modern Times*. "Styne, I'm a pig-head, so sue me. The listening device you sent me was tracked to a sophisticated wireless transcriber able to convert spoken English words into instantaneous typescript. It seems the Ruskies have a satellite relay system our own intelligence doesn't even know about. You get a star, Styne. Now, get your ass back here, pronto."

"Instantaneous text?"

"Abstracted and translated into Russian, broken down into major patterns of thought and cross-linked to bibliographic material."

"Is that all?"

"No." The captain leaned back in his chair and placed the thumb of his free hand under a suspender. He waved away a secretary who had some message she thought was urgent.

"Using a helicopter and a three-point GPS sensor, the fee-bees located the transmitter on a roof just twenty-five blocks from your apartment."

Whitmore got up, paced the room, then stood at the window and watched the pedestrians float down Fifth Avenue. "Inside was an Oriental, probably a Tajik, and a whole host of equipment. The station figured to be monitoring easily a half-dozen conversations from in and around the city, but as the chink walked out the door, handcuffed by two agents, he nailed his foot down on an explosive device. Half the place was destroyed, and one of the agents had his legs blown off.

"He bled to death before the medics could get there. The other man is critical, and the asshole got away by rolling into a shielded pocket in the hallway as he triggered the explosion. The whole place had been jury-rigged. Guy knew exactly what he was doing.

"Now, Rudy, I don't think I have to tell you, a lot of this is not the kind of thing that makes the papers. That's from the top. The fee-bees are unnerved, and they don't want the embarrassment of exposure, particularly when they found out some CIA liaison officer held back vital information about the whole frigging thing.

"We shouldn't even be talking about this on the phone, and I'm not even sure what we can, or even should, publish. New terrorism rules and all that bullshit. But I want you to know, you can continue your research."

"So, I can congratulate myself for not being as dumb as you thought?"

"Yeah. Something like that."

Rudy smiled to himself as he hung up the phone.

Purchasing a pair of sneakers, a new fishing rod and a case of multi-feathered lures, Rudy returned to the old fisherman's shack and placed them by the bed. Antigua had hardly begun to reveal its secrets. Nevertheless, by midnight he was back in Chessie's arms, pleased with the current turn of events.

BHUTAN

Shafts of sunlight broke into Chessie's bedroom. It was one of the reasons why she got the place, a window with a view to the east, the sun coming up in the morning over the Brooklyn skyline. She even told the real estate agent, who sold her the place, it was his best line because it was true.

"Chessie, I'm totally lost," Rudy said upon awakening. "God, or whatever it is we call God, spoke to me yesterday."

"How so?" Chess was just waking up. She stretched, scratched her scalp vigorously, much as a cat would, and then sat up to look at him.

Rudy related the episode with the fisherman. "I know it was just dolphins, but it was more than that. It was mystical, religious."

"You could look at anything that way, Rudy--the flowers, spring-time, a newborn baby...."

"Maybe you're right. But this seemed different. More direct. Like it was a message just for me."

"Oh, so now you're the One."

"No. Well, yes, well, you know what I mean."

"You mean, like that guy who marches all night on that Holy Rollers cable station with a bible tucked in his arm."

"Kind of," Rudy half jested.

"Rude, you're starting to sound weird. You're not going to become one of those bible thumpers on me, are you, because if you are....."

"Because if I are, what?"

"Oh, you know what I mean. Too much of this religion stuff. Praise be the Lord." Chessie stood on the bed, raised her arms, bounced and shook her wrists. "God-a-mighty. Praise be the Lord," she repeated in her best bible-thumping accent.

Rudy reached over and ran his hand up her thigh.

"Oh, so you're not that crazy after all." She sank back down to the bed and pressed her lips against his. As she reached under the blanket and mumbled, "Praise be to God," he rolled on top of her.

The following day Rudy asked Captain Whitmore if he could fly to Bhutan to write a piece on a Buddhist monk named Swami Baba. "Somehow, Styne, I can't say no. You have plane fare, expenses and two weeks...and do me a favor," the captain grinned, "if you find Ronald Coleman, give him a wink for me."

There was no direct route. Rudy would have to fly to Calcutta and from there transfer to Thimphu, the capital of Bhutan. Baba was in a city called Dzingdup. The travel agent told Rudy that a guide would take him over a mountain trail on a two-day trek, from the capitol to the refuge.

"This trip is not for the timid," the agent warned.

"I'll be all right," Rudy assured her.

"Bring your best winter coat and one of those thermal hoods. The Himalayas are notorious for incredible temperature shifts. Days could be in the 70s this time of year, but the nights could plunge so far below zero that your lungs could freeze. Don't worry, though. These guides know what they are doing. Just wear layers and..."

"And what, pray?"

"Yeah. I'm sure you'll be all right."

Rudy texted Dzingdup to announce his arrival in a few days, and was surprised to receive the following reply almost immediately:

> Looking forward to *Modern Times*!
> See Sherpa guide Yavi upon arrival
> in Capitol for mule ride to Ashram.
> *Felona*

Rudy printed it out, and placed the comforting report in his pocket, and then packed for the airport.

The jet streamed towards India, pausing to refuel in Morocco. A group of Indian medical doctors boarded. One of them who spoke English sat next to Rudy. The man was bony thin, with sharp features and sallow complexion. Dressed in a sleek gray suit, thatched shoes, pink shirt and cufflinks, he pulled out a leather incased over-sized touch-screen smart phone from a side pouch, and began to play with it. Time zones, maps, statistical information and moving pictures manifested themselves on a crystal clear LCD.

"OK calculator," Subash said in a rich Indian accent.

Beepbeepbeepbeep, the smart phone responded.

"OK." Rudy smiled in assent.

The Indian grabbed Rudy's hand with wiry fingers and yanked it for precisely two shakes. "I am returning to Calcutta to visit my cousin, Achmed." The Indian spoke in rhythmic staccato hitting high and low notes with every third or fifth word.

Subash told an impressive story of a heritage which spanned three continents. Schooled in England, he had been raised in Kenya, his grandparents having emigrated from India in 1907. His grandfather had been a cobbler for the British army, transferring to Africa when the platoon moved there. The family had stayed ever since. Rolling each *r,* he continued, "My older brothers still run a shoe factory there."

"Have you seen witch-doctors?" Styne shifted topics.

"Most certainly. I have seeen shamanism many times in Africa. I have met yõgis in India as vell, who also were endowed with powers."

"Tell me."

"Well, there was Yõgi Onnn-da, about seven years ago, who I met in New Delhi. He smelled of wild roses. I photographed him with my Yeshika." Subash smiled and then fished into his wallet to produce a picture of the master. "I'm sorry you vill not be able to seee his face."

"Why is that?"

"It vas just his vay." Subash handed Rudy the weather-beaten photo. Wrinkled, with edges torn, the picture was slightly out of focus. However, there where the head should have been, was instead, an image of a yellow rose.

"It is unfortunate that the picture is so shabby." Rudy suggested.

"Does it really matter?" Subash responded in his melodic way. "The picture is in my mind, not on paper. OK?"

Rudy's stop in India was brief. He lunched with Subash in a local restaurant not far from the university.

"And then there is Baba," the doctor added with a tone to his voice that seemed to say, 'but that goes without saying'.

"But he is in Bhutan," Rudy responded, while picking through the slim bones of a curry chicken lunch. Piling them up on the back of the plate, he searched with his fork for some meat.

"He appears, Rudee. He appears."

"How do you know? What do you mean?"

"I have seeen. He appears. And many others have seen." His smart phone beeped again. Subash checked it for a message. "Vell, I must be off," he said apologized. Subash yanked at Rudy's hand twice again, grabbed both checks and settled with the cashier before parting.

With almost six days devoted to travel, Rudy wanted to spend as much time as he could in Bhutan. He did not need to get trapped in Calcutta, although he had never been there before. As he made his way back to the airport, the Westerner became overwhelmed by the local crowds. Having been oblivious to them in the heat of conversation, now that he was alone he began to study them as he made his way back to the airport. The reporter passed beggars, fakirs and cripples walking sacred cows, tourists and school children, chickens and small herds of goats and packs of wild gibbons. He snapped some photos, but traveled through the city quickly. The masses seemed subhuman to him, not too different from the drek of Manhattan, he thought uncaringly.

A small WWII transport plane awaited his arrival at the airport. It would take a limited entourage to Paro International Airport, and from there, they could taxi to Thimphu. An eight-seater, Rudy was traveling with seven other tourists. He stepped gingerly into the half-century old relic. Weathered yet sturdy, it smelled of cold metal and gasoline.

One young lady became perturbed when parachutes were handed out. Beet-faced, she took one or two steps towards the terminal hangar, wheeled around, climbed back on board, and punched her husband's arm three times before returning to her seat. The engines fired; the plane lifted.

Rudy watched Calcutta Indians diminish to ant size as the antique flying machine put the mecca behind. Through trustworthy World War II portals, he watched green and barren patches rolling underneath. Farm lands, jungle, foot-hills; upwards into the Himalayas they plodded. The plane dipped, dropped and bobbed through turbulent winds, gluing Rudy's stomach to the ceiling above and the floor beneath him. The beet-faced girl puked green.

Punching through puffed clouds above majestic mountain ranges, the Westerners witnessed a fleeting grandeur of geologic splendor. A camel-etched caravan circled a precipice.

With a pair of glasses on his forehead, another pair at the tip of his nose, a pencil behind each ear, and a silver-colored Salvador Dali waxed moustache turned up like two antlers above his lips, the man sitting next to Rudy appeared scholarly. Heavyset, about fifty-seven years old and about twenty pounds overweight, he wore a brown woolen vest, a scarlet ascot and matching brown pants. He broke the silence first. "I am here to see Swami Baba," he said.

The man turned out to be a parapsychologist from the University of Sydney, a Dr. Wilfred Coomesberry.

"How is parapsychology accepted in Australia?" Rudy inquired.

"There are a few organizations, what, what, and one or two periodicals in the field, but we are, as you say, on the fringe."

"Then, how do you survive?"

"Tenure, my good man."

"But, you do experiments?"

"Of course, of course. We have a laboratory where we study brain-waves and the MRI. My traditional field is stroke victims. But we also use the equipment in telepathy tests, life after life studies, and telekinetic experiments. One way or another, it all helps to map out the brain."

"And you've had success in ESP?"

"Certainly," he humphed.

During the odd moment of silence, each man returned to their respective readings. Coomesberry looked bored with his book, however, and after a brief period, he started up again.

"What about you? Are you in parapsychology as well?"

"No. I'm a reporter."

"Oh. So that explains it."

"What?"

"All the questions."

"You didn't tell me what your main interest was in," Rudy said.

"My parents died with I was just a tot. I dreamt of them all the time. Still do. So, I would have to say, my main interest is in cross-over manifestations."

"That's a hard one to prove, isn't it?"

"No harder than say, materialization."

"And, that's why you're here to see Shri Baba?"

"What other reasons could there be, mate?" Coomesberry spoke in a odd mixture of feigned upper-crust British accent and Australian idioms. "Besides some occasional ectoplasmic manifestations by Miss Lilly, most of which, I have to tell you, occurred more than fifteen years ago, I have never really witnessed materializations."

"How about psychokinesis?"

"Well, we've had table levitations, ouija board communication and various and sundry poltergeist activity, but, as you know, repeatability is a big issue."

Coomesberry somehow seemed preoccupied with the way he said things rather than concentrating on content, but Styne reasoned that if the man was serious enough to travel to Bhutan, there must be some substance to his otherwise superficial manner.

"So, you believe in life after death?" Rudy asked.

"Certainly, what, what. The evidence is extraordinary. This is only one trip, old man."

The professor seemed to Rudy as if he was trying to convince himself, but he let it go and moved to a related subject. "What about Abdullah Manu."

"What about him?"

"With all the scientific studies he's done, why is he still not accepted by the mainstream?"

"Scientific studies! Bah! He's a bloom'n fake--a paltry charlatan. This Fandango fellow has duplicated every trick Manu can do and he does it better! And what about you, mate?"

"What can I say?" At a loss for words, Rudy now wanted to change the subject even though he had introduced it. He did not want to appear the fool to this Australian boor. "I've seen Manu do some astounding things."

"Such as," Coomesberry probed.

"This was in his apartment," Rudy began. "I was sitting next to him as close as I am to you...and, I saw him, with my own eyes...levitate some coins and other objects."

"Levitate?!"

Rudy nodded.

"It wasn't only that. It was his aura, so bright and animated, extending visibly beyond the body. He looked like a walking neon sign. Electric sparks around his head. Hell, I know you are not going to believe this, and I myself cannot explain it, but a girl drifted across the room. It was no trick. What can I say? I simply saw it as I see the plane we are sitting in." Trying vigorously to place the event in some reality framework, Rudy continued his description. Nevertheless, he felt a recurring need to qualify each statement. He watched himself as he spoke. The more he said, the more he realized the need to find a wiseman, a real guru, so that he could somehow make sense out of his new-found reality.

"He's a trickster, and he took you, mate. Simple hypnosis. That is all there is to it."

Coomesberry returned to his book, but soon turned back again to Rudy. "My advice, sir is, you are best off to forget him. Pass it up to experience. There are a lot of gullible blokes out there who believe in astrology, palmistry, UFOs and a lot of other rubbish, too. We have to draw the line somewhere."

"Do we? Is it really a matter of line drawing?"

"Albert Garner wrote a piece on Manu in the *American Scientist.* Devastating, simply devastating. They've got film footage of him using wires and simple misdirection. Manu has no credibility whatsoever. You know all that, Mr. Styne. Everybody knows that. No one will study him. Not a single parapsychologist.... Now mind you, I'm not saying that you did not see something. But what did you see? What could you have seen? Did you search him before he began?"

Rudy could only shake his head no.

"Did you look for mirrors, or a false ceiling perhaps? Have you ever seen anything else levitate in your entire life?"

"No."

"Of course you haven't. He's out for the publicity...for money and fame. Now, I'm hoping this Baba fellow is a different sort entirely."

The old war plane dipped from a downdraft and then nosed along through a windy Himalayan chasm, cruising over disappearing paths and isolated stone dwellings, on towards the center of Bhutan, over hovels and hamlets, stepped farmlands and cascading fields of rice paddies. Rudy saw herds of yak grazing, and then, as the plane descended and they neared the metropolis, isolated clusters of cars and mini-vans, a clump of bicyclists on tour, pack animals and tradesman on oxcarts.

Due east, a small airstrip appeared, the legendary city of Thimphu nestled a good distance away in a wooded valley. As the plane banked to land, Rudy looked west. The sun was beating down on a large mountain range off in the distance. The captain said over the intercom that the largest mass on the horizon was Everest. The machine touched down at Paro International Airport, a small urban center west of the capitol.

Set on a plateau, Rudy was surprised to see a tangerine orchid field near the airport and a welcoming banner by their entranceway which read: "The Land of Gross Happiness!" Grabbing his bags, and passing through customs, Rudy, Professor Coomesberry and two other travelers took the first minibus to Thimphu.

The van passed fields of wild flowers surrounding a large monastery which resembled a great sailing ship. Set on a rise, the grounds were inhabited by monks in long orange robes, rambling goats, turquoise peacocks and strutting tall gray cranes. The Byradingka Temple, for that was its name, was headquarters for the regional abbot.

Driving through juniper and cypress groves, the van sputtered into the ancient capitol. Thimphu was a small city surrounded by snow-capped peaks set along the Pho Chhu River, famous for its trout. There were surprisingly few cars in town and no traffic lights.

After putting his luggage into the hotel, the reporter scouted out the village and royal grounds. The streets were filled with small shops and quiet, leather-skinned craftsmen. Rudy toured Tashichoe Dzong, the largest fortress in the country, and also the Drubthob Goemgba Nunnery.

On the way back to the hotel, he found himself shopping. He bought a three-foot rice paper wood-cut for 50¢ from a man with a kind eye, and then purchased five more. Carefully, the artist rolled them into a burlap satchel and handed them to him. A group of hardy mountain climbers jogged past, and, occasionally, a few hippies still lost somewhere in the late 1960s drifted by. The air was thin, the view inspiring, with the great white-capped summits set majestically in the background.

Rudy met up with Professor Coomesberry again and together they planned their trip to Dzingdup. They would have to locate the Sherpa Yavi to take them on the two-day mule ride to reach the ashram. The hotel called ahead and confirmed the details.

That evening Rudy went to the local nightclub recommended by the concierge. Pushing through saloon doors, peering into a smoke-tinged room, he felt as if he had stepped back in time to 1935. Half expecting William Powell or Charlie Chan to prance in with Myrna Loy, he continued to peruse the place. The decor was of wicker and bamboo with musty curtains on the windows, the kind with off-white tassels. He ordered Chang, the local beer and a plate of emadatse, which was a luke warm chili and cheese stew. A Chinese piano player spun melodies from decades past. His rendition of *Something Wonderful* from the play *The King and I* particularly touched Rudy, and he applauded vigorously when the piece ended.

"Thank you," the man said in English, as he stood, bowed, and then returned to the piano bench to play another tune. This time, it was the romantic lead song *Beauty & the Beast*, from the Disney cartoon of the same title.

At a far away table, an old Tibetan palmist sat by candlelight reading the hands of her customers. Snatching Rudy's attention, she silently called him over. His curiosity piqued, he approached and sat down. The lady grabbed each hand, squeezed the palms and bent back each finger. Rudy took this time to peer into her weather-beaten face. It took him home to North America, to an upstate Indian reservation he had visited with his Uncle Abe when he was a boy. Her eyes were deep, her grip firm and assured, yet gentle, her English broken but adequate.

"Your lines...very peculiar. Major ones narrow but shallow at the same time. You have powers of concentration, but distract easily. Your fingers very flexible, but thumb strong--open to new learning yet boneheaded."

"Boneheaded?"

"Stubborn, like yak," she said firmly, nodding her head in agreement with herself. "See there," she said, almost in a whisper, "the mystic cross." The old gypsy pointed with a gnarled first finger to the center of his hand. There between the two major creases was an unmistakable X. She allowed him to view it and then stared into his eyes. "Much interest in spirit."

"What about my love life?" Rudy inquired, still staring at the X.

"Many lines of affection, and grid on Venus. You too easily influenced, especially in matters of romance." She smiled. "You will marry twice--may already be married to first girl." She stared a little longer and then said, "I see much nervousness and trickiness in pursuit of goals."

"Where?"

"There." The palmist pointed to the scattering of fine lines and curved first finger.

"I see great indecision in path. Many dents in heart line; you have much recent emotional upset and brush with death. You search for secrets to the mysteries. Are you to see Sri Baba?"

"Yes."

"Baba can not help. Great danger lies ahead. There was a death within this month, bad. Very dark."

"How can you tell?"

"There." The palmist pointed to a red-colored star which was newly formed inside his life line. The old gypsy grabbed his hand and held it to her heart. She closed her eyes. "I see bear and eagle fighting. Bear ripping feathers from eagle but blinding himself in the process. Manu Beware!"

Rudy gasped.

"Much brain troubles with acquaintances--watch for secret enemies. Heartache, despair, triumph and knowledge." She came out of her trance and smiled. Pointing to the porpoise around his neck, she concluded, "Nature is your guide and savior. Trust your higher self."

Rudy handed her a $20.00 bill. Her crinkled eyes smiled as he turned and walked outside. The night was crisp, the air thin. Cold and crystal clear.

Stepping into shadow and tilting his head back, he gazed up to the sky. A large three-quarter moon winked from behind a nearby mountain range. It looked so close, he felt he could pluck it, able to easily discern the outline of the missing quarter. Red, green, blue, orange, white and pink glitters perforated the black abyss. Constellations he had never seen before pierced his consciousness as a tiny white glow traversing the darkness caught his attention. A satellite, he figured. How magnificent.

Coomesberry knocked on his door at 5:15 the next morning. "Are you up, Mr. Styne?" Rudy looked at his watch and rolled out of bed. He went to the door and opened it.

"Time's a wasting, mate" Coomesberry said.

After breakfast, they waited by the hotel entrance next to a seated man and four mules. "Are you our coolie?" Coomesberry demanded.

"Guide," Rudy interjected trying to place the word over Coomesberry's. "Yavi?" he added.

"Yavi," the Sherpa said, bowing. They handed over their travel bags and some money and helped the guide to strap them to the sides of one mule as they climbed aboard the others.

The reporter could smell the animal's pungent sweat as the cold leather saddle bit into his inner thighs. Shifting his center of gravity in an attempt to stop the chafing, Rudy grabbed the thick mane tightly. He was trying to show the animal who was boss. But the ornery beast knew otherwise. Finally, the city slicker resigned to the dominance hierarchy ingrained in the pack, and settled into the journey.

Oblivious to the dangers that lie ahead, Coomesberry began belting out *Waltzing Matilda* as if he were alone in a shower, and he kept the song up for twenty minutes until Yavi interrupted.

"Yonder," the guide said in unusually well-spoken English, "is the holy Mountain, secret dweller of the life force." Rudy gazed to the left to see a tall, thin, spikelike ridge protruding into the clouds. "Baba lies on the other side."

They lumbered up byroads which seemed impassable and trudged down paths pitted with small boulders and the skeletons of less cautious beasts. Sometimes they were in valleys surrounded by massive crests and other times they turned upon overlooks that descended 8,000 feet. Overpowered by the awesome size of the Himalayas, the newcomers responded like timid explorers on an unknown planet.

Exhausted, yet inspired, at 2:45 P.M., they paused for lunch: tsampa and thermos-warmed barley soup. A group of lamas in long orange robes and shaved heads crossed their path. On a more treacherous route, the lamas climbed down a cliff and dropped out of sight.

Everything seems to move in slow motion except for the fleeing sun. They passed a craftsman chiseling Buddhas out of stone and also a number of hermit monks in prayer. So many different people living such varied realities, Rudy thought.

They spent the night at the Chomolhari Hermitage, or Castle of the Hornbill. A regional priest who spoke broken English told the travelers that the castle was the meeting grounds for the Four Winds. When the Professor began to ask about the history of Bhutan, the priest said, "Druk Yul. We not use name Bhutan."

"Druk Yul?" Rudy asked.

"Land of the Thunder Dragon."

The building was made of stone, and the night was cold, but Rudy had brought a second set of long johns and that is what he wore, along with an extra pair of socks and polar-tek hood.

After breakfast, they packed and continued their journey.

The sun dazzled, the sky such a rich deep blue it almost looked green. Bright puffed clouds drifted by like a floating column of albino elephants.

They passed through a forest of spruce and hemlock, and a field of wheat grass inhabited by musk deer. A rushing stream, which had cut a path from the foothills, cascaded by. "That is our way." Yavi pointed upwards, towards its source.

The jaunt was slow, the breathing becoming more difficult, as the small caravan continued to climb the circuitous path. Above them through billowy sun-lit clouds lay Baba's ashram.

Upwards into fog they rode, as faint echoes of rhythmic chants bounded off their stone passageway. Large, condor-like birds glided by as the small caravan hooked around another ledge. Coomesberry huddled low on the mule, hugging its neck with both arms, peering over yet another unprotected cliff. His singing having ceased long ago, he had realized after a time that his life depended upon this four-legged ass.

The mist thickened as they ascended, until Rudy could barely see the tail of the animal in front of him. Blinded from the afternoon sun, they emerged through the haze completely above the clouds! Rudy prayed that the mules would stay surefooted. Upwards they continued to push.

As the chanting grew louder the seven creatures surfaced. With a cottony blanket below and the music beyond, they arrived at Swami Baba's landing, their eyes now parallel with the setting sun.

Much to the surprise of the travelers there were over 600 people there. Most of the community was sitting in a huge circle swaying, clapping and chanting. There were mothers with babies, lamas and gurus, children with shaved heads and orange robes, and long-legged charcoal gray cats, a few businessmen, some Western-dressed tourists and about thirty-five hippies. At the periphery, black-necked cranes stalked, and a few individuals meandered through a small marketplace. But all of the energy was directed towards the center, for there stood Baba.

Dressed in a lavender robe with red stitching, the dark-skinned guru looked more like an African then an Oriental, although he could have easily passed for a Semite. He wore a modern afro hairdo, and gaudy golden rings on every finger of his left hand. His aura shimmered in the light in iridescent purples and yellows as he moved with grace and authority. The master began to strut the circle, spinning his hands in quick spirals as he materialized fruits and vegetables and jars of honey with advertising labels on them!

Rudy watched for a full fifteen minutes still sitting on the donkey and during that time he saw Baba toss out over 180 peaches, a dozen cantaloupes, watermelons, bunches of grapes and bananas, myriad oranges and plums and 40 canisters of the bees' golden nectar. All he wore was that single robe. A walking cornucopia, Baba seemed to hover slightly above ground, periodically fading into mist only to reappear in super-realistic clarity--almost as if he were a strobe-lit hologram.

The Swami broke through the first line of the circle and began to walk behind them. Everyone reached out to touch and kiss his hands. Sometimes daffodils, iris and roses would sprout from his hair, mouth and navel. Streams of energy pouring from the sun entered through the top of his head as he stopped and prayed with the sitters. The Maharishi then returned to the center and collected letters from some of the more scholarly-looking people, as well as the tourists, natives and peasants. He also pointed to five or six on-lookers and together they departed up a path and out of sight. As many colored auras began glowing from the crowd, Coomesberry fell to the ground in a faint.

Jumping to the Australian's side, the guide placed the professor's head in his lap and began to soothe Coomesberry's forehead with a moistened rag.

When the professor awoke, his beautiful smile turned to shock as he saw that he was in the hands of a Bhutanese peasant native. "My word," he scowled as he dusted himself off. "Quite a show, what!"

Rudy and the guide broke into laughter, and then they removed the travel bags from the back of the pack mule.

An American girl in her late teens or early 20s approached. "Hello, my name is Felona. You must be Rudolf Styne and Professor Coomesberry. We received your emails a few days ago. Congratulations on being on time. As you can see, we are a far cry from a technological metropolis."

"Thank you for your wire," Rudy said.

"When can we see Baba?" Coomesberry sounded somewhat irritated and demanding.

"You have." She smiled and bowed to both of them. "I'll show you to your quarters." There was an odd sweetness to her, although her mouth was tight and her face a little frozen. Felona wore beads in her hair and a nature dress, yak jacket and sandals. She walked in long rapid strides, insisting on carrying the two bags herself. "You must write Swami the reason why you wish to see him tomorrow; he will collect the letters and decide."

By the time they unpacked it was nightfall. Rudy was too tired to do anything but go to sleep. His cot was soft straw, heat supplied through forced air vents in the floor.

The next morning as the first light shown along the eastern horizon, the chanting could again be heard. Rudy looked at his watch: 5:35 A.M. Jesus, he thought, these people never sleep. There was a knock at the door.

"May I come in?" Felona entered, without waiting for a reply. "Services begin in ten minutes. Breakfast is at 7:30."

She dropped a card and envelope on the table and poured a pitcher of warm water into the sink by his bureau.

Rudy forced himself out of bed, washed up, dressed and walked outside. The sky was an orange violet, the mountains loomed. To the east, Rudy watched the dawn give way as the tip of the sun began to peek above a distant mountain range. The air chilled. Small birds fluttered. He stopped to write:

```
Dear Swami Baba,
     I am a reporter for Modern Times Magazine of
New York City, and have come to see you as part of
```

```
a report I am doing on parapsychology. Recently, I
have  seen  what  I  believe  are  psychic  events,
materializations,  levitation,  telepathy  and  so
forth, and I have reached an impasse regarding what
I had believed was reality and what I now perceive.
I would like to know if you consciously speak with
spiritual entities higher than man, and if so, can
they do anything about the use of parapsychology
for evil work?
```

Yours sincerely,
Rudolf Styne

With chest expanded, Coomesberry showed Styne his own epistle. The professor had penned:

```
Dear Sri Baba:
    I have come all the way from Australia to see
you perform. I am a teacher of parapsychology.
```

Professor W.H. Coomesberry, M.A.,Ph.D.

"Very good, what what," Coomesberry declared. Reading Rudy's note, he commented, "Reality is a tough nut to crack, old chap. Very good."

They walked to the circle of people and sat in the front row on the left, where Felona had placed them. Zithers and gongs, chimes and cymbals melodically resounded. Three robed lamas with shaved heads, swayed in the center, and led the chant. Six belly dancers appeared, wriggling their way through the congregation, as they snapped clanging castanets and created poses of Shiva and Rita Hayworth. Spirituality and festivity permeated the atmosphere.

After a time Rudy and, occasionally, Coomesberry, would join in singing the catchy tunes.

Finally as the chanting reached a crescendo, Baba appeared. Gliding to the center, the fuzzy-haired magi sat and prayed.

The music stopped. There was silence on the mountain.

Then he rose, fluttering about five inches above the ground. Settling, he smoothed his lavender vestment, strutted the circle once and collected the letters from Rudy, Coomesberry and from some of the others. The meeting broke. Felona led the way to the breakfast table: hot barley soup, eggs and oat bread, honeycakes, fresh fruit and goats milk.

"It will be four hours until the next service," Felona suggested. "Perhaps you would like to go swimming?" The duo looked at her as if she were crazy, as the temperature was only about 50. But she persisted. "Follow me."

Leading them down a winding lane, Felona guided them to an ominous looking stone precipice. Drilled into the rock was a large, cumbersome pulley system. Two young men handled its wheel.

When the elevator arose, Felona placed an arm around each man's waist, and took them aboard. The platform dropped slowly along 3,500 feet of scaffolding to the chasm below. Little dots became boulders as they continued their downward journey. Into the depths of the tiny canyon they rode, changing elevators about every 500 feet.

Rudy felt the mysteries of life flood through his veins as they descended a length equivalent to three Empire State Buildings. Although there were various paths and landings along the route, and extraordinary changes in the flora, they dropped as a staggered plum line, all the way to the bottom.

"Who built this system?" Rudy queried.

"The people of Druk Yul are extraordinary. They did the labor, but the construction of this multi-tram advanced pulley-lift was the creation of a French engineer, Claude René. It took four years to complete, the larger equipment and support structure having been dropped here by a high-altitude helicopter. René is now back in France, currently completing a design for a bridge over the English Channel. Perhaps you know of his work in Peru?"

Passing through an array of changing air currents, the lift settled in a small fertile valley where hot springs from ancient volcanoes steamed.

"This is our holy basin of the curative herbs," Felona said. "The waters you see rushing out of that rock, have been heated by volcanic action for thousands of centuries. Here, we gather sacred medicinal herbs." She pointed to a grove of strange plants. "We also grow certain fruits and nuts and go swimming in a natural bath. Come, I will show you." She smiled simply.

A few people could be seen picking herbs, strange fruits and nuts. Others were swimming. Felona shed her robes. Her body was youthful, sleek, her nipples erect. With toes pointed, she dove off a low cliff about twenty-five feet into a steaming lagoon. Rudy stripped and climbed down to the water's edge. The temperature was unusually warm, the water clear. Testing it with his hands, he could smell natural mineral oils. Double-checking the depth, he plunged in, and swam towards the center. The water was purifying, hot in spots, bizarre and bubbly.

Every pore in his body seemed to open to the soft liquids as he floated contentedly. Finally, when he emerged, his body shimmered in an iridescent glitter. He felt tingly and giddy.

"Curly moustache! Curly moustache!" A small group of children chanted in English as they pointed towards the Professor. Coomesberry pretended great anger as he plunged in and rushed towards the children, splashing and slapping his hands. The gleam in his eye gave it all away, and they giggled. "Squiggly moustache," one small girl continued.

"Squiggly!" the Professor boomed. Scooping her up and kissing her on the fly, he heaved her easily into a deeper part of the waters.

"We're in paradise, old man!" he said as he tossed another child and then another.

"Try these," Felona said, handing Rudy a pair of goggles. Diving like a porpoise, she led the way through a chasm to a deeper crystal clear pool. Sea horse-looking creatures, tropical fish and small turtles flitted about them.

She dove and Rudy followed her through an underwater tunnel. They surfaced at a slice in the valley where the sun screamed through. "Sit," she said, patting the rock next to hers.

She placed his hand on her beating heart. "I love here."

The rock was warm. They sat in silence and baked until the sun passed by, their pinkies touching. A cold wind pierced the atmosphere.

Felona led Rudy back to the main pool where they emerged. He felt, somehow, reborn. Coomesberry was sitting by the pool playing "Guess which hand the rock is in" with the children. They gathered their clothes, and Felona led them to a cabin where they could warm themselves by a wood burning stove. Time slipped by too quickly.

Back on the lift they found themselves, rising from the hot springs to, perhaps, an even more peculiar place. The lift creaked past interesting rock formations, a series of caves where monks were praying, a nest inhabited by two large eggs, herds of mountain goats, a fleeing animal Rudy thought to be a lynx, and on up through a fog to the summit.

Baba had already begun his service. He spoke mainly in a dialect of Bhutanese, but occasionally switched to French, English and Chinese. Prancing like a mountain cougar, with fingers together and pointed hands, he bent his elbows and positioned his arms into primeval poses. Pausing in a stalking position, with every muscle frozen, the "Avatar, Incarnate" turned his gaze upon two young women, one of whom was pregnant. And then he looked at an Indian yŏgi and the American journalist. All four stood and followed him up the path.

Rudy's heart pounded as he fell in line. They circled the mountain and shuffled into a small cave that was carved into the side of a colossal ridge. Baba entered first and sat on the bare floor.

Behind him, through a large octagon-shaped portal, above a sheer drop to unknown depths, Rudy could see a string of snow-capped mountain ranges. The four visitors sat in a line by the far wall.

The Swami began to chant, the room resonating with his melody. Rudy found himself envisioning the notes as tangible musical entities dancing about the room, bouncing off the walls. Bringing the melody to a close, the wizard waited for the reverberations to diminish to a palpable stillness.

Then he turned to the girl carrying child.

"Bless my little one, Swami?" she asked.

Baba placed one hand over her head and the other on her heart and sat in meditation. The young lady cried and thanked him as she kissed his hands.

He turned to the other girl.

"My father," was all she said.

"There is nothing I can do."

"I know that, Swami."

"Then, how can I be of help?"

"I ask only that you guide him to the Bardo plane."

"I will try." The Holy Man sat himself into the lotus position, and created circles with the thumb and first finger of each hand. Then he rested them on his knees and went into trance. Sinking like an empty sack of potatoes, his body went limp.

"Baba will be gone for quite a while," the yōgi whispered to Rudy. The reporter decided to question this bearded fellow in the interim.

"When Baba meditated over the girl, I thought I saw a Buddha appear in his aura."

"Very good," the yōgi commented. "Once, when Baba was visiting a lamasery in Tibet, quite unexpectedly he granted the monks a Vision of Avatar, the 'Man Lion of Vishnu'. The High Lama fainted and did not recover for close to a day. Another time while in India, Baba showed a professor the flame emanating from between his eyebrows. The man was so overwhelmed that his family chided Baba for taking their father so near to death's door. In such cases, other persons that were present did not see these visions for they were not intended to do so."

"How did Swami know he was an avatar?"

"Baba came from a family of fine stature. His date of birth corresponded to the next coming of the Great Nilaya Avatar who had died in 1887. Since his mother had had vivid dreams announcing the reincarnation, priests from Thimphu came to her to see the child. The late Nilaya Avatar had been a healer and spiritual guide and had first walked the earth in 1375 AD. He has lived in Tibet, Nepal, Bhutan, India and Mongolia during various incarnations. To assure themselves, the priests consulted an oracle before returning to Baba's father's house. They erected the child's horoscope, and took his palm prints. When Baba was two years old, he was asked questions regarding the secret life and teachings of Vishnu. It was on that day that the boy became Nilaya Baba, the reincarnation of Nilaya Avatar. When he was five he entered the great monastery near Katmandu, but also spent time in schools in Tibet and Bhutan. Through clairvoyance and bi-location, thousands have seen him in two places at once.

"After this training, Baba disappeared for a period of eight years. He was 19 at the time of his disappearance, and 27 at the time of his return. It is believed that during this time he met with a being which you Western people call Jehovah."

A shaft of golden light streamed through the octagon-shaped portal, entering the crown chakra of the slumped Master. He awoke just as a wind swept into the cave. The shaft morphed into a ring of light about his head. "I have taken your father to Vishnu," Baba said to the girl. "His work on the Earth has ended."

The daughter began to weep. Amidst her sorrow she asked if she could say goodbye. Baba cocked his head and turned one eye towards her. He stared for many moments, raised both his hands and spread them apart. Between his palms and above his head a luminance appeared. Oscillating, it formed into a three-dimensional apparition of her father! The man's expression seemed to be an odd combination of sorrow and joy. Reluctantly, the image waved good-bye, and father and daughter exchanged parting thoughts. "Thank you," she said.

Baba then began a duel chant with the yŏgi, and the girls and Rudy joined in. Fruit appeared so they stopped and ate.

While enjoying Nature's nourishment, Baba turned. "You have questions for me?" Rudy was speechless. He nodded yes. Baba waited. His bold eyes displayed a quiet compassion. Silently and reverently the Swami sat, his eyes drifting towards a distant chasm in the mountain range.

"I have lost reality, Swami," Rudy said, "and I fear evil--psychic evil between the United States and some of the new Eurasian republics."

Baba waited patiently as Rudy paused.

"Only a month ago I would have laughed at this field you are lumped into, which we Westerners call parapsychology, and yet, today, I have had telepathic and telekinetic experiences, have seen levitation, and," as he talked his voice dropped to a murmur, "have seen murder and other great dangers."

"Who was murdered?" Baba asked.

"Professor Ketchembach, a physicist from New York University active in this field."

"I know of Ketchembach, his work with Bohm, Bohr and Einstein, his attempts to integrate consciousness with quantum theory. He was close to revealing many secrets...And who was the taker of his life?"

"A Ukrainian agent known as Georgi Boshtov."

"I know of him, too." Baba paused. "You see this as terrible, and rightly it is so, but the Holy One works in strange ways. The Law of Karma, action and reaction, shall rule. Our creator has endowed the human with the capacity for self-evolution. He gave us free will, He cannot take it away. Do you see? But humans misuse this will, and this is what you have seen."

"Is Bash the incarnation of evil?"

"There is no such thing as Divine Evil, only ignorance of higher laws and misuse of transforming energies. Do you follow?"

Remembering Professor Ketchembach's talk on Lucifer, Rudy nodded assent.

"And?" Baba saw another question on Rudy's face.

"Why," Rudy began again, "are psychic powers so," he searched for a word, "uncommon? And why do so few people believe in them?" Rudy rambled on spewing non-sequiturs, pouring out subconscious thorns that had kept themselves wriggling in convoluted recesses of his mind. "Perhaps that is why I have felt so lost these past weeks. What I thought was real turns out to be false, and what I thought was fiction turns out to be fact. No one will believe my description of you either, Swami."

A twinkle in his eye, Baba looked at him knowingly. The Swami twirled his hand and produced a small amulet with his portrait imbedded in porcelain. He handed it to Rudy who stared in wonderment. "Turn it over, turn it over," Baba repeated. There in small letters it said: *Made In Bhutan.* Rudy looked a bit shocked, and the yõgi and Baba burst into laughter.

Baba rose up and turned, his body glowing brightly, a rainbow surrounding his being. "Reality is a learning curve, you know." Rudy nodded. "One level of development and understanding is quite different than another. People live in different strata all the time.

"First, Rudy, learn to walk before you ride. But remember, you are still in crawling stage." He looked over for understanding.

Rudy nodded.

"What is most interesting of all is that faith is a higher value than psychic tricks."

"I agree in your case, but it seems in my case they pointed the way."

"A door was opened, but only a little. After Atlantis fell, which was 100 generations before the Great Pyramids were built, it was decided that man's higher powers would become more subtle. Dormant for most. But man made this decision. Do you see."

"We fell from grace?"

"Precisely. The post-Atlantean evolution has come in waves. It is not a linear progression: Mesopotamia, Ming Dynasty, Inca, Egypt, Athens, Rome, Maya, Magellan, Minkowski, Edison, the Wright brothers, Einstein, RCA, CNN, Google, Microsoft, Shutterfly.

"The wheel spins upon its only route," Baba continued, "and with the rise of technology comes a corresponding revolution spiritual to counterpoint. The New World, Rudy, is in your heart and in your actions. Trust the miracle of existence, never limit its power, and you have already entered the Kingdom. Have I answered all your questions?"

"I have one more, Swami."

"Yes?"

"Are you in conscious communication with higher beings?"

"This is a complex question," Baba replied. "And the answer partly depends upon your definition of conscious and my definition of spirit. All human souls, that is, their higher selves, are constantly in communication with the higher realm. Let me ask you a question, my inquisitive seeker. When you dream who is the author of your dream?"

"I am."

"That is the easy answer, Rudy. Are you? Think about it. Do you, Rudolf Styne, consciously plan out the dream, design it, or do you watch it as if you were partaking in a virtual reality game?"

"I partake," Rudy agreed.

"So, you do not know what will happen during the course of this dream?"

"No, I do not," Rudy agreed.

Baba smiled. "So, then, who is the author?"

"I don't know. My higher self?"

"Exactly! And is this higher self conscious?" Baba continued.

"I guess, in its own way."

"In its own way," Baba echoed. "Think about it. While you sleep, It considers. And one last question for you. Is this higher self keeping your heart beating?"

Rudy looked at the teacher and then a light seemed to go on inside him. "I am beginning to see," Rudy said.

"So my answer to you is, bring Earth consciousness into your dream world and you will converse with the higher one. Have I answered you adequately?"

"Yes." Rudy said, now truly aware of how little he knew about his own mind, the source of his thoughts.

"Your dreams are your door to the world of Spirit." Baba then bowed his head in prayer. Shortly thereafter, he motioned for the yõgi to take Rudy and the girls out of the cave and down the path.

The American turned to the yõgi, "You have known Baba long?"

"Twenty years. I first met him when I was sixteen, and he took me in when I turned twenty-one. You used your time well."

"How can I learn to become more in touch?"

The yõgi stopped and placed a hand to his ear. "Think like the mountains, sense like the shrubs. The cosmic planes which reside beyond space and time cannot be grasped with the material body. Man is also composed of six other more subtle astral selves. Only with the spiritual senses can one reach beyond gross matter."

"Thank you," Rudy said.

When he returned to the main encampment Professor Coomesberry sauntered up. "All the way from Australia to be treated like a common bushman! The nerve. Well, how was it, mate?"

Rudy related the experience as best he could and then returned to his room to write notes. He realized no one, including himself of only three weeks ago, could believe what he had just witnessed. But it all seemed natural when it was happening. Spiritually uplifted, he felt in some other sense more alienated, not just from all his newfound reality, but also from a society that he now saw as vastly asleep. He wrote in his notes, "Civilization has not even the faintest notion of what realities lie hidden and what potentialities could be actualized." And then he began to describe the experiences he had just witnessed. *No one will ever believe this,* he thought to himself.

That evening he talked to Felona about occult phenomena and Baba's life. She spoke quietly but assuredly, "Remember this credo: To Will, To Know, To Dare, To Keep Silent. You must learn to live by these words.

"Rudy," she went on, "you are obtaining knowledge here. You must learn to differentiate these proceedings from mere belief. I can intellectually describe to you how to ride a camel, but until you get on that animal yourself you can never know it. This is why silence is so important. Without direct communication, the world cannot know Baba. Your articles can never be read."

"You mean that if I write the truth, no one will believe it?"

"Some believe, but no one will know. I have seen others leave to tell the world of Swami's greatness. It is folly."

"I do not agree, Felona. I think Baba should come to America to show that God exists. Why is he shut off from the world here in Bhutan? Why does God work in such unfair ways?"

"I don't know, Rudy, but let me ask you a question. Why are humans so greedy? I left my husband to come here. Every year he had to get a raise in salary: $80,000, $90, $135. For what? More heartache? Selling your soul for a bigger car? America has everything: foods of all types, housing for its people, entertainment, mass transportation, fresh orange juice...so why do prices keep going up? Why do people keep ripping off other people? Do you think Baba can change that? Utopia is in their hands as much as it is here on this mountain, but America still prays to the almighty dollar."

The next day Coomesberry sat at Baba's feet with five women and fourteen children. The Swami materialized a peach for the professor. Inside was a pit with a picture of an aborigine carved into it. "At first, I didn't understand. But then," he later told Rudy, "something happened. I *can* be a buffoon, can't I?"

The duo exchanged glances as Rudy nodded acknowledgement.

When the third day arrived, Baba called Rudy again and spoke to him briefly. "Humans create their own reality. Confusion exists when one accepts cultural beliefs over the miracle of existence. You, my son, are an external expression of the one Godhead. See your body as divine, and pray to that divinity as if you are already a wise man. True knowledge can only be received through perception of this higher self, your self. It is only from within that you meet and work with the Holy One."

The trip down the mountain was painful. Baba had not solved the problem with the Eurasian agent, yet Rudy wanted to stay and learn more of his ways. Coomesberry also felt the pull. But Baba was also sending them away. He had materialized amulets for each of them as a sign that higher laws operate, and he wanted this word passed on. Felona led them to the edge of the precipice where Yavi and the small convoy awaited them.

"I hope you have enjoyed your stay," she said. Her eyes seemed tearful. She paused, and then leaned over, kissed Coomesberry on the cheek and Rudy on the lips. Her mouth was soft and amazingly sensual.

"Say hello to the Big Apple," she whispered, as the two men got aboard their respective mules to begin their downward trek.

EGYPT

Routing himself through Cairo, Rudy emailed Chessie at the hotel when he arrived. He missed her and would tell all when he came home. Then he reflected on recent events. Baba had said that Manu, like himself, and like any child, is born a messenger from a higher existence. "Some speak louder than others," he said.

The taxi from the airport transported the reporter only a few miles in distance, but hundreds, perhaps even thousands of years back in time in terms of his normal frame of reference. Cairo reeked of butchered goats and camel dung. Rudy weaved through narrow alleyways lined with open bazaars with pushy street venders and donkeys and brothels and belly dancers in dingy bars, gray-shawled women and tacky shops packed with postcards of pyramids and fake artifacts. Arab men in striped head-dresses played cards as Bedouin nomads with hot-breathing camels hustled tourists saddled with their smart phones and digital cameras. At the periphery, the sphinx and regal pyramids loomed.

Following a mama goat and two of her progeny up a winding path, Rudy came upon the house of Abdullah's parents. Mrs. Manu, who had been kneading dough, asked him in. She was a plump woman with fierce eyes, yet kindly wrinkles.

The front hall was decorated with pictures of Nasser, Sedat, Mubarik and Zedoffil, and religious figures as well as a number of framed magazine covers with Abdul's face upon them.

"Come into the kitchen. I finish work....We moved back to our home four years ago after wrangling settled," she spoke in a heavy Egyptian accent. "Abdul can go levitate in Japan and America," she laughed.

Rudy questioned her about Abdullah's childhood, and she related one story accenting important points with a wooden rolling pin. "During Abdullah's fifth birthday we had big celebration and I invited all relatives over for dinner. Feizel, Abdul's great uncle, got into a heated discussion with Grandpappa, his brother, may he rest in peace, over British occupation of Suez. There was great tension, each beginning to yell louder...when suddenly, *whoosh!* descended upon room."

Mrs. Manu paused in her story to turn the dough over and size up her guest, resuming with her gaze still upon him. "Silverware and dinner table began to rattle and vibrate. Mama says, 'Lord, it's an earthquake, Allah help us!' and then mama began to scurry towards the door. As she reached threshold, sofa spat cushion which bounced over and blocked entrance. Snapping sounds erupted from walls and table. Forks, plates and food levitate. And then my son arose...*floated* up to ceiling to collect utensils and return them back to table! 'It work of Devil,' my sister kept shouting as she pointed her accusing finger at poor Abdullah. But our beloved Feizel, praise Allah, spoke up, 'If this be Satan's hand, then all of our food has turned to poison!' With that, and twinkle in eye, he gobbled up a floating sandwich and the tension was released."

Smiling in self-reflection as she related the event, Mother Manu reached into a drawer and pulled out a scrapbook of newspaper and magazine clippings devoted to her psychic son. She gave Rudy the names of some of the relatives involved and directions to a church where priests had taken time to train the boy. She also listed other witnesses to similar events.

"You go to others and verify. You take care of my boy when you get back to crazy New York....It true, all true."

As Rudy set to go, a small and shriveled woman peeked out from behind a large closet. "Go to bed, Momma," Mrs. Manu commanded, as she ushered Rudy to the door.

One of the most convincing stories Rudy was able to uncover was from an elderly schoolteacher who said that Manu had "levitated chairs and pencils in school. I very sincere," the old lady concluded. Extending a wizened hand for a remarkably warm handshake, she pointed the reporter in the general direction of the houses of other witnesses. Verification of these kinds of school incidents were obtained in interviews with two former students, Gabal Nessin, now an accountant, and, Rameesh Homel, a brick layer. Where Gabal told Rudy stories of how pencils and books levitated one afternoon when Abdullah came in late one day to school, Rameesh remembered a baseball game they played when they were twelve.

Rudy found Rameesh at a construction site where he was building a wall for a new bank that was going up. Having received Rudy's text message earlier in the day, after quick amenities, Rameesh simply launched into his story. Using a trowel to augment points being made, Remeesh continued laying bricks as he talked.

"Abdullah took one swipe at the ball, and he missed it, but the ball bounced out of the catcher's glove and he took another swipe and knocked it over the fence. It just seemed to hover there waiting to be hit. It was as if Allah had willed it. The referee ruled in Manu's favor, and the other team was simply too amazed to argue too much against it. Will you tell Abdullah that I think of him always?" Rameesh asked, as he offered the reporter a cement-powered handshake.

Rudy spent the last hours in Egypt visiting the Sphinx and the Great Pyramid of Giza. Ancient hieroglyphs and animal-god statues triggered a déjà vu sense of wonder deep within him. It became clear to the acolyte that humans had been more highly evolved spiritually at another time in their existence. Ancient Egyptian technology was not separate from its religion. Intertwined, they complimented each other. Such things as survival of bodily death were part of their way of life. As he sat in the King's chamber to meditate, essence was revealed. A higher conscious force, Rudy came to realize, was responsible for Earth's existence, let alone human existence. This was a self-evident necessity, prerequisite for human evolution.

Boarding the plane with a new sense of appreciation for the achievement of the ancients, Rudy jotted down his memories and emailed them to his office computer in New York, as the large metal flying ship sailed silently through the ionosphere.

Rudy was also aware, however, that these experiences were too incredible to be published at face value. Whitmore would never accept them as is, so he worked hard to compose a conservative version, which met both the tenets of accurate news reporting and the dictates of his conscience.

Realizing the need for scientific corroboration in order to substantiate at least some of the more astonishing phenomena, Styne decided to schedule interviews with leading American parapsychologists. After going through customs, he searched the crowd for Chessie. Not seeing her, he used his cell and gave her a call.

"Nice to hear from you," Chessie said distantly.

"I don't get it."

"You don't get it? One email from Cairo. How do I know it was even from you? You could have been dead for all I know, and that could have been a trap by that tall horrible man that almost killed you in the subway."

Why do women always do this to you? Rudy thought as a tune from the play *My Fair Lady* ran through his head. "Why can't you be more like a man?"

"Oh, just shut up," she said, and hung up the phone. He took a cab to his apartment, and slept alone that night.

Rudy got up at 5AM the following morning and hopped a cab to Chessie's block. Stopping at Pazzi's bakery, he purchased bagels, her favorite Danish, fresh-squeezed orange juice from the grocery shop next door, and buzzed her apartment. She released the doorlock and climbed back into bed.

He peaked in, and tip-toed into the bedroom. Their eyes met.

"What, are you taking beautiness pills?"

"No," was all she said.

Over breakfast, the ice thawed. He told her of his meeting with Baba.

"It sounds too unbelievable. Too much like a storybook." Chessie poured the coffee and sliced off another piece of Danish. "My third," she smiled up at him. "But who's counting." She reached over and gave Rudy a kiss, the first of the morning. Her eyes crinkled, and he fell in love with her all over again.

"What do you think fairy-tails are based on? Most fiction is based on reality. In fact, what I am finding is that I may have to either tone this experience down or write it as fiction if I want to get it into print. Chess, it's so strange, but reality is much more fantastic than any made up tale. Why just look at the size and complexity of New York City. If you had never seen this city, would you have ever believed it could actually exist?"

"But that's different, Rudy. That's something people can see and verify. The other is all, and please excuse me, based on your say-so. You have absolutely no proof."

"How 'bout Auntie Velma, Chess. We saw her, didn't we?"

"You mean the ghost in Vermont, huh? I had forgotten. I can't answer that Rudy. I know it makes no sense, but, it just seems like, well, like religion. Because we can't really prove it wasn't some shared delusion. When all is said and done, all we are really left with is just plain old faith."

"Is that so terrible?"

"No," she said as she stood to give him another kiss. "You go ahead to work. It will take me awhile to get out of here."

Rudy took the subway to 42nd and Fifth and walked the few blocks to his building. He motioned "Hi" to the red-headed janitor, the guy whose name he never could remember, and then walked on over to the elevators. Entering the office and then acknowledging his colleagues with a nod, he entered Captain Whitmore's office, and handed over his preliminary notes.

"You're going to need some scientific substantiation for some of this," the captain said, using the same word Rudy had been thinking.

"Yes, I know, captain. I've scheduled meetings with two American parapsychologists this week. One is at the University of Wisconsin, with Dr. P. Karl, the famous neurophysiologist. The other is with B.K. Pine in South Carolina.

"Make sure you see that magician, the Fantastic Fandango, or whatever his name is."

"Yes, sir."

"And cut out this crap about levitation and materialization."

Rudy glared back.

"Well, soften it, Styne. You know what I mean."

SWAPPING HEADS

Rudy phoned the Wisconsin Primate Center and spoke directly to Dr. P. Karl, the world's foremost expert on neurological states in humans and apes. "I want to warn you, Mr. Styne," Dr. Karl said, "parapsychology is just a hobby with me."

"You do perform psionic experiments?"

"Yes, of course."

"Then, may I see you tomorrow?"

"You may."

The following morning, Rudy flew out to Madison. Upon his arrival on campus, he inadvertently overheard two students talking about the scientist he was about to meet.

"The guy is barbaric. He should be caged instead of those poor monkeys," the girl said, shaking her head from side to side as she locked up her ten-speed bike and removed the front wheel. "I get sick every time I think about him. Patricia, how can you work there?" She rapped her tongue ring against her teeth as she waited for a response.

"Barb, it's three credits and I'm learning a lot. Dr. Karl's work with chimps and orangs is world-known. He has established single-handedly that schizophrenia is environmentally determined--at least in some cases. Would you rather he work with humans?"

"Damn it, Pat, he has! Why do you think he drinks so much? The asshole did his doctoral work with Penmeadow in New Orleans when they were sticking depth electrodes into the craniums of so-called volunteers. Many were schizoid or mentally deficient....I've heard that he still performs lobotomies. He's an evil man who has the sanction of a prestigious university because of his fame. God, Barb, just go to the Madison Zoo. You can see his butchery all over the place. They limp around with missing limbs, open wounds from past operations and half their brains torn out...."

Rudy decided to walk on rather than interrupt them, but he was disturbed. He came upon Karl's building complex. Above the entrance, carved crudely in wood were the words GORILLA-HOMME. He entered.

In the front display case was a stuffed orangutan. Cobwebs hung from its chin. In the next glassed compartment, plastic models of the evolution of the brain were presented. And in a third, there was a stuffed Bonobo. Its glazed eyes stared vacantly into space focusing somewhere beyond the plastic banana it held in its left hand.

Lining each side of the hallway behind the exhibits were a long line of stacked crates of live monkeys marked for shipment for laboratories all over the globe. Gibbering and shitting, many leered at Rudy as he walked by. *"Getoutofhere. Getoutofhere. Getoutofhere,"* they seemed to say in a high-pitched wail. Occasionally, a lab assistant would pass, holding or walking any of a variety of primate species. Off to the right was a room marked AUTOPSY and on pure inspiration, the reporter walked in.

Six students were bent over a reclining figure. Rudy inched closer. Lying on a slab was an old naked woman with long gray hair. Her entire middle section was zipped open and half of her skull was removed. Her left eyeball dangled from its socket. Rudy could see her stomach, liver, small intestines and heart, the cool fluorescent lights reflecting slickly off their shininess. One female student, scalpel in one hand, part of the spleen in the other, looked up and approached. She reeked of formaldehyde. "Can I help you?" she said disdainfully.

"Dr. Karl's office?" Styne gasped.

"Third floor at the end of the hall." She gestured with the spleen.

Styne left quickly, entered an elevator and pressed 3. He came upon the office. An older man with a cheap, dyed-brown hairdo was seated at his desk looking over papers. "Mr. Styne?" he smiled mechanically as a stream of sweaty brown trailed down the side of his left temple.

"Dr. Karl."

"Mr. Styne, Mr. Styne, how nice to meet you." He gripped Rudy's hand much too hard and shook it endlessly. The whites of Dr. Karl's eyes bled deep sorrowful veins; his pupils were icy black. "Let me show you around and then I can answer some questions." As he talked, he mechanically wiped his head with a sleeve of the lab coat. "I should alert you that my research in parapsychology is really peripheral to my, so to say, 'real' work in the neurophysiology and genesis of schizophrenia." His voice sounded rhythmic and upbeat, but his carriage betrayed a lonely man.

"I remember your work with monkeys from college psychology," Rudy offered. He wanted to be more friendly than he felt. There was great psychic distance between them. "I remember a movie about monkeys raised on surrogate dummy mothers, some of terry-cloth and some of wire-mesh. I believe that the wire-mesh raised monkeys became schizophrenic because of the lack of warmth in their upbringing, whereas the terry-cloth raised monkeys were pretty much normal. Jeeze, I must have seen that film over 15 years ago."

"Well, the evidence seems to suggest this." Dr. Karl spoke as he took Rudy out the office and down a back staircase to a basement floor. "This is where most of the experimentation takes place."

"Is this them?"

"Yessiree." Dr. Karl beamed. And there in various compartments were wire mesh and also terry-cloth Mickey Mouse-looking dummy mothers with milk bottles protruding from their chest areas. "We still use these surrogates so we can produce the kind of monkey we need. We have found it very difficult to breed schizophrenic monkeys, but have had some success. Then we take the children and raise them on the wire and terry-cloth mothers, and so on. Those chimps over there," he pointed to a cordoned off area, "have never had contact with another living being. It's a perfect experiment! Come, I'll show you." Dr. Karl led the way to an isolation booth and peered through the one-way mirror. "In this cage we have a third generation wire mesh monkey raised by normal real surrogate parents." The monkey sat silently in a corner as the mother searched its fur for imaginary lice.

"He seems normal," Rudy said.

"Yes, he does. We'll be sacrificing him on Wednesday to take neurochemical readings. Over here," he pointed to another sector of the lab, "we raise monkeys in over-crowded conditions, and here," he pointed to a third set of cages, "these are raised for brain studies.

"The next room can be a bit shocking for lay people and the freshmen, but the older students get used to it." Inside were a small group of apes with rows of sprouting electrodes and antennae drilled into their craniums. Each animal resembled a pin cushion with eyes, ears, arms and legs attached. "By stimulating various areas of their cortex, we can make a neurophysiological map of schizophrenic and normal brains."

Rudy stared at the little creatures. "They seem so human," he said blankly.

Dr. Karl walked over to a panel with dials on it. "Remote control," he grinned as he turned one of the dials to the right.

A small monkey suddenly shuddered, snapped his head about, first in befuddlement, and then in anger. Karl turned the knob further. The monkey flew into a rage, jumping around and banging its face repeatedly against the cage. Karl pressed another dial and a second monkey leaped to attack a third. Again he pressed and the first monkey fell to the floor shaking violently; the cage was a frenzy. Rudy looked on in horror. Karl paused and then turned more dials. All three apes collapsed into unconsciousness. "Yes, Mr. Styne, they do look human. That is why we use them."

"You did your doctoral thesis with Dr. Penmeadow?"

"Why yes, at the time we were able to use depth electrodes on people to map different areas of the brain." Dr. Karl had clearly anticipated Rudy's next questions.

"Wasn't there a danger of causing damage?"

"Very slight. The electrodes were quite thin, about a micron in diameter. And most of the subjects had to undergo brain surgery anyway....One of our studies on the amygdala led directly to the use of partial amydgdalectomies in cases of severe aggression. We have saved many lives."

"Amydgdalectomy?"

"Partial removal of the amygdala, a part of the mid-brain associated with temperament and aggressive behavior." He nodded to the unconscious monkeys. "A person with an overactive amygdala can smash his fists or head into walls, bite himself or others, or fall into manic fits of rage. This operation has been highly successful, and we are considering using it with specialized prisoners. You know, the hard-core violent ones--mass murderers, death-row lifers....Don't want to take too much, however, it seems the amygdala plays a role in face recognition and memory as well, but that's getting too technical."

"How about frontal lobotomies?" Since Dr. Karl had brought up the subject, Rudy decided to continue it.

"You mean *pre*-frontal?" Dr. Karl wanted to be completely precise. "Oh yes, standard procedure...in cases of severe depression mostly."

"You're kidding?"

"No, quite serious. Dr. Monitz first performed a technique in the 40s which I perfected a number of years later, and the key is, it can be done right in the doctor's office. One simply holds back the eyelids, and plunges a special scraping device, much like the ones you see at the dentist's office, up through that avenue, directly into the prefrontal area. And the patient can go home shortly thereafter without being hospitalized."

"Do you go up through one eye-lid or both?"

"Generally one, but in severe cases, definitely both."

"And, how many of these operations have you performed?"

"Well, I don't know the exact figures. We did quite a lot of them early on. But, you know, when that whole counterculture/antiVietnam thing came in, well, the operation went out of favor. But with MRI's and new lasers, I've been able to perfect this procedure greatly, and I hope to reintroduce it to humans in the near future."

"Won't prefrontal lobotomies destroy the higher functions?"

"There just isn't much evidence to support that premise. Many of these patients who had been totally incapable of working in society were then able to function in 9 to 5 environments after the procedure. And, they were no longer suicidal. Come, let me show you my most delicate work. You've seen the great advances in the mechanical heart, and the use of pigs' valves in bypass surgery, well we in Wisconsin are working on brain transplants."

Strutting now, Dr. Karl led the way to another room. A lab assistant let him in. They nodded their hellos, and the professor introduced the reporter. Instinctively, Rudy reached out to shake hands, but the lab assistant was wearing gloves and begged off. They walked to the center of the room.

Lying on the floor in a sheer plastic bag was the face of a monkey floating in a warm pool of blood. Its dead eyes appeared to express puzzlement. Next to it, in another clear bag, lay a bloody headless torso. Karl dropped both satchels into a hamper; they landed with a thud. Then he motioned to the assistant, who pulled back a curtain to reveal a table and chair where a whole animal with white bandages wrapped tightly around its neck, head and shoulders was strapped. "I must admit, we are not at the stage where we can transplant a brain, but this monkey body, with another ape's head connected on top should live about two weeks. And if we add neurogenic proteins to enhance dendritic growth, maybe a couple of months. We're trying to use twin monkeys or close relatives, as in this case, a mother and son, and eventually have the one body accept the other head and visa versa. In this case, we got the mother body and the baby head. Right Bob?" he called out.

"No," the assistant corrected. "The old lady's body was pretty wretched, so we reversed and put her head on the kid's body."

"No matter," Dr. Karl said. "We need data on both situations. Male on female, female on male. It's all good, and in either case, a very delicate operation particularly when it comes to splicing the brainstem onto the host spinal cord. No end to the possibilities. "

"Can you imagine if this were used on humans?" Rudy led him on. He had entered what he perceived to be a house of madness and wanted to find out as much as he could.

"It is possible. Suppose a man is dying from a bad heart or a cancer-ridden body and another subject comes into the hospital with irreparable brain-damage, you know, like that Terry Schiavo case."

"Yes," Rudy remembered. She had been in a coma for years.

"Theoretically," the doctor went on, "you could take the head of the conscious man and place it on the healthy body, you know, like that coma victim, but in a much shorter time period. And...why that person, theoretically, may have one, two or even five years left of productive existence. Of course, we are not there yet, but we're getting there, and that's the important point.

"We're also experimenting with adding additional lobes, taking parts of brains from one subject and grafting them to a host."

"To?" Rudy prompted.

"Oh," the doctor continued, "to enhance certain processes. And we can do the same thing with computer machinery, adding chips, depth electrodes or lobe specific protein synthesis. Of course with these head transplants, if you include the spinal cord as a parallel circuit, by interconnecting one with the other, success should be enhanced. The person should be able to walk more quickly. There's no telling where the possibilities will lead."

"What about the moral considerations of some of your work?"

"Yes, Mr. Styne, there has been controversy. However, just my brain mapping work alone performed here at WU has helped literally tens of thousands of people who were in need of various forms of brain surgery. You remember Ted Kennedy with his brain tumor?"

"Yes, of course," Rudy did indeed remember.

"Well, he got easily an extra year of life because of our work, or work much like ours. That's real progress. And, of course, the monkey experiments in schizophrenia speak for themselves. No longer is the burden of schizophrenia placed on God's shoulders, that is, on a genetic trait. Our work supports rather dramatically that a sick environment will create a sick child. My work is in virtually every major textbook in abnormal and freshman psychology. Government grants exceed $3.4 million per year. Brain transplant work and computer interfacement must be performed. It is our destiny. One must suffer in the short-run for benefits in the long-run. My conscience is clear Mr. Styne, for my work has helped humanity. Let us have dinner and we can discuss my research in parapsychology."

They went to one of the university cafeterias, Dr. Karl still wearing his lab coat. He grabbed a tray and piled it with two meatloaf sandwiches, glad-wrapped apple pie, Jello and machine-made coffee. Rudy chose a salad. They walked over to a microwave oven.

"I became interested in telepathy due to a strange dream I had." Dr. Karl reached into an inside pocket and produced a vile which he emptied into his coffee. "Dewar's tonic," he quipped as he placed most of his dinner into the oven, pressed a few buttons, and then found them a table. "One night I dreamt that one of my students had liberated a young female monkey from the lab. The following morning I approached this student, not realizing the event had been a dream." Dr. Karl raised a hand to inform Rudy he would be right back, and shortly thereafter, returned with his steaming meal. "I thought she had actually performed the theft. It had been so real....But, as it turned out, the student hadn't stolen any monkeys, but she had seen a TV show the night before about a young girl who frees a gorilla from the Bronx Zoo! The show was a modern-day reverse characterization of King Kong. Well, I never watch TV, nor am I in contact with it, and I think I was able to rule out all possibility of subliminal perception. Sure, it could have been a coincidence, but I came to the conclusion that it may have been telepathy. Interestingly, the girl's name in the TV show was the same as that of the student.

"You know Sir John Eccles, the Nobel prize winning neurophysiologist, has talked about the synapse, the connection *between* the nerves, as being the possible sight for telepathic transmissions. But I had never thought too deeply about ESP until that very day.

"When I began a bit of research, I was amazed at the profusion of information on parapsychology right here in our own library. Some of the best modern work in the field is by a psychiatrist by the name of Lillian Monty. In the 70s and 80s she wrote a series of books on psychoanalysis, telepathy and the dreaming mind. Since that time, we have conducted numerous successful dream telepathy experiments here at the lab. The most simple and satisfying situation is when we use two subjects, a sender who is looking at a picture, and a receiver, who is sleeping. They are separated into different rooms and the brain-waves of each are monitored. When the receiver is in REM-beta or dream state, we wait until he is finished and then we wake him (or her) up. At that time he describes his dream. We've had tons of hits. I'm continually amazed at how common telepathy is once you start looking for it."

"Can you give our readers a good example?"

"Why yes. We had one girl dream of a huge clock ticking in an ocean and the target that night was a Timex advertisement depicting a wristwatch attached to the hull of a ship."

"What did the EEG tell you?"

"We have discovered a peculiar brain-wave pattern which appears in a number of different telepathic subjects. This is to say, we have linked telepathic dreams to specific brain-wave states."

Ready for dessert, Dr. Karl palmed the apple pie and chomped into it as if it were a sandwich. Sipping coffee with the other hand he continued. "We have also conducted a few ESP experiments with other primates, but nothing conclusive has yet occurred."

"Have you worked with Abdul Manu at all?"

"Yes, we have. Particularly in telepathy studies. Manu was able to correctly identify ten out of ten pictures while located in a Faraday cage, which, I'm sure you know, screens out all electromagnetic energy. The sender, who was randomly chosen, was a lady located in another building."

"Did you take his EEG's?"

"Yes, but his brain-waves did not conform to our other subjects. They were much slower. He seemed to be in a totally different state of consciousness."

"Did he levitate any objects?"

"A few things did seem to float up, but I was not convinced about the authenticity of what I had seen. Subsequent to these experiments I believe Manu has been caught in a number of instances of blatant trickery, so we decided to discount the whole levitation episode. His ESP studies are now also under reinvestigation."

"Seems to me that you are attempting to alter the past."

"What do you mean?"

"Well, you had positive results with this guy, and because of some controversy, you want to rearrange the information to conform to findings that are acceptable by others."

"Reinvestigation is standard procedure. We always go back..."

"And reinterpret the data?"

"I'm not sure what you are driving at, Mr. Styne."

"Bottom line, do you think Manu's a fake?"

"I think he is a superb psychic, but I remain unconvinced as to his supposed PK powers. Fake, however, may be too harsh a word. Magician is much more apropos."

Unable to contain himself, Rudy blurted out, "But I have been in his apartment and have seen him levitate...books, coins...my God, even a girl floated across the room. There was no trickery, Dr. Karl."

"You see, Mr. Styne, you were at *his* apartment. Have him do it in *your* apartment--with his shirt off. Do you see my point? He is controlling all the variables. Misdirection and various special contrivances are common ploys in this field--Blavatsky, Pallidino, Dunninger, Geller, Kreskin, etc. Take Pallidino, for instance; she was a great psychic from the turn-of-the-century, studied by Sir Arthur Conan Doyle for one. She was caught lifting a table with her foot during one session and substituting that same famous foot for a hand during another séance. Her real hand was thereby able to, quote, materialize a, quote, spirit hand. She was clever, but she got caught....And then there was the 19th century Russian spiritualist Madam Blavatsky. She started the Theosophical movement, you know. Blavatsky had secret panels in her sitting room in India. Hodgson reported it all in the *Journal of Psychical Research* 100 years ago. It's all there." Pinching the flesh between his two nostrils, fiddling with his ear, Dr. Karl rattled on. "You know, of course, Houdini became famous exposing numerous fraudulent mediums." Karl poured the last drops of coffee onto his extended tongue and continued, "Don't waste your time with this Manu fellow. He's a clever shyster. At best," he added as an afterthought, "he's merely involved with low level poltergeist activity."

Frustrated, Rudy bid adieu. The monkey experiments upset him, as did the lobotomy work, but Dr. Karl was the expert. Maybe he was right about Manu...but how could he be a fake? Since, in another breath, he also said Manu was a psychic. Dr. Karl may be brilliant, Rudy concluded, but he is also asleep. "Tinkering with the Great Mysteries, Dr. Karl gives lip service to objectivity, boldly dissecting primate brains while carefully avoiding their souls." Rudy shuddered as he scribbled these passages in his notebook, rolled himself into his hotel blanket and tried to get some sleep.

The next morning Styne showered early. It seemed as though he could not get the scent of formaldehyde out of his clothes or his hair. Crumpling the shirt and pants he had worn to Karl's laboratory, he dumped them into the incinerator chute and grabbed an early cab for the airport. Entering the building, and validating his ticket, he punched out more ideas on a laptop, as he sat in the waiting area for his flight to South Carolina and his scheduled meeting with B.K. Pine. "See Fandango, appease captain," he typed out as his flight was announced.

Styne boarded somehow reassured in his beliefs in ESP. Absentmindedly, he took his seat by the window and glanced over to the man at the aisle seat next to his. A jovial looking fellow, he had long strands of silver hair tied into a ponytail, orange suspenders and a substantial white beard. *Skeptics are a waste of time*, Rudy reasoned in his mind, trying to somehow talk himself out of a meeting with Fandango, as he continued to watch the curious gentleman.

"Is there something in my beard?" the man said jokingly.

"Sorry," Rudy responded and turned back to his notes.

"Wait, wait," the man interjected. "It's coming. My God, it's coming." He raised his voice loudly as a few other travelers turned toward him.

"What's going on?" One man called out, as the white-bearded gentleman reached deep into his beard and pulled out a live, flapping pigeon!

"I thought I felt something," he laughed, releasing the bird in flight. Rudy's eyes lit up. "Excuse me," the magician continued, as he fluttered a second bird down the aisle. It disappeared behind the steward's curtains near the kitchen. Causing a bit of a commotion, the man took off after it. Upon his return, various colored ping-pong balls appeared, as did candle flares, scarves for lady passengers and coins and toys for the children. A cornucopia of objects became manifest from chins, ears and armpits. Amidst spontaneous applause, the man sat back down and tipped his head in appreciation.

"Amazing," a boy shouted.

"No, incredible," the magician retorted.

"It's the Incredible Fandango," another boy said, running up to get an autograph. As two more children approached, a stewardess came by and gently returned them to their seats.

"Mr. Fandango, you will have to refrain from any other prestidigitation, at least until we are soundly airborne."

"Big word," Fandango said with a feigned sense of awe.

"Crossword puzzles. Sixteen-letters for magic."

"Hmmm."

"And, sir, you will have to cage your birds as well, I'm afraid."

"Don't be. They're harmless."

Rudy couldn't believe his senses. This was the very man he was just thinking about. "How odd," he exclaimed.

"Oh, that, it's an old gimmick of mine. Gives the pilot something to tell his wife when he gets home. Hah!"

"No," Rudy continued. "No. It wasn't that at all. You're not going to believe this, but I had been meaning to call you, and was thinking about you this very moment, and here you are, sitting next to me. My name is Rudolf Styne, reporter for *Modern Times*. I'm doing a report on parapsychology and my editor suggested I contact the Incredible Fandango this week to get the skeptical point of view."

"Small world," Fandango said. "Well, here I am."

"I think I've just had a psychic experience!"

"Hogwash, and you can quote me."

"Don't you think that it is the least bit peculiar that I was just thinking about a particular man I have never seen and did not know, and here he, er, you are, right next to me?"

"Not odd at all. Just a coincidence. We both travel a lot. It's bound to happen to some people every day. It happens to be us this day--happens all the time."

"You mean, you don't think there is anything to coincidence?"

"You mean Carl Jung's prehistoric theory on synchronicity?"

"Yes, that's exactly what I was thinking."

"I'll say it again. Hogwash. It's just plain old chance. Synchronicity is a short-term illusion in the long term of our lives."

"But the odds!"

"How many times have you traveled on a plane?"

"I don't know."

"Well, how many times per year?"

"Oh, fifteen, twenty," Rudy calculated.

"And how many times do you run into the very person you are looking for?"

"Never. Not like this."

"There, you see. Exactly my point. Random events, such as our meeting must occur occasionally if they are truly random." Fandango pulled the four of spades from behind Rudy's ear. "Randomness demands occasional coincidence. Now, if coincidences did not occur, then *that* would be something!"

"But, we could have even traveled on the same plane, and I would have never known. Look, I just typed your name into my laptop!" Rudy showed him.

"You misspelled *Incredible*," Fandango said, pointing out a typo.

"Thanks," Rudy said, correcting the transposition of two letters. But that's besides the point."

"Not to me," Fandango said. "That's my name."

They exchanged fake smiles as Rudy continued. "Look, the odds of us even sitting next to each other, even if we are booked on the same flight are 100 to 1."

"So you think the Almighty set up this meeting?" Fandango looked to the ceiling and turned his overhead reading lamp on. Lifting his hands, he said, "Praise the Lord." Dropping his eyes in prayer, Fandango continued, "Kiddo, I've seen much more amazing coincidences than this. It's just a statistical anomaly. From your point of view it's synchronicity. But from my point of view.... Why, I'm famous. I'll bet there are a dozen people in this plane right now who would think it was a fantastic coincidence to sit next to the Incredible Fandango." Opening his eyes and turning back to Rudy he continued, "Now your odds are less than 10 to 1. Soon you'll be telling me you believe in Abdullah Manu. You're not one of those people who suffer from Manu-itis, are you?"

"I'm afraid I am. I've been to his apartment and seen him levitate objects. His abilities to psychically bend metal are scientifically documented."

"Hey, let me show you something," Fandango interjected. "Do you have any keys on you?"

Rudy took out his set of keys and removed one.

"Watch closely." Fandango said. He took the key in his palm and began to rub it gently. "Bend, bend, bend," Fandango said. Rudy felt he could see the metal bend before his eyes. Sure enough when Fandango handed it back to him the key was bent at a 30° angle. "I'm going to draw an animal," Fandango said. "And I want you to concentrate and then guess what I drew. Now hide your eyes."

Rudy hid his eyes and saw before him a "Rhinoceros."

"Right!" Fandango exclaimed. "You're telepathic. That's exactly what I was thinking of!" He reached to his side and produced a crude hand drawing of a rhino.

"So you think Manu is simply a magician?" Rudy inquired, his mind now beginning to fill with skepticism.

"Think! Hah! His act is so primitive, it amazes me he has lasted as long as he has. That's his real trick. The man is worse than a fraud." Fandango's face seemed to twist into subdued rage as he continued, "He's a liar and a fraud. Appearing as a magician is one thing, but claiming you're psychic to a gullible public, and then performing crude magic tricks in half the parapsychology laboratories in the world...and getting away with it! Hah! Manu's incredible. We should call him the Unbelievable Abdullah. We could tour together and include a dance routine. Everyone wants to see the Great Miracle Man and so he gives them what they want....

"You know of course, he was caught cheating in telepathy tests at Oak Ridge. Read Greatle's book on it. It's all there--the layout of the laboratory. Greatle measured the size of the key hole between the rooms and determined that the angle of vision was sufficient for viewing. Can you imagine, he actually got away with it! He simply peeked through the door to see the ESP cards that were being 'transmitted.' Paul Frogg claims he saw Manu through a one-way window crouching by the door during the experiment. Shit, I can do every one of his tricks, and have proven myself to almost everyone who ever tested him. ESP is a figment of B.K. Pine's fertile imagination.

"I'm talking today to the Board of Directors who help fund Pine's parapsycho ward down there. Did you ever read Jenson's report on Pine's so-called air-tight card tests? His best subjects performed miserably when Jenson tested them, and of course, Pine's cards were transparent! Can you imagine the stupidity of people! Telepathy tests with see-through cards. Why, there's more evidence for Peter Pan than for ESP. And at least we know what color Pan's suit is."

"So you think that there is nothing whatever to parapsychology?"

"Absolutely. There hasn't been one test that has been repeated consistently. Hell, look seriously at the claims. Levitation, come on! Psychokinesis, hah! Precognition. Give me a break. Now, tell me, can you see the future? Why, ESP violates every natural law known to man. Show me a psychic who can read my mind and I'll buy that man a Rolls Royce."

The plane landed softly in South Carolina. Fandango was greeted at the airport by a statesmanly-looking gentleman and a chauffeured limousine.

"I'll see you, Mr. Styne," Fandango said as he rolled up his sleeves. Twisting his hand in the air he produced a small plastic rhinoceros and handed it to Rudy.

The reporter stood by the terminal and watched the magician drive off. Nagging doubts began dragging him down...down. "Fight it, fight it, fight it," Styne kept repeating.

THE MADAM RETURNS

Tight-lipped Uzbek soldiers marched Vladimir to a blank cement wall. One dressed in African war-paint, pointed a machine gun at his heart.

"*F I R E,*" the commandant shouted. Kopensky tried to duck, but it was futile, his obese torso impaled with a barrage of poisonous syringes. Awakening to the nightmare, Kopensky looked about the room. He was lying on a simple cot with an intravenous needle plugged into his vein. The pain in his shoulder, where Madam Grotchka had stabbed him, continued to throb. He plucked the stainless thorn from his arm and climbed out of bed. The hospital was asleep.

Shoving his nose out the door, Kopensky tip-toed into the corridor. Sweat-covered ripples of flesh stuck to the thin fabric of his gown as he cautiously crept along the shadows and into Grotchka's room. The fat man leaned over and shoved her shoulder a few times.

"It's me, Vladimir," he whispered.

"What do you want, you son-of-a-bitch."

"A bargain."

"Terms?"

"We forget this incident, and I let you go to Yakutski," he said with a sigh. "Remember, if you expose this fight, we will both suffer."

"Humans."

"What?"

"Do I get to work with humans?" She glared at him waiting impatiently.

"Madam, when you get there, you can do as you please."

Wiping her dripping nose along the pillow case, Madam Grotchka nodded agreement. They fabricated an absurd explanation about showing each other Samurai war moves, but Kopensky knew that his trips to Siberia would soon be over. He had lost the edge.

The following morning Kopensky took the offensive and called the Academy and spoke to Gorkii Slomov. "Professor Slomov, how has your work been going? I have written up my research on holographic brain theory, left/right hemispheric interference patterns and neuroelectric states. I would like to send you some reports and invite you to our laboratory."

"I would be glad to come, Dr. Kopensky. Your work sounds very exciting. Let's meet for lunch."

With politics out of the way, Vladimir felt on more solid footing. As soon as Madam Grotchka recovered, he would send her to Yakutksi and take over the St. Petersburg lab once again; but he was unhappy about her mixed alliances and treacherous nature. He sent a telegram to Siberia warning Patrenko of her arrival. She would be given two human subjects, but the lab's work in psychokinesis would remain secret.

The prison conviction of parapsychologist Boris Raudow was disturbing to Kopensky, especially since he and Patrenko were so close to a major breakthrough in PK. Another major point of concern was how Raudow's imprisonment would affect Imo, who saw the arrest as it happened while his high-jumping brother was at the Olympic tryouts in Tashkent. But Raudow had been foolish by seeking international publicity and by inviting parapsychologists from the West to come to his laboratory. Raudow had also served to revitalize interest in superstition and religion. He had become a propaganda liability to the Kremlin and the Academy of Pedagogical Sciences. On top of that, Raudow had the audacity to imply that he belonged to an organization which in truth only existed on letterhead. Handing a report on telepathy and brain-wave biofeedback to an American news reporter was the straw that had been his final undoing. Since the Academy was still not sure where Bonzovalivitch's true motives were aligned, in sending Raudow to a hard labor camp in Siberia, the Academy was warning the entire parapsychological community: stay away from publicity, avoid or minimize contact with the West. "The policy of glasnost does not extend to the field of parapsychology," the Academy said in no uncertain terms.

Kopensky reflected on Raudow during his plane ride to Yakutski. Clearly, the upstart had been too cozy with American and British scientists, but he liked Raudow, and the man was a creative researcher. Luckily, Patrenko had stressed total secrecy in their own PK work. They had no direct connection with Raudow, and they also had the backing of the all-powerful Dr. Georgi Bash. But if discrepancies in later editions of *Eurasian Parapsychology* made headlines, or if Madam Grotchka uncovered their work and decided to push her power, there was no telling what could happen. Just knowing that Bash has something on that butcher-slut enabled Kopensky to carry on a calm exterior when Dr. Slomov stopped over for lunch. Nevertheless, it still amazed Kopensky how Slomov and most of his colleagues in neurophysiology refused to acknowledge any of the validity to psionic research when the evidence was so overwhelming.

Going back to the time of the Russian Revolution, parapsychology had always had a mixed reception. In 1921, V.M. Bekhterev, co-worker of Pavlov and founder of the Institute for Brain Research in Moscow, began a study with a number of other prominent scientists researching hypnosis at a distance. Throughout the 1920s and 30s the All Russian Congress of Psychoneurology not only backed, but even supported this work. But when it was discovered by L.L. Vasiliev that telepathy could not be screened out by lead shields or other electromagnetic barriers, hysteria erupted amongst factions of the Eurasian psychological community. If telepathy turned out to be a non-material form of communication, the whole spiritualistic platform with all of its mystico-religious ramifications might take hold. Proof of this nature would oppose the Eurasian position of materialism and atheism. Thus, most of the scientists backed away.

Kopensky remembered that *Pravda* had never printed a serious story about psionic research, except for the infamous rehash of the 1950s American experiment in telepathy aboard the submarine Nautilus. And *New Commonwealth*, the newspaper that replaced *Pravda*, simply followed suit. Fearing the Americans would get credit for studies in telepathy already validated by Eurasian scientists, Kopensky used this ruse to siphon more funding. With Patrenko, they made the case that national security might be in jeopardy, and further, that if the West had a scientific breakthrough, the new Commonwealth would be at a disadvantage. Thus, parapsychology was allowed to flourish once again in Uzbekistan, Russia and Siberia, although in guarded fashion.

When the Americans came to Russia in the mid-1960s, and Kopensky was a graduate student writing a history paper on Pavlov and Vasiliev, he remembered how the Americans were welcomed. But by the late 60s with the Vietnam War and the new advances in mind control, psychokinesis, hypnosis and information retrieval, Russian security clamped down. Just as Kopensky was getting started in the field during his post-graduate studies, parapsychology was once again driven underground. Raudow had been one of the last open-door holdouts.

Kopensky reflected on the endless battles between the believers and non-believers. Fortunately for the field, the influence of a few powerful individuals, such as former KGB agent Georgi Bash, allowed significant portions of the military budget to be appropriated for covert psionic research. Thus, Yakutski was built not only for strategic placement of military hardware, but also to continue this important, albeit controversial, area of scientific investigation.

In the beginning, over a decade ago, Madam Grotchka had been drawn in with doctors Bash, Patrenko and Kopensky because of her unmatched knowledge of neurophysiology and because of her audacity in human experimentation. However, her abrasive nature and refusal to acknowledge the findings in PK and telepathy, proved fatal for her stay in Yakutski. Nevertheless, Madam Grotchka's work on mapping neurological states and EEG patterns enhanced Patrenko and Kopensky's research on PK and brain-wave states. Also, the Madam's conservative nature served as a smoke screen, proving invaluable for keeping channels open with skeptical factions of the Academy.

Kopensky needed Imo because of his association with the renown Dr. Floria. He was a researcher who could integrate the neurophysiological data along with quantum theory and the parapsychological work. As Patrenko's library was situated in Yakutski, Imo had to be taken there. In time, Kopensky hoped, Imo would get used to the esoteric aspects of the research, and hopefully, if he played his cards right, he could even get Imo into the forbidden rooms. He knew that Imo's brother was a friend of Raudow, and this was a problem. It was Patrenko's idea to keep Imo at Yakutski for as long as possible and slowly acclimate him to the difficult work. The arrival of Madam Grotchka might speed this along, but even Patrenko feared this could also backfire.

"Dr. Bern," Dr. Patrenko said, "fortunately or unfortunately, the answers to many of our problems lie buried in these books." He pulled out a stack which included the *Old* and *New Testaments, Tibetan Book of the Dead,* early works in Theosophy, Anthroposophy, the Cabala, Tarot and also astrology. He smoothed non-existent hair back along his left temporal lobe with a brush of his hand, and presented the texts to Imo.

"Why unfortunately?" Imo asked.

"You know we have adversity from the Academy of Pedogical Sciences, comrade, and even from the new leaders from the Kremlin. Some of our colleagues have been sent to hard labor for allowing their minds to stray from Commonwealth principles."

Imo could tell that Patrenko was talking specifically about Boris Raudow, but he was also aware that to mention his name at this time was verboten. He allowed Patrenko to continue without interrupting.

"It is a warning for all of us. Do not get philosophically involved in writings such as these." Dr. Patrenko patted the *Old Testament.* "We can only apply them to science. As I'm sure you realize, most of these occult ideas are based on outmoded religious beliefs. But, every once and awhile you may get lucky and find hidden herein certain natural canons...laws of mind, if you will. And, it is in those rubrics, tidbits here and there, where insights for our work may be gleaned. Be careful, Dr. Bern. These writings can trap and shake you from your patriotic convictions....I don't want you reading this contagious lore without a break. Madam Grotchka will be arriving within the week. I want you to assist her, and it would be good to learn how to stay with this literature and not end up *persona non-grata."*

"Yes, sir."

As much as Imo despised Madam Grotchka, he did not want to be alienated from the Academy. And as far as he knew, he had never had a direct run-in with her, having kept his feelings to himself. But even though warned, after just a few weeks with Patrenko's incredible collection, the metaphysical message had taken hold. In one obscure book he read:

> Man's arrival upon the earth was not a random process. Just as it takes planning to build a house, it took preparation to create life. Although science assumes an orderly universe, it ignores the fact that order presupposes conscious design. Supernatural mentation is responsible for human creation, for man did not invent himself....
>
> Psychic phenomena is but one proof that the human species is only a shadow of its potentiality. But what man usually fails to realize is that lack of knowledge of his own occult powers is not a chance occurrence. The Fall of Man was not a mythological fable. Higher worlds can only be safely attained through knowledge of one's soul...
>
> Mysticism involves rediscovery of ancient foundations of authority. Divine revelation and supersensible understanding are

inherent in this journey. Psychic powers are only the natural accompaniment ....

Evil results in lack of perception of the whole. Incomplete knowledge of higher worlds and use of the psychic for dishonest goals will always result in self-destruction; for man reaps only what he sows.... In God's mansion there are many rooms.

Aside from the conscious discovery of his own soul, or his rediscovery, Imo also uncovered certain ancient statutes:

In Laws of the Mind, like attracts like.
Mind transcends both space and time.
The Will is the liaison from mental realm to the physical.
Divine Law operates regardless of human realization.
At deeper levels of mind all beings are One.

"Dr. Patrenko, I think I have discovered the mechanism for telepathy!" Imo came running down the hall, slamming his face and shoulder into Madam Grotchka's breasts and upper torso. "Madam, I'm sorry. How good to see you again."

"You fumbling idiot! Dr. Patrenko says you will be working with me full time. Humph!"

"But Alexi, I am on to something. The Universal Mind--it is the most obvious and logical choice for the mechanism of telepathy." Dr. Patrenko lifted a threatening eyebrow. Imo clamped his mouth shut.

"Occult horseshit, Bern," Madam Grotchka cajoled. "At least I will be able to continue my work with Tajiks!"

It was as if Imo had been hit in the stomach with a sledge hammer. His eyes were glazed and he just stood and stared at Patrenko with mouth open. "Alex," he barely said.

Dr. Patrenko turned to him. "It is about time you got back into the experimental work. We are at war, comrade. If we don't prove what we know in experimental ways, the Academy will take away our funding. Who do you think was the first and only country to utilize the Atomic bomb?.... Dr. Bern?"

Imo was still trying to digest Madam Grotchka's comment. She stood there gloating, her buxom chest expanding to its full extent. "Bern," she said, continuing Dr. Patrenko's line of reasoning, "the United States threatens our very identity-- every day. They have infiltrated Korea, South East Asia, the African and South American continents, Turkey, China, Afghanistan and of course most of Europe, and now they are setting up Coca Cola plants and MacDonald's hamburger places in most of our satellite countries, and even in downtown Moscow! They are fast-food pigs, and they must be put back in their place." Madam Grotchka didn't care much for politics, nor did she really care about what she was saying, but she did want Imo to be obedient. Also, she was well aware of Patrenko and Bash's paranoia concerning Bonzovalivitch's dreams of Empire and America's competing interest in parapsychology.

"Imo," Dr. Patrenko went on, "America's work in parapsychology dates back to the 1930s. In terms of their interest in national defense, their telepathy work in the 1950s on the Nautilus submarine is well-known, as is their current research in remote viewing of our military installations. PK ability of superpsychics is also directed towards infiltration and disruption of our vital interests, and now they are using even more sophisticated forms of mind control. Grow up, Dr. Bern. Your work is important, but realize that the security of our Federation is at stake."

Madam Grotchka turned to Patrenko. She looked perplexed, because she really was ignorant about parapsychology, and except for reading a few successful telepathy and PK tests, she knew very little about findings from the West, or even from her own country. "Alexi, you will have to show me your research," she said.

"In time, Madam. First you must prove you are capable of appreciating the work. Vladimir tells me that you have great resistance to parapsychology. Working with Imo here and your old friend," he winked at Grotchka, "I find it hard to believe."

"How will you explain astral projection to the High Command, comrade? If your work causes a rebirth of religious dogma, Russia will digress back a hundred years. You know the Academy's posture on this." Coyly she turned to Imo. "Son," she said sycophantically, "do you believe in life after death?"

"I don't know," Imo said.

"Alexi," she turned suddenly, "do you?"

A door-lock clicked. Silence overpowered the conversation as Georgi Bash entered the hallway. Imo felt his chemistry change, as he also discerned a distinct magnetic pull towards Bash's presence. He fought hard to maintain a semblance of self-consciousness. The tall dark man's square-boned brow cast a glare in Madam Grotchka's direction. Fear struck. She pivoted and scurried out of sight. Alexi became automaton-like as Bash spoke, "I don't like that whore here. Her work is tedious and redundant." He put his hand on Alexi's shoulder and smiled through his long down-turned moustache. Dr. Patrenko seemed to come back to life.

"That is not totally true," Alexi said cautiously. "Her EEG mapping of the mid-brain and cerebellum is unprecedented. If she gives us one tenth of that kind of research on mapping more subtle occipital, parietal, temporal, frontal and prefrontal lobes...one tenth, then we should have a hold on the repeatability that we desire."

Imo had rarely spoken to Dr. Bash, having avoided his hypnosis demonstrations after that first time in the theater, but he had great respect for Bash's power, and knew that he would not throw words around carelessly. "Why did you call Madam Grotchka a whore?"

The sorcerer began to laugh. Deep booming hearty-ha-has erupted from his solar-plexus as his moustache bobbed up and down. He stared at Imo and placed a ponderous hand on the intern's shoulder. The youngster's body went limp, but also he was aware that he felt this. From his research he had come across the Russian writer P.D. Ouspensky and his text *Fragments of an Unknown Teaching,* a work about the mysterious Turk, Gurdjieff. Man is mechanical, he had read. In order to awaken, man must remember himself.

The hand remained; Imo began to dissociate his thoughts from his body's physical reaction. Dr. Patrenko interrupted the moment in quick rapid bursts of muttered speech. He was shocked that Imo could resist the mesmerist, but proud of himself for correcting Bash. "Dr. Bern will be working with Madam Grotchka," Dr. Patrenko said. "He is spending too many hours in the library and not enough time in the lab."

"Alexi tells me that you have discovered the mechanism for telepathy?" Dr. Bash said. He was now staring at Imo, a bit curious as to how this Bern fellow was able to maintain consciousness under the magnetic power of his stare and touch.

"Why, I only just told Dr. Patrenko!"

"I know... his thoughts," Bash smiled.

"It's no big secret. It just suddenly made sense to me," Imo went on. "It's the Universal Mind. Each human has his own conscious and personal unconscious, but every person also shares or taps into a collective unconscious. What you know, everyone on the planet knows at deeper levels of their own psyches, because at deeper levels we are all interconnected."

"Exactly, Dr. Bern, exactly." Bash turned to Alexi. "Keep him in the library. He can work with Grotchka on Tuesdays and Thursdays." He turned back placing both hot palms firmly on Imo's shoulders and gazed deep into his pupils. "Good work, young man. You learn quickly."

"Is Madam Grotchka a whore?" Imo spoke quietly, timing the question accurately. Dr. Bash boomed more laughter, turned, and walked down the hall, his heavy footsteps vibrating throughout the floor and walls. Imo turned to Alexi. "If I'm to work with her, I believe I should know."

"Only when Dr. Bash is around." Dr. Patrenko smiled for the first time. "Come, I'll show you. You were quite something to oppose Dr. Bash that way." Alexi's voice sounded desperate. "Imo, can you teach me? I know he has such power...." Even as Dr. Patrenko spoke, he seemed to slip in and out of trance.

"You must feel the power of your own will," Imo said. "But, Dr. Patrenko, exercise of the will through conscious means is realization," Imo leaned forward and whispered, "of the soul."

"I know, Imo, I know. Come." Dr. Patrenko put his arm around Imo's shoulder and led the way. An important barrier had broken down between them. They walked into the movie projection room and Dr. Patrenko closed and locked the door behind them. Using a separate set of keys, he went to a distant file cabinet and pulled out a film canister entitled "Experiments in Primitive Behavior." Dr. Patrenko began to talk as he loaded the film into the projector, "Bash knew the day he met her, that Madam Grotchka had an unusual propensity towards

nymphomania. He hypnotized her immediately and brought her into his apartment-
-kept her there for weeks, yet neither he nor Madam would talk of it. We would
occasionally see her at dinner, but her normal mind never seemed to be localized in
her body. Then one day he took her to his lecture room and called down twenty
Tajiks. Let me show you...for it's on the film."

The movie was photographed from different cameras positioned from the
ceiling. It was poorly edited and the quality was grainy. Imo could see the group of
soldiers standing up on the stage. Madam Grotchka, deep in trance, disrobed.
Standing naked she began fondling her gruff dimpled skin, as she dropped to the
floor writhing. Twenty youths were called up and then two more sets of twenty.
Madam tackled them all. As Patrenko sped the film up, hysterical tears cascaded
down the cheeks of the viewers. The next segment was an interview with Grotchka
while she was still unclean. Tortuous to watch, she described in detail her erotic
and sadistic fantasies and the lack of fulfillment which she felt in her life and
research. Dr. Bash left the stage and returned with a male Bonobo. He told
Grotchka the excited male was an ice cream cone. She took him at his word. The
wizard snapped his fingers, and she came out of trance in the midst of it all, her
face quickly contorting in horror. Her mind had snapped.

Imo sat stunned for many moments. Sweating profusely, he could feel his
underwear sticking to his body. Bash's power was awesome; the realization of this
fact only became more unfathomable, never less. As vile as her sybaricity
appeared, its fascination caused disquieting reverberations. Rasputin's legacy had
tapped deep archaic centers.

"Does she know?" Imo asked.

"No. He de-programmed her to forget with post-hypnotic suggestions."

"Does she suspect?"

"Yes." Dr. Patrenko still had tear tracks down his face, yet fear had re-entered
his brow. "Bash had her go through this ritual with upwards of eighty subjects and
several primates on four occasions! Imo, I hate to say this, and soon you will
understand, but she deserved it. I transferred her out. She's a butcher -- her god-
forsaken experiments. Kopensky called her to Moscow and kept her with the
monkeys and gorillas. The idiot actually thought he was in love with her! Can you
imagine?"

"But I never knew," Imo said.... "I mean, that there was anything between
them."

"Bash showed him the film. Kopensky has never fully recovered. Something
in him died that afternoon." Dr. Patrenko held his head down in self-realization of
his own shame. "Bash broke his spirit, my friend. Hold on to it, Dr. Bern."

"Who really is Dr. Bash?"

"Georgi Boshtov, for that is his real name -- descended from a long line of
holy men." Patrenko led Imo back to his library as he talked. "His grandfather
Talon Boshtov, was a prelate and half-brother to Grigory Rasputin, healer of the
feeble Tzarovitch, Prince Alexis, son of Tzar Nicholas."

"The hemophiliac?" Imo recalled.

"Exactly. Talon had traced the bloodline of the young prince's mother, the Tzarina Alexandra, back to her grandmother, Queen Victoria of England, and her husband and first cousin, Prince Albert of Saxony. Rasputin had sent Talon to Victoria's castle to steal an artifact of Albert's so that a resonator horoscope of the Tzarovitch's planets could be cast. It was through this tuning device that the Tzar's son was healed.

"Bash was to have been the godson of Rasputin, but he was poisoned and assassinated decades before the boy was delivered. And so, Georgi Boshtov grew up with the Revolution. Born with second sight, he was known to speak in the voice of his deceased great uncle. Occasionally, he would discuss experiences he could not have known about in any rational way. The family feared possession and took young Georgi to an exorcist. He was only three at the time. But the priest said that he could not help in such cases because this was not a case of possession, but one of reincarnation!"

"But you don't really believe in reincarnation?"

"Look." Dr. Patrenko pulled out three volumes on reincarnation. "Many cases of alleged rebirth occur in this fashion. See Dr. Beaverton's research with Aleutian tribes and Weaver's study of the Micronesians."

"If Dr. Bash was linked so deeply to the occult and to an enemy of the Revolution, how could he get into such a high position in our government?"

"Dr. Bash was born with the charisma of the Staretz. He was an excellent hypnotist even as a youth, and was used in debriefing German scientists during the nuclear arms race in the 60s. He taught brainwashing techniques to Ho Chi Minh during the Vietnam War. All this is listed in his access files. His work in America, however, remains top secret.

"Only recently was he able to reveal to me his plan for world domination. Kopensky and I have been part of that plan for seven years, and now he has Bonzovalivitch in the palm of his hand. I am telling you this, Imo, for one reason." Patrenko held Imo's hand with both of his. "I am under his spell. I need an ally to prevent him from...." He tried to motion to the film. "From losing control. His magic is awesome, perhaps bordering on the diabolical...but his goals are for the good of the Federation. Dr. Bash is a patriot and a seer. I was not quoting propaganda about American involvement in ESP for warfare. With the loss of our country's unification we are even more vulnerable." Dr. Patrenko handed over a photograph of Abdullah Manu being tested in a laboratory with electrodes pasted to his head. "This is the kind of work we are up against."

Imo could not sleep that night. He kept envisioning Madam Grotchka destroying her dignity so readily; and yet, he, himself, was not immune from thoughts of decadence. He tried to understand why sometimes his dreams included immoral encounters. Having had only scant reading in Freudian doctrine, Dr. Bern's concept of the id was only partly recognized. But what would occult literature tell him about this darker side? Early that morning he had dreamt of the Earth as a globe pierced by a towering phallus which traversed a straight path from New York to Moscow. The next day he read more of the mystical literature.

From such turn-of-the-century books as *History and Power of Mind* by Richard Ingalese, and works by Rudolf Steiner, he compiled his thoughts: In the human we have to differentiate between the world that is visible and the one concealed. For during life, a continual battle must be waged against the material substances of man's animal drives, and the supersensible nature which lies hidden deep within. Just as the physical body decays with death, so too it may decay the non-material body in life if it is allowed the controlling position.

The lower realms of the astral plane harbor the "obscene and licentious thoughts" of both sexes and they also harbor the "elementals," or "dwellers of the threshold" that prevent the average human from penetrating too deeply into the mental realm. These elementals are seen as evil and immoral beings in dreams and they are known to possess and embody themselves in the weak of will in the living. Drunks, prostitutes, the promiscuous and misers are temples for their existence; but also "elementals become embodied in the creeping crawling bugs and vermin that infest untidy houses, second and third rate hotels and public buildings. These are the biting and stinging thoughts manifesting on the physical plane as wasps, roaches and mosquitoes, and the poisonous thoughts which become spiders and reptiles. These miserable creatures born of the human lower mind cannot use the atoms of a higher rate of vibration for their bodies, but must use atoms which they vibrate harmoniously with." It is we who create the destructive things of the Earth.

In the Gurdjieffian literature he came across the following passage on evolution and devolution:

> Humans are born incomplete and must attain higher frequency astral body during the course of living on Earth. This vehicle, later used in the process of transmigration, is activated with exercise of the Will and through Intentional Suffering. Very few reach this level. Same with acorn. Out of hundreds that fall from tree, only handful become tall oaks. The rest are fertilizer for growing sapling.... My teachings are not fertilizer.

The library phone rang. It was Madam Grotchka. "Dr. Bern, you will come to level II immediately. I want you to conduct occult blood tests on the fecal matter of six of our orangutans."

"I'm sorry, Madam, I am to work with you only on Tuesdays and Thursdays."

"Dr. Bern, come at once!"

"These are Dr. Bash's orders. But if you want, I shall tell him that you take me away from the library and my work so that I can conduct routine procedures which your orderlies should be doing. I will be meeting with Dr. Bash in two hours." He liked repeating the name. "You may come up then and discuss it with him. And Madam, do not call me here again." He hung up the phone.

Bash was in his apartment listening to classical music as he painted colorful abstractions upon a freshly primed canvas. "Come Imo, we must go to Vladivostok. I will show you how to use hypnosis as an anesthetic." Bash led the way into his bathroom and pulled Imo into the shower. Revolving around like a turnstile, it emptied into a narrow staircase. Imo did his best to try and stifle his fear as Bash began to laugh. "It's faster this way," he said.

They walked up four flights to the ground floor airplane hangar. Imo had not been to Vladivostok Hospital in over three weeks. He realized the need to make another appearance.

SEA HOUSE

In long heavy strides the master led the way to a small jet plane. It sat next to one of the Sukhoi-67s. Imo looked excitedly at the swept forward wing design, the leading edge flaps and small vertical wings on the tail.

"Not today," Bash said, referring to the 67. "Here, slip this on." He gave Imo a parachute as he put one on himself. "You have great strength, young man. You are wise to resist, but never oppose me." The smile vanished as he burned holes with his eyes through to Imo's core.

Bash climbed into the control seat as Imo took over the co-pilot's. "Today is your first lesson," he said.

"What about the 67?"

"In time, my little man. You want to start on the steak before you have even had a hamburger?"

The sleek machine seemed to glisten in response as they taxied from the hangar and turned out onto the tundra runway. With a mighty thrust, the plane ascended. The old Brezhnev-era trained pilot began to show Imo the various dials and meters and allowed the youngster to take over the controls. After slicing through myriad cloud formations, Bash took back the craft and began to weave it in and around the fluffy drifts.

Without warning, he cut the engine.

They sank like a stone in free fall.

As the ground approached, the Master reignited the engines one at a time. The plane continued on its path but began to roll in a corkscrew pattern which Bash ended in the flipped position. And then he took the plane to supersonic speeds. For timeless moments they traversed mountainous terrain with the horizon upside down.

Bash looked over and grinned. "Here, you take control." He let go of the steering wheel in such a way as to cause the ship to wobble.

"No, don't! Don't!" Imo blubbered, fright overwhelming him. The pilot righted the plane and asked his passenger if he was all right. Although obviously amused, Bash seemed genuinely concerned since the lad looked so green. Imo barfed upon the dials and floor as he looked up in between heaves in silent apologies.

They rode for the next three hours in complete silence, the young doctor tying to clean up the mess as best he could. Finally, the airport was in sight. Bash circled once, and then landed smoothly taxiing to a private gate.

As the stepped out onto the tarmac, Bash turned to the youngster, "You will be unable to attend today, so we will go to the hospital tomorrow."

"But I am to work with Madam Grotchka tomorrow. I'm sorry." He nodded to the cockpit, implying that within twenty-four hours, he would have to fly back.

"To hell with that witch." Bash had fire in his eyes. "She can wait another day." As he spoke, he began to rub his huge hands on Imo's back in attempts to soothe the plane-sick traveler. Bash made long passes along Imo's spine and softly told him to sleep. Imo tried to resist, but the warmth of Bash's great hands was too soothing, and in time, the intern collapsed into oblivion. Easily, Bash lifted the youngster into his arms and carried him to a waiting car.

Later that evening, Imo awoke in the Master's Vladivostok hide-away. Bewildered and disoriented, he looked at his watch. There was nearly five hours he could not account for. He jumped to his feet as the terror that had swept over Dr. Patrenko began to rush through him. His face began to flush, his breath shortened. He remembered something Gurdjieff had written about self-remembering. Thus, total panic was held at bay.

The inside of Bash's house was decorated in gothic style, with 18th century guns, cross-bows and heads of wild animals mounted boldly on the walls. A large picture window opened to the Sea of Japan.

Staring out at a number of fishing vessels which dotted the water, Imo watched the tall silhouette of a solitary figure stalk the beach. He followed the image until it slowly disappeared from view.

Imo felt drawn to an adjacent room, Bash's study. On the right was a poorly-lit wall of books with texts on Voodoo, hypnotism, remote viewing, quantum physics, consciousness, witchcraft, spells, black magic, possession and reincarnation. He approached the desk and began quickly opening and closing various drawers. He knew he was crazy to risk his life in such a way, yet he felt compelled.

Scattered without order in the middle compartment, were modern pictures of places and women, turn-of-the-century, auburn-tinted family portraits, newspaper clippings of Rasputin and the royal family, and portraits of Lenin and Stalin, FDR, Churchill and Hitler. The interloper moved too quickly. He was so nervous that he pulled one of the drawers off its track. *Crash!* He scooped up the photos and tried to jam the drawer back in place. It could not be closed all the way. Becoming somewhat frantic, Imo blindly reached into the opening and ripped out a manila envelope that had been taped underneath to the inside of the framework. The packet remained unscarred as it peeled off easily from the over-used adhesive. With sweat pouring from every pore, Bern slowly opened it.

On top of the pile were news clippings from English and American papers, and a list of names of Western parapsychologists. One, two, or three stars were placed next to each scientist's name. He scanned an article which featured a British researcher, Gregory Hereward, who had died of a heart attack while at a dinner in his honor. Imo recognized his name from his work in PK at a distance and from his popular book *Eurasian Parapsychology*. Another was an obituary about a physicist, a Professor Ketchembach, who was hit by a taxi cab and killed in downtown New York City. This accident had occurred only weeks earlier. Imo racked his brains in his attempts to try and place the name. Underneath was a pamphlet which read:

TOP SECRET
WARP DETENTE NIMROD CONTINGENCY
Dr. Georgi Boshtov Solely Responsible
History of Parapsychology for Military Uses
ESPionage, offensive and defensive weaponry.

A slow, stomping noise caught Imo's attention. His ears perked to the steps of his host returning. He tried not to panic, placed the papers carefully back in the envelope, reached in and taped it to the appropriate drawer bottom. *Click.* Bash placed his hand on the door knob and turned to look once more at the misty waters. Bern squeezed the drawer shut and high-tailed it for the bathroom, turned the shower on, threw his clothes to the floor and jumped in. The icy waters froze his innards as he tried to adjust the hot water handle. Bash entered the bathroom and spoke through the translucent shower curtain. "How are you feeling? I thought you would never awaken." Since his voice was subdued, Imo feared that somehow Bash would hear his knees clattering, they were shaking so badly.

"I'm fine," he managed. "What happened to me?" Imo really was not sure. His knees continued to vibrate as he rubbed his body vigorously with a slim bar of soap.

"I put you to sleep. You'll have to get used to my flying if you want to come with me again." Bash laughed quietly. "It was tactics such as those that kept me alive during the East-West Berlin fracas in the late 60s. I was one of the first Soviet pilots to violate Berlin's air space in those days. Knocked out a train station and bridge near Lubeck on that first run. Of course, NATO never reported any of our successes. But we had many. They simply got to the higher ups at the newspapers, and got them to 'hide behind the cloak of the tinderbox.' And they complain that we don't have a free press. Hah!....Are you hungry? I'll go make dinner."

Imo turned the shower to hot. Steam filled the room and warmed his rattled soul. Still somewhat shaken, he prayed to himself. *"Don't lose it, Imo,"* he repeated over and over quietly, remaining beneath the curative waters as long as possible without attracting undue attention. The scent of sizzling onions drifted through the slatted bathroom door.

After putting on the outfit that had been laid out for him, a lavender tunic and matching pull-on pants suit, Imo took a deep breath, and walked cautiously into the living room. Bash was seated cross-legged on a thick fur rug. He wore a black and maroon-colored V-necked velveteen shirt open to a hairy breastplate, shiny white pants and white buckskin shoes.

Imo felt that he was seeing this strange man's face for the first time, having never really looked beyond the wing-like eyebrows before. The nose was broad and bony, as was his Neanderthal forehead and rectangular jaw. Bash had a stern mouth and fattened upper lip. His large bushy Foo Manchu moustache seemed never to hang quite right. Hair erupted in auburn tufts from his nostrils and ear holes, his monstrous forearms and brawny neck betraying the deeply rooted animal essence of his being. The wizard sat beneath the head of a horned rhinoceros as he puffed away at a long hookah. An unusual odor drifted around the room. "Opium," he said matter-of-factly. "Try some."

The novice approached hesitatingly, and grasped a second tentacle of the snakelike water-pipe. He stared dumbly at the glowing bowl and then inhaled deeply. The room began to swirl and pulsate slowly as Imo became aware of the weight of his brain for the first time in his life.

Bash stood up as in slow motion to go back to the kitchen. He seemed over eight feet tall, as all his movements became mythologically exaggerated.

Imo tipped himself slowly backwards. As his head sank into the soft rug he became aware of the capillaries in his lungs, the flow of blood through his veins and arteries, and the shifting of his consciousness, as brain fluids changed their relationship with his tilting. Closing his eyes, he had visions of his cranium as an Earth-like planet with a map of the continents engraved on each lobe. He could feel the light from every star and planet permeating his mind. Knew the answers to all questions and laughed at how obvious everything was. Every thought profound. Even the lint on the rug contained the solution to the mystery of the cosmos.

Bash returned with a tray of steamed lichens and multi-colored mushrooms. Popping one into his mouth, Imo had visions of every fruited fungus that had ever grown and every one that had ever been eaten.

Within the tall gawky mystery that stood before him, Imo felt a moment of...yes, he felt tenderness. Bash stared back stoically. Pushing the tray aside, he staggered out of the house and headed to the sea. Imo stood and chased after. Out the front door, down a slate-path, Imo found himself at an embankment. The sand was sticky and coarse. Great latent power was detected as the quiet sea rhythmically lapped the shore.

The tall man stopped by a dock to watch the surf.

Imo felt at one with the ocean and the stars; the metronomic waters seemed soft and compassionate. He did not know what to do.

Bash approached. Grabbing Imo with two large tendrils, the tall Ukrainian pulled him closer, as he leaned over and rested his head on the young man's shoulder. Perhaps through instinct, or fear, or a combination of both, Imo reached out, and gently stroked the wizard's thick wooly hair. It felt so peculiar. The assassin shook loose, stood back, and peered at the young doctor. "I have killed many times, little man. And there is great weight on my shoulders. Sometimes I feel the world will collapse upon my brain." They stood there in silence watching the boats bob upon the primordial waters. "Come, let us eat."

Georgi the chef served baked fish and stir-fried vegetables. The meal was a feast containing subtleties of herbs and other strange flavors. "Is there fruit in here?" Imo realized that he had never really tasted food before this moment. He had merely eaten food, never appreciating its actual pleasures.

"Fresh plum and peach preserves," said the cook. "But, enough of food. Come see my prize collection." Bash pulled a staircase down from the ceiling and led the way to a loft filled with dust and strange icons, weapons and ancient artifacts. "Here are shrunken heads from a cannibal tribe on the Amazon, and these are from Kenya. Note the difference in the color and textures of the skins.

Imo saw one head, obviously that of a Negro man, and the other head had long red hair and was light-skinned.

"Brazilian natives use hot sand, cure their heads in herbs, and hang them in the sun, while the Africans keep them in pickled fluids." He placed the two tiny human heads into Imo's hands.

"What do these letters mean?" Imo said, referring to the Western letters ACW. He stared at the small faces.

"Each tribe in Brazil carries a different acronym," Bash said. "That head came from an English researcher who claimed that the cannibal tribe involved may have cured it as recently as sixty-five years ago.

Imo stared at the large cleft in the chin. "But it looks Caucasian?"

"May very well be. The Brazilians were notorious for killing and eating Western travelers, particularly missionaries who came there with naïve plans of converting the tribes. Frankly, if it is Caucasian, I believed he probably deserved what he got."

Bash placed the two shrunken heads on two small mantles, and then he took out a number of other artifacts including Bronze statues from Tibet, a turquoise colored porcelain mummy from Egypt which he said was 2,000 years old, contraband ivory carvings from China, Voodoo dolls from Haiti, shaman masks, peace pipes and sacred bones from the Congo, South America and New Guinea. He also displayed stuffed lizards, squirrels, frogs and turtles, human and other fetuses in formaldehyde, darts, blow-guns, arrows and cross-bows.

Staring down at Imo, the old master donned a taut zebra-skinned mask, grabbed a spear, whirled and hurled it forcefully into the far wall, nailing a hanging elephant skin that stood along its path. Picking up some rattles, two in each hand, Bash began to chant to a primitive rhythm that rocked the hermitage as his heavy feet stomped on the wooden floor.

Although Imo was frightened, he was also entranced, able to witness the power of the mystic's beat amplified by the drug, the sea, and the magnetism of the moment. Transcending his present-day reality, he began to glimpse worlds undreamed.

Bash took off the mask and placed it carefully on Imo's lap. "You are now the Initiate," Bash declared. "Your first lesson: survival of the fittest. Never forget that."

Ripping loose a board from the rafters, Bash grabbed a hammer and nails and pinned the board across the door entrance.

Striking poses remindful of the art of Kung Fu, the Master pointed his hands with knuckles bent, and performed a sacred dance. *"Hee Yaaa!"* he yelled, as he threw an outstretched fist at the board and smashed it. The jolt rattled the house, and knocked the red-haired shrunken head off its mantle. Bash looked at Imo with an expression of triumph, as he waited.

Imo reached down, picked up the little head and placed it back on the shelf. It seemed to stare back at him with an odd expression.

"Come," Bash said, and then led Imo back down the stairs into the living room, and over to a dimly lit bookcase.

Choosing an old Romanian text on possession, Bash handed another on Voodoo to Imo. "PK at a distance," he winked. The night turned thick. The sky boomed. Lightning spit. As the storm approached, Imo felt electrified. *Crack!* A miniature thunder-bolt leapt from an outlet plug to a lamp on the very desk Imo had rifled through. A lightbulb exploded, *Pop!* The two men stared at each other; neither said a word. The storm moved west.

The following morning the two doctors exited the sea shanty and walked along the protected beach to a lot where Bash's car was parked. After heading back towards the city, Imo found himself surprised by the modernization of the surrounding area.

"Vladivostok is a crossroads for the whole of the Pacific Rim," Bash said.

"I am surprised to see so many Chinese," Imo responded.

"They probably outnumber the Russians here. Some, I imagine you know, use the port as a means to funnel their relatives out of China to Europe and the Americas."

"I knew we were close to the Chinese border, but I didn't know that," Imo said.

Although an international city, like many former Soviet urban centers, it seemed that the prevailing color of the buildings was a ubiquitous drab gray, but in this case offset by the percolating and colorful harbor. Bash turned up from the sea, took a right turn off the main turnpike and pulled into the hospital parking lot.

"Dr. Bern," Bash said, "This is Nurse Jabinsk. She will be your guide for the day. Nurse Jabinsk, Dr. Imo Bern."

Imo looked at the young lady and read her name badge. Irina was her first name. She had long brown hair tucked under a nurse's cap, shapely legs, caring eyes and a solid, yet tender, handshake.

"And you are from?"

"Tashkent," Imo said.

"Uzbekistan?"

"Yes."

"The only person I know from Uzbekistan is that high jumper, Heinreich something or other."

"Bern." Imo's face lit up.

"Yes, that's it. Heinreich Bern."

"He's my brother."

"That's so amazing. But he's so..."

"Tall?"

"Yes," she blushed. "I work mainly with geriatric patients," she said, changing the subject.

Imo could taste the sterilized walls as they marched down the main hall. "Come, let me show you some things." Nurse Jabinsk gave Imo a general tour of the entire hospital and then led the way to a cancer ward where Bash was working with several patients.

"I met Dr. Bash because of his work with hypnotherapy," she said, her eyes expressing great interest in this subject. Out of earshot, she continued in a whisper, "He has a 14% remission rate in cancer patients right here in our hospital."

Imo spent the next three hours with the nurse in mental healing sessions with Dr. Bash.

"He uses guided imagery, behavior modification, therapeutic touch and bioplasmic healing," she said.

Bash meditated with them, and with each patient in the ward. He also gave the patients magnetized water to drink.

"By use of the power of visualization and auto-suggestions for health, I have achieved spontaneous remission rates in third-stage cancer patients exceeding 14%," Bash said.

Imo looked over at Nurse Jabinsk. She mouthed the words, "I told you so," as both broke out into a smile.

"The national average is only 3%, Bash went on. "Many cancers are psychosomatically induced or triggered. I have the patients realize that their minds do indeed control their bodies, and I accompany this ritual with a short intensive course on the immune system. We discuss the production of the T and B cells, the role that bone marrow plays for white cell production, and how the thymus gland modifies the anti-bodies. We then have exercises in visualization rituals, whereby the patients picture their cancers in the process of disintegration by the anti-bodies. We have documented many cures."

"How often do you work here?" Imo inquired.

"As you know, I can only come about once a month. I do have subordinates, however." He smiled at the nurse.

"You have great healing powers, Dr. Bash," she said.

"So did Rasputin."

"It was nice to meet you," Nurse Jabinsk turned to Imo and shook his hand.

"Irina," he finally said.

She exchanged a warm smile with Imo and then departed.

While at lunch, Imo sat and listened to the Master's psychophysiological theories on hypnosis. In the afternoon, Bash put a woman under hypnotic anesthesia, while a hysterectomy was performed by a surgeon and his crew. No drugs were used, and the patient claimed no pain. The following morning Imo and Bash flew back to Yakutski.

As expected, Madam Grotchka had left a note on Imo's door to "come immediately" to her laboratory. Imo lowered his head and marched down. When he entered her space he almost vomited. Lying unconscious on an operating table were two Tajiks whom he had casually known from the cafeteria. One had a fourth of his skull removed, his brain glaringly bared. "Extirpate the occipital plate on Number 2," she said as she handed him a small buzz saw. "And hurry, I want these computer chips implanted simultaneously."

"God damn you...you butcher slut," he blurted as he spat out a wad of green bile. Slamming the door, and smashing the window, he raced down the corridor blindly searching for Dr. Patrenko. Running from room to room, he became frantic and burst madly through the FORBIDDEN door, running past rows of dismantled missiles and closed and locked supply closets. He began opening doors that would open, getting more and more frustrated.

Finally he barged into one more doorway only to discover Alexi sitting by a computer monitor which resembled the cockpit of an airplane, there were so many dials. He was there with a strange lab assistant, monitoring a subject whose entire forehead had been removed and replaced by plastic and wires. A lightbulb was lit where his right eye should have been. The subject appeared alert and in a state of deep concentration. Imo noticed large black tufts of eyebrow above the remaining eye and dark tufts sprouting from the chest area. The man was Caucasian.

In milliseconds, he flashed to his brother Heinreich, that day in Tashkent on the track, that parapsychologist who was arrested right there, in front of him. But that man, Imo couldn't think of his name, had gone to a labor camp.

"My God!" the young intern gasped. The subject turned.

"Imo," Boris Raudow managed to say.

"Boris!" Imo exclaimed. The name just popped into his mind. He turned to face Patrenko. "How could you?" he said horrified.

Alexi Patrenko just looked up silently, his hands frozen on the dials.

Imo slammed the door shut and began to run back towards the main hallway. Crashing out the FORBIDDEN door, he disappeared into the catacombs.

Dr. Patrenko rushed to a phone to call Bash. "Imo has seen the human subjects. He's seen Raudow, and now he's gone berserk. Stop him."

Bash grabbed the intercom to summon his elite crew. His directives boomed throughout the complex. "Capture Dr. Bern alive! Do not harm him."

The small platoon poured into the halls and scattered. Patrenko studied the overhead monitors, forwarding a continuous stream of information via an ear-piece Bash always carried with him. The sorcerer took the elevator to the plane hangar as Imo smashed through two guards and raced up the stairs. Bursting through a barred exit door, he lit out into the open air, fleeing as fast as he could away from the barn and out onto the desolate tundra.

B. K. PINE

It was a humid day in South Carolina, the kind that causes you to sweat, but does not allow the perspiration to leave the inside of your clothes. Even Rudy's suitcase felt clammy; nevertheless, he felt exhilarated to be far away from Wisconsin, far away from headless monkeys, and dog and rat shit, and he was looking forward to meeting the world famous Father of Parapsychology.

A jet-black cabbie picked Rudy up at the airport. His skin reflected rainbows in oils, his gaze radiated depth, but his eyes were bloodshot from a life of drink. "Where to, son?" he said as he threw Rudy's case into the truck.

"I'm going to Dr. Pine's laboratory." Rudy sat on a worn leather seat, crackled and torn from decades of daily service.

"Sure...ole Pine's a good cat," the cabbie spoke as he turned onto the highway. "Why, he despooked my sister Pearl's house. My great-granddaddy used to walk de halls at night moving pi'tures, cups and all kinds of things. De old slave juzz wouldn't stay in heaven. Lordie, every night was a racket until Mssr. Pine hears of it. He brings a spirit lady who talks to my great-granddaddy and tells him he's dead!"

The old yellow cab rolled through pungent swampland and endless patches of leafy greenery. "Tabakee," he said as they continued past hamlets, and then crawled by a ramshackle house seeded with flower pots, colored clothes lines and five little children who frolicked with some kittens and a large mangy dog. The cabbie slowed to wave and grin at his brood, and the children excitedly waved back. He picked up speed again and continued his story. "And granddaddy says, I knows I'm dead, but I fears leav'n dis place. And da spirit lady scolds granddaddy and says 'it's time to trust God and come to heaven,' and he starts crying. Pearl's crying and I got streamers too, but it worked. We haven't heard him since. Yeah, dat Dr. Pine's A numba one in my Bible. In fact, he wrote a letter ah recommendation for my daughter when the young'n entered Atlanta University."

Dr. Pine's laboratory was buried behind a long network of red brick factory buildings that covered three city blocks. In towering letters at the main entrance Rudy read: LUCKY STRIKE. "Jeez," he exclaimed, "This place smells like a giant carton of cigarettes."

"Yuk, yuk, yuk," the old man guffawed. "Yeah," he said between chuckles, "I believe it do."

Dr. Pine's laboratory surprised Rudy. It was just an old shingled building with a sign on the doorway:

INSTITUTE FOR PSIONIC STUDIES
Founded: 1937

The vehicle was greeted by a young college girl dressed in cut-off jeans and a white tea shirt. Her nipples jiggled through the thin cloth as she shook Rudy's hand. "B.K. is napping right now," she confided. "You may see him at two. Let me show you around." Rudy was taken to see the library, offices and lab rooms. In all, the building had no more than nine rooms. "This place was a small country store before Dr. Pine moved in," the girl said. "Built a hundred years before the cigarette factory."

"What do you do?"

"Research."

"On..."

"Oh," her eyes gleamed. "I'm trying to teach mice to become telepathic." She looked to the ground and nuzzled her toe into the rug as she spoke. Rudy smiled.

"What could you possibly do with a telepathic mouse?" he wondered aloud....

"Breed it, of course."

"I guess you could charge one helluva stud fee."

Rudy sat in the library and waited for two. He read turn-of-the-century books on materialization and spirit photography. Finally, he was called into Pine's chambers. The old man was still in bed stretching. "Come on in, youngster." An elderly lady teetered into the room carrying a tray with orange juice on it. "My wife, Rowena."

"Hi," Rudy said.

Pine was well into his 90s. Every line on his face showed depth and humor, but also there was a deep sense of seriousness tucked beneath his furrowed brow. The elderly professor finished his juice, sipping from the small glass slowly. Then he leaped gingerly out of bed, creaking, but still with a little bounce to his step, winked at his guest and made his way into the other room to get dressed. "Only a minute," he said. Mrs. Pine sat down.

"So you're interested in psionic research?"

"Yes. I've had a number of psychic experiences and have seen some incredible instances of telekinesis recently with Swami Baba and Abdullah Manu," Rudy said.

"Oh, how interesting."

"Did someone mention Abdul Manu?" Pine had reentered. "We had him here at the lab. Fantastic, just fantastic. I've seen some perplexing phenomena in my day, but he tops them all. He jerked around the place so rapidly I thought I was going to have a nervous breakdown. But he was serious about his work. No denying that. Perplexing, very perplexing."

"So you think his powers are real?" Styne inquired.

"Well, let's say I lean in that direction. Of course I'd like to test him again. Somewhere I read some controversy about him. I think the magician that Incredible Fandango was able to replicate some of his feats. That's the problem with psychics and psionics. There is a real lack of consistency and repeatability. Manu is as unreliable as you can get. The second time he stopped by absolutely nothing paranormal occurred."

"What do you attribute the inconsistency to?"

Rowena answered. "ESP is such a subtle force. Why, B.K. has friends who have been interested in his work for a half a century, and during that time they have never once had a psychic experience. Never! Can you imagine? And two or three of these non-ESP types, as I like to call them, are some of the most well-known names in the field."

"Dr. Pine," Rudy asked, "What percentage of the parapsychological community believes in Manu's abilities?"

"Mr. Styne, perhaps this is an important question to you; but in terms of the development of the field, or Manu's contribution, it makes practically no difference whether 50, 80, or only 7 percent believe in Manu. I say this because before Manu was born we were able to establish the scientific validity of telepathy, precognition and telekinesis. Nothing has changed since."

"What about Jensen's report on your card reading experiments? He claims that the cards were transparent and that the controls were not tight."

"Jensen's book created quite a stir, it's true," Pine said. "But what he didn't tell you was that the only way he could see through the cards was with a flood light." Pine reached down into a desk drawer and produced two sets of ESP cards. "These are the old ones, and these the new." Pine held them up to a light bulb. Rudy could not see through either one. "Now look at this." Pine produced a flood lamp and shined it through the old cards.

Rudy could see an outline within the card. "Circle." Rudy guessed.

"Close," Dr. Pine said. "It's a square." He turned the card around to display it.

"My main complaint with Jensen is that he never attempted these experiments himself. Never in any real sense, that is. For the last thirty-five years he has been criticizing me, but only once would he allow us to perform a telepathy test on him."

"What happened?"

"In a run of 25 cards he got everyone wrong. We had quite a laugh, didn't we, Rowena! It was a delightful occurrence of negative ESP. He was so embarrassed that he hasn't forgotten me since. It's a shame though. Deep down he knows, but his defense structure just cannot allow any mystery that smacks of metaphysics. It's a real shame.

"The mind, Mr. Styne, transcends time. It transcends space and it is not limited to the material dimension. More important than the existence of any one great psychic is the understanding of the laws involved. No scientist, as far as I know, has really figured out how these laws operate. There are some good guesses, but they remain only guesses. Come, let me show you something."

Dr. Pine took Rudy's arm and led him down to a back stairway. The old man's bones creaked with each step he took as he led the way out to a green field. They walked over to an anthill and sat beside it. Two of the six-legged insects were cooperating in carrying a dead moth over the grass. Other ants were busy building an entrance to their home below. Rudy watched one after another appear from the hole and place a single grain of earth outside the entrance.

"These ants have a consciousness," Dr. Pine said. "We are all expressions of the Universal Mind. We are all emanations from the One. The universe is like a giant mandala with God at its center." Pine drew a circle in the dirt with spokes leading from the mid-point out to the edges. "At the periphery we are individual humans, or animals, or ants." He pointed to each spoke of the hub. "Science is seeking to uncover the laws that verify this oneness of existence."

"For a scientist you sound very religious."

"It depends on what you mean by religion," Dr. Pine said. "I have lived many years and watched the great mystery. I was born not too long after the invention of the airplane. Now we send rocket ships to Saturn and Neptune. Telepathy, precognition, even psychokinesis are all factual abilities easily substantiated. But to the unenlightened these abilities are like airplanes before 1904. Religion to me is no more than the acceptance of an order that supersedes human existence. Telepathy is kids' stuff compared to the mystery and complexity of this little society below us." He pointed to the ant colony. "Manu is child's play when you compare the levitation of a human to the mystery of birth.

"Mr. Styne, I worry about America and its continual battle with Eurasia. Humans have still not conquered this physical plane of existence, but they seek to uncover the non-material realm. It is tricky business and there are dangers ahead-- not only in terms of traversing unchartered territory, but also in terms of releasing great powers, energies that dwarf the atom bomb. There is vast evil in our scientific community. I perceived great deception when Rowena and I visited Russia and some other countries from the old Soviet Union twenty-eight years ago. Why, do you know, we were not allowed to step foot into a single laboratory! Not a one. And my colleagues tell me that they have had similar experiences."

As Pine spoke, Rudy felt as though his mind was being read, for the old man discussed exactly the questions he had considered asking.

"The irony is that their very aims will bring about their own destruction. Of course the United States suffers from the same malady. The government spends more money building a single nuclear warhead than on the total funding for investigations into man's supersenses. Am I carrying on too much, youngster?"

"No, go right ahead, sir. How do you know that evil will bring upon its own end? There are so many bad people living very high on the hog."

"There are two reasons, Mr. Styne. Number one, life after death, and number two, the Law of Karma. Newton told us that every action has an opposite and equal reaction. This is also true in the world of affairs. Take President Nixon, for example. He lived a treacherous life, bending the Constitution to suit his own needs, building enemy lists, infiltrating psychiatrists' and opponents' headquarters, and here, a man at the top of the world, at the very height of power, visiting Red China, transmitting live to the men who were walking on the moon...ends the war in Vietnam...Even he falls. Action and reaction. Sometimes, however, Karma does not fulfill its mission until after death. So this is the irony to the study of parapsychology. With the uncovering of the new laws that rule the finer dimensions of matter comes the certainty, even the proof, that we do not die.

"Come," Pine said, placing a gentle arm on Rudy's shoulder. "We shall do some experiments with my psychic mice."

Styne flew back to New York with the feeling that he had been blessed. He had a great story and, due to his exhilaration, he was able to piece it all together in one night. He recounted some of the history of the field, surveyed on-going laboratory work in the United States and throughout Eurasia, alluded to the potential military uses and repercussions, described his interviews with Pine, Ketchembach, Karl and Fandango and described in measured tone his meetings with Swami Baba and Abdul Manu. Concerning the latter two occasions he stressed more the spiritual and mysterious aspects and played down the fantastical. Styne felt it was a much wiser decision to follow the occult credo of "silence" due to the overbearing skepticism in the country and also to his need to appear objective. If Styne lost credibility, his career as a reporter could suffer irreparable damage. He concluded thusly:

> The science of parapsychology has discovered and validated many unusual human abilities including telepathy, psychokinesis and out-of-body experiences. But are these "alleged" phenomena more miraculous than the fact that we exist? Knowledge about parapsychology can be sought in laboratories, with gurus on mountains and through introspection. However the real mystery lies not in these abilities themselves, but in the force that created them. In the human species, consciousness is but a shadow.

Captain Whitmore was pleased with the report and scheduled it as a main article in the next issue of *Modern Times.* In a moment of irrationality, Whitmore indicated that any reference to the *San Francisco Chronicle* story be crossed out, but aside from that, the piece ran as Styne wrote it. He felt elated. He could not change the past anyway, and Moth's article had died on the starting block. No one had picked it up. Rudy couldn't carry the weight of the world on his shoulders. He rushed over to tell Chessie the good news. When he got to her apartment and knocked, she took too long to answer. He turned to leave just as the door clicked. Chessie was dressed in a robe and the look of her troubled face told Rudy she was not alone.

"Why haven't you called me?" she asked. Her face was worried and saddened, her eyes lost and she was not going to let him in. His mouth dropped.

Rudy turned and walked back to the stairway. All his happiness seemed like a sour taste in his mouth. He felt as if his very life had all but been drained from him.

He popped down a subway and surfaced near the garage by his apartment that housed his car. He needed to depart for anywhere out of the city.

The attendant took forever. No. He wouldn't take a credit card. "Jesus fucking Christ," Rudy screamed. "I don't have any fucking money. You've seen me every fucking day for three fucking years."

"I'm sorry, sir. The sign says no credit cards."

Rudy stormed out. He needed cash.

"Wait," the man ran after him. "Look. I can defer the fee till next month. I just can't take your credit card."

The man looked sincere. A real person. "I'm sorry I got so angry," Rudy said. And then he waited over twenty minutes for the man to retrieve his car.

Where the fuck could he have possibly gone? Rudy thought as he watched the elevator retrieve yet another vehicle that was not his. *What had he done to deserve this?* He thought about his so-called girlfriend. It hadn't even been a goddamn week. There, finally, his little Gazelle. For an instant, as he stepped inside and sat behind the wheel, his face lit up. He felt free.

Squeezing around a double-parked truck, Rudy derived some satisfaction that his little car could fit. But, once on the avenue, traffic was murderous. He honked and jammed the accelerator and brake in alternating rhythms, as trucks and cars spit black exhaust around the windshield. Finally, he inched to the FDR Drive. Then it began to pour. Droplets of water pelted the roof, with traffic at a standstill. Rudy was trapped--next exit ten blocks away. Ineffectual wiper blades smeared the view. All he could see were the blurry yellow images of the taxies that surrounded him. It took forty-five minutes to travel those few measly streets. A stalled vehicle blocked one lane and a tow truck had to be called to remove it. It's flashing colored lights, whipped round and around, as it reflected yellow and red rainbows off every droplet on his windshield, the extreme brightness of the light piercing his already taxed brain.

Although he had finally reached the exit, Rudy was still in the heart of the city. "Fuck it," he said to himself. "I'll go home." He turned up 59th only to be caught in another snarl. The line of cars extended as far as his eye could see. It was gridlock. *How could anyone live like this?* he thought to himself. Gripping the steering wheel hard in his hands he began to rock and scream through the closed windows as tears flowed down his cheeks. "Get me out of here. I hate this city, this goddamn car...it's all a farce. Get me out of here."

CYBERNETIC SKULLCAPS

Bash darted out onto the tundra and spotted a lone figure vanishing into darkness. Waving off the henchmen, the lanky wizard set out after his young protégé alone, pacing himself in a steady rhythm, timing his stride to a digital wristwatch which beeped every fifth second. He was in no rush.

Imo could not stop. He ran until his lungs burned and the muscles in his back and thighs began to ache. Angry, resentful tears drove him through his second and third winds past the fourth and fifth over thick, moss-covered terrain. He had been betrayed. Although his feet became tons of lead and the pain in his side split him in two, on and on he pushed. He knew Bash was on his trail, but he didn't care. "That bastard. He'll have to follow me to the goddamn Arctic Ocean," he spat.

Bash, on the other hand, had been on many chases and was mentally prepared for such a jog. He kept a deliberate gait and monitored his energy level carefully. He watched a lone fox dip into shadow as Imo finally dropped in complete exhaustion. He tried to crawl, to persist in his futile journey away from the underground complex, but his arms gave out. His heart thumped against his rib cage, yet he attempted to continue. But all he could do was collapse, heaving, awful tears of conscience streaming down his face.

A few minutes later Georgi arrived. He stood over the lad, one hand on his hip, as he paused to catch his wind. If Imo remained a threat, he would have to be eliminated. He sat down and cradled Imo's head and rubbed his spine with huge-boned hands. They sat silently. Well into the evening a glow-green meteor streaked overhead. As new constellations emerged, they made the long trek back to the subterranean complex. "No one likes this business, Dr. Bern. But we are at war. You do realize this?"

"No."

"Do you not know that the Americans have spent hundreds of billions of dollars on their war machine?"

"War is obsolete," Imo said. "Finally, our borders are open to the West."

"Imo, the Americans are subversives. Look at their history. Every year they spend more than the year before on military equipment, as they continue to dismantle our nuclear stockpile while they set up outposts in Crimea and the Middle East and take their arsenal into space.

"They supply arms to the Israelis, Egyptians and Turks and now have a bases in Afghanistan and Iraq. They have fought us politically and through espionage in continuous fashion for over fifty years. They interfere with our internal affairs, threaten us economically with half the countries that used to belong to the old Soviet Union. They have spy satellites. Do you see that light traveling silently across the sky?" Bash pointed. "That's an American surveillance device. As incredible as it may seem, that tiny dot could be monitoring our conversation at this very moment! They drop antennae that look like rocks. Why do you think we have a pasture growing above Yukutski Science City? They might have already uncovered our laboratory's location. Their own military has admitted that they test biological warfare on their own citizens, right on their own city streets and in the subways! And Imo," Bash stopped walking and firmly grasped Dr. Bern hard on the shoulders, "they are using psychic energy for defense purposes. Don't think the Cold War is over. They are not only close to uncovering our hard-fought advances, they have already attempted remote viewing of our most top secret installations. They use psychics for deployment of radar jamming and interference of our telecommunications and computer systems. On the surface, it is detente. But underneath we are at war, not just overtly military, but clandestinely psionic. Do not forget that. A few must be sacrificed for a greater good -- the good of hundreds of millions... for the good of Bonzo's Empire. Dr. Bern, talk to me."

"Dr. Bash, I know what you are saying, but I do not see it your way, and I cannot, and will not, accept human experimentation. And, even if I could, Tajiks are one thing. But Boris Raudow! How could you? How could anybody?"

"He volunteered, Imo."

"Don't." Imo said. "It's hard enough to accept the potential necessity of all this, but don't insult my intelligence by lying to me."

"You can ask him yourself."

Imo stopped and looked into Bash's eyes. "Was he out of his mind?"

"He'd been arrested. The secret police. They had him in one of their psychiatric reprogramming facilities in the Gulag. Isolated. Sub-zero weather, no heat. You know I have nothing to do with them. Shock treatments, neuroleptic drugs. Mental torture. He got into a fight with a lunatic. That's when he lost his eye. I saw him at the hospital in Vladivostok, shortly thereafter. Got him off the drugs. He knew all about Yakutski. That's when he volunteered.

"I don't believe you."

"He wanted to become psychokinetic. Maybe it was a way to get back at those who had arrested him, or just get back into the game anyway he could. I told him it would involve surgery. He agreed.

"Well, you can imagine. Not like one of those peasants. Raudow was one of us. He could tell us exactly what was going on in his brain as he worked through the biofeedback machines. It was a marvelous opportunity, and we took it. He took it."

Imo was staggered by all of this. "What about the killing of Western parapsychologists?"

"What about it?"

"The Law of Karma, Dr. Bash. Action and reaction. You don't think you will pay for this?"

"Oh, so, you read a few occult books, and now you are an expert? What do you really know about the Karma of nations, of epochs? These override mere individuals. Don't you think I know what I am doing? You will understand one day. Go speak to Raudow yourself. I encourage you."

"Believe me, I will."

"Good. And after that, you will work with Madam Grotchka. Starting next Tuesday."

Imo was trapped. He had reached the point of no return. "Can I go home for the weekend, to Uzbekistan?"

"Your oath, Bern." Bash grabbed him by the scruff of his collar and stared deeply into his eyes. Imo shuddered with the truth.

"Of course, damn it. Damn you," Bern said.

"Say it."

"I won't say a word."

Imo flew home without the knowledge that a listening device had been placed in his watch. Bash and Patrenko would record the entire stay. He was welcomed by a proud father at the airport. "Son, you look drawn. Is everything all right?" His old weathered hands grabbed the luggage.

"Of course, papa. How is mother?" He found comfort in his father's simple honesty during the ride home.

"Fine. Heinreich is home as well, you know. This will be a rare treat." Mr. Bern's forehead was clear of wrinkles, his eyes sparkled.

During Mother Bern's home-cooked meal, the family laughed and shared each other's company. Heinreich told stories of his escapades in New York and Steamboat Springs, Colorado, as his two children cavorted with "Uncle MooMoo."

"The people are not afraid in America, Imo. They party; they tell the government when they are unhappy; they write what they want; they travel wherever they want, when they want." Heinreich's face glowed as he reflected on his happy times.

"So why don't you just live there?" his brother blurted out.

Heinreich physically retreated at the force of this uncharacteristic display of anger.

"Hey, what's wrong with this house?" Mrs. Bern said tactfully.

"The West is at war with us, Heinreich," Imo continued as he looked down at his plate and mashed his leftover vegetables until they were pulverized.

Heinreich spoke softly. "That's nonsense; I have many friends there."

"Just look at Serbia, Afghanistan, Iraq! What percentage of their national budget goes toward armaments?"

"I don't know, a third?" Heinreich's voice dropped.

The evening ended bitterly.

Imo retreated to his upstairs room. Even his familiar bed could not calm the distressed initiate. Intense nightmares tore into his sleep. Giant wolves with dagger-like teeth ripped his flesh apart. He screamed in searing pain as Heinreich rushed in to rescue his frightened brother.

"Shush, Imo, shush. Let me show you something." Heinreich coaxed his brother out of bed and into his own room. He opened a black portfolio and displayed pictures of his various track meets. Imo perked up when he saw a picture of Heinreich at a Mayan pyramid in the Yucatan peninsular, but as his mood lightened, palpable lumps of anxiety formed in his chest. The dam broke and he began to wail uncontrollably. Imo sobbed so deeply that Heinreich began to cry with him. "What's wrong, my brother? What's wrong?" Heinreich whispered.

"Nothing, Heinreich, nothing." Blackness began to overtake his heart.

"Imo, tell me."

"Nothing, I can't. Nothing, nothing. Heinreich," Imo managed, "we are at war. I can't tell you anymore." He felt the veil close, yet gripped his brother tightly until dawn.

All things considered, Saturday and Sunday passed in relative calm. Sunday night, however, Heinreich spoke: "If you ever want to reach me, you know how." An address book was opened, a finger to the lips sealed the episode.

On Monday, Dr. Bern flew back to Siberia. Boris Raudow was in the clinic recovering from a biofeedback exercise that had left him with a partial stroke. The doctors expected full recovery. Imo sat at his bedside.

Raudow corroborated Bash's statements. He had lost an eye in a food fight with a lunatic in the asylum where he was stationed. And when he saw Bash in the hospital in Vladivostok, the doctor offered his services. He would do anything to get out of the situation he was in.

"Did you know that the top of your skull would be replaced with plastic and wires?"

"Well, I had an idea. I had seen one of the cyborgs in the hospital. And look at this." Raudow pointed to a bulge on the side of his stomach. It was the rest of his skull being kept alive while the experiments continued. "They can always put it back!" The duo exchanged smiles. "Imo, you just cannot imagine how horrible that first camp I ended up in, was. For six months, I shared a room ten feet by six feet with seven other men."

"You're joking," Imo said incredulously.

"No. And that was considered luxurious as compared to some of the other wards. We were not allowed to move or talk for all that time. We sat along two benches and communicated with hand signals."

"Where was it?"

"It was in a shit hole near Novyy, just south of the Gulf of Ob."

Imo stared at the glass eye that was embedded where Raudow's real eye should have been. It seemed to track, and with a toque over the cerebral paraphernalia, Raudow did not even look so bad.

"How did you survive?"

"The whole camp was set up to break you down so that you would do anything to get into a better cell. The goal was not so much to kill you, but to make you a servant of the state. They let us eat in a central dining hall once a week, and some crazy man just attacked me out of nowhere."

"You didn't know him?"

"No. That's the way it always was, only this time, it was me. The guards really encouraged the fights. They bet on them. And if a man got hurt bad enough, he got to go to a hospital."

"Are you happier now?"

"Who are we kidding, Imo? My life ended with my arrest. Maybe I can be reborn." He patted his stomach. "That's all I'm hoping for. And to contribute."

Imo lowered his voice. "To helping murder our Western competitors?"

"What are you talking about?"

Imo told him.

Resolutely, Imo returned to his station and began his work with Madam Grotchka and the human subjects. Raudow disappeared. Imo decided, at least for now, to leave it alone.

To maintain some semblance of sanity, he changed his reading habits, concentrating only on quantum physics and experimental papers. He now feared occult literature and curtailed his study of it, as he began to harden to the situation. As with Bash, however, he found himself over-extending his efforts in helping the sick at the hospital in Vladivostok. At those times, he found himself thinking about Nurse Jabinsk, Irina, making sure his off time matched hers so he could sit with her at lunch. For the restless nights a glass of vodka and a sleeping pill usually did the trick. By preventing himself from seeing the Tajik youths as individuals, Dr. Bern was able to proceed. His face grew taut, his heart became cold. The research continued. Madam Grotchka had already killed three subjects, butchering one of them quite badly. Imo snuffed another; but their mapping of EEG differentials deep within the interior of the human cortex and their continual virgin discoveries in the localization of brain functions, and corresponding states of consciousness, proceeded smoothly.

Imo tried to look for the positive qualities in Madam Grotchka. Certainly this was no easy task, but the excitement of charting previously unknown neurological territory and the fact that he too had killed, aided each of them in communicating. He withdrew from personal understanding of himself, existing only on "work" mode, as he began to identify more and more with the equipment and less and less with the other people at the underground complex. He learned to write up the experiments as if the subjects had consented for electrode probing during standard brain surgery, and Dr.'s Patrenko and Kopensky began to release some of the "safe" research for international exposure--all under Imo's name. Bern did have some bad moments when he occasionally caught the soulful looks of the subjects, or when he noticed a calendar, but he proceeded so well with his work, that Dr. Patrenko called Dr. Kopensky back to Yakutski so that together they could show their young protégé the psychokinetic experiments.

Dr. Kopensky swaggered in one Tuesday afternoon. As usual, he smelled of yesterday's perspiration. Together with Dr. Patrenko, they escorted Dr. Bern and Madam Grotchka through the FORBIDDEN door. Passing down a corridor lined with laser-gun toting military personnel, Imo noticed at least six Tajik cyborgs walking leisurely down the halls. Conversing in Russian, they were well-fed and in good humor. The top third of their skulls had been removed and replaced by black plastic caps with plugs and wires neatly arranged in circular rows. One of them, obviously the leader, was packing a shoulder holster and pistol. Dressed in a pin-striped suit, he appeared rested and tan.

Carrying a leather attaché case, Dr. Patrenko made every effort to stay one step ahead of Dr. Kopensky. As he led the way, he said, "These Tajiks are useless without this baby." He patted the suitcase. "We keep them happy by feeding them fresh chicken, providing them exercise and simulated coital stimulation by triggering their hypothalamic pleasure centers after they achieve the brainwave state we require." Patrenko shot Madam Grotchka a self-satisfied glare. "And, all of this can be done by wireless communication."

"What about the fellow with the gun?" Dr. Bern inquired. Madam Grotchka's ears perked.

"Secret Police," Vladimir said softly and assuredly. "One of Dr. Bash's finest...has international clearance." Grotchka's eyebrows raised as the cybernetic soldier passed by. The terror that swept over her for an instant, did not go unnoticed by Imo, as she had inadvertently killed the man's younger brother only weeks before, and had subconsciously mistaken the living for the dead.

Finally, they came to a room that could only be entered via a push-button coded lock of which the combination was changed every other week. Alexi led the other three into a large laboratory room where he lifted up the black suitcase and placed it sacredly onto an electronically equipped pedestal. Opening it in meticulous fashion, pinkies slightly raised, he revealed a multi-media G-72 computer complete with mouse, DVD-Rom re-writeable drive and 600,000 gigabytes of hard disk memory. These in turn were linked to a complex display board of lights, dials and outlet jacks. He plugged another hand-held computer into a wall socket. "Now watch this," Dr. Alexi Patrenko grinned, as he smoothed his shiny skull.

"Remote control," Dr. Kopensky added, bobbing his double chin in support.

Dr. Patrenko inserted a small zip-drive into a top slot and sat down onto a nearby table. Crossing his legs dramatically, he leaned back on both elbows. His muscular forearms bulged in taut anticipation. One by one, six Tajiks filed into the room, all adorned with matching maroon woolen berets. After a moment of contemplation, as a unit, although still standing, they went into a deep trance. Dr. Kopensky handed each a brown oblong-shaped pill and a small cup of water. "Megavitamins," he said.

Some dials were adjusted as they reached up in unison with a right hand to remove their hats. Each had an identical black plastic skull-cap in place of the skeletal crown, their flesh neatly fused with the artificial skin that ran around the cybernetic edges. There were nubs and sockets for 34 different depth-connector cyberchips and a series of colored LEDs between some of them.

A small aerial was extended on the premotor cortex of each man, as Dr. Patrenko played his computer much as if he were a concert pianist. Oftentimes, he would shake his head back and forth or side to side as if he wore a long mane. This affectation particularly intrigued Imo, as Patrenko was completely bald. The doctor shook his head once again and typed in a ten digit code. Little lights ignited on the cybernetic units. He became delighted as the subjects marched to the wall, and he smiled at Kopensky who beamed back. One man climbed into a closet and handed out six chairs. Back to the center they moved, positioning their seats on six prescribed cross-marks on the floor. Grabbing a rope which was attached to a hexagon-shaped steel frame which hung from the ceiling, Dr. Kopensky lowered the contraption over their heads.

"Rather primitive," Madam Grotchka mumbled in mild disdain. Kopensky stared her down as he attached each brain to the six nodule fulcrums, wiring the antennae to a central radio dish which protruded from the hub of the apparatus. Tiny alligator clips linked premotor, occipital and other connector electrodes to colored wires attached to each angle of the hovering hexagon.

"We decided on the hexagram because of the presence of this design in the benzene ring which appears in the atomic structure of most neurotransmitters," Patrenko explained. "The wires from their brains are, in turn, hooked to this central cable which feeds into our EEG machine and corresponding MRI virtual reality screen." He continued talking as he pushed a button which illuminated the control panel monitoring their brain-waves. "Not only can we get a 3-D visual of practically their entire brains in operation, we can also influence their neural processes. We can work by either remote control or through direct connections. The resonant frequency generated by this geometric configuration is transferred by means of induction back to various key synaptic sites in the cerebral cortex, thalamic pathway and brain-stem of each subject.

"In this way," Dr. Kopensky added, as he stretched out his fleshy arms to emphasize the point, "we create one giant superbrain with a synchronized control for states of consciousness and psionic energy emissions."

Dr. Patrenko continued, "With the MRI virtual reality screen hook-ins, all cyborgs can synchronize their thinking patterns through biofeedback and electronic manipulation. The geometry of their seating pattern improves reception and serves to increase harmonic and other resonance effects in order to create the superbrain." With that, Patrenko flashed on the large computer screen a composite MRI of all six brains superimposed and color-coded to show their separate brain-wave patterns. Digital DVD cameras recorded the entire event.

Both Madam Grotchka and Dr. Bern sat as they looked on in subdued wonder, unable to reconcile how Alexi and Vladimir could have kept such complicated work hidden for so long.

"We are not at the stage of total synchronization, but by connecting all brains together, and superimposing them this way, we are able to monitor the various neurological circuits so that when one of these men begins to produce the correct

PK brain-wave pattern, we can put the others in synchrony with him. These, of course, are our best subjects. Their trances are cued to hypnogogic frequencies, so they can maintain partial conscious control over their own states. Thus, they are also partially conscious of this conversation. Naturally, it is to their advantage to produce the correct frequencies."

Dr. Patrenko pointed to one of the dials. "We also have a fail-safe. If any individual goes into catalepsy, he can be knocked unconscious and separated from the others. When this occurs, we revert to a five-sided configuration and rearrange the seats accordingly."

As he spoke, Dr. Kopensky placed a large handful of ping pong balls in the middle of the cybernetic circle. The floor had a slight depression to it so all balls rolled towards the center.

The Tajiks stared intently at their target and then one by one, closed their eyes. "Each of these subjects has been tested earlier for PK ability--even before their operations, and then we trained and treated them with kid gloves. We have found that the shape of the neurotransmitter molecules hold important keys for non-local or psychokinetic intercerebral effects." Kopensky glanced over to Madam Grotchka. "We handle them like VIP's. And they know that if they can perform well, Dr. Bash may release them for more exciting duties. We also use our graduates to recruit some of the younger students. That fellow out in the hall, for instance, was in this circle only seventeen months ago."

Dr. Patrenko stepped forward as Dr. Kopensky became silent. "Behold," Alexi announced. He removed a small disk and inserted it into the DVD-Rom instrument panel. "Keep your eye on the EEG." His manner became excited as he moved the mouse with authority over the cybernetic keyboard. The superbrain disappeared, replaced on the screen by six separate flowing iridescent green lines bobbing horizontally to each other. "This, of course, is the reproduction or their brain-waves, one line for each subject. Below the sixth line is a computerized EEG pattern showing the correct wavelength necessary for producing synergistic PK states."

Beep. Beep. Beep. Beep.

"Number 4," Kopensky called out. One of the ping pong balls began to oscillate slightly as it gently knocked lightly into some of the others. Number 4's brain-waves matched quite closely the computerized PK pattern. Alexi pushed some buttons. Number 2 and 5 began to beep, their brain-waves synchronizing with that of Number 4. Dr. Kopensky rolled another bunch of ping-pong balls into the circle. Some began to bounce vigorously away from each other as if they were magnetized to the same electric charge, others hovered or floated precariously above the floor.

Patrenko ran to a closet and brought out a large carton of more ping-pong balls and dumped them into the center. Balls shot to the sides of the room, vigorously attaching to or repelling from one another, as they collided and bounced about. The room became a frenzy, little white whirlwinds ricocheting erratically off the ceiling, walls, chairs, and floor. Caught in the reverie of the moment, the three male scientists began to toss some of the bouncing spheres at each other, ecstatic with their capture of telekinetic brain-wave states.

"Is this all these bastards can do?" Madam Grotchka shouted above the din, allowing ping-pong balls to bounce off her callous exterior as she spoke.

Alexi's face grew stern. He crumpled a handful of the globes in his hand as he placed another DVD into the machine. Gradually the beeping ceased, the balls bounced down. Each humanoid dropped neatly into unconsciousness, as his respective EEG flattened into the slow, steady undulations of the delta wave sleep.

Mechanically, Vladimir went around the room with a vacuum cleaner, and dutifully sucked up all the ping pong balls. Subconsciously, Imo placed one into his pocket, and waited for their next move. As the subjects slept, Alexi left the room. Madam Grotchka sat in contemplation.

In short order, Alexi returned with four mottled kittens. Glancing at Madam, who was sitting sternly with arms folded, he placed the young animals onto the central depression and then pointed to the fat man. Kopensky approached the black briefcase and inserted another DVD.

The computerized EEG flashed another simulated brain-wave pattern similar to the first, but more erratic. Periodic spindle bursts between rapid oscillations scurried across the screen in seemingly arrhythmic pulsations. Subject Number 4 began to beep again, as his brain-waves came into synch with the demo pattern. Dr. Kopensky manipulated the dials.

"It took us nine years to find this," he called out.

Number 1 began beeping, as did Number 5. A red selenium cell implanted in their foreheads started to emanate. The kittens jumped about changing their behaviors rapidly from passive postures to aggressive predator stances to frightened, arched-back poses, hair furrowed rages to unconsciousness. Primordial behavior patterns expressed themselves in seeming non-sequiturs, as each animal repeated again and again its repertoire of instincts.

All cyborgs were now producing similar PK EEG patterns. The red lights from their foreheads met at the center of the circle, as a focused beam struck one of the animals. Ear-splitting *MEOWS* erupted from its mouth in gyrating attempts to shake off the negative energy. Another kitten flipped over and over.

Number 2 began to shake violently. He spit and retched phlegm from his mouth. Kopensky dropped him into unconsciousness, and moved the other five subjects into the pentagram configuration. Number 4's arms became spastic even though the rest of his body appeared calm. There seemed no unity of his body to his mind. Another kitten started rolling around; suddenly an eyeball exploded from its socket as the animal imploded. A second apparently died as well. Although it lay on the ground like a lifeless sack, its tail continued to oscillate, the nerves apparently still charged with PK energy.

Above the delirium Madam Grotchka was cackling, her face contorted in horrific jealousy, one side drooping markedly. Imo could feel the pain and pressure in his own brain as his eyes began to blur and his breath became labored. "Stop!" he yelled as blood oozed from his nose. Alexi inserted another DVD and the beeping ceased as each Tajik dropped once more into a deep state of unconsciousness.

Number 4's arm continued to vibrate spastically and Kopensky rushed over to smooth it down, kneading it vigorously as it persisted. He administered a vile of medicine directly into a chute at the top of the cybernetic gear of the subject. Attached to his premotor cortex, his shaking soon ceased. Patrenko unplugged each Tajik and gave them all injections. He directed Imo to grab the kittens, dead and alive, and toss them into a garbage can. Patrenko took its contents and dumped it into the incinerator, and then led Madam Grotchka and Dr. Bern back to their own lab stations.

CHESSIE

"Be back by 1:45, Chess," Duncan, her boss, said as she left for lunch. "I'll have a memo for you to type."

Right out of art school, Chessie had been hired to log artwork, price it, help substantiate its provenance and prepare the works for auction. She knew it was a little thing, but Duncan asking her to type his memo, just hit her the wrong way. He pretended otherwise, but he was a chauvinist, part of the old boys' network, and she resented it. Maybe she was overreacting.

It was funny that it seemed to be the little things that irked her the most. For her age, she actually had landed a prestigious position in a very competitive field, but she began to worry that she was become pigeon-holed. She had to figure how to rise to the next rung. But what rung would that be? She wasn't ready to open a gallery herself, and she certainly was no auctioneer. When people like Duncan left her alone, the truth was, she absolutely loved what she did, even if she did still find herself bitten by the Peggy Lee bug.

Like many New Yorkers, Chess began to look for more excitement on her hours off. She worked hard in pottery class and continued dating other men, but Rudy held that special place. Free moments at work were spent speaking to him on the phone or fantasizing about life together. She returned at 1:45 only to find Duncan late himself. Bastard, she thought as she sat and waited. He does it every time. She returned to her office to continue logging the new works, but her mind drifted from the task at hand. She reflected on her life as a child. She remembered her favorite closet above the third floor stairs of her parents' house. Hours were spent there in her favorite hide-away. Why had this memory surfaced now, she thought. Chess loved everything about the spot; the smell of folded winter blankets and cedar chest, the low slanted ceiling, thick raw wooden two-by-fours with blurred penciled numbers dating from the time the construction workers nailed them in. This was her special nest, a place for Rapunzel to let down her hair. Rudy was the materialization of the secret knight she had always loved. She knew it their first night. He had smelled of cedar.

Chessie saw Rudy only three times a week including weekends. Free sex was out for her. That day Rudy caught her was the worst of her life. She had begun to run after him in the moment of sheer madness, but fortunately he had disappeared. Her partner, an unhappily married business executive, understood. But then, what choice did he have? Jed was one of the few men in her life that she had trusted, and it turned out to be a good choice. When she told him that it could not work for them, he nodded and hugged her, his penis shriveling back into semi-coma. For Jed, companionship with a striking and intellectual female was satisfying enough...for the time being anyway. He had a stringer at the office, but was currently "down on sex." Jed was searching for a female friend more than anything. One night, however, while they were watching a TV show together, Chess could feel his heart pounding. "We live in a difficult world, Jed." She helped him achieve orgasm, but both tried hard to keep the romance out. It was true that he continued to massage her back and breasts, but the relationship was mostly in a different dimension. Sex could only complicate things. On their nights together, Jed would take her to French restaurants, Broadway plays, museums and TV shows. He knew the city night-life, and Chessie got to meet some of the interesting people. They usually went out Mondays and Wednesdays. She would discuss Rudy, and Jed might tell of his impending divorce, or tidbits about the people at his office. When he left at night, oftentimes they only shook hands or hugged. This was the first "male-friend" Chess really had for herself since high-school, and Jed had told her that this was the first "female-friend" he had ever had.

Chessie occasionally spoke to Rudy about Jed. If they ended up together, she wanted to keep Jed as a friend. But she knew, at least for now, that the two must stay separated. If only Rudy had not disappeared for so long. She took a cab to his building. "Hello, Mrs. Brown," she said, as she followed the lady into the lobby and rode the elevator with her.

"You're that whippersnapper's gal, aren't ya?"

"He has apologized to you, hasn't he?"

"You mean, for knocking me down and taking ten years off of my life." There was a meanness in her eye, so Chess decided to give her the New York smile, as she stepped out of the elevator and walked past Mrs. Brown's apartment to Rudy's.

With her fingernails, as she always did, she rattled the metal door. "Rudee."

"Who wants to know?" He spoke through a crack.

"It was Jed. I told you about him. You travel all over the world. Don't call me for a week." She paused. "He's just a friend."

"I know. It's my fault."

"No, it isn't, not totally." He opened the door part way and gave her an unmistakable glare. The guy was still pissed. His silence unbearable, she knew he couldn't help himself.

"I'm sorry, Rudy. I just wanted some freedom."

Rudy saw an opening for a half dozen sarcastic lines, but she had said the two magic words. "I've made the psychic connection," he said, changing the topic, as he opened the door fully. But he wouldn't (couldn't) kiss her.

"Mon," she said in a deep Jamaican accent, "you can take your Tarot deck, get your'd own cable show and tell da people's future." She nipped his cheek with a quick peck as she stepped by him.

"You read it?"

"Of course I read your article. *Parapsychology Today* by Rudy Q. Styne." She made up a middle initial. "That whole section on Baba. Awesome. But, I agree with the captain. You had to hold back."

"I don't want to hold back," Rudy replied. "Let me move in. This place is a dive."

"Can I see the bedroom?"

"Look at all the money we'd save." He led the way, and then turned around and just looked at her. "We could use it to go to Europe, or the Caribbean."

"Or buy a house?" She spoke before she knew.

His eyes looked away. "Yeah, or a yacht."

"I want to, Rudy. I mean, part of me wants to. But I like my own place, my free nights." She took off her clothes and stood there facing him.

"I won't interfere with those." He reached over and held her. Her body quivered and then simply melted. Their lips met. He was simply amazed at how soft her skin could become. And how hot.

She undid his belt buckle....

Twenty minutes later.

"Rudy, didn't you ever think that maybe we get along so well because we don't live together."

"I don't buy it, Chess. We love each other, don't we?"

"I'm afraid, Rudy, of losing myself. Just when I feel that I'm finally finding myself. After all that time with Luke."

Rudy bit his tongue. Decided just to look at her. Let her unwind.

"When I got out of college," she said, her body glistening in the soft light, "the first thing I wanted to do was get married. My parents wanted it. His parents wanted it. And, now, as I look back, I think I may have been more into the idea of marriage than into Luke. You know what I mean? I was young. But then, our first few years were fine. He did that movie poster for *Lord of the Rings.*"

There she goes again with the poster, he thought.

"We saw it all over the city. In magazines. His poster. It was cool. On nights out, friends would bring their friends just to get his autograph. I thought we were on our way."

Rudy did not want to hear again about Luke. Yet, at the same time he wanted to know everything about her. No secrets; he stifled jealousy. "Then what happened?"

"The security we had, the symbol of the wedding rings, the mutual commitment. It was all there, that sense of no longer being an outsider, of being whole. The first year was magical."

Rudy flinched, but she went on. "Then he lost a major client, and it changed everything. He became bitter, stopped looking for work, and he began drawing those endless pictures of nubile women, with castles in the mist and dragons, that whole heavy metal thing. Nobody wanted it, but he wouldn't quit. He'd stay at home and fax or email them all over the country, to his old clients, to anyone he could think of.

"And then it was just the two of us. In the apartment. Every day. I can't tell you how many hours we sat by the tube fighting over the remote to find something, anything, because neither of us wanted to get off the sofa.

"I almost didn't mind his affair with little twaddle-tits, as much as the reason he gave for it. He told me I was boring. Me! He was stoned all the time, headed nowhere. But he also had a point. And it was at that very moment that I decided to change my life. I left him, walked out and never looked back."

As she sat up in bed, her eyes turned to Rudy, her upturned breasts and neat tips peering over the covers. "It was then that I found myself. And now I found you." She smiled.

They studied the colors of each other's eyes. Hers were gray with a radiating inner circle of sienna; his, hazel with floating golden flecks. Their pupils pulsed. Rudy reached over, and nibbled her eyelids. She sighed as he worked his way down to rest his head on her belly. "If you kiss another man again, I think I might die." Her vibes were soothing, her hands affectionately resting on his shoulders. Suddenly he felt her chemistry change. He reached up to kiss the nape of her neck, her lips, and forehead. Chessie always smiled when he looked at her. She could light up an entire restaurant with that smile. She smiled in her sleep, and Rudy loved her just for that.

They spent the next hour in a quiet lovers embrace. Chambers opened in Chessie she had never known existed as Rudy expanded and plunged deeper. There was not this macho thrust Luke used to lay on her; this man found dimensions Luke could never know. Sweat poured down the two of them as the climax inevitably drew near. Rhythms built in a rapid steady pace. The Earth continued to traverse the solar system. Explosive streams of energy traveled along their spines and out their toes. With eyes closed, they witnessed stars and whirlpools of light, visions of glowing gods, the constellations and moons of Jupiter. They watched for endless seconds the history of the galaxy and birth of the sun, and then they drifted back into slumber.

She awoke sharply to a phone call. "That was Kranz," Rudy said. "He just invited me to speak at the up-and-coming psychotronics convention to be held in Florence. The guy's world famous."

"What will you speak on?"

"Parapsychology and the mass media, of course.... Now if I can just get the captain to agree...."

Chessie looked at him.

"And don't think you are going to make me go to Florence all by myself!"

* * *

The following day Rudy told the people in the office of his invitation. "Why, you just came back from Bhutan!" Sally cried, obviously jealous of Rudy's travel expenditures. She, herself, was planning on asking the captain to allow her to go to the Middle East and Turkey. She also was fantasizing again about Rudy. Just this past weekend she had envisioned his entering passages within herself she had never known existed. "Rudy, I had a dream about you."

"And?"

"It wasn't PG."

"I'm afraid to ask."

"You're going to marry her, aren't you?"

"Chess?"

"No, the lady you knocked down in the apartment."

"We may move in together. But marriage. I have to tell you, Sal, I haven't thought that far."

"Uh huh. You gotta let me go in first." Placing a sizzling hand on his shoulder, she motioned to the captain's office. "I've got to meet with Egyptian, Israeli and Syrian officials and then go on to that NATO alliance meeting in Turkey. If he OK's your trip, I may not be able to talk him into mine."

"You're paranoid, but go ahead."

Smirking, she bumped her limber tush against his arm and pranced into the captain's office. Ten minutes later she bounced back out, beaming. Rudy could not understand the continual feelings of lust he had for Sally when he was content with Chessie. *Am I merely a product of animal forces?* he thought to himself.

"Rudy, you are not a parapsychologist," the captain said. "If you want to, you can go into it full-time, but not here. You know we have other work more pressing--like politics, the natural gas shutdown, life extension, the Gore proposal on that Lunar station, virtual money, thievery on the info-highway...."

"Captain, I'm not in disagreement. I ask for this trip out of respect for the people who invited me. It could be helpful in the long run if they have a breakthrough, and *Modern Times* becomes their liaison. Two of the speakers are Nobel prizewinners."

"Don't take advantage of me, Styne. I want a report on Tuscan life styles. Get a link to their medieval past, and match it to the on-going conflagration in the neighboring region of Croatia, Bosnia, Serbia. You know, living at the edge of a civilized Europe. Spend a day or two in Zadar or Dubrovnik and try to get to the border areas. Do a *National Geographic* thing. Get that photographer, what's-his-name from Budapest."

"Vienna."

"That's what I said, Vienna. Maybe do a retrospective on the history of Balkan states. Set up a meeting with that Tito lady."

"Sir, how much time do you think I'll have? I'm covering a conference."

"Okay, okay. Do what you want. Just don't forget, you don't leave for a month." The captain dropped his head to get back to work, and then looked up as an afterthought. "Florence is a beautiful town, Rudy. Just don't drive it. If you get a car from the airport, drop it at the parking garage at the edge of town and call a cab."

"But, I'm sure we can get around."

The captain reached into a lower draw and shuffled through some papers. "Here," he said, taking out a city map. "Don't be an idiot. This is the route to the parking garage." He took out a magic marker and outlined the path carefully. "Leave the car here," he slapped the map, "and take cabs."

Rudy put in twelve-hour days for the next four weeks. He cut his Tuesday nights with Chessie to work on cyberspace pedophilia, New York politics, the problem with ghetto funding and a critical article on the doctors who perform vasectomies, hysterectomies and sex change operations.

"Chess, we're going weekend after next. I can cover air-fare and lodging. Clear it now with your boss. I don't want any screw-ups. The conference starts on a Thursday night. We should be gone about five days."

Rudy sounded excited on the phone. He told Chess about the captain. "He doesn't want me to drive. Wants us to take taxies! I got this trip covered. You can take me out to a restaurant if you want."

"Sounds good. But let me do the booking. I say we land in Pisa and drive from there to Florence."

"Fine with me."

"I may stay longer, if you don't mind...as long as I'm there.... Could do Verona and Venice, take my new Nikon megapix."

"Captain mentioned Zadar and Dubrovnik. How 'bout going there instead? You could do some background shots on that whole Serbo-Croatian thing."

"Pisa, Dubrovnik. Hmmm, maybe I'll even skip that whole boring Florence thing." As Chess got up and flashed her can, Rudy smacked it as she headed for the shower.

"Ow!" she yelped scooting. "Last one in is a rotten egg."

THE CONFERENCE

The young couple packed their bags for Florence. Chessie fantasized the trip as a kind of honeymoon. She was looking forward to being in a foreign place with this man. Rudy focused on his talk. He was happy to be in a country whose language he had in high school, and he brought along an *Italian At A Glance* guidebook to help brush up. He was also gratified not to leave Chessie at home. Having been a product of the wholesale ignorance concerning scientific discoveries in telepathy, psychokinesis and the rest of parapsychology, he planned his talk accordingly, sketching out ideas in a powerbook he brought along. He noted his own prejudices, and the biased reporting by the skeptic Garner concerning B.K. Pine's research. He described and sought reasons for the attempts of the mass media to continue false accusations against Pine; he described the hedging of real issues, and the peculiar tactic of labeling past and present parapsychologists as pseudoscientists; and he discussed his own revelations in self-discovery when personally witnessing both fantastic and incidental cases of paranormalacy. Each and every psychic researcher has a tremendous responsibility, he wrote, towards waking up, not only the lay person, but also in enlightening the scientific establishment, constituencies who continue to perpetuate false realities concerning the nature and potentialities of human existence.

One particular tactic, he noted, was the stigma placed on parapsychologists by falsely accusing them of belief in the supernatural, and thus irrational, modes of thinking. No psychic researcher worth his salt thinks ESP falls outside the laws of nature. Humans simply have not as yet uncovered the particular tenets involved. Styne planned to conclude his talk by offering his services in helping establish a better relationship between parapsychology and the press, and by suggesting that the researchers involved attempt to invite newspaper and TV journalists to their labs. He punched in his notes, "Try and get in the habit of sending continuing reports as a matter of course."

As the plane circled the approach to the airport at Pisa, Chessie tried unsuccessfully to spot the Leaning Tower through her window.

The plane landed on the tarmac. They walked towards the terminal, and Chessie searched the horizon again. The sun etched a ragged rim of gold around a jagged blackened sky. Off in the distance, steamy yellow shafts from the cloud's interior punched down upon an area that Chessie guessed was where the Leaning Tower stood.

"Multo bello," Rudy said, as he planted an exaggerated kiss on Chessie's cheek.

"Bonjorno, signore," she jested in a heavy sexy accent.

They found their Eurocar, got directions, and drove out of the airport to try and locate the famous landmark.

"Why don't we just GPS it?" Rudy said.

"These cars don't come equipped," Chessie said, "and anyhow, that's no fun!"

"Sounds like famous last words," Rudy said.

"There it is!" Chessie shouted, as they looked right to see the tower peek its slanted apex above nearby fields.

Turning a corner, Rudy parked at the fortified entrance of the walled city which housed not only the tower, but also the Baptistery and accompanying medieval Duomo. The size of the church and the work involved were awe-inspiring.

"Now, you know, we can't spend too much time here if we want to get to the conference before the opening speech."

"I know, I know," Chessie said, as she raced over the cobblestones towards the great leaning edifice. Following at a slower pace, Rudy contemplated the giant marble wonder built 1,000 years ago. He ambled over to the fence which surrounded the tower to watch some workmen place yet another counterweight at the upside portion of the base. The guide-book said over the last forty years before these countermeasures, the tower had been increasing its lean at a rate of a half inch each year! This seemed unbelievable. The Italians, however, believed the calculations and they spent millions to return the landmark to its lean of the early 1800's and thereby keep it from toppling.

It was a long shadow at the tip of the crest of the downside end that caught Rudy's eye. He looked up into sunlight to see what he thought was a tall man with bushy eyebrows standing in the most precarious position. As he squinted to adjust to the harsh light, the image faded and disappeared. By this time, Chessie had grabbed his arm and guided him to the tchotchke stands, to look at junk and buy some postcards.

"Look at this." Rudy shook his head in disbelief as he pointed to the headline of an English newspaper that was at one of the stands:

700 DIE IN MASS SUICIDE IN PAKISTAN
UKRANIAN SORCERESS DEUS MAXIMA
BELIEVED TO BE AMONG DEAD

In an apparent attempt to persuade the Pakistani people into joining a new Russian Empire, the self-proclaimed messiah, Deus Maxima, made good on her gruesome promise by persuading 700 of her followers into undertaking a mass suicide. Bodies lay strewn....

"That is so crazy, Rudy," Chessie reflected as they walked back to the car, and made their way out to the Autostrada.

Humming along at 120 kph, Rudy and Chess coasted easily into the region of Fiorenze.

"Florence," Chessie said.

"I'm not that dumb," Rudy retorted as he patted his watch. "Right on schedule. Now, get out the captain's map, and let's see how to get to that garage."

"Oh, come on, Rudy. Where's your sense of adventure? We've got a car. There's no point in wasting money on a taxi when we can drive ourselves right to the hotel."

Passing an overlook, the couple stopped to take in the bird's-eye view. It encompassed not only the surrounding area of Tuscan estates, but also the river, the bridges, and the entire city. A replica of the statue of David lay on a rise above them.

"There it is, right off Via Zanobi, Rudy. See. There's at least three bridges we can take." They pulled back into traffic as the car rolled onwards towards the Arno River, the picturesque gateway to Florence. "Look at the tower," Chessie shouted, "by that great Duomo!"

"I think that's the one at the Uffizi Museum," Rudy hypothesized. "What's on that bridge?"

"Let me get the guide book out. That's the Ponte Vecchio. According to this," she said, with a gleam in her eye, "those are covered shops on the bridge, and they all sell jewelry. In fact, if we look at the map, it looks like that route leads almost directly into Zanobi."

"What do you mean *almost?*" Rudy inquired.

"Here, we take Via Romana, right over the bridge, and follow it up De Gineri, hang a left on Arazzieri, and a right on Zanobi."

"Let me see that," Rudy said, trying to drive, shift gears and read the map, as his eyes squinted to make out the words. "How the heck can you read this. We should have brought a magnifying glass!"

"Oh, come on, Rudy. It's very simple."

"Okay, you shout out the names as we get close."

Unfortunately, they found out quickly that the Ponte Vecchio was a pedestrian walk only. The car continued on.

"So, we'll take the next one. There are about five," Chessie declared, pointing to the numerous small bridges that crossed over the Arno River. "Here, we can just follow Via Del Morro right into Ariento."

"But what happened to Arazzieri?"

"Well, we won't have to go that way."

They continued on the road, only to find that the next bridge was one-way leading out, and the flow of the cars forced them to branch left. Quickly, they found themselves on a narrow back street in an urban area, still on the wrong side of the river. After a few heated arguments, and two or three discussions with non-English speaking natives, they found themselves back at the overlook where they attempted a new strategy.

"I say we just follow the traffic flow," Rudy suggested. "Most of these people are probably going downtown."

"My God, Rudy. That has got to be the dumbest idea I have ever heard." Chessie grabbed the map, left the car, and approached a tour bus driver, and then she returned with a Cheshire grin. "He said to take Via Gransci and follow it around to Spartaco Lavagnini." She pointed out the route on their trusty map.

"Well, if we're going to do that, why don't we just hang a left on Borgo LaCroce and take it to Guelta?" Rudy offered. "The bus guy's way is a big curve. This is practically a straight line."

"But he said..."

"Where's your sense of adventure?" Rudy challenged, as he put the car in gear and took them across the correct bridge into Florence. Once on Via Gransci, Rudy made a sharp left where Borgo La Croce seemed to be. Suddenly the road became a cobblestone lane which led to byways too narrow to negotiate with an automobile. Three motor scooters sliced around them.

"We can't be very far," he fumed, as he tried to avoid a pedestrian while driving in reverse to get back to a road that was one-way leading in his direction.

"I told you we should have followed the busman's directions," Chessie stormed. "Now, let's go back, and do it right!"

What seemed to be such a simple task, that is, to turn the car around and return to Via Gransci (or one of its connectors--as it changes its name as it goes along), was not. But after twenty-five minutes and numerous questions to numerous friendly pedestrians, the couple found their way back to the place where Rudy had diverted left.

"Now, all we have to do is follow this avenue around Piazale Donatello. We go right and..."

"Left," Rudy said, looking over to Chessie's lap. Suddenly, he stick-shifted down and hit the brake to avoid hitting a pair of women on a motor scooter who had cut them off to weave between a truck and a bus that were cruising nearby them.

"That's a right."

"Left."

"RIGHT!"

"Are you out of your mind?? That's a LEFT!!!" Rudy slapped the map, his face flushing. And so they continued shouting at one another, until each realized that the other was pointing to a slightly different part of an S-curve that did, indeed, bend right and then left. "By the way," Rudy said in a completely calm voice, "Did you see that chick on the back of the bike?"

"So she was nearly topless," Chessie responded testily.

"I didn't think you saw her." Suddenly laughing, Rudy pulled over to the right curb-side to regroup. "Hey, let's try to enjoy this, even though we're freaking out. We're in Italy, right?"

"Then don't snap at me!" Chessie said. "You were wrong. I'm the one reading the map."

"I was RIGHT...."

"If I remember correctly, Rudy, you were left. I was right."

Calmer, "Yeah, I guess you were."

"Can we agree that we take a left on Viale Spartaco Lavaggnini?" Rudy said as even-temperedly as he could.

"Yes." Chessie was fighting back tears.

After the traffic passed, Rudy moved back onto the roadway and pulled up to a red light. Cars, cabs and motor scooters bunched up and revved their engines, waiting for the change to green. The light turned, and like thoroughbreds at the starting block, they all lurched forward, and raced like demons to the next intersection. The road forked, and the mass of vehicles split rapidly in two. Unable to go left, Rudy was forced right. "We'll just take the next left," he said, naively, not realizing that in Florence there's no such thing as a second chance.

Completely and utterly lost, and completely and utterly flabbergasted that this could be so, in such a relatively small city, when they had a map *in hand,* each traveler drove on dumbfounded in silence. For reasons totally unexplained, they found their way once again across the Arno, exactly back to where they had started, at the same overlook. With the fight knocked out of them, all they could do was look at each other sheepishly. Rudy started out again but quickly found himself stuck down some back street in a narrow urban off-shoot still on the wrong side of the river. Somewhat by instinct, he simply rolled on.

"There. Do it!" Chessie yelled, pointing out a Eurocar drop-off center they had stumbled upon. They rolled in, settled on the costs of the rental, and hailed a cab.

"Hotel Zanobi," Rudy said.

Like a man possessed, the cabbie shifted from first to third to fourth, as he gunned it over the river, made a hairpin turn, weaved between busses and motor scooters, avoided the many pedestrians, and performed even more startling maneuvers that caused the hair to stand up on Rudy's arms. Down a small cobblestone road the automobile bumped, as the driver hung a sharp right, then left, back onto a major road, up to racing speeds, and back onto what seemed to be a pedestrian walk. Shooting onto the sidewalk, with the two left wheels still on the narrow byway, the cabbie allowed just enough space for a car to pass, as the vehicle screeched to a halt. "Hotel Zanobi," the cabbie announced in his native accent.

"I could have done that," Rudy mumbled. Having given up over an hour ago any attempt to have gotten to the conference in time to cover opening ceremonies, they took their bags to the front desk. Although well after 9 PM, fortunately the place was still very much alive. Conference attendees milled about in the familiar humm that every symposium seems to exude.

Rudy looked at the register and recognized many of the names. One sent shivers down his spine: Alexi Patrenko. Rudy had practically forgotten the incidents that nearly cost him his life. He realized how asleep he really must be. P.

Karl, Hanley Kranz and Professor Coomesberry were also attending. Jay Ketchembach's name was crossed out, and the word "deceased" was written next to it.

Coomesberry was slated to speak about Swami Baba and materialization on Saturday, followed by Karl on localization of brain functions in lower primates and man. Alexi Patrenko along with a co-worker, Dr. Imo Bern, was scheduled to discuss neurophysiology and telepathy. Hanley Kranz would read the paper Ketchembach had been working on at the time of his death. It was titled "Brain-wave Biofeedback and PK States." Kranz would also "MC" the program, with his first talk scheduled for the following night.

"Come on," Chessie said, after freshening up in the room. Cheerfully, she grabbed Rudy's arm and dragged him to the elevator, and down a ramp which led to a large hallway bounded on each side by demonstration booths.

Rudy was surprised that Chessie whizzed so quickly past the UFOlogists, palm readers, astrologers and transmediums to stop at a booth that had the following sign:

PROFESSOR DUCAM'S DBA NEURAL NETWORK

"DBA?" Rudy inquired.

"Direct Brain Activation," Chessie said. "This guy wants to hook up human brains directly to computers through thought power alone. Virtual telepathy, they call it."

"How do you know that?"

"Rudy, if you would read the symposium booklet, maybe you'd learn something too," Chessie said as her nose turned up.

"Hmmm," Rudy said.

The couple stood and listened as Professor Horatio Delano Ducam gave a brief lecture on biofeedback, neural mapping of brain-wave states and neurogenesis, the ability to enhance or restore specific areas of the brain by using targeted genetically engineered proteins. A short, balding man with tufts of white hair sprouting on both sides of his head, the professor had just started his demonstration.

"I began this quest a quarter century ago teaching monkeys, with depth electrodes in their brains to play video games while mapping out their neural architecture with the MRI. My own brainstorm occurred, ha, ha, ha, when I realized that I could simply remove the attachment to the joystick and have the monkeys play the games through wireless transmission of their thoughts, even though they assumed the joysticks were still operational." Professor Ducam turned on a television and showed a short clip of the monkeys playing video games.

Behind Ducam was a young boy who sat in what looked to be a dentist's chair adorned with golf-cart wheels and robot arms. The boy's head was encased in a porcupine-like helmet with numerous electrodes attached. "Since my goal had always been to help the handicapped while doing the least amount of harm, I have now refined the procedure so that neurosurgery is no longer necessary." The professor graciously waved his arm as if to announce the boy.

"Billy here can do a variety of functions just by thinking about them," Ducam said. "Each mental state he envisions generates a corresponding brain-wave pattern that is hooked up to trigger the correct sequence to activate the machines. Here, we can see the architecture of his actual brain, and also see which areas are intensified on this computer screen. It's true, we inject into the bloodstream specific proteins to enhance the functioning of various areas of the brain, but we do not use any form of brain surgery. This is a very effective non-invasive technique which has cross applications for other brain disorders as well." As he spoke, a few more onlookers joined the group. "OK," he said, turning to the boy. "Do your thing."

Billy, who looked to be no more than 8-years-old, stared off to the side and curled up his bottom lip. Suddenly, one of the arms of the chair extended itself and grabbed a small accordion. Rudy and Chessie and the other onlookers saw the boy's frontal and occipital lobes and motor cortex light up on the computer screen. Then the other metallic appendage reached out, and a simple musical tune was played. The instrument was put down, the left arm reached out and turned on a computer. A video game came on screen.

"Keep in mind," the professor pointed out, "Billy is playing this game by thought alone. That joy-stick that you see moving is set up with a remote-controlled impulse switch that is synchronized to electrodes placed along his motor cortex at the top of his scalp. Naturally, if we could sink electrodes or computer chips into his brain, which we prefer not to do with humans, his precision would increase dramatically."

The computer screen changed and the words "GOOD BYE" appeared.

The arms of the chair receded back into position, and the chair moved smoothly forward, turned right at the Astrology booth and headed up the ramp. As Billy departed, one of the robot arms was raised again to wave good-bye.

"Oh, I'm sure he'll be back before the evening is over," Dr. Ducam said. "Do I have any more volunteers for the other chair?"

Chessie stepped forward and the scientist strapped her in.

"How long did it take the boy to learn that?" she inquired, as another porcupine-shaped helmet was placed on her head.

"Some of it in just a few minutes, but the most difficult procedures, about six weeks."

"So, what's the big deal," another observer commented. "My boy can ride a bicycle no hands down our street...and play a clarinet at the same time," he added with a laugh.

"Your boy isn't paralyzed from the neck down, I take it?"

"Oh my God," the man said.

"OK, young lady," the professor said on a more upbeat note, "I want you to look at this screen. Do you see the dot in the center?" He pointed to a television screen that was attached to the chair.

"Yes."

"Well, this dot is linked to a computer that is attached to electrodes that surround your cranium. If you can change your brain-wave patterns and make that dot go to the right, your chair will go to the right; if you can make that dot go to the left, your chair will go to the left; up to top is straight ahead; and down to bottom is backwards. Essentially, if you think right, you usually cause a corresponding energy change on the right side of the motor cortex. This happens so as to prepare the right side of your body for movement. The same thing with the left side, and so on. What we have done is tap into this preactivation series of neural processes. Any questions?"

"No."

"Ready?"

"Sure," Chessie said, and winked at Rudy.

"OK, go ahead," said the scientist.

Nothing happened. Chessie wrinkled her nose, lifted one eyebrow, puffed up her cheeks. Nothing. She looked up at the professor with a pleading expression.

"THINK LEFT!" he commanded, and the chair suddenly lurched to the left, knocking over one of the display tables that separated Dr. Ducam's booth from a palmist's. The chair continued on in a slap-dash, start-and-stop fashion down the hallway. Chessie just grinned and apologized as she slammed into another counter while still going backwards. Orthorotating, she waved with her other hand and disappeared 'round a corner.

Friday morning was a free period set up to allow the attendees time for sightseeing. Many were taking prescheduled tours. Rudy spotted Professor Coomesberry, but ducked away before he was seen, as he wanted his free time with Chessie. There was little doubt in his mind that he would have plenty of time to spend with his old friend from Bhutan.

On foot, and in rapid order, Rudy and Chessie toured the city, meandering through the piazzas, taking in Michaelangelo's great statue of David at the Academy, and then going down to the Ponte Vecchio. As they had read the day before in their guide book, the famous bridge was, indeed, lined on both sides with what seemed to be a hundred jewelry shops. They stood in line at the Pitti Palace and gawked at the numerous well-known renaissance paintings, many of which depicted Madonna and Child. Rudy was particularly taken by one of the works of Raphael. It was a picture of a dragonslayer. "Look at the depth, the use of color and the detail," he said.

"Just like Luke's," Chessie said.

"Exactimondo." He gave her a not so gentle pinch on her left buttock. She wriggled slightly in cadence with their walk.

The highlight for both of them, was the exploration of the magnificent Duomo at Piazza San Giovanni. The size of the cathedral was awesome. Built a thousand years ago, and set in alternating bricks of white, pink and black marble, the couple marveled at the workmanship and great strength of the building.

Having prearranged the time, they met with their photographer from Vienna, Bruno. Rudy directed him to take some shots by the Duomo, and use the telephoto lens to capture the complex front of the church. Rising up four stories were mosaics and numerous pristine statues of Madonna and Child, Jesus and the Saints, all imbedded into alcoves in the front exterior wall. Bruno also had instructions to photograph Pisa, Venice and Belgrade, so he said good-bye, and Rudy and Chessie continued their excursion.

At the south side of the Duomo were numerous artists set up to sell drawings of local street scenes or to create portraits or caricatures of the tourists.

"Hey, lady, I make pretty picture of you," one of the artists said, coaxing Chessie to take a seat.

"I don't want a cartoon," Chessie told the man, and to Rudy under her breath, "All they do is emphasize what's ugly."

"No, no, I make lovely exact picture. You like, you definitely like." The man proudly showed off well-worn drawings he had made of Sofia Loren and Lauran Bacall when they were young. "80,000 lira, but for you, special price, 50,000."

"Yeah, he probably drew them when they were that young," Rudy whispered under his breath.

"Shush," Chessie whispered back. "They're lovely," she said to the artist.

"It will look just like her? *Stesso?*" Rudy pointed to Chessie's features.

"Si, si. Stesso."

Chessie looked so happy that Rudy nodded agreement, and she took a seat.

Rudy could see, right off, that the artist began with a wrong depiction of Chessie's eyes, but he hoped for the best and wandered away for fifteen minutes, only to return to see that the portrait, although lovely, was not Chessie. If anything, it looked like Sofia Loren. He turned the portrait around, as Chessie had not seen it yet, and said, "I'm sorry. You did not capture her. We don't want it." And with that proclamation, he took Chessie's hand and walked away.

"You pay 50,000 lira. American must pay. You pay," the artist hounded.

"It's pretty, but it's not her."

"It her, you pay." The man tried to push the portrait into the couple's hands.

"Maybe we should just pay him," Chessie said.

"What for? We are never going to hang it up. It doesn't look like you."

"I know, but it's pretty."

"I make you deal," Rudy said to the artist. "I bring my girl and this picture to your other friends, and if they say that you have captured her, we pay. They say *facia stesso,* we pay."

The artist looked once again at the picture, once again at Chessie, and then glanced quickly over to his colleagues who had their stands next to his. It did not take him long to realize a decision. Shooing them away with a flick of the wrist. "You go now," he motioned. *"Se ne vada!"*

"Con piacere," Rudy said. "With pleasure," he translated to Chessie.

"Capisco," Chessie said. "I brushed up a little before the trip, myself."

"Molto buono," Rudy smiled, as he led the way to the town square where the Uffizi Museum was located.

Dr. Kranz opened the Friday night dinner with a toast to the parapsychologists from all around the world who were attending "this Seventh Annual International Meeting." His message was that it was "imperative for the scientists of the Earth to work together to bring this planet towards unity, while we search the deeper recesses of the mind." Dr. Kranz gave a stirring speech and received a rigorous round of applause.

Rudy became obsessed with finding Dr. Patrenko. During dinner, he took the time to search the crowd for men with shaved heads, and proceeded to locate three of them.

"Rudy, you don't mind if I go to the Ponte Vecchio on my own," Chessie said. "There's a couple of jewelry shops we missed."

"Thanks," Rudy said, impressed with her ability to read his need to be alone. Methodically, he went from one bald man to the next, and was thereby able to rule out a psychoanalyst from the Mid-west and a Rumanian researcher in Kirlian photography. His heart began to pound as he approached the third man.

The man was quite muscular. He had an odd habit of stroking his shaved cranium with his fingertips as he talked to a sleek dark-skinned women who looked to be Filipino or Malaysian, and a man who appeared to be Chinese. Not quite sure what he was going to say if it was Patrenko, Rudy felt his armpits begin to sweat. He stepped forward.

"Aye mate," Professor Coomesberry cut him off.

"Buon giorno, Professor, how are you?" Rudy was genuinely happy to see the "old chap" again. It was just the timing that upset him. Stuck, he tried to keep his eye on the third bald man as he relived the experience in Bhutan with his Australian friend.

The reporter's interest in the events surrounding Jay Ketchembach's death rekindled, his mind jogged into a new state of awareness. As he spoke, he felt as if he had awakened for the first time. "Did you get my article? I hope you enjoyed my rendition of our mule ride through the Himalayas."

"Si, si, Rudy-old-chap-old-mate, got a big kick out of it, what what. I hope you don't mind me referring to some passages when I discuss the Baba." Coomesberry twisted his fingers along the curve of his moustache as a way of further lightening the moment.

"Not at all," Rudy said, his face breaking into a smile.

"You know," Coomesberry went on, "ever since our swim in that spring, I have been going to an indoor pool in Sydney. The water...."

As the professor droned on, Rudy returned his gaze to the bald man who nodded adieu to the young couple. They bowed in return. Then the man approached Dr. P. Karl and another young man, who, by the look of his body language, knew the bald man well. Nodding yes, and smiling at the appropriate times, as Coomesberry rattled on, Styne waited for a suitable pause, and an excuse to leave, when a tall dark figure by the window caught his attention. The bald man departed suddenly, leaving the younger man with Dr. Karl. The bald man's sense of purpose, and the foreboding shadow by the veranda, sunk into the pit of Rudy's stomach. An image of Rasputin flashed into his mind. As sweat poured out his forehead, Rudy excused himself and walked over to Dr. Karl.

"Rudolf, how good to see you again." Karl's breath reeked of beer and wine. "I want you to meet one of our Eurasian colleagues, Dr. Imo Bern." Karl's red eyes lit up. He was enjoying himself immensely. "Dr. Bern is partially responsible for some of the newest brain-wave research, such as the mapping of frontal, prefrontal and midbrain feedback circuitry."

Barely giving Dr. Bern acknowledgement, Rudy inquired of Dr. Karl, "Have you learned anything of significance with your brain transplant work?" His voice appeared casual, but he was still angry with himself for not taking a moral stand on that score. One of Rudy's friend's mother had been saved by brain surgery when a malignant tumor was removed from deep in the right temporal lobe, and Rudy was well aware that work such a Dr. Karl's made such surgery possible. As Karl replied, Rudy realized that he was having difficulty following the conversation. He was preoccupied... contemplating various ways to assassinate the Russian Georgi Boshtov.

It's either Bash or me, that bastard, Rudy thought to himself. *I'll kill that son-of-a-bitch if I get half a chance.* His violent thoughts shocked his innards. "How exactly do you shift one brain to another body?" Thinking on two levels, Rudy felt queasy and spaced out.

Karl lifted one eyebrow, but did not appear uncomfortable by the question. "We only use monkeys," Dr. Karl said. "Dr. Bern, here, has been fortunate to work with human subjects."

"Dr. Karl," Imo said, "if you remember correctly, you worked with Dr. Penmeadow on depth electrode work in humans." Imo was upset about the tone of the conversation and did not want the focus of attention to shift his way.

"You work with human brains, Dr. Bern?" Rudy asked.

This question cut through Imo like a knife. Who in hell was this Styne fellow? Yet, Imo sensed his own hate and incredible waves of resentment for Dr.'s Karl, Patrenko, Kopensky, Bash, and for Madam Grotchka. *God damn it, I hate my own guts. I loathe myself,* Imo thought. He began to feel the pang of his conscience--a pain he had fought off since the first night on the tundra. Sounds of a buzz-saw cutting through human skull echoed deep within his right temporal lobe. If he let it get a hold, it would overtake him. His knees began to buckle. Grabbing a drink from the waiter, he was able to control it. He had to.

"Mr. Styne, I hear you are a reporter from the American popular press. I saw your talk listed on the schedule. In our country, there remains some mixed feelings about parapsychology. Even our own science journals are reluctant to print our research. I'm sure you will agree, however, that great humanitarian strides can be made in this field."

"Oh, I agree," Rudy replied. "Ironically, the situation in America is similar. There is very little positive reporting on parapsychology. Nevertheless, there is my article. I'll have to give you a reprint."

"Thank you. I'll look forward to reading it."

"Come to my room, 307, and I'll give you a copy." They walked up together. Rudy had no intention of sleeping in 307 after seeing what he believed to be the tall Ukrainian assassin, so he decided to make sure the Eurasians knew what his assigned room was. Yet Rudy instinctively connected to Imo as well. Similar in age and interest, they took to each other quickly. They discussed many topics, the subject having changed a number of times. Imo covered techniques of mind-control, the concept of the universal psyche and Jung's theories on the archetypes; Rudy talked about telekinesis and as a change of pace, his crazy ride into Florence.

Imo's eyes gazed beyond Rudy. "I hope she's coming to say hello to me," he said as he smiled at the glowing young lady who walked towards them.

"Chess, this is Dr. Imo Bern, a parapsychologist from Eurasia. Imo, this is the lady I was telling you about, Chessie Barnsworth." Rudy smelled the unmistakable aroma of liquor on Chessie's breath.

"Hello," she said giddily. "Perhaps Dr. Bern would be interested in where I have just been." She looked at Rudy coyly.

"And where might that be?" Rudy inquired. "The Pitti Palace?"

"Nooo, Rudee. Guess again."

"The Major Duomo?" Imo tried.

"The Major Duomo. I get it," Chessie laughed. "No."

"The Uffizi Museum?" Rudy guessed.

"No, silly. I was at a PK party!"

"I am unfamiliar with..." Dr. Bern began.

"As am I, Chess."

"Well, it seems," she began, "that they began in the late 1970s...in reaction to that handsome Israeli psychic, Uri Geller, and his key bending performances."

"Handsome?" Rudy noted.

"Someone had his picture downstairs. Where was I? Oh, yes. I met one man whooo, who worked as a scientist for the Pentagon who claimed to have run over ten, twenty, thirty, fifty of these parties back in the 80s. Everyone gets together on a weekend evening and they all bring old keys, knives, spoons and..."

"Booze?" Rudy interjected.

"Booze. Yes. That's it, booze, and they get drunk...Do I look tipsy, Rude? And everyone shouts Bend! Bend! Bend! Well, we did it!" Chessie giggled as she reached into her handbag and produced a very large thick metal spoon with a very impressive pretzel-like double twist to it. "I can't explain it. The energy suddenly changed in the room, and my spoon became plastic and malley...malley..."

"Malleable?"

"Yes. That's exactly the word I was looking for. Malley-able. I twirled it round and around and around, round, round, round, and then it stopped."

"I'm impressed, young lady. Dr. Bern, what is your professional opinion?"

Imo picked up the spoon and eyed it carefully. Holding it up to the light, he twisted it to get a better view, and then paused for a considerable amount of time to consider his findings. "It looks bent to me," he said.

The three erupted into laughter, and then decided to continue their conversation over dinner.

"La Fontana," Chessie sang out.

"La Fontana?" Rudy asked.

"El restaurante," Imo said in a horrible Italian accent. "I hear it's a delightful establishment..."

"Not far from the hotel," Chessie cut in.

Chessie grabbed them both at the elbows, and led them out of the hotel, where they took a right and turned down a small cobblestone alleyway. Stores were open on both sides including a butcher shop which displayed six entire pigs hanging in its main window, rows of sausages and Italian salamis. They passed a store which specialized in masks and puppets, and then came upon the restaurant.

A debonair maitre de with sleek black hair and penetrating eyes of blue, greeted them with a smile. Guiding the trio gracefully to the back of the small establishment, he sat them amidst a group of hip locals, disappearing and reappearing with menus, a basket of bread and olive oil. Talk drifted from Italian pastry to Eurasian and American home life, sports and Heinreich, Imo's high-jumping brother.

"I've seen him jump, Imo!" Rudy said excitedly. "He's very impressive."

Upon their return, Imo thanked Rudy for the article, shaking his hand vigorously. He congratulated Chessie for her psychokinetic feat, held her hand for a timeless instant and returned to his room to read.

Dr. Bern read about the spiritual teachings of Manu and Baba, 19th century occult tenets on mind power and also the Law of Karma. He read once again that human presence on Earth is proof in and of itself that higher thinking entities exist, and he reviewed some of the studies in life after death.

But then, his conscience erupted as his body began to shake violently, and he knew he had sinned deeply. Imo felt lost and conflicted. Tajik cyborgs and soulful gorilla faces flashed like overbearing holographic images before his mind. He ran to the bathroom to puke in the toilet. Hugging the cold porcelain bowl with both arms for support, he draped his head over the clear water and continued to dry heave for many minutes. Each time a wave came over him acid from his stomach rose towards his palate, its bitterness refueling the nauseous feelings. His chest expanded rapidly. Tears flowed forth. As he washed his mouth and chin by the sink, he had trouble looking at his face in the mirror, he felt so ashamed. The reflected image became blurred and transfigured as a Spockish rendition of Imo, complete with pointy ears and bushy eyebrows, superimposed before his eyes. The floor and ceiling vanished as the young occultist hovered in limbo in harrowing communication with his oversoul. Imo witnessed his past and future lives, each flashing in rapid succession in the mirror. Telepathically, one of them spoke to him. "Murder Madam Grotchka," the being said. It seemed the only way to atone for his sins. With this obsession implanted, Imo found some relief. "Yes, I must do this," he whispered as he slumped down to the tile floor to sleep.

Chessie spoke after Dr. Bern departed. "He looks troubled. What do you think is wrong?"

"His boss is Alexi Patrenko, one of the Russian scientists missing from all the later editions of *Eurasian Parapsychology*."

"I had forgotten about that." She placed a forefinger to her lips reflectively.

"Chess, we are not sleeping here tonight, and tomorrow morning you will take a plane to Dubrovnik. I'll meet you there at the Filipov Hotel, Monday at 3 P.M. sharp."

"But Rudy, I want to hear you speak."

"Chess, I saw the man who tried to kill me, Georgi Boshtov. He may try again even though everything has blown over. Come, we will sleep in an empty room." Rudy took the pillows and propped them under the blankets, shaping them into two sleeping figures. "I know this sounds crazy Chess, but you must do this. Tomorrow morning you leave for Dubrovnik."

"But Rudy, I'm a bit taller than that!" She pointed to one of the dummies under the blanket, as Rudy ushered her out and down to the lobby.

While Chessie charmed the desk clerk, Rudy palmed a key for a room on the fourth floor. He only hoped no one was staying there. Stalking into the strange room, they undid the covers and climbed into bed. There was some trouble sleeping, but finally they succumbed to the night's power.

Rudy awoke about 6 A.M. and darted back downstairs. Quietly, he opened his room, but could not ascertain whether anyone had been there. He thought he heard a bottle move in the bathroom. Slamming the door, he raced back to the fourth floor hideout. No one followed. From the house phone he called Hanley Kranz. It was only 6:15 and Kranz sounded perturbed.

"Dr. Kranz, there is something I think you should know. The murderer of Dr. Jay Ketchembach is in this building, and I think he tried to murder me during the night."

Though tired and annoyed, Kranz came quickly to the hideout, meeting Rudy outside in the hall. After fashioning a weapon from a towel rack, Rudy led the way back down to his assigned room. Quickly, they burst in. The bed was perfectly made, the bathroom in order, the telephone in its proper place. Kranz looked peculiarly at Rudy.

"Ten minutes ago this bed was unmade. Wait a minute, doctor." Rudy removed the set of drawers and turned the cabinet upside-down. Under the left rear leg was a small bugging device. Somehow he knew it would be there.

"How do I know...." Kranz began.

Rudy grabbed the man's mouth shut and spoke as he pointed to the device. "You must move us to another room. Can we stay in 406? I think it is unoccupied....Please do not tell anyone about the change." Rudy motioned to quietly help turn the cabinet back right side-up. Dr. Kranz followed his reasoning.

When they got out into the hall, Rudy told Kranz to come to 406 where Chessie was still asleep. While she dozed, the reporter quietly reviewed the entire chain of events from Patrenko's and Kopensky's names missing from the later editions of *Eurasian Parapsychology*, to the bugging device at Professor Ketchembach's office, to the subway chase, Boshtov's name and description, the Oriental agent that Rudy hit with the croquet mallet, Ketchembach's murder...the entire story. Kranz said it sounded far-fetched, but he would get a security guard posted by 406 for that night.

"What could Dr. Patrenko have discovered that was worth killing for?"

"Dr. Kranz, this is exactly the question only men such as yourself can answer. Patrenko was studying dematerialization and anti-matter, and Kopensky, PK and brain-waves. That's about all I know. As far as I could figure, Ketchembach was killed because he was going to substantiate my findings about the changed names in *Eurasian Parapsychology*. The scientists probably feared that they would become security risks for their stupidity in gaining publicity for work that was strictly top secret."

"Perhaps," Kranz said, "but let's dig a little deeper. Murder is a big move. Granted, Ketchembach was not just any run-of-the-mill parapsychologist."

Rudy interrupted, "He was studying precisely what Patrenko and Kopensky were into."

"That may be. However, I'm not convinced he really was murdered. Certainly it's possible, but let's not get into a paranoia trip here. Could his knowledge have been worthy of murder? Maybe if we go through his notes..." Kranz murmured to himself.

"That big gawky bastard is here. I felt him. I've seen him. Damn it, he didn't chase *you* through the shit and muck of the subways until your lungs almost burst." Rudy was getting perturbed but did not want to alienate himself from his newfound ally. "And why was there an attempt on my life in the first place? I'm no parapsychologist."

"OK. OK. Let's assume you are accurately describing the events as they occurred. Then I would guess that you were hunted for two reasons: One, you were the only other person who knew about the name changes, and, two, you knew Ketchembach's death was not an accident....Now mind you, Styne, I don't know if I believe any of this; I'm just speculating.

"So, if we continue the speculation, we can deduce that some other parapsychologists who also were involved in the same area as Ketchembach may also have been killed ...." Kranz paused as he reflected.

"Dr. Kranz, could you make a list of parapsychologists who would seem to be likely candidates? And include any that may have died unusual deaths within the past, say, fifteen years?"

"Off the bat, I can think of a number of them: Chogyam Trungpa, the Tibetan, he was only 47, cause of death unknown; Gertmann Flatt, parapsychologist, heart attack; Arthur Koestler, author extraordinaire, very strange, double suicide with his wife. Then, of course, there were a number of the old guard, but they were in their 80's. Oh, and of course, Bill Scofield and Bob Atcheson, that was that crazy fire in their lab...."

"Bill and Bob, I remember that. University of Georgia wasn't it?"

"Yes."

"I didn't know they were parapsychologists."

"Well, the press played up the quantum physical angle. They were into hidden variables. Is that enough?"

"No, please go on."

"OK, let's see. There was D. Scott Rogo, summer of 1990; and that was a real shocker. He was only 40, or something like that, and already he had easily over a dozen parapsychology books under his belt. Murdered in his apartment, prime of his life, during a so-called robbery. They supposedly got one of the killers, but as I understand it, the other person, who was probably the mastermind, has not only never been caught, there isn't even a description of him, even though his supposed partner rots in jail. And then of course, there was Allan Churchway, a plane crash, and Itzhak Bentov, another plane crash. But that one's going way back. Jeeze, I guess I'm really dating myself."

"Why is that?"

"Well, that one's gotta be twenty-five, thirty years ago. Seems like yesterday." Kranz stopped, looked down and shook his head before he continued. "Fact of the matter is, it was sometime after Watergate. That bum Nixon, Jesus Christ!...."

"Dr. Kranz," Rudy interrupted. The professor had obviously lost his train of thought. They exchanged glances. "Bentov," Rudy reminded him.

"Oh, yeah, Itzhak Bentov. I remember his jet-black eye-brows. He was important, an Israeli. And, of course his death sticks out in my mind because he died in one of those famous plane crashes that everyone suspected involved foul play. It was in Chicago, maybe 1977, sometime, late 70s, anyway. This crash took some *Playboy* executive and E. Howard Hunt's wife. You know Hunt, Bay of Pigs, JFK, the grassy knoll, Watergate break-in, and all that?"

"But if Hunt's *wife* was the target...so, who's Churchway?"

"Ah," Kranz sighed. "Now there was a brain. This guy could control natural forces, he could astral travel to any point in the solar system, saw the rings of

Jupiter before the spacecraft got there. Churchway, with his enormous head and shock of red hair, major cleft in his chin. What a site when he would go to Wall Street. Made an absolute fortune on the stock market by tuning that incredible brain into the moves of all the greed-is-good guys like Ivan Boesky and Sloan Turner...you know, Michael Douglas?"

"Yeah, I know. The Oliver Stone movie," Rudy responded.

"You got it, but *this* wasn't in any movie! Churchway, was simply fantastic. You should have seen the statues in his apartment! He had one of a boy on a dolphin which was 4,000 years old, though he claimed 40,000. It was really tragic."

"What happened?"

"No one knows. Disappeared without a trace. Most think his plane went down somewhere in Tanzania. He was doing a weather control experiment with an agricultural company."

"Weather control?"

"Churchway was one of those rare individuals who had the ability to recalibrate the forces that control the weather, and he was successful on a number of occasions."

"You're kidding?"

"Not at all. I had seen him control a dirt devil, out on a field at a conference in Oklahoma. That was back in the early 1980s. Other people saw him manifest rain clouds and even generate lightning. The Tanzanians had heard about him, and brought him to Africa with the hopes that he would end a three-year drought. And the drought *did* end after Churchway's visit, but he simply vanished, and was never heard from again."

"And what about Hereward?"

"How could I skip him? I was at the dinner in his honor when he died suddenly of a heart attack, and that was just a few years ago." Kranz paused. "Head fell into the dessert cakes.... His pacemaker was found to be defective." Kranz stopped once more to reflect on the passing of so many parapsychologists. "It was a great tragedy." He gazed at his watch. "Well, maybe you got something, maybe you don't. This conspiracy stuff, and I got a conference to run. Look, I think you'll be all right for now. I've simply got to get some rest."

"Were there any Eurasians present at the dinner?" Rudy ignored Kranz's attempt to leave."

"You mean, Hereward's dinner?"

"Yeah."

"Well," Kranz paused to consider. "Patrenko was there, so was Nicholiev, and Kopensky. But Hereward had already had two heart attacks and with a defective pacemaker...." Kranz began to pace the room in deep contemplation. "Microwaves, of course, it's possible. The Ukrainians had been experimenting with microwaves for years. In fact, one Czech told me about...now what was it...some sort of psychotronic devise that looked like a clump of pencils that the powers-that-be in Minsk have used to zap flies on the wall with...."

Rudy spoke. "And of course there is the periodic bombardment of our Moscow embassy with microwaves. Rumors about health risks and so on."

"Mr. Styne." Kranz stopped pacing as Chessie moaned slightly in her sleep. She seemed to awaken for a second, recognized Rudy's voice, moaned again, and then tumbled back to slumber. "I'm going to share some top secret information, not for your magazine, off the record. Am I understood?"

"Yes."

"There are a number of scientists who believe that the Russians and Ukrainians have decoded the telekinetic formulations for directing psychic energy to any point on the earth. This is all, of course, with no diminution of power over distance."

"Telekinetic formulations?"

"Ultra-dimensional energy fronts in synchrony with special brain-wave patterns that transcend light speed."

"Ultra-dimensional?"

"Hyperspace, man, hyperspace. Don't you know anything?"

"Tachyons?"

"In part. Yeah, if you want, tachyons."

"Please go on."

"Right. There's evidence that Eastern bloc scientists can direct telekinetic effects either through or around the earth; and if this is true, they may also have the capability for transmitting any number of lethal rays."

"I don't think I'm following you."

"I thought you knew something about this field." Kranz sounded exasperated, but he went on. "Just as the body is made up of specific atoms and corresponding energy fields, so are viruses and bacteria."

"What does that have to do with the mind?"

"That is their discovery. The interference juncture from the pre-physical to the material. Once the psionic transformations are understood, such diseases as leukemia and cancer could theoretically be beamed to any point on the globe. Coupled with laser technology, their potential weaponry could make a mockery of conventional warfare. Some of the frequencies include the so-called ELF or extremely low frequencies which are synchronous to brain-wave states and neuro-molecular gestalt patterns. Genetic molecules such as viral RNA, which have crystalline structures that oscillate in resonance to the Earth's magnetic pulse, are also synchronous to these ELF waves. There's a whole host of less vicious psycho-physiological states that could also be affected, like headaches, strokes, even thought patterns."

"What about that bizarre epidemic that wiped 175 people out in that small village in northern Montana?" Rudy asked.

"You mean Scobey's galloping carcinoma?"

"Yeah."

"So, you do know something! And Legionnaires' Disease, AIDS, Marburg filovirus. It's a dirty business, Mr. Styne, and difficult to separate the facts from the crap. That's why a lot of this is top secret. *Capisce?*"

"*Capisco.*"

"I don't really have much more information than I told you, except that valuable documents have been passed to the West which discuss a number of these nefarious studies and concepts. Ketchembach was telling me about it....That's it. Gotta go. If I don't get some sleep before the first meeting, I'm going to be fried by the end of the day. Your talk is at four, I believe?"

A shadow passed under the door as Kranz got up to depart. He rushed to open it. Blocking the hall light stood the massive frame of Georgi Bash. His winged eyebrows and drooping moustache cast a long crescent of blackness onto the floor.

"*Buon giorno,*" he said in an Italian/Russian accent, his feathered appendants bobbing with each word. "How nice to see you again Dr. Kranz." He smoothed his moustache in seeming calm detachment.

"*Buona sera,* Dr. Bash, we were hoping you would arrive." Bash looked at Rudy and smiled.

"You *know* him!" Rudy shouted, waking Chessie with a start. She gasped at the dark presence.

"Of course, this is Dr. Georgi Bash, the great Russo-Ukrainian hypnotherapist."

"*Mólte gràzie,*" Bash responded obsequiously.

"*Prègo,*" Kranz mumbled, as he continued. "Why, he spoke in D.C. just two years ago."

"Why yes," Bash said, echoing Kranz' phraseology, "I seem to have the wrong room. But this was where I was assigned, #406. I had some business on the Finnish border and my plane only arrived a few minutes ago." Bash held out the key. It read 406.

Styne froze. His would-be assassin stood before him, yet protocol dictated that he could do nothing. I should kill him right now, he thought to himself, searching for a weapon in his mind. "I thought your name was Boshtov?" Rudy's eyes bore into the eyes of the Ukrainian.

Bash stepped forward and placed a heavy hand on his shoulder. Rudy slapped it off. He was struck by the magnetic power of the man. "Bash, Boshtov, what's in a name, young man?" Bash curled the ends of his lips upwards, and nodded with his eyes to both men. "Dr. Kranz, I'll have to show you some new healing techniques I picked up in Ethiopia. [He pronounced it, Etopia.] Come, get me another room. This one seems to be occupied. *Buona notte,*" Bash said, as he put his arm around Kranz's shoulder and loped down the hall with him. Rudy was about to run after them, but something stopped him. He locked the door and took Chessie to the shower. She seemed shocked by the tall Ukrainian's presence.

"That was him, Chess! He tried to kill me. That was him."

"Are you sure?"

"Jesus Christ!" Rudy managed in a controlled scream. "Goddamn bastard chased me through half the city, in and out of taxis, through the goddamn shit and piss of the subway trenches. Goddamn it Chess, yes, yes, YES!"

"OK, OK," Chessie said somewhat reluctantly. "He just had such interesting eyes."

"You are going to the airport right now. I'll meet you at the Filipov Hotel in Dubrovnik, Sunday afternoon at 4 P.M. sharp. Stay at another hotel of your own choosing until then." Rudy called a cab, grabbed his laptop and accompanied Chess to the airport. He was determined to get her on board and was even tempted to go himself. Consciousness awakened again and again in Rudy, as he planned in fear and excitement how to handle the swollen ogre, and the other Eurasians as well. By the time Chessie's flight was straightened out, the sun had risen.

Rudy used some of the downtime to search the internet for more information on Allan Churchway. He punched in AskGod.com and the powerful search engine popped into view. He played awhile and then said to Chessie, "I can't find anything on his death."

"Did you punch in obituary?"

"Yes, and death notice, Tanzania, nothing."

"That's strange." Chessie's nimble fingers moved over to the key pad. "There," she said as a photo of Churchway appeared with his shock of red hair, along with a full biography. "Woman's intuition."

"Hmmm," he said as Chess left to wander through the local news-stand. He took this time to read through the information. According to the article, when it came to out-of-body experiences, Churchway never claimed to actually leave his body. What he did claim was that he had the ability to tap the noosphere, or what he called, the Galactic Grid, and shift his consciousness, or point of reference, to any sector of the globe or solar system. He simply thought of himself *as* the galaxy, and then focused into the part of it he knew the best.

"I utilize Mother," Churchway said in a video portion of the site, which was a segment of the Düvid Russkind Show. On the panel with the superpsychic was Sydney Sahl, the satirist, and B.K. Pine, the parapsychologist. The event took place in the late 1980s. "Father Nature is a bit more scary," Churchway said.

"You mean Mother Nature has a husband?" Russkind probed.

"Diana and Thor, that's how they were introduced to me."

"You mix metaphors," Sahl commented.

"You know these entities?" Pine asked.

"Of course. Diana is the god of life and consciousness. Thor controls darker elements, including the weather, disease, war. But the same principles operate."

"And so, you control the weather, by how?" Russkind asked. "By asking Thor?"

"Well, a lot of this is ultra-secret, but, essentially, yes. I contact him and work, in a sense, as a liaison or transducer. As you know, I told you we would have a snow storm in May, and, well, I think the storm speaks for itself."

"I was wondering," Sahl said, "If you could get the Jets to win another Superbowl."

The intercom announced Chessie's flight. Rudy walked her towards her first check-in point. "Chessie, Dr. Coomesberry is talking on Baba at 10:15. Will you be all right? I don't want to miss him. Now get on that plane and I'll see you in a few days."

"Sure, I'll be OK. Good luck tonight and be careful." She held him close, kissed him softly on the lips and turned to her gate.

"RUDEE!" a strange woman called out rushing forward lugging a cumbersome satchel. She was large and awkward, teetering. Instinctively, Rudy and Chessie began to duck and seek refuge as the lady waddled past them. "Dear, you forgot your briefcase." She handed one to her waiting husband who stood close by. Rudy looked at Chessie with a sheepish grin.

* * *

As he rode back to the conference, Rudy contemplated the enemy. Relieved that Chessie would be in another county, he exited the airport and hailed a cab.

What seemed like minutes later, he felt a sharp jarring to his shoulder. "Meester, meester," the cabbie said poking him awake. "Hotel Zanobi."

Rudy looked up. His head was groggy, he had been in a very deep sleep. Momentarily disoriented, he paid the fair, entered the hotel and got directions to the talk.

As he approached the auditorium, he became aware of an eerie quietness. The echo of his footsteps bounded off concrete floors. Heads turned as he passed through the cold clanging doors. "That's Coomesberry's partner," a man whispered. "He's the one who met with the great Baba." Rudy took a nearby seat and looked up at a large poster which was taped to the front of the lectern. It was a flattering picture of himself with the Professor, each on their respective mules near Baba's ashram.

There was a problem with the equipment. The Professor was going to show slides and the projector they were using was on the fritz. Professor Coomesberry took the opportunity to scan the audience and nod to many of the scientists he knew.

Where was Rudy, he thought, when suddenly his eyes caught sight of the faithful friend, prompting his silver-gray moustache to turn up accenting his smile. He nodded hello to the man with whom he had shared so much. Rudy tipped a finger to his eyebrow in return.

As the audience waited for the lecture to continue, some used the opportunity to talk to people sitting next to them, a few jotted notes, and others simply watched the AV man connect another wire.

Imo approached. "May I?"

"Of course," Rudy gestured to the empty seat that was next to him.

"I read your paper last night," the young Eurasian doctor said. "And yes, I agree with the necessity for higher conscious forces above humankind. One of the problems I am working on is the link between neuronal complexity and the nature and substance of these higher forces."

"You mean, for instance, the link between the cerebral cortex, the brainstem and the energy that designed this set up?"

"Yes," Imo said

Upon exit of the AV man, the Professor resumed his lecture. Imo and Rudy continued their conversation in low voices with eyes forward.

"When I went with that chap who just sat down," Professor Coomesberry continued, "through Bhutan, to my meeting with an avatar, I realized for the first time, how ridiculous this world really is. Materialization could not possibly occur. It must be balderdash. That is why I smuggled a metal detector under my coat to Baba's meeting room, so that I could continually record metal readings during the course of the interview."

For security reasons, the Australian had neglected to tell Rudy he had brought the device. He feared that word would get out and some other parapsychologist would publish *Metal Detection Recordings of Alleged Materialization with Sri Baba as Agent* before he did!

"So Professor Coomesberry tells the truth about this guru, Sri Baba? He materializes fruit and honey?"

"Yes," Rudy whispered cautiously.

"I've seen dematerialization and levitation myself, but *creating* something from empty space!" Dr. Bern looked up and away in reflection. "Mr. Rudy Styne, I like your writing."

"Do you know Dr. Alexi Patrenko."

"Of course. He is my overseer."

"Dr. Boshtov?" The journalist was going on instinct.

"Oh, you mean Georgi Bash. All the time," he said, anticipating Rudy's next question. "We are colleagues. I work hand and hand with Dr. Bash in Vladivostok. He's a powerful hypnotist and great healer. He sees me as a protégé."

"I suppose you know he is also a murderer?" Rudy was solemn and direct.

"As a soldier for the state, Dr. Bash has been a hero since the 1960s," Imo countered. "You should thank your lucky stars that you have not had to fight to protect your way of life. Dr. Bash was the first Soviet pilot to successfully invade West Berlin's air space."

The American looked at Imo eye to eye. The man seemed sincere, but looked deeply troubled. "Imo, I hardly know you, but I feel that I know you." Rudy meant what he said.

"I feel it too."

Rudy took out a sheet of paper and wrote: "Bash murdered Professor Ketchembach in New York City and almost killed me." Imo read the note as Styne crumpled and destroyed it. Imo was stunned. He did not know what to do. His immediate impulse was to sock the American in the face. The truth wounded him deeply.

"I'd love you to meet my brother Heinreich." The lights dimmed and darkness engulfed the audience. A chart flashed up onto the screen. It depicted a jagged line representing the amount of metal present in the room with obvious changes in the reading whenever Baba allegedly materialized something.

They tuned back to Coomesberry's voice. "Dressed in orange caftan, Baba displayed the small gold ring on his finger, and another through his left nostril. I wore a belt and had some pocket change," Coomesberry said. "Other men and women present, including a psychic researcher from Malaysia, also had small amounts of coinage or jewelry on them. This created a baseline reading of about one and one half units of metal present. Note the chart."

Coomesberry used a laser pointer to highlight various areas of his diagram as he spoke. "The detector gives an accurate reading for a radius of approximately 15 meters. Baba swirled his right palm in a circular motion. This lasted 1.37 seconds. We can see that the metal detector registered briefly the presence of no metal, and then the baseline reading increased proportionately to the introduction of the gold amulet which Baba allegedly materialized. This occurred again during a second materialization as well, just 12.4 seconds later. I considered the possibility that the machine had actually been momentarily turned off, or that it malfunctioned, perhaps by PK, and this in turn could account for the differences in baseline readings before and after the materializations. However, we had the machine checked out properly and it has never jumped a baseline reading before nor since the experiment." Coomesberry concluded with a slight bow. The crowd gave him a standing ovation, and many walked over to question him further.

Imo turned to Rudy with a surreptitious glance about the room, "Can we go onto the veranda? It's too close here." He seemed to be referring to a man in a trench coat who turned away and exited the room.

"Yes, I've seen him jump. He's quite an athlete." Rudy nodded slyly.

"How'd I do?" Professor Coomesberry had pushed through the crowd to be with his partner.

"Fine," Rudy responded. "I thought you would want to bask in the accolades."

"I was concerned when you weren't here at the beginning of my talk."

"You must be mistaken," Imo said looking at Rudy. He could not accept Rudy's words. *Bash was no cold-blooded murderer. If anyone, Grotchka, maybe. But Patrenko works with humans as well, he thought to himself. So do I.* He turned to Coomesberry. "Professor, you were quite more than 'fine'. You were magnificent." They shook hands vigorously.

The Professor began to rattle on and a small group of interested attendees formed around him. The day went by.

Styne prepared for his "before dinner" speech. He was tempted to tell the group exactly what he felt about Boshtov or Bash, whatever his name was, and about Dr. Patrenko and the other missing scientist from *Eurasian Parapsychology*...and Ketchembach's death. Everything. The more he thought, the more his amygdala became agitated. He would have to use his frontal lobes to fight back the fear. Rudy decided to locate Imo again. Bash would never attempt anything with his protegé around. Where the hell was he?

As he tried to find Imo and ready himself for the impending talk, a glitter caught his eye. It was a reflection of a stage light off a small metal object being held by the bald man. Dr. Patrenko was mixing with other attendees at the far side of the room near stage left. Wanting to get a better look at the device, Rudy inched forward.

Dr. Kranz tapped the microphone. "I am pleased to announce our next speaker, Rudolf Styne, reporter for *Modern Times*. This young writer is quite a rarity among journalists." Kranz paused and smiled. "Ah, there he is," he said as he pointed Rudy out. "He's actually written an article with the word "psionic" in it!" The crowd laughed as Rudy flashed glances with Alexi Patrenko.

Rudy turned and walked up the steps to the podium.

"I am honored to speak before you this afternoon," he began. "I feel a bit ashamed of saying this, but I have only been aware of the word psionic for about three months," he paused, "let alone tachyonic non-local hyper-dimensional psychotronics." The audience chuckled.

"I began this quest after I experienced a dream, part of which consisted of me simply walking across a street. The most amazing thing about it was that I thought I really was walking across a street, and was totally startled to find that I was still in bed.

"After a serious investigation and talks with Shri Baba and leading members of your community, including the late Professor Jay Ketchembach, I have come to the realization that we, as a species, are, no doubt, still in bed.

"Yes, this is a talk about ESP, psychic phenomena, including my own telepathic experience, and the research by such brilliant scientists as B.K. Pine, and Dr. P. Karl. But this is also a discussion of a more difficult aspect, the shadow of man, and how it has infected this little international psychic community."

Rudy planned to ease into the Eurasian angle.

The back doors banged open.

Bash entered with Chessie. Holding hands, they sauntered down the center aisle and sat in the fourth row from the rear. Like an overgrown turkey-vulture, the agent placed a hairy limb about the lady, smiled and looked intently up at the lectern feigning interest in the speech. Overtly reaching into an inside pocket with his free hand, he allowed Rudy to see what looked to be a syringe which he then placed back into its compartment.

Rudy stared back and shifted gears. "Colleagues of yours have died in mysterious ways, as far back as the 1970s, Itzhak Bentov, Israeli researcher, in a plane crash in Chicago, Arthur Koestler and his wife in a supposed double suicide in the 1980s, in the 90s, D. Scott Rogo, one of your most prolific authors, murdered in his apartment, and then a few years after that, a whole slew of deaths-- Allan Churchway, possibly the greatest astral traveler in a century, lost in Africa, body never recovered, Bill & Bob in that strange fire at their university, Gregory Hereward, of a bizarre heart attack at a dinner in his honor, and now, just a few months back, Dr. Jay Ketchembach, colleague of Bohr and Einstein, possibly your greatest credibility booster, run over by a taxi in New York City.

"I met with Professor Ketchembach just a day before he died. He was testing himself on a PK machine in my presence, and his experiments resulted in negative psi. Ladies and gentleman, negative psi. He was picking something up."

Rudy noticed some members of the audience shifting their position, trying to be polite, losing interest. He had diverted from his intended speech, and tried to return to a more positive venue.

"The teachings of your field suggest that each and every human is a microcosm. But, of what? Do I have within me true access to the highest strata? In theory, this sounds great, my connection to the very soul of the universe."

"Religious jumbo," a large poorly-dressed American man called out, as he got up loudly to leave the room. A few others followed.

Rudy's connection with the remaining group had become tenuous. Dr. Patrenko raised a hand. Automatically, the speaker called on him.

"Tell us about your string of psychic experiences. Not all of us have read your article, and as for myself, I'd just like to hear it from, as they say in your country, the mouth of the horse." Alexi spoke in a rich Russian accent.

"Ah, the mouth of the horse," Rudy used the faux pas as a springboard. "How about a pigeon and a rhinoceros on a passenger plane?" The moment lightened. Rudy grabbed back the attention of the audience as he recounted his chance meeting with the magician Fandango. His voice recounted story after story, how Fandango released a living pigeon on the plane while it was in flight, how he read Rudy's mind when he was thinking about a rhinoceros and produced a toy model of one, how, like Abdullah Manu, Fandango could levitate small objects, and how amazing it was to run into Fandango precisely when he had been assigned to interview the man, but his mind stayed glued to Bash, a man who returned a hypnotic stare that caused the room to spin. Rudy felt the Ukrainian was about to leave with his girl. God, she seemed normal, but Styne knew that she was not totally present. The sexy spark that had always been between them was just not there. He tried looking into her eyes, but she would only smile and focus hers about his chest.

"The big question remains," Rudy paused to create eye-contact with as many pairs of eyes as he could, "what is the purpose of man's higher powers? Surely, it is not for mere control over others." He looked at Patrenko, and then found Imo, who sat in the back of the room, transfixed. "We are an expression of higher and more complex activity. Evolution, devolution, reciprocal maintenance. Awareness of the connection to the source, and potential communication with that source. That is the only thing that makes any sense to me."

Staring at Bash, the speaker concluded, "You people out there should remember one thing about parapsychology. There is a world invisible and one beyond. The Law of Karma shall reign. What we do on the planet determines where our vibe must take us afterwards." He pointed directly to Bash, "Remember, you reap what you sow. My girlfriend, Miss Chessie Barnsworth, is asking me to hurry so we can go to dinner. She's sitting with the great hypnotist Dr. Boshtov. I hope he hasn't put her under a spell." Rudy leapt from the stage and trotted to her. The applause was vigorous. Bash stood up to give a standing ovation.

The "phantom leaf" effect.

Dr. Kranz tapped the microphone once more. "The dining area is through the large hall on your left when you exit the auditorium."

Scooping Chessie from Bash's arms without a word, hungry and out of sorts, Rudy found himself walking into the dining room with Professor Coomesberry. Chessie saw Imo, and so, they joined him at a round table, just as Alexi Patrenko and Georgi Bash entered the room with Hanley Kranz.

"Do you mind?" Kranz said, as he brought Patrenko and Bash to the same table.

Rudy did not know what to do. His sense of self was being torn at the seams as mixed feelings of protocol and persona waged war against a more volatile impulse.

"You were great. *Magnifico*," Chessie said. "Doctor Bash was so kind to talk me into coming back. I cannot figure out why I ever wanted to go in the first place." She spoke automatically, with no particular inflection in her voice, even in her use of Italian.

Rudy felt his confidence quiver. Perhaps he had mistaken Bash for someone else. Certainly it was possible. He kept questioning his relationship to the chase in the subway with the man who sat across from him now so calmly sipping tea. Finally, Rudy grabbed Chessie's arm and started to walk out.

She said loudly, "Don't be rude! We have come to eat dinner. *Mangiare*."

It was not at all like her. The vulture just smiled. Rudy sat back down, watching, as if it were a dream. Chessie had been loud and some of the other scientists had stared at them. He decided it was best to take things slowly with her. At the moment he was safe, but his eyes kept returning to Bash, double and triple checking. Was it him?? It must be him. He began to rub Chessie's hand under the table to bring her back to reality. He could visualize Bash staring at him from the church steps at Ketchembach's funeral. If I leave now, he thought, that bastard sorcerer would win.

Drawn to the power of this primordial moment, the reporter remained seated. He was curious as well. It was a unique opportunity to see the assassin up close. Primitive instincts pulled the city man in many directions as he watched Bash's awkward and gnarled hands lie passively by his plate. The reporter also noticed beads of sweat manifesting in equidistant droplets upon Dr. Patrenko's bald head, as the scientist kept patting them with a grimy handkerchief while he talked with Professor Coomesberry about the Ukrainian psychic Nubea Lanilov.

Rudy shot a question at Bash, "Dr. Boshtov," his eyes beginning to glare with hate, "I hear you are part of Bonzo's secret police force."

Dr. Kranz, who had been roaming the tables, arrived in time to hear the question. "Mr. Styne, that question is out of line."

"It's all right," Bash replied.

Imo was becoming uncomfortable with the turn of the conversation. He knew, of course, that Bash was connected to Bonzovalivitch, but he didn't know to what extent. He began to think of that envelope taped to the inside of Bash's private desk drawer, crossing eyes with Bash for an instant, before looking away. His mind returned to Styne's question. The names on the envelope, Hereward, Ketchembach, Kranz? Kranz? Did his name have stars by it also? Imo had assumed that these names were starred because these men were already dead....

Bash on the other hand, enjoyed the question. The more emotion he elicited from Rudy, the better. Patrenko looked worried. The table stopped all chatter to hear Bash's response.

"Do you think Foster Pullman was involved in the Kennedy assassination?" Bash rebounded coolly. "There is plenty of evidence linking his group with Savak, you know, the old torture crew of the former Shah of Iran."

What does that have to do with my question, Rudy thought. Pullman? Oh yes, former head of the CIA and ambassador to Iran. "Certainly one has to be a killer to be in a Secret Service," Rudy said icily. He was vigorously rubbing Chessie's hand under the table. She heard his words and began slowly to return to her senses. "I ask again, Dr. Boshtov, are you in the employ of Bonzo's secret service?"

Imo looked at Patrenko, whose expression was intense and disquieting. Coomesberry showed great interest, Kranz, intense concern. Chessie seemed oblivious.

"Petar Bonzovalivitch does not need secrecy to achieve his aims. The world knows that he has the support of the Russian people, and that it will only be a short time before they rally around him as we rebuild our empire."

Dr. Kranz tried to change the subject to Bash's talk for the night. Bash murmured, "You're still here?" His voice was almost nonchalant. Patrenko wanted to excuse himself and started to get up. He accidentally dropped a knife on the floor, his shirt soaked at the armpits in sweat. "Alexi," Bash said, "didn't you meet Oswald when he was in Moscow?"

Patrenko replied in monotone, "I was called in as a graduate student intern under the consulting psychiatrist, Dr. Grinkov. We diagnosed Lee Harvey Oswald borderline psychotic with hostile tendencies, and Grinkov recommended immediate deportation." He turned to Kranz.

Imo thought he saw tears in Patrenko's eyes. He was definitely going to eliminate Madam Grotchka when they returned to Yakutski. It would be the only way he could make peace with God and himself.

Bash spoke, "Back in the early 1960s I joined the KGB as a consultant in hypnosis."

"I recommended Dr. Bash to the Kremlin," Patrenko added. "It occurred to me from the start that Oswald might have been under hypnotic command from a right-wing faction of our own military." He dabbed his cranium more vigorously with the dampened handkerchief. "Fortunately, that speculation has been proven wrong."

Bash continued looking directly at Rudy. "Pullman had his top field agents trained in trance techniques and psionic practices you people naively call voodoo. The CIA deployed hypnosis many times to commit murder. I was called in as a consultant by my people. At the time, we thought Oswald was sent to commit high-level assassination in our country. How ironic!" Bash smiled and turned to all who listened.

"How about your secret service? Do they also use hypnosis for murder, such as for inciting mass suicide to rebuild a crumbling empire?" Rudy sliced.

"Deus Maxima was a misguided zealot." Bash kept a quiet tone. "If only we were that powerful. Yours is the government that coined the phrase Executive Action."

"Executive action?" Coomesberry chimed in.

"Assassination by order from the top," Kranz told him.

As the conversation continued, Rudy mentally began shouting to Chessie to wake up. She gripped his hand. It was a sign, but she was surfacing too slowly.

The gawking figure settled on its prey. He smiled at Rudy and continued. "You have lone gunman shooting presidents, presidential candidates, a civil rights leader, a talk show host and rock stars. You have bands of fanatics bombing federal buildings, mailing out biological poison pen letters, attacking civilian airports. You have other elements taking using commercial airplanes as guided missiles, or spreading auto-immune diseases to your own gay community or even attempting to wipe out whole civilizations on other continents. You think all this is coincidence?" Bash inquired, his eyebrows bobbing with each point made.

The sorcerer began twiddling a spoon with his long bony fingers. "Your government has plotted deaths in Cuba, Latin America, South East Asia, Africa, Europe, the Middle East and even in your own Waco, Texas and Ruby Ridge. In fact, your own covert forces, just recently, have knocked off at least two U.S. senators in rigged airplane crashes, and the same group has created wars in Serbia, Afghanistan, and Iraq. I admit, we Russians have had our own troubles in Moscow, Chechnya and Odessa, but we are in the midst of cultural revolution, not master plans to set up military and propaganda bases in Moslem territory abroad, and create hypnotically trained assassins to reshape local political policy at home. The evidence is overwhelming, wouldn't you say? Take the Middle East. Who do you think trained the Libyan terrorists who bombed those American planes? Who initially armed bin Laden, and gave anthrax to Saddam Hussein? How do you think the terror organizations you now target learned to use suicide bombers and mass hypnosis? And who do you think initially armed and trained Iraq's elite Republican Guard? So, to get back to Oswald, sure, he was a double agent. That's why we kicked him out of Russia. And then with Kennedy's death, it was your government that almost caused World War III, blaming us for your misdeeds."

Rudy was losing his cool. He could not let Bash get to his emotions like this. Kranz was quite uneasy, as were Patrenko and Bern. The mystic held firm, but Coomesberry moved into the conversation. "Are you saying that the killers of John and Robert Kennedy, Martin Luther King, George Wallace and John Lennon were under hypnotic trances, sir?"

"You certainly know a lot for an Australian," Bash said, "even if Wallace didn't die. Mr. Styne's countrymen should know better than I. Just ask Oliver Stone, or better yet, go see *Manchurian Candidate*," he added with a guffaw.

While looking directly at Rudy, he continued answering Coomesberry. "Certainly they all died at opportune moments and for political reasons. For instance, knocking Robert Kennedy out of the race for the presidency assured victory for Richard Nixon in his first election, and the shooting of Wallace assured his victory in the second election. It is well known that Nixon was a man obsessed for over a decade with trying to assassinate our ally, Fidel Castro. And then he created a virtual league of assassins under code name Project Phoenix in Vietnam, and look more recently at the assassinations in Serbia, Venezuela, Columbia and Iraq.

"Note, also, how easily the lone assassins were caught in America. All were listed as undesirables in your CIA files. And all had unusual mental problems. My guess is, yes, they were each hypnotized by covert agents well trained in their profession... factions of your American government, Dr. Styne." Bash stuck a pinky into his left ear and twirled it. "Even the Beatle, George Harrison, was stabbed for the same reason, to intimidate and control the masses."

"Fascinating," Coomesberry exclaimed.

"Diabolical," Bash added.

"Could you demonstrate hypnosis for us?" Coomesberry asked.

Bash stared at the small ball of wax he had just dislodged. "I thought you would never ask." He turned to Chessie. "Young lady, would you agree to accompany me for a demonstration of my powers?" The gawky doctor smiled as best he could.

"Not on your life," Rudy almost shouted.

"Why yes, I'd love to." Her voice sounded almost normal.

"No," Rudy held her firm, answering tightly between clenched teeth. He kept her pinned to the seat.

Imo spoke, "I'll volunteer." He stood up to move over.

"Now, Dr. Bern, they'll think we are in, how you say, cahoots. Professor Coomesberry?" Bash asked.

"Absolutely! What fun, what what?"

Scooting through the tables, Dr. Kranz ran up to the stage and grabbed the microphone. "Ladies and Gentlemen. Ladies and Gentlemen! May I have your attention! Dr. Georgi Bash has consented to demonstrate hypnosis for us."

The audience broke out into enthusiastic applause.

Bash walked to the front. His movements seemed almost magical, an aura of dark blue/black glimmering about him. All talk ceased, as the overpowering figure reached center stage. Every gesture, although exaggerated, was gracefully macabre, self-assured, commanding. Coomesberry dutifully followed. Rasputin reincarnate turned to his subject and suddenly snapped his fingers, "Sleep!" he commanded. The Professor collapsed onto the cold stage floor like a time-lapse sequence of a shrinking violet. Chessie dropped as well, as did three other people from the tables. Bash turned to the audience, pulled unconsciously at his crotch, and cocked his head. The crowd gasped.

"You are in a deep sleep," Bash said to Coomesberry.

Summoning his strength, Rudy lifted Chessie into his arms. She was still asleep, and he carried her out amidst chuckles from some of the crowd. Bash nodded to Patrenko who got up to leave, and Imo followed.

Rudy carried Chessie quickly into the ladies' room. He looked upon his lady, her eyes delicately closed. Taking a cup from a Dixie dispenser, he doused her face. "Come on, come on, wake up," he said in a hoarse whisper. He undid the top of her blouse and rubbed cold water between her breasts. Her skin felt warm and smooth to his cool hands. It was strange, but he desperately wanted to witness the end of the performance. *Why should I give a shit?* he thought. "Hurry up, Chess, come to!" He slapped her briskly on the cheek. She awoke in a jerk.

"Where am I? Did you hit me?" She rubbed her reddened cheek.

"Hey, Peabrain," he said. "Bash hypnotized you."

"He, what? That's ridiculous."

"Then why aren't you in Dubrovnik?"

"What do you mean? I came here to see you speak."

"Rudy reached into his jacket pocket and removed an itinerary he had taken from the airport."

"What's that?"

"You have a choice, Chess. You can trust me, or you can trust Bash. Which is it going to be?"

"Hotel Filipov?" she said, meekly.

"Yes. Now, give me a kiss. We are going to go back in there. Can you handle it? Do not look at him and always hold my hand. Remember who you are. Keep saying, 'Chessie, I'm Chessie, Rudy's girl. I will not be hypnotized.'"

"But, suppose I don't want to be Rudy's girl?"

"Ah, that's better. Now, let's get in there."

They walked back into the auditorium. Rigid as a board, Professor Coomesberry lay suspended between two chairs, and Bash, now in stocking feet, was standing on his chest, hands uplifted, the air electric, his King Kong eyes glaring.

"Rise, rise," Bash commanded and two hypnotized subjects from the audience stood and came forward. One was Dr. P. Karl, the other a man Rudy did not know.

"Too bizarre," Rudy said to Chessie. "We are leaving tonight, with a police escort." She had dropped back into a slight trance. "Hotel Filipov," Rudy whispered.

"Hotel Filipov," Chessie replied. "I'm sorry. I'm Rudy, Chessie's girl. I won't be hypnotized."

"That's better," Rudy said. "Only I'm Rudy. You're Chessie."

"That's what I said. You're Chessie's guy."

"Um hmmm."

The two scientists had reached the stage by now, both walking like zombies. Carefully stepping down off of Professor Coomesberry, Bash turned to them and spoke, "When I say the word 'moon'," he said to Dr. Karl, "you will become an elephant. And when I say the word 'dream'," he continued, turning to the other subject, "you will become a gorilla. The word 'dinner' will bring you both to consciousness.

"Sleep!" he commanded. Both men slunk to the floor, but were helped back up. They stood there immobile like Easter Island monuments. Removing a long thin needle from a vest pocket, the sorcerer proceeded to plunge it, with great authority, through the cheeks of each man. If he had a thread he could have sewn them together. With energetic spunk, Bash placed their hands like two slices of bread and drove the needle through the top of one and out the bottom of the other. Holding the nailed-together palms up to the audience, he glared in egocentric ecstasy demanding his applause. Swiftly the thin spike was removed, and a command was whispered in their ears. Bash then returned to Professor Coomesberry who had remained rigidly suspended throughout the performance.

"Well, I guess it's time for dinner," Bash said enunciating the last word. The two men awoke somewhat befuddled. Puzzled as to how they had gotten to the stage amidst a few snickers, they made their way hesitantly back to their seats. "By the way," Bash went on, "does anyone know what night is the full moon?"

Dr. Karl got up, hunched his back and walked on three limbs, dangling his free arm in front of his face as if it were a trunk. His sense of concentration and purpose rang true. The audience began to laugh nervously. They had great respect for this famous neurologist, and did not really know how to respond.

"What do you think of that?" Bash called out to the other man.

"He looks ridiculous."

"Yes, he does," Bash agreed. "It seems almost as if it were a dream."

With that, the other man jerked his body into gorilla shape, made two fists, expanded his chest and started beating it rhythmically. Eyes glaring, on bowed legs, the man/gorilla pounded his way down the aisle posturing as if to protect his territory, threatening as if he was going to attack. Dr. Karl roared like an elephant, as the two continued their strange duet. "Dinner!" Bash said again, and the men clicked back to their previous "normal" realities. "Moon, dream," Bash repeated and the men returned to their animal modes. Bash repeated this sequence three more times before ending his show.

Rudy was struck by the ultimate belief these subjects had in the roles Bash had chosen for them. Karl was not a man playing an elephant. He *was* an elephant; the other scientist *was* a gorilla. There was no room for doubt. The group was astounded.

Bash helped Professor Coomesberry off the chair and brought him back to consciousness. "So, mate, when are you going to hypnotize me?" Coomesberry asked straightforwardly. He had no memory of the entire episode.

"Perhaps another time. You are just too difficult to put under, Professor," Bash concluded to the delight of the audience.

"Well, I thought as much," Coomesberry grumbled half to himself, as he dusted off his jacket and returned to his seat.

"Incredible, incredible," Kranz repeated over the thunderous round of applause. "I saw you two leave," he said to Rudy and Chessie. "I'm so glad you are all right, Miss Barnsworth."

"Thank you. I am fine, Dr. Kranz."

"Splendid! I'm so pleased that you did not miss this extraordinary demonstration. This could be the last time in one's life to witness such a performance."

"I'm all right, I'm all right," Chessie repeated in a whisper as Bash glided back to the table.

"May I see your needle," Rudy queried. He wanted to put it through the bastard's heart. Gad, what a performance. The sorcerer handed it over. Rudy took it between both hands and snapped it in two.

"I have others, Mr. Styne."

Dr. Kranz had stepped up to the microphone by now in order to quiet the audience for the rest of the evening's events. Dr.'s Patrenko and Bern watched from the back of the room.

"Alexi, you don't appear quite yourself."

"I'm fine, Imo," Patrenko lied. "I only hope that the Styne boy and his girlfriend will be all right."

"Come, you look like you need to sit," Imo said.

"No, I think it better that I..."

Bash interrupted. "Ah, Alexi, Dr. Bern, come, come. Things are just starting to warm up." With that, Georgi Bash coaxed Patrenko and Bern back to their seats.

Rudy summoned his courage. "Dr. Patrenko, would you happen to know why your name is missing from all editions of Hereward's text *Eurasian Parapsychology* except for the first edition?"

Imo turned to look at his colleague, as Patrenko responded. "I wouldn't know. I haven't read the book."

From the podium, Dr. Kranz took over the microphone, "To end the events of this evening," he began, as people continued to talk at their seats. He waited, and when he got the attention of the crowd, continued. "Although, ladies and gentlemen, it will be impossible to top the performance we have just seen, we have compiled some beautiful Kirlian slides from Great Britain, America, Czechoslovakia, Russia, the Ukraine, and Uzbekistan. And after the Powerpoint presentation we will demonstrate the Kirlian technique."

A large white screen lowered from the ceiling and the lights dimmed. Psychedelic pictures of leaves, finger tips, coins and metals were displayed from a projector positioned at the rear. "By sending a high electrical frequency through the objects," Dr. Kranz explained, "we can see these beautiful auras thereupon displayed. Note that every specimen radiates its own particular luminescent blueprint.

"And this is the famous phantom leaf," Kranz said, walking over to the screen and indicating with his finger. With a portion of his face in the spotlight, a ghostly Kranz pointed to the electrical outline of where the physical leaf had been clipped. "Although an electrified aura of the entire leaf is present, part of the leaf has actually been cut away." The crowd could clearly see the aura continue its outline around the empty space where the cut-out section of the leaf used to be.

"This proves the theory that a non-physical energy-body separate from the physical leaf exits. Although part of the physical leaf is missing, the code for the entire leaf remains."

Kranz changed the slide and displayed another phantom. "And here again the whole aura is present even though part of the leaf is gone! This technique supports the theory that a holographic-like representation is inherent in the non-physical, or bioelectrical structure of the leaf. Here are some more phantoms."

Kranz flashed a number of similar slides, and then went on to display Kirlian photographs of the hands and fingers of diseased patients and psychic healers. One image clearly depicted a beam of psychic energy spurting from the finger of a psychic healer. "Now, we look at the weak aura of the diseased person before the healing and after. Notice how his aura becomes much brighter."

"This is amazing," Chessie commented.

"Yes, it is," Imo concurred.

"OK," Kranz continued, "now I'll try to make a normal Kirlian picture of my own hand and then one in meditation. If I'm lucky, the aura should be brighter in the second photo."

Dr. Kranz placed his hand into a developing bag, plugged in the Kirlian device and turned it on. "There is absolutely no pain. I don't even feel it. It will take about 15 seconds to develop the film. There." Dr. Kranz displayed a normal Kirlian photograph of his fingertips encircled by a modest sized electrical corona.

"Now, I shall meditate, and try to raise my energy level. Please give me a moment." Dr. Kranz closed his eyes and stood quietly in meditation for about thirty seconds. Imo watched a bead of sweat roll down the forehead of Dr. Patrenko and suspend itself at the tip of his nose. "OK, I think I am ready," Dr. Kranz said quietly. Gently he placed his hand back into the lightproof pouch and turned the device on.

"**aaaaaaoo ooo O O O hhh HHHHHHHHHH H H H H!**" the parapsychologist cried. Soul-wrenching shrieks erupted as the lights in the room dimmed. With the bag exploding in sparks of orange and green, and the hair on Kranz's head standing on end, he twisted and sputtered in excruciating display. Fighting to maintain himself, the man crumbled to the ground writhing. Shimmering as he fell, flashing bursts issued from his nostrils and ear holes before he expired, his charred hand still seared to the flaming pouch. Two men rushed forward. One grabbed the cord and yanked it from the outlet, flicking his hand quickly to shake off the pain. Kranz's eyes were frozen open, his hair still extended, as he lay on the stage floor smoldering. The room smelled of burning flesh. And then, almost as an after thought, his whole body jerked once again, as it released his life-force towards dimensions unknown.

"**MURDERER, M U R D E R E R ! ! !**" Rudy screamed. Lurching across the table, he knocked it on top of Bash, and grabbed him by the throat, pinning the Ukrainian's arms underneath. Rudy's thumbs dug deep into the agent's neck, ripping into flesh, inching towards the Adam's apple as Bash struggled to free himself from the table. Possessed fingers dug still deeper, as Bash got weaker. Professor Coomesberry and Dr. Patrenko grabbed Styne's head and hands, and tried to pull him off, prying each finger, one by one, from the sorcerer's throat until they finally freed him.

Having almost fainted from the pain and shock, Bash slowly climbed out from under the table. Yet, like a caged beast, Rudy lurched again for one more attack. "Murderer," Styne repeated as his eyes circled the room, and rested for an instant on Imo's.

Bash lifted his foot so swiftly that no one had time to stop him. It caught Rudy on the side of the head and sent him back into the tables behind, taking Patrenko and Coomesberry with him.

"I would say you deserved that, old man," Coomesberry commented, brushing himself off as he rose. "Accidents happen, mate."

With a hand from Imo, Patrenko arose and walked over to their leader to help him towards the exit. Still quite weak, Bash staggered slowly towards the door.

Rudy's face was scraped, but the kick had been off center; he was fully awake. Grabbing a steak knife that had fallen beside him, leaping back to his feet, Rudy barreled over chairs and tables, as he catapulted his body onto the wobbling threesome. Bash turned with raised forearm in time to deflect the lethal course of the descending weapon. Still, it landed deep into his shoulder, tearing into tendons and flesh as it sliced towards bone. With wounded fist, the magi caught his assailant on the chin, flipping Rudy backwards, but the blade remained. Gobs of blood spewed forth as four men grappled with the American, pinning him to the ground until the police arrived.

While the doctors tended to Bash's wound, Rudy, crazed with anger, was taken from the room by four law officers. He tried to regain some sense of self as he was handcuffed and escorted outside. Lined up along the hotel were two police cars and a paddy wagon. Rudy was placed in the wagon. As a procession with lights flashing, the vehicles pulled out and headed for the precinct. It was then that it dawned on him that Chessie was by herself somewhere.

"Officer, my girlfriend is *solo,*" he said quietly. "I know you think I'm *crazy-loco,* but that Russian electrocuted Dr. Kranz. *Non capisco* how he did it, but he did do it. And he could kill Chessie as well. Morté Chessie!"

"*Silenzio!*"

"Per favore, you must help me. Bash, the man I stabbed, is dangerous, *molto* dangerous. *Il mio ragazzo solo. Per favor,* she is all alone."

The officer sitting beside Rudy looked him over, and then took out a cell phone. "We - send - for - her," he said in broken English.

"Gracia."

The van slashed its way to prison in a blinding thunder shower. Ineffectual windshield wipers mushed the view and served to magnify the lights of oncoming traffic as a barrage of hail pelted the roof in pinging cacophony.

Rudy felt an odd sense of security there in the van with the heat on, next to two armed guards, with his wrists cuffed together. *It was good to have someone else drive in this weather,* he thought. *Will Chess be safe? That bastard.* Rudy looked down at his shackled hands. They were stained with Eurasian blood. *My God, I almost killed a man. Such emotions. I could kill him now....* And then it began to dawn on the journalist that he could go to jail for years over this. *That bastard.*

The vehicle stopped and the guards marched Styne into the front office of the precinct. There, they removed his wallet and belt, checked his rectum for hidden weapons and ushered him down into a dimly lit hall, shoving him into a dark, dank cell. Just a toilet, a cold metal bed, damp and sticky unwashed blanket, and an impenetrable pervasive metal grill. Rudy felt insignificant, trapped. The bars seemed to move closer together, and he thought for an instant that he might go crazy. He wanted to escape, to pick the lock or squeak between the bars and flee. He felt "loco," as if he was going to lose it completely. Shaking terribly, he thought, I've only been jailed for two hours. How do the criminals make it? Make it, make it....Oh, my God, oh, Chessie....Rudy kicked the cover off with his foot to lay down limply on the bare hard bunk. Draping his jacket over himself for protection, and laying his head on an arm, he tried to fall asleep. The storm continued to bombard his brain. He could not bear to have that horrible stained blanket near him.

THE RUSSIAN FLU

Imo dressed Dr. Bash's wound and wrapped it securely in sheets of gauze. Bash was conscious but had lost a lot of blood. "Did you see Kranz fry," he chuckled beneath the pain.

"Shut up," Patrenko said.

"Then it's true!" Imo blurted out.

Patrenko retorted quickly, "Don't be a fool."

Bash suddenly perked up, glaring with the primeval intensity of the shaman master.

Imo retreated as Patrenko continued the offensive. "You know we are at war," Patrenko said. "It's covert, to be sure, but, we've gone through it with you. Don't be naïve, the Americans have their own cadre as well. That is what Dr. Bash was trying to tell you at dinner. This man before you is a great patriot. He flew over forty missions into Vietnam and West Berlin before you were even born."

"I've exterminated two American double agents just this past year." Bash added quietly. "Dr. Bern, do not live in a vacuum. Our work makes Russia strong. Gain some perspective. The Americans are war-mongers." Although weak and in anguish, Bash seemed to pick up steam as he continued, "They, and when I say they, I mean the ones that really are in power, are out to destroy us. Do you know that your Dr. Karl, who you were talking to, was a great supporter of Senator Joseph McCarthy, that anti-Soviet zealot from the 1950s? We are still recovering from injuries suffered because of his campaign to wipe us off the face of the Earth. Dr. Karl actually toured with him, getting him votes throughout his home state of Wisconsin, and preaching against the Red Plague! They liken us to rats! And Kranz, who seemed so liberal, he'd tell you right out, he voted for Presidents Kennedy and Johnson, the men most responsible for building a war against our allies, blocking our route to Southeast Asia. Kranz has lived in Thailand and Spain and spent nine months in South Vietnam. Who knows what he did there."

"And Professor Ketchembach?" Imo asked, playing his hand with the rhythm of the moment.

"Goddamn Jew. Trying to stir up trouble with refusniks in our country, pressuring the United Nations to meddle in our internal affairs. Dr. Patrenko can tell you about him and his remote viewing of our old Soviet military bases. He's the one who probably found Yakutski for the Americans in the first place. I've had enough," he gasped. "I must rest. Now get out, and don't come back. We will fly tomorrow morning. Get the plane ready."

"Imo," Patrenko said as he closed the door on the ailing Bash, "Ketchembach was on to us. He had ties with the CIA and FBI going back twenty years. He was their pipeline to our most secret psionic endeavors. He left us little choice. Ketchembach was preparing dossiers on our laboratories....And Imo, he was close to cracking the EEG PK code that took us so long to find. I don't like this anymore than you, but we must face reality for what it is."

"For what we are, Alexi? I'm tired. I'm going back to my room."

"Do you want me to stay with you? You know I have wanted to tell you all about our operations, but only when you became ready. We are soldiers as well as scientists."

"No," Imo retreated quickly so that Dr. Patrenko would not see his tears. Bursting into primal pain, he shut the door behind him, and broke down by the inside wall. He cried for his lost innocence, and for the death of Kranz, and the blood of Rasputin's legacy. He cried for the suppressed jealousy he had for his brother Heinreich, and for his love for him... and for Heinreich's children. He cried for the children he would never have, the ones that would call him in the night when he was alone. Frantically, he tore his way through his luggage to read once again Rudy's article, turning to the passage about Sri Baba:

> I asked Baba about black magic and this was his reply: "You see evil as terrible, and rightly this is so; but the Holy One works in strange ways. And the Law of Karma, action and reaction, shall rule. Transformation on Earth is like transformation of one's soul at death. They are one and the same, separated only by octaves or dimensions. God has given man the capacity to change, that is, he has given him free will. If he gave it, he cannot take it away, or he limits his own freedom. Do you see? But man misuses his will. Evil is ignorance of higher laws...."

Through tears and sobs, Imo re-read the conclusion:

> The real mystery is not in these psychic abilities, but in the force that created them. Consciousness is but a shadow in man.

Imo had to find Chessie and get her to safety. There was no telling what Bash might do. He went to the door and opened it slightly, and then crept out past the elevator to the stairway, making his way to room 406. He paused and knocked. Chessie was quietly weeping; Professor Coomesberry and a police guard were by her side.

"What do you want, mate?" the professor asked.

"I came to see if the young lady is all right. Can I come in?"

The guard barred the threshold. "Get away," he said.

"No," Chessie interrupted, "I'll see him."

"May we have some privacy?" Imo asked.

"I'm afraid that is impossible," the guard explained.

"How is Dr. Bash?" Coomesberry inquired. "That was a nasty wound, what."

"He is well, considering. How are you, young lady? Your boyfriend is quite an emotional type. I came to return his article."

"You may keep it if you like," she said, managing a smile.

"No, here, take it." He smoothed out the wrinkles and handed it to her. "I'm sorry for you." Leaning over, Imo kissed her on the forehead, allowing his lips to linger perhaps a bit longer than he had anticipated. He started for the door and reached for the handle, turning to say, "Maybe I will keep a reprint."

"Here," she handed him back the article.

"Do you have another? I already read that one."

"Oh," she said somewhat puzzled. Their eyes clung, two souls entwining, and then his eyes dropped to the article he had returned. Scribbled in pencil she read, "All will be revealed!"

That night, Chessie prayed to God. It had been the first time she had spoken to Him in twenty-five years. Kneeling by the bed, she clasped her hands...then climbed back in and drifted into slumber.

* * *

Imo had trouble facing the night. Slipping out of the sheets, he tip-toed down the long cold corridor of the sleeping hotel, and stepped into a phone booth. He could not risk using his cell. There, he dialed a number his brother had given him. The name was Marcel, the country, France.

"Marcel," he whispered, "it's Imo Bern, Heinreich's brother. Do you know where he is?"

"He's in Munich. I'll give you his phone number."

Imo dialed. It always amazed him that no matter where his brother traveled, he was only a phone call away. The mystery of how electricity could transfer the voice instantaneously to any point on the globe almost made him choose engineering over the medical profession. Now, a good part of him wished he had. He waited impatiently, counting each ring. Heinreich picked up after two.

"Heinreich," he said.

"Are you OK?"

"I feel like my brain is dissolving. I'm losing," there was a long pause, "contact."

"Contact?"

"With...with who I am."

"You're my kid brother."

"I must see you."

"Come to Japan. I'll be at a track meet there in four days."

"Four days! My God, Heinreich, I'm not sure I can make it."

"Hold on until then, Uncle MooMoo. I'm sure you can get a weekend off if you ask."

"Four days can be a lifetime, Hein."

"I know. I know."

Imo hung up the phone with a dull click. Cold sweat had permeated his night clothes, causing them to stick about his arm-pits and the small of his back. He scurried to his room to curl once again into the depths.

* * *

Hanley Kranz's wife, Eleanor, who was in Sacramento at the time, wrote down her dream that following morning because it was so unusual.

She saw her husband flying above the tables of a dining room, while peering down at a mirror-image of himself, melting like a candle. He hovered for a while, trying to figure out just where he was, watching his own death and the ensuing fight in perplexed detachment. "I'm not ready to die," he told his wife, "but my brain is too fried." She saw Professor Jay Ketchembach, whom she had known socially through her husband, and Hanley's grandmother trying together to coax him into the astral planes. It took what seemed to be half the night to convince him that he was indeed dead. "My dear, my kids... Honey, tell them I will miss them," Kranz said.

With that, Ketchembach seemed to dissolve as Kranz turned to face his wife. She saw him walk up the stairs to greet her, and then he took her in his arms and walked her to a couch where they sat, as they always did in the sunlight. "My work now, my dearest," Kranz said, "is not over. It will involve interfacing between the dead and the living. I have known for years that many on the Earth are really reincarnations of former selves from previous times in history, but others, as we are now learning, have come from different solar systems and galaxies." Kranz reached over and wrapped his arms around his wife and wiped away her tears. "Eleanor, my love, you must be brave."

Mrs. Kranz had guessed some of the dialogue, upon awakening, as she scribbled the dream in a notebook, but the message was clear. The following morning she received confirmation when the Italian consulate called to notify her.

* * *

In the morning, the policeman took Chessie to the house of correction. At the same time, as Dr. Bash busily unwrapped his bandages, Imo stared on in wonderment at the well-healed shoulder. Dressing the wound once more, and helping Bash as best he could, Imo also knew his allegiances had changed. His fate was sealed. He felt deep commitment to help Chessie and Rudy to avenge the deaths of Dr. Kranz and the others, in whatever way he could. He had already planned the execution of Madam Grotchka, but he now knew that it was Bash who was the real source of evil. No longer torn with conflict, he now understood, and decided to write down all he knew, and release the information to the West. *I've got to get hold of Bash's envelope in Vladivostok,* he thought, as soon as he left Bash's sight, *and then get it to Heinreich, or to one of his contacts.*

Alexi came out to the corridor to join him. "I now see you are right," Imo said. "We are at war."

Rudy was in a waiting room when Chess arrived. He was talking to Dr. Karl and the man in the trench coat he had seen with Imo. It was an American CIA agent, Paul Templar. He motioned for Chessie to stay back. Dr. Karl spoke. "I need a hell of a lot more evidence than a misprint in a book and a few coincidental deaths."

"Doctor, why is it that you don't believe me when I tell you that Bash chased me eight blocks through a subway tunnel?"

"It's not that I don't believe you. I do believe that you think it was Bash. You simply have been mistaken. You have to understand, I've known Dr. Bash at these kinds of conferences for years."

"Professor Karl," the agent spoke, "don't be an idiot. Although, we are not yet able to prove that the Kirlian device was tampered with, we have been watching this Bash, or Boshtov fellow, for nearly a decade. He flies to the United States frequently for no apparent purpose, and some of those flights have correlated with strange deaths of scientists or politicians."

"But..." Dr. Karl tried.

"Look sir," Templar continued, "if it squawks like a duck...." Dr. Karl stood there dumbfounded, so the agent went on. "To put it bluntly, we believe that you and two or three other scientists here at the conference may have been targets as well. Thus, we at the Agency want you to publish all the information you have on brain-waves and telekinesis. If you die suddenly, it will be because of what you have not shared with the world."

Templar turned to Rudy, "Mr. Styne, you, of course, are also in danger, but more because of your power as a journalist than because of your scientific expertise. We would like to change your apartment. We have agents in New York who will keep you under surveillance. Bash will not stay here to press charges, so you will probably be released. We are suggesting that your girlfriend change identities and move out of New York. Your immediate family, however, should be out of danger..." and then added, "An unwritten law."

"Who the hell are you? And why didn't you tell us this before Kranz got electrocuted?!" Rudy demanded too loudly.

"We try to interfere as little as possible with domestic affairs. You became our concern when you came to Europe. We were working with Professor Ketchembach, whose job he saw as that of having to warn the American parapsychological community of a possible danger. He had no idea of the extent of his intuitions. And, in fact, I must admit, I didn't even believe any of this psychic bullshit until last night when I saw Boshtov's performance."

"You were there?" Rudy responded. "That wasn't parapsychology. That was only hypnosis."

"Only!" the agent said. "Only! I can tell you this, and then I must leave. There are very few secret police that take this field seriously. Very few. Psychotronics and related work has been riddled with deception and fraud. Most of us think it's plain old hokum."

"Most of it is, Mr. Templar," Dr. Karl interjected. "But certainly there is something to telepathy, which, I can tell you is legions more of an impressive feat than that amateurish hypnosis demonstration we embarrassingly had to sit through last night."

"Dr. Karl, you astound me," Templar retorted. "Do you not remember what happened to you?"

"What are you talking about? All he did was stretch that bore Coomesberry between two chairs, and stand on him like King Kong. That's the oldest parlor trick in the book."

"You mean to say you have absolutely no memory of becoming an elephant at Boshtov's simple command?"

"Don't be absurd!" Karl said. "I did no such thing."

"I'm afraid you ..."

Chessie could wait no longer. She ran over and hugged Rudy tightly. Tears streamed down her cheeks as she kissed his lips and neck. He was still upset by Karl's idiocy as a so-called expert in his own field, and by Templar's impotence when it came to saving Kranz's life, and so he had difficulty shifting gears back to his girlfriend. Preoccupied, he was even having difficulty being thankful to be out of his cell. It was only later on the plane ride to America that it struck him how lucky he had really been.

As the craft left the ground, Rudy turned to his girlfriend. "Chess, you must leave New York and change your name for awhile." Strangely wistful, he watched the coastline disappear. "I will move into a hidden apartment down near Wall Street." He continued as he peered out the window. "I want you to cut your hair and lie low. We can check a map to see where you can relocate. If Boshtov had pressed charges, I'd still be in Italy. I could have died there. It's all so crazy."

Chessie's lips began quivering as fear seemed to overtake her. She started rubbing both her legs vigorously with her hands. "Rudy, I don't feel well." Suddenly her forehead erupted in perspiration as hundreds of tiny beads of sweat began streaming down her face; hives broke out all over her body. She was breathing deeply and started rocking quickly back and forth as she continued to knead her legs. "I'm cold, Rudy...deep inside. Hold me."

Rudy removed his jacket and placed it over her. He called the stewardess over to take her temperature. One-hundred-and-three. He carried Chessie to a seat in the rear to hold her close and rock her in his arms. He soothed her back with firm loving strokes as he looked at the small firm red bumps multiply all over her skin.

"All I want to do is sleep," she managed as her eyes closed.

Love for this lady poured out from Rudy in overwhelming undulations, as he continued to hold her tightly throughout the remaining six-hour flight. By the time the plane touched down in New York, Chessie was in a delusional state.

* * *

Unbeknownst to Imo, whose plan was to return to Siberia with Patrenko via St. Petersburg, Bash rerouted his flight from Paris, to New York. He left Alexi and Imo, and boarded a Concord, a plane that could travel at Mach II. It was one that the public had no idea was still being used. Bash's shoulder ached terribly, but he knew it would heal. He needed to beat Rudy to the city, where he could catch him unawares.

On the slower flight, Chessie was sleeping under some blankets, as were a few other passengers who apparently had the same illness. In fact, upon their arrival at the gate at JFK, all of the travelers and crew were placed under quarantine, unable to pass through customs. As impudent businessmen and obese women shouted with authorities, the travelers and crew were shuffled to a makeshift hospital located at an old World War II Quonset hut at the eastern edge of the pavilions. This new way-station resembled a gigantic tin can lying on its side, half of which seemed buried in pavement.

Rudy counted at least seven other people from the Psychotronic Conference there, four of whom, including Chessie, were exceedingly ill.

Dr. Wedge approached. An ex-hippie from the Vietnam days, he was dressed in a sparkling Jerry Garcia tie and what looked to be a brand new jacket, but he also wore old faded jeans ripped at a knee. Picking unconsciously at the stubble on his chin, he opened the conversation. "Mr. Styne, frankly, I thought you'd be in jail for the next ten years. Dr.'s Ducam, Harpin and Schultz are all quite ill. Come with me." Wedge pulled Rudy over to an empty corner and whispered, barely moving his lips, "There are rumors circulating that they may have Legionnaires' Disease, or some reasonable facsimile."

A loudspeaker bellowed: "All passengers from Florence flight 704 shall be kept in quarantine until the cause and cure of the disease is determined. Please stay calm."

Then it was announced that Dr. Ducam, the DBA neural network wizard, had died. Chessie, Harpin and Schultz were losing strength rapidly.

The Concord had landed at a VIP terminal at the same airport three hours earlier. Deplaning, Bash slipped rapidly through customs. At a special hangar, he stepped aboard a helicopter which took off towards the city. They landed downtown nine minutes later. As Rudy and Dr. Wedge moved into a TV room inside the hut to watch the 6 o'clock news, Bash summoned two of his Tajik henchmen.

"Another strange outbreak of a Legionnaires-type disease was discovered at a scientific conference in Florence, Italy, today," blared the TV. "Two victims have already died and five more are in serious condition. We have with us the head of the U.S. Department for Disease Control, Dr. Philip K. Bundle. Dr. Bundle?"

"Yes."

"Is this disease contagious."

"If it is Legionnaires' Disease, or a close relation to it, then our experience is that after the first gestation period, it is not contagious. However, we know very little about the etiology of these kinds of infestations, and so to answer your question, we do not know. We are certainly checking the air-conditioning system at the Italian Hotel where all the patients were staying."

"What exactly is Legionnaires' Disease?"

"It's a bacteria, that is, a microscopic organism that can infect and grow in the body of its victim. *Legionellis bacteris* turns out to be very unstable. Even the slight change in climate or exposure to the sun can modify its genetic structure. Therefore it is very difficult for the host's immunological defense system to eradicate it. There have been a number of outbreaks such as in Providence, Rhode Island a couple of years ago, and of course the well-known micro-epidemic in 1976 at the Legionnaires' convention in Philadelphia when 180 people were afflicted. But again, we have yet to confirm the bacteria as *Legionellis.*"

"How long will the quarantine last?" The broadcaster asked.

"We have separated the sick from the healthy, and so far there have been no new outbreaks. If this situation remains stable after 24 hours, we will reconsider our position."

"Thank you Dr. Bundle. In an unrelated incident at the same conference, one scientist, Dr. Hanley Kranz, was accidentally electrocuted during a routine experiment with an electronic photography device. His body will be flown back to Sacramento, California where a private funeral will be held. Dr. Kranz is well known for his studies on memory recall...." The newscast trailed off.

"Why didn't they mention that it was a parapsychology convention? Or the fight I had with Bash afterwards?" Rudy asked.

"They might not have known about the fight. And as for the parapsychology connection, I'll wager, they don't want to risk a panic situation. You know how irrational people can be about psychic research," Dr. Wedge suggested.

"Got a cell I could borrow?" Rudy asked. "Mine died a week ago."

"Never carry them," Wedge said stoically.

"Here, you can borrow mine," an elderly lady with kindly eyes interrupted.

"Thank you," Rudy said, and then he dialed Abdul Manu's number. "Hello, Abdullah?"

"Yes."

"Good to hear your voice. This is Rudy Styne."

"How are you?"

"Terrible. My girlfriend has this Legionnaires' Disease with some others from the Psychotronics Conference. You may have heard this on the news?"

"Yes."

"I believe it is a form of biological warfare from the Eurasians....You heard about Dr. Kranz?"

"I did. Very tragic accident."

"That was no accident, Abdullah. The hypnotist Georgi Boshtov rigged the Kirlian device. He's out to kill a number of the top parapsychologists. He may even be after the superpsychics as well. I'm calling to warn you, and to ask you to pray for my girlfriend. Dr. Ducam has already died, and I don't know if she can last much longer."

"She girl that was here?"

"No, that was my associate from work."

"How many have disease?"

"About nine or ten. Three are at a makeshift hospital here on the outskirts of Kennedy Airport, behind the Pan Am building in an old military hangar."

"Rudy, listen. I have dreams about Rasputin meeting Kojak....You're laughing, but I got to tell you, it very true."

"Kojak is Alexi Patrenko. The Secret agent and hypnotist that I told you about, Georgi Bash, resembles Rasputin. I think he's a relative, a nephew."

"That's amazing. I can't believe it. Rudy, I must warn you. These dreams were of evil."

"These are evil men, Abdullah. They killed Professor Hereward and your friend Professor Ketchembach. Can you help Chessie and the others?"

"I am not healer. Look, it not my thing."

"She's dying, Abdullah. I know you don't...but your mother told me ..."

"My mother?"

"I met her in Egypt. She said to call her, and be a good boy."

"Look, I have done some healing, but this all hush, hush. I can't believe you met my mother. I'll phone some major people I know and together we meditate. But I don't want this out there, Rudy. I can't be seen as healer."

"I understand," Rudy replied.

"Good, we send healing to airplane building you are in, encase with blue light. I think of your girlfriend. What is her name?"

"Chessie Barnsworth."

"Chessie Barnsworth. Let me write that down. But you tell no one. You pray too, but you keep my involvement out of this."

"Thank you, Abdul. What can I say? Let's meet again when this is over."

"Yes, of course. And Rudy," Abdullah paused and then said quickly, "do not go back to apartment. I don't know why. It just a strong feeling. By 10:30 tonight, there will be a sign. Crisis should be resolved."

Styne rushed back and told Dr. Wedge that he had contacted some powerful healers.

"Manu too?"

"He's not a healer," Rudy side-stepped.

"I knew it! All that guy does is levitate and make money. You would think someone like him would care about really helping when it counts. OK, Rudy, I'll get the interested parapsychologists here to meditate as well. The least we ESP nuts can do is put our money where our mouth is."

Rudy tried to cross the quarantine line to see Chessie, but the guard would not let him through, as he was considered to be one of the healthy ones.

He went to the bathroom and rubbed some soap in his eyes and staggered back to another guard. His eyes bleary, he bent over and began to hack. "I am not feeling well." He drooled a little towards the guard's boot.

"Medic!" the guard screamed as he jumped back.

This maneuver created the desired effect, and Rudy was ushered to the other side, placed on a hospital bed, and given a thermometer to hold under his tongue.

Now within the restricted zone, he confessed to one of the nurses. "I must be by my girlfriend's side. Please."

The nurse led the way. "I'm putting in the report you have weird symptoms," she said.

"That's certainly true. Thank you."

He entered Chessie's room.

Above her hospital bed was suspended a clear plastic sack filled with nutrients and antibiotics, and a long tube leading into an IV attached to a vein in her arm. Chessie was unconscious, lying in a pool of sweat. Her hair was drenched and pasted to the side of her face. He reached over to hold one limp clammy hand, as he silently watched an oscilloscope monitor her heartbeat, her life reduced to a jagged pulsing line of luminescent green.

"Chess," he whispered gently as he pushed the hair away from her face and dabbed it with a white towel. "Chess, wake up."

Ever so slowly, her eyes opened. She looked exhausted and barely recognized him. "Rudy," she whispered. They were both quietly crying.

"Chess, hold on and fight. Use your will. Picture yourself completely healthy." She nodded, then started to fall back asleep. "Chess," Rudy put his lips by her ears, "you are getting better. I promise to never take you to Florence again."

"Oh, Rudy, stop." She smiled barely, her life's breath dwindling, she dropped off as her mate sat and prayed.

JUMPING SHIP

When the Russian plane touched down in Paris, Imo slipped away, happy to lose sight of Bash and Patrenko, at least, for awhile. Finding a pay phone, he used one of Heinreich's credit card phone numbers to call his brother's friend again. "Marcel, please tell my brother to leave his itinerary at Suchan. There will be a package for him there in four days. Do you have that?"

"Yes, Suchan in four days."

"Marcel, this is very important. Tell no one but Heinreich."

"I understand."

By the time Imo returned to the plane to plan his next move, Bash was nowhere to be seen. As far as Imo could determine, the wounded arm had miraculously recovered, considering the depth of the wound. "Alexi, do you know where Dr. Bash is?"

"I think he is on a military flight to St. Petersburg. There is an excellent surgeon there who can look after him."

"That Dr. Bash is incredible," Imo said, trying to keep the conversation on safe ground. "When we get back, I'd like to do the final run-through on the anti-matter studies."

As they boarded their plane, the two doctors heard over the loudspeaker: "Will all passengers arriving from Florence please go to the rear of Gate Seven. Do not, we repeat, do not board another aircraft, or leave the airport." The announcement was repeated in four languages.

"Why, that's us, Alexi!"

"We have to get out of here. They could keep us for days. The disease is not contagious."

"What disease?"

"Sir," the pilot informed Dr. Patrenko, "We cannot obtain permission to take off. Our orders are to take all passengers to the back of Gate Seven."

"Damn it," Patrenko whispered to Imo. "I bet you Bash had no trouble getting out of here."

"What's going on?" Imo asked.

"You'll find out soon enough."

"Alexi," Imo held him with both hands, "don't play games with me. What in blazes are you talking about?"

"We introduced bacilli #73146 to some of the people at the conference through microwave induction and resonance effects."

"You what?"

Alexi produced from his bag a small device and a number of pin-shaped objects. "By placing this small resonator on the clothing of the victims and activating this device, we have found the period of vibration for T-cell production and inhibition. The resonator incapacitates a significant number of pluripotent stem cells leaving the body susceptible to all sorts of diseases. This pin contains bacteria that attacks the mitochondria of various fat and muscle tissue, thus affecting cell metabolism. Once inhaled, ingested or introduced by scratching the skin, it only becomes a matter of time before a 'strange new disease' is created. Because the DNA of this strain is unstable, yet subject to rapid maturation, it is difficult to track down, and therefore very difficult to defend against."

"How many people did you infect?"

"About 14. We expect about a 65% mortality rate."

Bern and Patrenko entered the waiting room. Only two people there had the disease, but reports from America, England and South Africa confirmed the success of the operation.

"Isn't there anything we can do for them, Alexi?"

"Of course, an injection of compatible white blood cells or the bacteriophage we have developed as the antidote, would help, but we can't very well tell the authorities this. However, we could suggest a simple blood transfusion."

Imo rushed over to one of the medical personnel.

* * *

Rudy was numb. Chessie was slipping away, and there was nothing he could think to do. Then, suddenly, her eyes opened wide. "I see them! I see them!"

"Who?"

"Monks chanting. Don't you see? They're all over the room, marching, chanting." Chessie sat up. "They're all in long robes. There!" She managed to lift her arm and point, and then she fainted.

Rudy ran out of the room shouting, "Nurse, nurse."

"Yes?"

"Help her, you must keep her alive, you must."

The nurse hurried in. "Oh dear," she muttered as she sponged down Chessie's body. "I'm going to put her on a respirator to help her breathing."

Rudy looked back at the oscilloscope: *Beep. Beep. Beep....*

By 9:15, Chessie began to resemble a death angel, her face having turned a pale green. One more victim in London had died, bringing the death toll to four. Traces of panic could be detected in the expressions of some of the medical personnel.

Rudy watched the white-clothed professionals march back and forth in determined fashion like a well-trained army or ant colony. The pungent smells of medicine vials permeated Rudy's nasal membranes, as he closed his eyes to return to prayer. He sought out Sri Baba in his mind's eye, and asked him to save Chess, his girlfriend. By now she was tossing and retching in her sleep, paradoxically trapped by a cumbersome respirator, a machine that promised her a chance for the breath of life.

A nurse came by. "How are the other two?" Rudy asked.

"They are holding steady. It seems as if the virus is at a critical moment."

"Yes, it does."

"Rudy," Chessie called out weakly.

Rudy rushed over and held her hand. Gradually, color began to reenter her forehead.

By 10:15 she was off the respirator, her breathing almost normal. By 10:35 she was conscious. A half-hour later she sat up to talk.

It was difficult to see that she had been so sick just a few short minutes ago. "I want to take a shower and get out of these sweaty sheets," she said with a smile. "Rudy, I thought I was a goner there for awhile." Cheers could be heard throughout the wing as doctors and nurses triumphed in a spontaneous expression of euphoric relief as both of the other patients recovered as well.

"It has passed. It has passed," a young intern came running in, shouting.

The following morning all traces of the disease had vanished. Both Rudy and Bash heard the American news broadcast:

> The virus, which has been suggested by some experts to be a form of Legionnaires' Disease, has miraculously abated here in the United States. While in Europe, due to the ingenuity of two Eurasian doctors, it appears that victims were cured with simple blood transfusions. In total, the strange infection left five people dead and nine more hospitalized. Coincidentally, all of the victims had attended the same science conference held in Florence, Italy. Authorities are checking the water and shower stalls and also the air conditioning system as possible sources of the infection. Doctors have not as yet isolated the bacteria involved.

IMO BERN

The two physicians arrived in St. Petersburg where they met with Vladimir Kopensky. Patrenko filled his colleague in on Kranz's death and the spread of the so-called Legionnaires' Disease.

Vladimir was visibly shaken. "I didn't want it to come to this, Alexi." Kopensky walked to the far side of the room and stared at the wall; then he returned to face Patrenko, stammering to try to hold back tears. "You've known Dr. Kranz for ten years."

"Excuse me, I must discharge some excrement," Patrenko left the room.

Vladimir looked searchingly at Imo as he scribbled a note on a pad and handed it to him: "Bonzo's denounced us. Get out while you can." Imo ripped it to shreds as Patrenko reentered.

"Now Vladimir," he began, "you know you get into these moods every now and again, but..."

"This is not what our country is about," Kopensky cried out.

"Vladimir," Patrenko began again.

"I'm disgusted with you." Kopensky showed a bravado Imo had never seen before. "Now get out. We have no further words for each other."

"The fat man's lost his nerve," Alexi declared, as they exited the building.

The following morning Imo and Alexi were on a flight for Yakutski. Kopensky went home and got drunk, too ashamed to retaliate and too afraid to commit suicide--for it was he who had discovered the simple way to transmit the disease.

After the plane landed, Imo overheard a rumor from one of the radar operators suggesting that Kopensky had defected. It was Bonzo's defection that was the real problem.

In a major speech, Bonzo had denounced "virulent psychic warfare," and, in a complete reversal of his former position, called for a "spirit of reconciliation" with the West. Yakutski Science City, although still a separately funded secret government operation, was now politically out in the cold.

Patrenko spoke, "Now that the rats have abandoned ship, we can get on with our telekinetic studies. I have left our subjects too long as it is."

Down to Alexi's lab they went, only to find one of his cabinets pried open. "Kopensky, that traitor son-of-a-bitch," Alexi cursed between gritted teeth.

"No, it was me." Madam Grotchka stood in the doorway, scowling, her barrel-chest puffed to its limit. She was holding one of Patrenko's notebooks. "I just borrowed your notes. I hope you don't mind."

"I could send you to a labor camp for this," Patrenko said. Grabbing back the book firmly in both hands, he glared at the woman's look of sheer insubordination.

"You won't with Vladimir gone, and your support in the toilet. I had a feeling about him all along. That's why I tipped off Bonzo's men two days ago, when he was here sniveling about the mishaps at the conference."

Patrenko was in a tight spot. "Next time, ask me!" He spoke with authority, trying to recapture the offensive, as he considered this potentially useful information about Kopensky. "Your conduct will be reported to Dr. Bash," he said, using the one advantage he still had over her.

"Imo," a voice called out from a dark corridor. It was Boris Raudow.

"How are you?"

"As well as can be expected. Bash had me in recovery in Vladivostok for many weeks."

They continued to talk as they walked towards the FORBIDDEN zone.

"Your head looks much better."

"Yes. Bash removed the plastic skull cap, put back my original cranium and grafted bone and artificial skin onto my scalp."

"Are you still bionic?"

"What do you think? I'm working with Madam Grotchka. I still have depth electrodes in three of my lobes, in the thalamus, and in my aggressive and pleasure centers."

"What's going on?"

"The stroke made me incapable of eliciting any additional PK states, but you know Grotchka. 'Why waste an asset, especially when it can speak Russian.'" He attempted a crude parody of Grotchka's gruff voice. "She's still interested in the link between the primal and higher centers."

Now bumped up to lab technician, when not acting as a subject, Raudow worked as Imo's assistant in the continuing experiments performed by Madam Grotchka and Alexi Patrenko.

With Raudow's help, Imo prepared two Tajik cyborgs. They had been well-fed and their bionics had been properly adjusted. In quiet communication, Imo and Boris watched Alexi as he pondered his dilemma. Even though Bonzo had supposedly abandoned psionic research, Alexi knew that if he obtained a real breakthrough, that would be the safest way to protect the work, and himself.

The two subjects had their brains wired to a large control panel somewhat like the one Madam Grotchka had used in St. Petersburg on her primates. Alexi attached two large dunce-shaped devices with Tesla coils and small particle accelerators to the artificial parts of their skulls.

Raudow cranked open a sun roof, and Imo activated a radar scope, as Patrenko positioned the subjects so that their headgear was aimed skyward.

"We are energizing their PK brain-wave states through biofeedback, neurogenesis and electrostimulation," Alexi explained. "When the buzzer goes off, one of our satellites will be tracked by these gun-shaped accelerators. By harnessing their brains, we are hoping to erase or interfere with a digital recording that we had programmed into the satellite."

Patrenko spoke as if there were a crowd of fifty people in the room. "The shape of the instruments and the turns of the coils are in precise mathematical ratios to the size of each lobe of their individualized brains. When this tone goes off, they will know that they are producing the correct frequencies, and they will be rewarded later with steak and potatoes for dinner, and a movie of their choice."

The first buzzer went off. Patrenko activated the biofeedback loop, and shortly thereafter the tone sounded on the first subject indicating that he was producing a correct frequency. Soon the second subject was responding favorably as well. "This particle accelerator attached to their brains releases electromagnetic waves in the direction of the satellite. Our hope is that these will act as carrier waves for the PK energy which their brains will produce."

A light bulb above exploded as one of the subjects began to go into convulsions. "Turn him off," Alexi shouted. Imo adjusted some knobs on the man's skull-cap, and Boris injected a powerful sedative. The other subject stayed calm; his eyes, however, appeared vapid.

* * *

Late that night, Boris Raudow stole into Imo's room. "Imo," he whispered, as he shook the doctor gently.

Imo awakened.

"Come."

Raudow led the way into the FORBIDDEN zone, to a hospital annex anti-chamber, assigned to Madam Grotchka. There, two Tajiks were lying on two beds in drug induced sleep.

"They look exactly alike," Imo exclaimed.

"They're identical twins."

Imo could see that their wrists and ankles were handcuffed, and their cortexes were being monitored with depth electrodes and EEG connections.

Imo was about to ask what this experiment was all about, when his eye caught sight of a hefty jar, with a sizeable human brain floating in a clear solution on a shelf behind them, on a back wall. Written on front of the jar in magic marker were three English letters.

"ACW?" Imo asked, a cold shiver running down his back.

"Allan Churchway."

"The American superpsychic?"

Raudow nodded yes.

"Did he have orange hair?"

"Yes," Raudow said. "Long and wild, down past his shoulders. And he was tall, easily 6'5", with a forehead as big as the Rock of Gibraltar and an enormous skull to match."

"And a big cleft in his chin?"

"Yes.

"My God," Imo gasped. "I saw those very letters on a shrunken head in Bash's Vladivostok retreat."

"And it had long orange hair?"

"Yes, and the face had a sizeable cleft in the chin. You don't think he...?"

"No, he didn't kill him. Grotchka did, but there is no doubt he shrunk Churchway's head. We all knew he'd done others. We'd see his mishaps. Some were monkeys, little shriveled faces stuffed in the garbage."

"You're sure it was Grotchka?"

Raudow nodded. "After that first horrible year in the labor camp, you remember, I told you?" Imo nodded, "I was transferred to the same prison where Churchway had been a decade before me. It's an underground facility, not as big as this, but similar, upriver near the Leptev Sea. It was a luxury hotel as compared to the hell hole I had come from."

"You had better living conditions?"

"No comparison. I shared a room with two other men. We even had a desk, and there was a library on site. We were not allowed to talk, except during dinner, and we were not allowed to look at the guards. A man getting caught looking at a guard was deprived of food for three days along with his two roommates. I can't tell you how demeaning that simple act was, having to spend your entire time with your head down, what it does to your neck muscles, to your soul..." Raudow trailed off, having lost his train of thought.

"How far away is this place?"

"By plane," Raudow snapped back, "maybe an hour, hour-and-a-half from here."

"How do you know it was Churchway?"

"One of the other prisoners, a lifer, had the same name as my mother's maiden name, Meyerhov. We're probably cousins. He'd been there twenty-five years. Churchway came in '92."

"After the fall!" Imo said, referring to the collapse of the Soviet Union, which took place in 1989.

"Of course. Nothing changed, at those depths. They kidnapped him out of Tanzania the winter he was there. And the funny thing was, it was all my fault."

"You don't mean that?"

"I'm afraid I do."

One of the Tajiks moaned and tried to turn over in his sleep. Imo had a mind to unshackle him, but, for now, he had to let him be. He placed another melatonin tablet into his reticular pathway.

"I had actually met Churchway at a conference in 1987 in America, in a place called Oklahoma."

"Like the American play?"

"Yes. It's a province in the southwest, on the way to California. The area there is all flat, for hundreds of miles."

"Like our tundra?"

"Well, it gets hot there, so there's no permafrost. But what Oklahoma is famous for is tornadoes, and that was why we were all there."

"To study tornadoes?"

"To study Churchway, a man who claimed he could manifest and tame tornadoes."

"You're joking with me."

"Not at all. The guy may have been an ego-maniac, he was into that whole extraterrestrial thing. You know, he was the One! But he tested positively on many occasions. Remote viewing and weather control were his two fortés.

"Did you ever test him?"

"No, but I saw him in action. Imo, this was not a day one could forget. It was a Saturday afternoon and the conference had reached that tiresome stage, and that's when Churchway called us all out to a field. We could see for maybe fifty, a hundred miles. A dark cloud came out of the East, cracking lighting, spitting down rain. We were in sunlight. It was way off in the distance. And then he said a funnel would appear, and bingo, there it was.

"The thing zigged along, back and forth across the plane. He would point left, and it would go to the left. He would point right, it would go right, and so on. He was like a conductor. It was darn spooky, and frightening, but also fascinating. We were spellbound. But, before it got close, he said, *'Poof!'* and the thing just disappeared, sucking itself right back up into the sky!"

"Did he have an explanation?"

"Well, some people thought we were all simply hypnotized. But I didn't buy it. That would have been one helluva collective hallucination, and would have been almost as amazing as what he had really done.

"Claimed his mind was an extension of, what he called, the Galactic Grid, a series of primary frequencies interwoven with thought waves responsible for the construction of the universe. He said he could tune into those frequencies, and thereby roam the grid, or manifest certain celestial events. By shifting his consciousness to any part of the solar system--he chose our solar system because he felt he knew it best--he could travel to other planets and describe what was going on there. By hooking into the grid in a different way, he claimed the ability to alter the weather. That's how he explained it...There was an American Indian present, and they hit it off tremendously."

"Because Churchway put a different spin on the concept of the rain dance?"

"Yes, Imo, exactly. So when I returned to Moscow, you know, I was a big man then, Bash wanted to know all about the conference. And I told him.

"A couple of years later, Churchway went to Tanzania to cure a drought. And it did indeed rain there for the first time in years. Two days after he got there, the rain started. But then, a couple of days after that, he disappeared."

"Did you suspect anything?"

"I was oblivious." Raudow looked down and took two paces. "I never made the connection to Bash, not until Meyerhov told me, jeeze, over ten years later, when I, myself, was locked up there. He had a high position, Meyerhov, somewhere between a prisoner and guard. There were four of those types at the facility. If you wanted to ask a guard something, you asked the middle man, and he then went to the guard."

The two men looked at each other--the absurdity of the moment, the world they had entered, the laws of science, the nature of reality. This was going to be a big night for Imo. He had much to do, but he had to hear the end of the story. "You said Grotchka killed him?"

"More than that. She decapitated him. According to Meyerhov, and from what I surmised, Bash treated the psychic with respect. Sure, he was in prison, but Bash flew in gourmet meals, gave him access to modern movies, took him for long walks on the tundra.

"Meyerhov said it wasn't just that Madam Grotchka was jealous, even though she was, but that Bash had done something to her that was simply awful. No one knew what it was, but she came back one time, and Meyerhov said, her eyes were looking in two different directions. She was different. 'As much as I despised her,' Meyerhov said, 'she became even more evil after that day.' She sacrificed one of the Tajiks way before her experimentation was through with him, vivisected the body and hung the different parts on a line to dry, and then, a few nights later, she went into Churchway's cell, shot him with a drug which put him into a coma-like state, wheeled him into her lab, and did the most vile tests on his brain. Everyone there was afraid to do anything, and Bash was out of town. A few technicians had planned a revolt, but it went nowhere. And then Churchway died.

"The body was disposed of, but no one knew what happened to his head until Bash returned. Grotchka had placed it in a solution in a jar, and put the jar in Bash's private study. When he saw it, Meyerhov said, he simply broke down into tears. No one understood why he didn't have Grotchka arrested, but he didn't. In point of fact, he told Grotchka that she could have the brain and do all the tests she wanted.

"I believe, if I hadn't been so enthusiastic about describing Churchway's ability to manipulate that tornado, Bash never would have been interested in him in the first place. Sure, he had known about him, but it was all too unbelievable until I convinced him otherwise."

"That he could control the weather?"

"Yes. And the irony of it was that Madam Grotchka didn't give two hoots about his psychic ability. She knew that Churchway had a high IQ, topping 200. That's what she was interested in. But this experiment," Raudow swept his hand to motion to the two sleeping Tajiks, "is the end of the line for me."

"What does she plan to do?"

"Her idea is to match the architecture of Churchway's brain by grafting parts from one of these subjects onto the brain of the other."

"And that's why she wanted twins?"

"Exactly. There would be no problem of rejection with the grafts. She wouldn't have to use immuno-suppressive drugs and so on."

"Has she decided which one of these men she will sacrifice?"

"The horror of it is that she is going to toss a coin. It seems, the subject on the left does well in math, and the subject on the right is advanced in reading. Their overall IQ's are pretty much the same.

"So, tomorrow, her idea is to open up their craniums, and begin the procedure. Once she gets into it, she thinks she will know which one would make the best donor."

Imo thought about what might go through the mind of the remaining living twin. It was too ghastly. This was the night it would all end.

"Watch the door," Imo said. "She's done her last experiment."

One by one, Imo removed the screws that held the clamps to the hands and feet of the two Tajiks, and replaced them with screws whose heads had been almost severed from the shaft. A quick jerk would easily snap them apart. Then he crossed the wires in each hemisphere of their brains so that when they awoke, their aggression centers would be triggered, and massive amounts of adrenaline would be pumped into their bloodstream.

The plan was for the subjects to produce a horrific burst of superhuman strength the moment Grotchka returned to awaken them in the morning. Any experiment she would perform would activate rage in each of the twins.

As he departed, Imo placed a box of large scalpels on a tray between the sleeping subjects, and a number of crowbars on a table across the room. In their own way, he hoped, the two lost souls should be able to take some revenge on the butcher who had placed them in this situation.

"You must arm yourself," he told Raudow.

"Only to finish her off, if they don't succeed," Raudow said. "Do not worry, Imo. One way or the other, she will be dead before the end of the day."

"And what about you?"

"In the chaos, I think I can get a boat for town." Raudow replied, showing some of his old swagger. "Imo, There will be a half-dozen ways to get out of here. All hell's going to break loose, and if I keep my wits about me, I should be able to pull this off."

Imo reached to embrace Boris Raudow in a bear hug. "I'm sorry for all that has happened to you," Imo said.

"I am as well, Imo. Tell Heinreich hello when you see him."

Back in his room, Imo popped a handful of vitamins and drank a bottle of juice to prepare himself for the night's work as he sat to write down all he knew about the experiments performed by Patrenko, Kopensky, Grotchka, Bash and himself. He described the human brain mapping and EEG experiments, scrawling everything in a small but legible hand. He told about what happened to Boris Raudow and Alan Churchway, described Bash's hypnosis techniques, and his telepathy at a distance experiments; he wrote about Deus Maxima and her mass hypnosis demonstrations with large groups of subjects, and he described what little he knew about Bash's connection with Bonzo and the Secret Police.

Then Imo wrote down in detail a description of the surgery, specifically, where electrodes were placed in the subjects he and Patrenko were involved with, and their theories on how various EEG biofeedback situations could trigger gross manifestations of psychokinesis. By correlating specific frequencies with corresponding areas of the cerebral cortex, wired-up subjects could move and sometimes even levitate small objects. Subjects could interfere with radar and radio waves and cause disruption on computer disks at close range, and on hard drives and also smart-phones within a vicinity of about five meters. Without immediate biofeedback, he noted, most of the subjects' psi abilities were essentially nonexistent. And without depth electrodes, the Western scientists could never use biofeedback to produce comparable results.

Imo described the strange helmet-shaped headgear that was used to enhance or "step-up" PK frequencies in the satellite experiments of the previous day. He followed with a blueprint drawing of the Yakutski lab with its many floors and military hardware, and also the longitude and latitude of the location.

Hounded by second thoughts about disclosing exact military information, he crossed out the location and any reference to physical weaponry with vigorous thrusts of the pen. He did not want to be a traitor to his country, he only wanted to eradicate the elements that poisoned it.

Now he wished he had somehow kept the digital camera Heinreich had given him from Patrenko. Had he done so, he could have broadcast all the details of the horror the minute he had gotten to a safe location. But at least he still had the Nikon. Imo loaded in a roll of film and began photographing the pages, two at a time. Out of a roll of thirty-six pictures, he had used seventeen to capture his full thirty-four pages of notes.

The sun peered above the tundra, as the last of his notes were burned and thrown into the toilet. He was able to catch about an hour-and-a-half of sleep at dawn before pursuing the next phase of his charted course.

By 7:15 A.M., Imo had dressed and ascended the stairs for the plane hangar, with his orders to gain his weekly release for the hospital in Vladivostok. As he was about to step onto the aircraft, camera and satchel in hand, Patrenko approached the runway, walking rapidly, almost breaking into a jog.

Patrenko appeared a macabre sight, for his head, which had just recently been shaved, was bleeding profusely from three separate locations. Having probably used a new blade, he had been careless.

"Dr. Bern," he said, dabbing the blood with both sleeves of his laboratory coat, "we think it unwise for you to travel today, having spent so much time in Florence." He used the pronoun "we" as if he had actually consulted someone else. He wanted simply to add credence to his precarious situation. "There is much more work to be done here, especially with Dr. Bash gone for the week."

"Alexi, with the publicity we received in Paris concerning the blood transfusions, I think it imperative to carry on as usual, and this is my scheduled run to Vladivostok. I've given Raudow instructions. He can fill in while I'm gone.

"There will probably by questions on our procedures when I get to the hospital, and," Imo patted Patrenko on the back for added emphasis, "after I report on your brilliant medical diagnosis and treatment of Legionnaires' Disease, you'll probably be up for a Pavlovian Medallion. I can already see how Bonzo is planning on reversing his position once again. If things are tight here, I can be back before midnight."

"Dr. Bern, I don't think so. Not today."

"Alexi," Imo tried again, "the higher-ups may think it odd if I don't show up at the hospital. With Dr. Bash gone, and our duties to perform, why should we risk toying with a procedure that has been our mainstay?"

Alexi pondered the logic. "You do have a point," he said. "Maybe it would be best not to break ritual," Alexi forced a smile, not fully reassured by Imo's confidence. "Pavlovian Medallion, huh?"

The flight was smooth and uneventful. Imo studied carefully how the pilot landed the craft, circling the airport to head into the wind, adjusting the various levers. He disembarked and took the shuttle for the hospital.

Dr. Bern performed his usual morning rounds but also stopped at a major drug supply outpost and requisitioned morphine, antibiotics, syringes and powerful tranquilizers. He stuffed his medical bag with the items and then made an unprecedented call to Suchan, one of the neighboring villages.

From a pay phone, Imo dialed Heinreich's friend, the well-known sports journalist. "Dubie?"

"At this stage in my life, I prefer Yon. May I help you?" the former Olympic champion answered.

"This is Imo Bern, Heinreich's brother."

"How are you? I've heard you were in Vladivostok."

"Yes, could we meet this afternoon? I'm at the hospital neurology division. I have Heinreich's eldest boy's blood tests and brain-wave scan. I've been told you will be seeing him soon, and was wondering if you could give these records to him for me?" As he talked, he heard the characteristic "beep" every so often, which implied that the phone call, as all phone calls, was being monitored. He only hoped it was routine, with no one actually listening on the other end. If it were only on tape then there would be no immediate danger.

"I'd love to see you, Imo," Yon said. "I'll be seeing Heinreich in Japan this week. However, I'm tied up today. Can we meet first thing tomorrow morning?"

"No, I'll be out of town tomorrow," Imo said. "It must be today."

"I'm sorry, Dr. Bern. Perhaps you could leave the records with a nurse, and I'll pick them up."

"Heinreich's son is gravelly ill, Mr. Dubinoff. My brother will not be pleased to hear that you treat this event so lightly. You know how records can be misplaced. You must come today."

"I'll see what I can do," Yon responded. "I did not realize."

"Then at three?"

"Three it shall be."

Imo hung up the phone and reflected upon how to get to Dr. Bash's house. He had achieved two difficult feats, that of fleeing Yakutski, and the planned mutilation of Madam Grotchka. He hated to have left his friend, but Boris had made it clear that he had a plan of escape. Although burdened by what was to be, he had to stay focused. His determination now centered on how best to pass state secrets to the people of the West. Imo could walk or take the bus to Bash's house, but that would take too long and could arouse suspicion. He had to get access to an automobile. He went over to the parking lot to consider the problem.

Nurse Jabinsk had just arrived from her duties. Imo had known her schedule. He also knew that she was one of the few staff members that owned a car, but he had other reasons for seeing her as well. He found himself staring at her shapely calves as she stepped from the vehicle.

"Miss Jabinsk." He called out. "Irina," he added.

"Dr. Bern." Nurse Jabinsk smiled and gazed directly into his eyes. Her expression struck Imo as not only sincere, but hopeful. "I've thought about you," she found herself saying.

"How are you doing?" He walked up close. Their eyes entwined and he reached out to hold both her hands.

"You look troubled."

"I am," Imo said, honestly.

"Is it something I can help you with?"

Imo looked back at her as if for the first time.

"I don't think so. I lost a patient yesterday, and..., well, you know, it begins to get to you."

"Many of my patients are in the 80s and 90s. I see death every week."

Imo walked her to the entrance of the hospital. "I need to ask you a favor."

"It isn't really the death of a patient that is bothering you, is it?"

"No."

"What is it?"

"I can't tell you right now. But if you have an email address, maybe later I can...." Imo paused. "I don't want to lie to you." Imo moved swiftly towards her and gave her a tender kiss on the cheek. She kissed his cheek back. "Can I borrow your car at lunch?"

"That's what you want. My car?"

"That's what I need right now. I need it for lunch, just need to get away for an hour or so."

"Maybe I could go with you? For lunch?"

"How about next time. Do you understand?"

"You're in danger?"

"If things work out, would you ever consider leaving Vladivostok?"

"With you?" Irina asked.

"Yes."

"I'll have to think about it."

"So, the car?" Imo said. "I really need to be alone today. I brought my camera. Thought I might take a few pictures before Vladivostok gets buried in snow!" He spoke in such a way to let Nurse Jabinsk know this was small talk. She played along.

"I didn't know you were a photographer."

"I'd like to build a darkroom, someday."

"When the world's gone digital?"

"I'm a purist, so shoot me," Imo boldly said.

"All right, Dr. Imo Bern. You may have the car. But I'm going to hold you to that invitation, so you can date a caring soul, instead of merely dating a cold vehicle." She looked into his eyes again searching his soul for some type of answer and then handed him the keys. "Be careful," she said, letting her fingers touch for many seconds longer than were necessary.

Her fingers were warm and delicate, yet firm at the same time. He had avoided any romantic side to his life for so long. Her small effort loomed large in his heart.

"Thank you. I look forward to a luncheon with you next time?" He knew he might never see her again.

"Certainly," she said as she blushed slightly. "I'll put it on my calendar." She touched an imaginary pen to her tongue, and then began to write in her imaginary calendar. "Now, how do you spell your middle name?"

Imo grabbed her and hugged. Both in need of affection, they stood there awkwardly experiencing the chemistry of the moment. He kissed her again gently on the cheek, and then walked her back inside. They waited by the elevator to prolong their moment of silent communion.

"I should straighten my desk before my break," Imo said blushing.

"Where do you live?" Nurse Jabinsk inquired. "We see you so rarely."

"I'm just a free spirit."

Before leaving, Dr. Bern xeroxed a random file of a young boy's blood analysis and EEG scan, superimposing Heinreich's son's name on the top and changing the index number. He made two copies and a bill, filing a dummy in its appropriate place, and also returning the original. Then he put the second copy in a folder and left it on his desk. Strolling out to the nurse's car, he turned the key, shifted into gear and sputtered away. Except for a few fishermen, young mothers and old women, he passed no one at all. Nonetheless, Imo tried to appear nonchalant as he drove to his destination. But the more he pretended, the more alienated from his true self he felt. He stopped about 200 yards beyond the last dock and walked the long stretch of beach to Bash's house. Stopping along the way, he pretended to take photographs.

The color of the ocean was clear green, and it seemed to beckon. He skipped a few flat stones, as he drifted back to family vacations along the River Elbe when he was a child, to mud castles he and Heinreich used to build, and the network of tunnels they created below. He passed a young girl and her mother playing by the shore. The sun was warm and bright as the little girl followed the edge of the surf in an untiring game of ebb and flow. Occasionally she would let the water caress her toes, and she raced with it back and forth, as if to tease the very sea. She giggled as she shot a smile in his direction.

A gull swooped.

Imo stopped to stare at a half-eaten squid washed upon the shore. It was nearly three feet long. Iridescent green flies darted and crawled along the weather-beaten carcass. Its tentacles appeared to wave to Imo with the movement of the shallows. He took the light measurements and brought it into focus. The squid's remaining swollen eye stared back; another wave lapped its flank. *Click!* He accidentally photographed the strange beast. The camera seemed to go off by itself. Only eighteen pictures left. He hoped they would be enough as he continued along the water's edge.

Bash's house appeared in the distance, its treacherous contents hidden beneath a quaint exterior. Imo approached with caution, pausing a moment to listen to the gentle waves before stepping onto the porch. *Knock!* He boldly rapped on the front door and waited, and then reached behind a loose shingle and produced a key, which Bash had once off-handedly tucked there one day after they had returned from an early morning stroll. He felt as if that strange giant was standing beside him. Even now as he turned the lock and crossed the threshold, his heart pounded so loudly that he thought the men on the nearby fishing boats would hear him.

Entering boldly, he walked into Bash's office. There on the desk, staring back at him, was the shrunken head of Allan Churchway. It caught him by surprise, as he had expected the head to be buried in the attic. As he stepped back, his knee knocked into a lamp, which in turn knocked over a Brazilian spear that lay on the wall. *Crash!* The sound resounded throughout the house, as it clanged in his ears. Bash's presence loomed. Imo's hands began to shake, and it took him fully three minutes to right the spear.

He had difficulty ignoring his emotions as he moved swiftly to the target drawer and removed it. The young doctor felt a retching in his throat, for when he reached for the envelope he found it missing! "That fucking asshole," Imo said, as bile and the morning's breakfast surged up his esophagus. He gulped hard, fearing that if he threw up, the authorities would be able to trace the puke back to him. He replaced the drawer, and sat down to weep, swallowing stomach juices as he pondered his dilemma.

In a controlled yet frantic manner, he began to remove every drawer and searched each thoroughly. On his third try, he found the envelope. Bash had simply taped it under a different drawer. Imo brought it to the center of the room and opened it.

TOP SECRET: NIMROD CLEARANCE
PSIONIC RECONNOITER File #236492
For Your Eyes Only: Georgi Bash, MD

NOTICE: Anyone found with these papers other than the authorized agent shall be considered traitor to the Commonwealth of Independent Republics and treated as such.

SECTION I: TELEPATHY: History and applications for offensive and defensive purposes: espionage, remote-viewing, mind-reading, the EEG and telepathic states, ELF frequencies and brain-wave entrainment/modulation, psychic harassment during sporting events, dream telepathy, dream control, psychometry, communication with unknown intelligences, mind-control, illness.

Chapters included: (a) Historical retrospective of brain-washing techniques from such countries as Argentina, Cambodia, Chile, China, Korea, Latvia, Nazi Germany, Panama, Russia, United States, Uruguay Uzbekistan and Vietnam. (b) speculations and other theoretical considerations; e.g., in the case of the United States, mind-control tactics were hypothesized to have been used in a number of major domestic attempts and successes in assassination. These included the Kennedys, Martin Luther King, George Wallace, Gerald Ford, Larry Flint, John Lennon, Ronald Reagan, Paul Wellstone, Michael Connell and Peter Alston. Bash speculated that CIA or factions thereof had created hypnotizable "soldiers" to carry out the killings or attempted killings. There also followed a description of the top living hypnotists and their accomplishments, and also they were ranked for telepathic inducement, PK capabilities and other attributes. Names included university psychologists and top American and European entertainers.

SECTION TWO, perhaps the most important, described uses of PK in espionage and as a military weapon.

As Imo began to glance through the papers, he realized that time was fleeting, and he had to be back to the hospital to meet Yon by 3 o'clock. Carefully, he removed the one staple and began laying out the pages, ganging together four at a time. By standing on a chair and focusing carefully, he was able to capture the entire package including the front cover.

As carefully as he could, he returned the staple to its original holes, and retaped the envelope under the drawer where he found it. Then he rolled up the film and opened his camera, removed it and wrote on a piece of tape in English: DELIVER TO Rudolf Styne, *Modern Times,* New York, USA, LIFE & DEATH, wrapped the tape around the film and placed it into his sock.

Leaving the beach house, Dr. Bern carefully restored the key to its original spot, and retraced his steps, walking briskly along the beach. Breaking into a jog every so often, he made his way back to the car...and back to the hospital. Yon was waiting for him; everything was going to plan. After exchanging greetings, Imo led the way to his office.

"Is Heinreich's son very ill?" Yon asked.

"No, but he has been complaining of headaches and chest pains, so I offered to take a blood sample, and do the scan analysis. As long as you are going to see Heinreich in Japan, I felt you could hand deliver these." Imo handed him the dummy medical records. Putting his arm around Yon's shoulder, Imo walked him back out to hospital entrance. "Yon, would you risk your life to bring some humanity to the world?"

"That's a peculiar question."

"Your life? Would you risk it?"

"If it was worth it, of course," Yon responded. He appeared honest, yet perplexed.

"World peace is at stake. I want you to do something for me." As Imo bent down to pull the film from his sock, two men dressed in pin-striped suits approached. One was carrying Imo's camera, which he had left on his desk, and also his medical bag.

"I am Dr. Bern. Can I be of some assistance?"

"Come with us Imo Bern and Yon Dubinoff." Imo was firmly grabbed by the arm.

"What's all this about?" Yon demanded.

"Just a routine check. You'll be free by dinner time if you have nothing to hide." The man grabbed the medical records and led Imo and Yon to a black sedan, and locked them into the back seat. Imo began to sweat. *What will I do? What will I do? Don't panic,* he told himself. *Think. Think. Figure it out.*

From a third story window, Nurse Jabinsk watched the car disappear down the road.

"They'll probably search us," Yon said, trying to make conversation. He was totally perplexed, but innocently oblivious to any danger.

The vehicle finally stopped, and the agents led the two captives into a modern building on the outskirts of Vladivostok. "Go into that room and sit."

Imo and Yon were escorted to a small sterile room with two plastic chairs and a four-foot wooden pulpit. Two large mirrors and a poster of Alaska with Russian flags surrounding it's borders adorned the walls, the odor of ammonia wafted in the air. Imo started pacing as Yon sat down. "Come sit, Imo, don't worry. They don't want us."

"I can't, I'm too edgy." He kept feeling the film shake in his sock. In a swift jerky motion, he sat and crossed his leg over his knee rotating his body away from those mirrors, palmed the film and got up again and began pacing as he worked the tape off. Just then the door opened again, Imo sat down. Surreptitiously, he reached under the seat, and taped the roll to the underside.

"Come here and strip," snarled the agent. Each, in turn, took off all their clothes and were searched thoroughly. "Bend over and spread your cheeks." Both men complied. "Open your mouth and step over here." They were led to a chest X-ray machine that folded out of the wall.... The two men searched their clothes as they stood. "OK, get dressed and wait there." He pointed back to the arrival room.

As they got dressed, Imo deftly placed the film back into his sock. He was so nervous that he jumped when Yon coughed only to clear his throat. Praying for the first time in his adult life, he felt God say, "Thy will be done."

The two agents returned after about forty-five minutes. "Everything is in order," one of the agents said as he gave Yon the medical records and Imo the camera and the bag.

"What is the morphine for?" he asked.

"Nothing sinister, sir. I can assure you. I have patients in a lot of pain."

"And why is it that there is no film in your camera? You were seen taking pictures."

"No film. It can't be!" Imo grabbed the camera and opened up the back. "Did you?..."

"No, there was no film. Why not?"

"I can't believe it," Imo continued. "All that time wasted. How could I be so dumb."

The agents and Yon laughed as Imo feigned embarrassment. He felt relief at pulling off the answer so well. "Dr. Bern, you will be taken to the airport. You are wanted at the base immediately--some virus broke out. Yon Dubinoff, we will take you to your bus back for Suchan."

Dr. Bern reached out to give Yon a hug and his hand. "Thank you for everything. I'm sorry for the trouble, but with world peace at stake," he said jokingly, "one can't be too careful." Imo smiled as he dropped the film into Yon's jacket pocket. "If you see Heinreich, try and give him those records," Imo said redundantly. "I'll try to make his track meet if I can."

"But it's in Japan..." Yon trailed off. Something was peculiar, and he thought it best to end the conversation before digging any deeper. They parted, and Imo was escorted to the airport. His bodyguards were cordial but cold. The fancy sleek Sukhoi-67 awaited with one of Bash's customary alternate pilots. "Hello, Kandinsky," Imo waved.

"Hello, Dr. Bern. Haven't seen you in eons. How was your trip to Italy?"

"Tragic, Colonel. Quite a few people died of Legionnaires' Disease, and another scientist was electrocuted during a scientific experiment."

"How terrible," the pilot said, as their jet ascended rapidly. "Any of our people?"

"Not possible."

"Huh?"

"Kandinsky, we Eurasians are impervious to illness, especially when the dice are loaded."

"I'm not sure I understand."

"I'm not sure you want to." Imo assumed he would be arrested at Yakutski, but he was pretty sure Kandinsky did not know this.

Imo rummaged through his medical bag as he continued his conversation. Easily able to obscure what he was doing, he found a syringe and plunged it into a vial of a potent tranquilizer.

"What you got there?" Colonel Kandinsky asked, as he craned his neck.

Imo palmed the needle with his right hand, and dropped it to the right of his thigh. "Trying to find an aspirin. I've got a ton of medical supplies," Imo added. "I know they are going to need it at the base."

"Yeah, I heard there was some trouble there. A small mutiny or something."

"Anybody injured?"

"Don't know. I guess we'll find out soon enough. Hey, look at that," Kandinsky said, changing the topic, as he pointed out a herd of animals running across a plateau.

"Horses?"

"We're too high. Most likely caribou," the Colonel said.

Imo adjusted his seat belt to give him a little room to move.

Within minutes they were 30,000 feet above the ground. "Colonel, how do you decide our flight pattern?"

"The computer usually does it."

"But I notice when we go to Yakutski, sometimes we take a southern route and sometimes a northern one."

"Well, that all depends on the winds."

"But, how would the plane know this?"

"It doesn't. When I punch in the numbers, the plane dials up a computer at central control, which contains the day's weather patterns. The jet stream is always essential to locate."

"Suppose you wanted to go to Japan, what would you do?"

"Well, we would have to go in the other direction, that's for starters," the Colonel kidded.

"Would you bank north or south?"

"You need to know the coordinates. Here, I'll show you." Kandinsky lit up the mid-section of the control panel. "Which city?"

"Say, Tokyo?"

The Colonel hit the buttons again. "Ah, here it is." His fingers moved easily over the keyboard. "There, do you see that?" Kandinsky pointed to the map, which was etched in oscilloscope green in a clear square LCD screen in front of them. "As you can see, the direct route is southeast, over the main island. But, here are today's flight patterns, the prevailing winds, and so on, so I would bank north for starters. You see this line?"

"Yes."

"That's the route the computer is suggesting. After we turn around, due east from Vladivostok, over the Tsuguru Strait to the other side of the island, and south along the coastline."

"And that's the way you would go?"

"Well, it's apparently a little longer, but that's the way it's telling me."

"Because of the winds?"

"That's part of it. But as I said before, you have to also take into account incoming and outgoing flight patterns. You see those blips?"

"Yes."

"Those are planes coming into the airports around Tokyo."

"Is that radar?"

"No. This is compiled from reported flight data to the computer we are hooked into."

"And our flight?"

"Well, as you know, we wouldn't let the international community know about this flight. But, if it is a postal run, or something along those lines, I often call it in. You know, I give it to the tower, and they send it in."

"Can we do another?"

"Why all this interest, Dr. Bern?"

"Dr. Bash has been giving me flight lessons, and some day I hope to get my pilot's license."

"So, you see this as a lesson?"

"Yes."

"And you've flown this plane?"

"A number of times, Colonel. Come on. How about San Francisco?"

The Colonel looked at Imo. "You know we don't haven't enough fuel for that?" he kidded.

"Well, then, Hawaii."

"All right, Hawaii. We'd easily get within 800 miles, and then we could just swim from there." As Kandinsky typed in the numbers Imo used his right hand to work off the protective top of the syringe.

"Which island?"

"The Big Island. That's where the volcano is, isn't it?"

"I'm not sure," Kandinsky said. "But the Big Island it is. See the map? That Big One's actually called Hawaii. There, you see? Most of the flight patterns go to Honolulu and Maui."

"What the hell was that?" Imo lurched his head forward in a rapid attempt to look out the left side of the window, as he released his seat belt. The Colonel turned his head to look. Imo grabbed the syringe and plunged it into the base of the Colonel's neck. The drug was fast-acting, and Kandinsky had little time to struggle before he went under. With luck, Imo hoped, he would be able to land the plane at an airport in Japan before the Colonel awoke.

Reconnecting his seatbelt, Imo took over the controls. He banked right, coming full circle, headed north of Vladivostok and then due east out to sea. As he flew over the ocean, he felt an unparalleled rush of joy. Pressing the "back" button on the LCD screen, he found the coordinates for Tokyo reappear, and when they did, a huge grin appeared on his face. He passed the time to review his life: his childhood with Heinreich in Uzbekistan, fighting as kids, his father's ever-present red fez and his fruit stand, his mother's warmth, the high school he spent his youth at, his first girlfriend, medical school, his first autopsy, the stay at the hospital in St. Petersburg with Kopensky, his interest in ESP, Alexandr Floria, the visit with Nubea Lanilov, her levitating the cigarette lighter and her soft-boiled eyes, the ape he killed, Madam Grotchka, the Tajik subjects he experimented on, Georgi Bash....The Islands of Japan could barely be discerned on the horizon, when, to his horror, Imo saw a fiery streak head inexorably towards him.

Captain Kenji Sugimura had his men set the nets, as he began to haul in their catch, when his eye caught sight of a pencil-thin flash of iridescence tear across the sky. Kenji had been a fisherman for thirty-five years. His father had been a fisherman, and his father, and his father before that. Since today was a calm day, he had taken his crew to the Niitaka Shoals, because that is where he guessed the fish would run.

His eye quickly scanned the sky ahead of the trail of light, and then he saw it, the miniscule outline of a military jet, screaming towards the east. Supersonic booms were commonplace in the Sea of Japan, but Kenji knew that the boom he was about to hear would be unlike any he had ever heard before.

"Look," he shouted, pointing upwards as the missile hit its mark. It took nearly two full minutes before the sound and the vibration of the detonation reached the boat, but he, and most of the crew saw it happen as it took place. The odd-shaped jet, with its wings swept forward, burst into a sizzling flash of orange, red and yellow light, much like the blast at the end of a major fireworks display. Kenji thought spy-plane, when he called in his sighting to the Japanese Coast Guard. His call was by no means, the only call the Coast Guard received.

FORTY-SECOND STREET

Chessie was packing her clothes, as an orderly wheeled out the hospital bed. "It was as if a storm that had taken me over, has simply passed. Like night and day, that's all I can say."

"It's a miracle, Chess." Rudy looked at her with a sense of wonderment, her face having regained an amazing expression of radiance. "What, are you taking loveliness pills?"

"No," she said modestly, looking back into his eyes.

The nurse entered the room. "Here are your charts," she said. "And, let me be the first to congratulate you."

Chessie looked down at the papers. "That's preposterous. I'm not pregnant!"

"Let me see those." Rudy looked the charts over. "Are you sure?"

"Well, let me put it this way," the nurse began. "You're carrying a fertilized egg."

"But, what about the illness I just had?"

"The doctor who took care of you, Dr. Roseman, conferred by internet with a group of specialists, and the consensus is, the embryo should develop normally."

Rudy experienced a feeling he had never had before. It was a deep sense of joy, and it took him by surprise. "Jeeze, Chess, that's wonderful."

"Yeah, just ducky. I don't want it."

"I know it's sudden, but, why not?"

"Why not? Why not!" Chessie had raised her voice.

"Well, I think that's my cue." The nurse turned to leave.

"Thank you," Chessie managed.

"You're welcome," the nurse replied and shut the door.

"Don't you understand, Rudy? I'm finally getting my life together. Experiencing a sense of freedom, maybe for the first time ever. I've always been living someone else's life, my parents', my husband's, even yours. Well, now it's time for me. I almost died in a sense, because of you, and now, I want my chance. I don't want to be saddled with," her face showed disgust, "a baby."

"But we love each other."

"Oh, that's just great. We love each other. I have to go back to the city, change my identity, and move to, where was it you want me to hide out?"

"Vermont."

"Yeah, Al's place. My friend's place. Great. And in six months, if we survive six months, I'll be this big fat tub. And a couple of months later... I'll have an anchor, a life-sucking anchor.... Do you get it?"

"No, I really don't."

"Oh, just get out! Leave me alone."

Rudy didn't know what to do. He tried to reach over to give Chessie a kiss, but she pushed him away.

Hurt, he had no choice. "Be careful," he forced himself to say, and then slipped away.

Released with a clean bill of health from the makeshift hospital, Chessie stepped out to the waiting line of taxis. The air was thick with the suffocating odor and black-flecked particles of airplane exhaust, and her mind was similarly clogged. "That's all I need," she said out loud, as she hailed the first cab and got in.

"Where you headed, little lady?" the hack mumbled lasciviously.

"The city."

The mustard-colored vehicle inched its way onto the highway. Traffic was miserable. "Cars moving like molasses," he said.

"You're very poetic."

"Yeah, I guess I am. Thanks. To tell the truth, I'd much rather be a writer than a rider. Get it? writer, rider?"

"I'm afraid I do."

Beyond the endless row of automobiles, Chessie could make out the Manhattan skyline. The sun was just setting directly behind the Empire State Building. It appeared as if set off completely by itself. "Ah, the great empire's phallic palace piercing hot-pink rays of the solar mandala," he cried.

"Take the Williamsburg Bridge, Ferlingetti" she ordered. "I'd like to see the view from the Brooklyn-Queens Expressway, as long as I'm driving with a connoisseur."

"Unreal," he exclaimed, as they gazed on the full-length panorama of the great metropolis. "An erector set of checker-board lights dotted the canvas of our smog-lit existence...." he began, as he attempted to scribble the words as he drove.

"Can you stop for a moment?" she asked. "I'd like to take a longer look....Don't worry, you can keep the meter running."

"Great. This'll give me time to write these gems down." Out loud he continued spouting, as she opened the door for a better view.

From the breakdown lane of the bustling overpass, they overlooked the entire skyline: Wall Street to the left, the great gap where the one-hundred-story King Kong twin towers once stood; moving right, the East Side docks, the bridges of Williamsburg and Brooklyn, Tri-star Oracle, Okidata, Empire State and Chrysler buildings, the UN, 59th Street Bridge and Randall's Island, and to the far right, the Triborough...and even part of the Bronx. Superimposed on the rise right before them stood endless rows of gravestones. "A dramatic juxtaposition of the human monuments of opportunity, illusion, industry and finality," he expounded.

"You're on a roll," she said. "Do you mind if I get out to get a better look?"

"Be my guest," he said, as he continued writing. "Take your time."

Chess stepped out onto the extra asphalt shoulder and catwalked along the edge, as a black sedan screeched to a halt about twenty yards in front. Two weapon-wielding Eurasian men came flying out and raced towards them. A shot careened off a side view mirror as Chessie leapt back into the cab and screamed, "Gun it!"

Instinctively, and without looking for a gap, the cabbie plunged his foot onto the gas peddle, side-swiping a moving van, and lurching his vehicle towards the two assailants, sending them flying to the guard rail. "What the fuck," the innocent driver ducked, as his cab was hit again on the right rear tail-light. He scraped by the black sedan careening back into traffic. The two Tajiks raced back to their car.

Vainly trying to lose them, the cabbie faked right, and veered left onto the Williamsburg Bridge, the chase now in full gear.

"They'll kill me if they grab me," Chessie blurted, digging her nails deep into the front seat, piercing the tough leather.

"Lady, I don't want no part of this shit. I got a wife and two kids." The cabbie yelled back as they barreled up the rickety entrance.

The black sedan was about five cars back and closing fast. Bridge support after support ticked by, causing a strobe effect upon the surrounding skyline as the hack skidded along obsolete trolley tracks, ran the red light at Houston and turned right onto the Bowery. Weaving in and out of traffic and wandering bums, jamming on the brake to avoid an accident, and flooring it every time there was an opening, the taxi sped uptown.

At 26th Street, a squad car zipped in behind, and followed the taxi with its flashers on, as it zigzagged west and north. Chessie's driver stayed on track until 41st Street for a little more lead time. He hung a left, raced up to Eighth Avenue, and pulled to a stop under a marquee which read "Fanny Flanagan: 3 shows daily." Skidding around the block, the squad car slid to a halt, positioning itself diagonally out in front of them.

Chessie opened the door and raced forward. Oblivious to the possibility that the gun-toting officers might see her as a potential enemy, she reached out and hugged the closest one. "Thank God," she cried. "Don't let them get me. Don't let them get me."

"Who?" the man said, puzzled at his lovely catch.

"THEM!" she screamed, pointing to the approaching vehicle. "They'll kill me."

Without a thought, she fell to the ground as shots rang out. One of the policemen dropped with a bullet in his chest, as the other fell on top of her, and started firing back at the attackers. The wounded cop shot one of the enemy in the arm and blood splattered onto the windows of some nearby storefronts.

Chessie's protector shouted "Come on!" He had run out of bullets, and was sprinting for cover as he left the girl totally exposed. She screamed, and darted down the bright neon street hurdling over innocent bystander bodies that had dropped when the shooting began. Both pursuers were gaining when a large Black man stepped out from a doorway and slammed one in the face with a fifth of gin, destroying him instantly. The other, the wounded one, continued to press on, plugging the citizen with a lethal bullet as he scooted by.

Frantically passing pimps, tourists, pushers and peep shows, Chess entered a 3-D j-max porno house, bursting into darkness to crouch under a nearby back seat. Asses, tits, cunts and pricks flashed upon the high definition screen, as she watched the entrance in animal horror. Heavy breathing would give her away, so she tried desperately to calm herself and keep hidden; but the man two seats over who was rustling under a newspaper, stared down with twisted grin. "Shush," she whispered. "Don't look at me."

Member in hand, he blurted, "Don't look at you!" and burst into hearty laughter. Other people in the audience turned their way.

"Shush!"

"WHERE IS SHE?" the Tajik shouted in broken English as he entered the theater.

YON DUBINOFF

When Yon returned home, his wife was waiting supper. "Yonnie, what took you?"

"Agents stopped and searched us. I think they were Secret Police."

"Do you think Heinreich's brother is in trouble?"

"I don't know? He did say something strange. He gave me Heinreich's son's medical records to hand deliver when I go to Japan this week, and then he said, 'Perhaps I'll see Heinreich next week.' If he was going to Japan himself, why would he give them to me?"

"He probably was not sure, and knew for certain that you were going," she reasoned.

"Yes, that must be it," Yon responded, "although he could have just as easily emailed them."

"Private medical records, hon, I don't know," Anna said.

Yon walked into the next room to get his favorite smoking pipe. He reached into his pocket to retrieve some matches and felt something that did not belong there. Pulling out the film, he read the tape: Rudolf Styne...MATTER OF LIFE AND DEATH, and dropped it as if it were radioactive.

He sat there, deliberating, and then reached into his camera drawer, and found an old unopened film carton, removed the pristine roll from the canister, and replaced it with the foreign one. Searching through another drawer for a glue-stick, he reglued the carton shut, wrapped Imo's spy package in a plastic bag, grabbed a spoon from the kitchen, and walked outside into the forest. Deep into the woods he trekked. Stopping by a big old elm tree, Yon buried the package, covering his tracks with leaves and pine needles. Looking up at the dwindling light, he cursed Imo Bern. "You bastard," he cried out to the silent tree limbs hovering.

"Honey, where are you? Dinner's getting cold," his wife called out.

Yon took his time walking back to the house. How secure he had felt that morning, and now how insecure. His work in sports journalism allowed him to travel to many international track meets. Having handled the 1980 Moscow Olympics (which had been boycotted by half the world) in diplomatic fashion, an Olympic champion in his own right, Moscow had allowed him to write his own ticket. His ability to capture the Russian spirit in competition was often quoted in high circles. He had been looking forward to the Japanese meet, and now he dreaded it. What could be on that film? he thought. I'm probably better off not knowing.

Yon ate his dinner in silence as his wife looked on. "Anything wrong?" Anna asked.

"I guess I'm a bit shaken by the day," he said.

It was nearly midnight when Yon heard pounding knocks at the front door. Nervously, he jogged down the stairs and hesitantly opened it. One of the agents from the morning, and two others whom he did not recognize, entered. The eldest man, a shriveled, thin-faced fellow with white wispy hair, fixed a piercing stare. "We must search your place," he said stoically.

After frisking Yon and his wife, two of the agents began to go through every room in the house carefully, searching every nook with sophisticated electronic devices and scrutinizing every cranny. With special care for order, they removed furniture seats, cabinet drawers, boxes, bags and boots and inspected each one in turn. The elder read through the medical records Imo had given Yon over and over, as he kept looking to Dubinoff for any signs of anxiety. He paced the floor increasing the speed of his gait, as the search continued. Anna stood by the kitchen doorway glaring.

"Is this all Dr. Bern gave you?"

"Yes, of course. What is this all about?"

"I am sorry," said the first agent, "but you will be unable to go to Japan this week, Mr. Dubinoff."

ILL REPUTE

Chi Jhenghis glanced up at the porn, before his eyes adjusted to the darkness. He had seen Madam Grotchka perform on a number of occasions, sometimes even as a beneficiary, but the size and clarity of the high definition action startled him. With his brain overloaded from the stress of the moment, and his arm numb from the wound, mixed signals were activated from various electrodes placed in his hypothalamus and frontal lobes. But, overall, aggressive instincts predominated. The goal of the chase prevailed.

"Tell me where she is!" Jhenghis waved the gun in dramatic display, waiting for a sign to direct him to his quarry. Two arms pointed in Chessie's direction. "Over there," someone said.

Five men screwed girl goddess in high definition and three dimensions, as Jhenghis lumbered forward.

"AHHHhhhhhh!" Chessie screamed, grabbing a nearby coat and flinging it at the approaching assailant. It caught him in the face like a wooly octopus.

Chessie shot down the aisle, and darted out a side exit into an alleyway. Leaping over and around corrugated trashcans and urine-soaked bums, she stumbled to the street, and clamored across to the bus terminal.

People were sitting or strolling leisurely as she zipped past. Down the escalator she rode, her eye tracking a mother glide up with a child in her knapsack, and another holding her hand. Ducking through a side exit, she threw off her coat, and grabbed a green jacket which hung on one of the clothing discount racks that lined her path.

On the run, she crossed Tenth Avenue and stepped into a ma and pa grocery store. It smelled nice and safe, but too close to the action. The grocery man had a Semitic olive-skinned complexion, he was corpulent with a clipped handlebar moustache. "Can I help?" He peered over the counter, thumbs stuck between his shirt and the big white smock that covered the rest of his body.

Chessie looked him in the eye, nodded a frightened no, and then sneaked her head back out. Stretching her gaze east towards Ninth Avenue, she saw no one. And so she turned west out the door and continued on her journey, dashing towards Eleventh Avenue, hugging the entrance ways to the apartment buildings, trying to remain as inconspicuous as she could, as she picked her way towards the Hudson. At Eleventh, she turned right, angled across the street and then left on 45th Street, and right on Twelfth.

Traffic was dangerous, cars screaming off West Side Drive en route to the theatre district, and who knows where else. Across the Avenue, tucked along the northwest corner, was a slimy luncheonette with a big broken round red Pepsi sign dangling over the entrance way. Three ladies in short dresses paced in front.

In desperation, Chess dashed diagonally across the busy street, dodging cars, as she zigzagged to the entranceway. Ducking her head, she snuck a glance at one of the gals as if to say, "Please, you never saw me," and slid into the place. It had a dappled gray counter on the left, eight or nine cheap plastic booths along the windows, and a door to the back.

The chef paid no mind as she skitted past, and entered a small hallway where the restrooms were. The door-handle of the Lady's Room was greasy. Wiping her hand on her pants, she entered, jogged past a sink, and scooted into the last of three raunchy booths. Closing the metal flap to lock it, she crouched on the toilet seat, and waited. With nothing to do but be silent, she found herself resting her hand on her stomach, quietly listening to a sink drip.

After what felt like eons, a gal entered, and peed in the first stall. While putting on make-up by the mirror, she spoke. "You gonna stay in their all day, girl?"

Chessie stepped cautiously from the stall. Dressed in mesh stockings, spiked heels, a mini-skirt and a coat which came to the top of tree-trunk thighs, she continued primping, as Chessie looked her over.

"See anything you like?"

"Could I borrow some lipstick?"

"You don't look too good."

"I know," Chessie replied, as she pasted her lips with large red strokes, and ripped off the bottom seven inches of each pant leg.

"I suppose you want to swap jackets, too?"

"How did you know?"

"You mean, that you were hiding?"

"Yes."

"Shit, girl, it's all over the street." The prostitute tied a bandanna around Chessie's hair, and made the jacket swap. "There you go. Now take this." She handed Chessie a big black purse, and patted her on the behind to usher her into the dining area.

With one deep breath, Chessie boldly approached a not-too-sleazy-looking blue-collar type at the counter. A husky man, he wore a bluejean mechanic's shirt with the name "Bill" sewn in above the pocket, matching pants and alligator leather cowboy boots. A cigarette dangling from his lips, smoke drifting into his eye, he turned to look her up and down.

"Can I do anything for you?" he said. His eyes were gray green, with a hint of intelligence between them, along with the dead-eye stare of a primate on the prowl.

Her underwear pasted to her skin, her mind crazed in fear, she said, "Honey...." Hating every word from her mouth, she continued. "I've seen you before?"

"Sure, doll."

"Would you like to come to my place for some fun?" she winced.

"Is this a date?" he asked sarcastically.

"You interested, or not?" Chessie turned to leave.

"Sure, baby cheeks. Let's go." He grabbed a brown leather flight jacket and her arm, and escorted her to the street. "Where do you live?"

"We can take a cab," she suggested. As they turned uptown, she planned on what to tell him, once they found a vehicle.

Trying tenaciously to hold herself together, all Chessie could see was the next step in front of her, and the next. If she had noticed her attacker, she might have panicked and run, but she didn't. The couple walked off the curb and hailed a cab.

Feeling like an actor in a bad play, Chessie watched from afar her own actions. She felt a modicum of security in her disguise, with the open cab awaiting and a "John" at her side.

"How do you know me, baby cheeks?" the man asked.

"Maybe from a previous life," she smiled. As Chess stepped into the taxi, the man fell backwards, and Chi Jhenghis slipped in beside her. Smelling of raunchy perspiration, and the pungent aroma of dried blood and clotting agents, he bared his teeth, and told the driver, "Vermont."

POSITIVE NEGATIVES

Yon turned to face the agent squarely. As a national hero and prominent citizen of the nascent Commonwealth of Independent Republics, he played his biggest card. "Now I don't know what this is all about," he spoke boldly, "but your request is going to upset my readers, which happen to be two-thirds of the Commonwealth...and nine-tenths of the Kremlin. With the upcoming Olympics, our people are sitting on the edge of their seats waiting for my reports on this preliminary meet. If this has something to do with those files or with Dr. Bern, then take them. I insist. Take them!" he shouted. "I only accepted them as a favor." Yon was amazed at his own strength, but he also felt safe...at least, for now. He needn't even take the film. To hell with Imo Bern. He handed the files over in a firm slapping manner.

"Alright, alright," said the older man reflectively. "You may keep these records for Dr. Bern's brother. However, if it turns out that you are lying to us, you will be tried for treason." They apologized to Anna who indignantly showed them the door.

"What the hell was that all about, Yon?" Anna demanded.

"We are both better off not knowing."

"I feel violated." Anna had never been frisked before.

"Take a shower," Yon suggested quietly. "Come on, and then let's go to bed."

Anna huffed under the blankets, read a few pages of the novel she was reading, and turned her light off. Yon did the same, but he was unable to surrender to the night. He waited for his wife to fall asleep, then slipped out of the covers, and walked over to the window. Looking out into the night, like an obsessive, he kept ruminating over what Imo had said: "Would you risk your life to bring some humanity to the world...world peace at stake...." What could be on that film? Tormented, he went down the stairs to his study. Rudolf Styne, *Modern Times*--that was the key. He knew he couldn't risk the internet at home. He had no doubts. They could track electronically his every move. He settled instead for a scotch on the rocks, and then made another.

The next morning, Yon Dubinoff took his truck to the airport and flew to Seoul, just 500 miles from Vladivostok. Going on the pretext that an important shot-putter from Korea was training for the upcoming meet there, he was thoroughly searched, none-the-less.

Yon really did want to preview the athlete, but it also gave him time to look up *Modern Times* in the American library situated at the U.S. base near the athletic complex. Fearing he might be followed, he logged on rapidly, and used the powerful search engine Dogpile to cross correlate Rudy Styne's name.

This American journalist seemed run of the mill: TV sex, political bribery, an article on sports and one on parapsychology. The last one seemed on target, so Yon clicked to it, and read its contents carefully: Life after death, telekinesis, materialization, ... "Yes," he thought, "this must be it." He had a clue. Something Styne said meshed with Imo's brief statement:

> Both Russia and the United States have experimented with military uses of parapsychology for reasons of espionage and guerrilla warfare. They have tried to harness telepathic and psychokinetic powers for potentially evil purposes; but let them not forget the myth of Atlantis and all who misuse the gift. Humans are but groping infants in this world invisible.

To protect himself, Yon hyperlinked to *Sports Illustrated,* read up on the history of shot-putting, and downloaded a few articles to stuff into his briefcase. Thus, he was able to integrate some of his research with the interview he had scheduled with the Korean athlete.

On his return to the airport, the sounds of the radio tore into his soul: "Last night a Russo-Siberian jet was shot down west of Japanese waters by one of their own surface-to-air missiles. It is believed that the pilot was an unhappy airforce captain who was trying to defect to the West...." There was no mention of Imo's name, but Yon knew he was gone.

On the flight back to Vladivostok, he decided to risk it. He would take the roll of film to Heinreich, and tell him that his brother, most likely, was dead.

After winning the gold metal in Mexico in the javelin throw so many years ago, Yon had gained perspective on his role as a world citizen, rather than merely a Commonwealth pawn. That's what brought him to journalism. He kept this global perspective in his writing, and that is why he had become one of the most widely read journalists in the Federation. Becoming a spy, hiding and smuggling, that was another thing entirely.

When he arrived home, Yon went back to the woods to meditate. He always found refuge in the forest. That is why he and Anna had bought the house they were living in, in the first place. The pine trees behind the house stretched out into hundreds of acres of woods and trails. Breathing in the scent of the needles and damp moss, he watched a chipmunk munch an acorn, as six blue herons flew silently in formation overhead.

At the local general store the following morning, Yon bought five packages of film which they continued to stock for the film diehards, and took them home. Having always kept his darkroom, he still had a natural cover. Out to the forest he returned, where he dug up Imo's roll. Carefully, he opened the seal on one of the purchased canisters, pulled the film two inches out of its holder, and cut off this end. Then he slipped this cut piece into the exposed roll that Imo had given him, so that it would look unused, ripped off the tape with Styne's address and placed the target film in the new canister. With the glue stick, he resealed the box. Two of the circles in the word Kodak on the outer cardboard container were filled in, and the box was placed in the bag with the other film. The filled in circles on the outside would be the only difference between Imo's film box and the other four. The opened roll was put into his camera. Then, Yon returned to the house to pack his bags.

At the airport he was frisked once more, and his bags searched thoroughly. And when he arrived at Hanedo Airport in Japan, he was approached by yet another Russian agent, and his luggage was searched again. They were making no secret of the fact that he was going to be followed wherever he went.

Gathering his things, trying to appear nonchalant, Yon took the long walk to the train station. There, he took the monorail to Hamamatsuscho Station, and changed for a bullet train for downtown Tokyo. He had booked a room at the Dai-Ichi Hotel in the Ginza district.

Planning to visit the grounds of the Imperial Palace, which was not far from his hotel, he would also take a bus tour to Mount Fuji and attempt to lose his tail before he took the railway out to the pre-Olympic site.

The Dai-Ichi had put him on the second floor. He asked if it was a smoking room and they said that it wasn't. He wanted a smoking room. They complied.

Once inside, he locked the door, took the camera to the desk, removed some masking tape he had brought with him, and rewrote Styne's name and *Modern Times* address and the words: WORLD HUMANITY AT STAKE on it before he wrapped the tape around the film, and resealed it back into the little box. Then he went down to the lobby and sauntered out onto Harumi Dori Avenue.

He passed a line of jewelry shops, a large computer/camera store and then the Nakajin Capsule Apartments where frugal workers lived in 9′ by 15′ cubicles. He took a photo, walked on past the Sony building and fashion district, and then turned up Shin Ohashi Don Street to make his way to the Buddhist temple.

Yon walked leisurely, pretending the tourist, haggling with out-door merchants, taking the occasional picture, weaving his way to the temple. Once inside, he found a side door and exited. Taking a back street to the fish market, he used the pedestrian walk to scurry through the many stands. Across the way was Tsukiji Subway. He scooted to it, jogged the stairs and jumped on a train for the athletic compound. His plan was to see Heinreich who was scheduled in a preliminary heat.

Passing tens of thousands of Japanese fans and a smaller hoard of Westerners, Yon felt a measure of triumph, having lost his tail so easily. A little too easily. He considered the possibility that he might have some type of tracking or listening device on his person. Flashing his press pass, he walked along the perimeter of the field and ducked into the locker rooms. There, he found a suitable place where he could take his clothes off and search them again. If he hadn't had trouble rethreading his belt, he may never have noticed the thin wire sewn into the inside of it. Carefully, he studied the belt and then stuffed it into an open locker, and proceeded back out to the field.

A ten-mile race was in progress. He waited for a group of runners to jog past, scooted over the track, and made his way to the high jump area.

There before him was Elway Bannistair, the great Jamaican long-jumper. Yon watched Bannistair chug down the launch pad, and sling-shot himself over the sand pit. He was two inches off a new world record. The crowd applauded.

Heinreich spotted him first, and nodded from his warm-up area. There were three jumpers ahead of him in rotation, so they talked at a small sitting booth as the crowd cheered a shot put.

"How's Anna?"

"Heinreich, Anna is fine. I saw Imo the other day, and he gave me your son's medical records."

"What?"

"They're fake, aren't they?" Yon handed him the folder.

"I guess so. What the hell is this all about?" Heinreich talked as he casually thumbed through the report.

"Heinreich, I think Imo is dead. I think it was he who stole that Russo-Siberian jet the other day. When he gave me these files, we were picked up by the Secret Police. We were searched and interrogated...and before that Imo asked me if I would risk my life to save humanity. He was edgy and overburdened....Heinreich, I'm sorry." Yon dropped his voice. "He gave me something else which has to be delivered to an American journalist from New York by the name of Rudolf Styne."

"What did he give you?"

"Perhaps I shouldn't tell you, Heinreich. The less you know the better off you will be. Try to contact him. I'm sorry though; I think your brother is gone. He was in trouble. If I can unload my package, you'll be in the clear. Siberian agents are watching my every move, and maybe yours too."

"Try Charles Koswell of the *York Tribune*. He's a sports journalist, but he also covers politics. The *Trib* is out of New York, so he should know this Styne fellow."

"How do you know him?" Yon scrutinized.

"I met him three years ago in New York, and then again here, in Japan, just last year at one of the bath houses. He was staying at the Prince Hotel in Shinjuku."

The loudspeaker announced Heinreich's name. "Gotta go," the high jumper said. Wiping a tear with the back of his hand, he patted Yon on the knee, turned, and in long bouncing strides, pranced down the runway. Up he sprung with the Fosbury Flop, and cleared 7 ′ 3 ″. That jump placed him third in the preliminaries.

Charles Koswell. Yon read his bio at one of the many internet outlets that dotted the stadium. "Kos", as he was often called, had been a news reporter since 1984. A graduate of Columbia University, the only newspaper he ever worked for or ever wanted to work for, was the *York Tribune*. He had interviewed them all: Willie Mays, Mohammad Ali, H. R. Halderman, Terry Bradshaw, Alexander Haig, Colin Powell, Michael Jordan, Al Gore. Politics and sports, that was his game.

Yon decided to retrieve his belt. There it was, still in the locker. He exited the arena, found the subway for Shinjuku and left his belt on the train when he exited. Winding his way to the Prince Hotel, he rang the American up.

"Charles Koswell, this is Yon Dubinoff, Eurasian sports journalist. I'm a friend of Heinreich Bern, the high jumper."

"Wait a minute. Dubinoff, Dubie. 1964, Mexico, right? The javelin, right?"

"I'm amazed."

"Sports is my game," Koswell sang. "What can I do you for?"

"Could we meet for coffee, perhaps. I'm right downstairs."

"I'm quite full up right now...." As Koswell driveled on, Yon noticed a Eurasian man in a pin-striped suit and fur hat coming towards him. He looked right at Dubinoff, never faltering in his concentrated stare. Yon began to get scared.

"Koswell, this is no bullshit. I've got to go. They're after me. World peace is at stake." He hung up the phone and walked right up to the agent. "Looking for me?"

The Eurasian, not programmed for this type of encounter, looked through him and spoke something in a language Yon could not understand. The man looked to be in trance, as he dropped to one knee to repeatedly tie and untie a shoelace. Dubinoff did not quite know what to make of it. He rushed out, leaving the Eurasian struggling with his special form of simulated sanity.

Back at the subway, he took the railway to the arena, where he interviewed the athletes and took their photos, all the while carrying Imo's roll of film mixed with the others. Yon saw Eurasian agents everywhere he looked, paranoia beginning to cloud his vision. The whole concept of being arrested for treason became more terrifying the more he thought about it. He knew he had to unload the film quickly, and so met Heinreich once again on the track.

"Heinreich, I can't meet Koswell right now, although we talked. I was followed by a strange man. The Secret Police are all over the place...."

"What is the package?" Heinreich interrupted, having completely shifted his focus away from the meet. Between screams of joy streaming from the tens of thousands that spanned the bleachers, Heinreich said, "I tried to call Imo after you left. I was unsuccessful."

"It's one of these rolls of film," Yon said in a hoarse whisper, as he patted his camera pouch. "I'm being followed. We may both be in danger."

"What will you do?" Heinreich said.

"Your cup will runneth over," Yon replied, shook hands, and brought Heinreich's hand in contact with another high jumper who stood near. He shot their picture, and then shot a single photo of the other jumper, as he watched what he thought were two agents coming in his direction.

Whipping out his notepad, Yon began interviewing the other two high jumpers who had placed ahead of Heinreich. He started with the long blond-haired favorite, Swedish jumper, Sven Hjamerscht. An athlete who had catapulted to celebrity status, Hjamerscht was already surrounded by other journalists and a television crew. Second place went to the 6'11'' giant, Sergi Muryvhvev, from Romania. With the crowd to block him, Yon dropped the film into the third place cup, and then walked over to the shot putters, interviewed two of them and took more pictures.

Two agents were only arms length away. Breaking into a trot, Yon weaved through the multitudes, as he made his way to an exit. He took a bullet train to his hotel room, packed his bags, and shot to the airport. There, he was detained yet again by officials from the Commonwealth.

"You bastards win," Yon said. "I can't work being harassed and followed like this. I will be going to Moscow to get sound clearance for the Olympics. I will not be treated like this in our new Commonwealth. You should be ashamed, and I will be sure to tell my buddies in the Kremlin about how you treat me." Dubinoff reached over to a recent issue of *Siberian Times* that was lying on the desk. Flipping the newspaper to the back page, he showed the agent his latest article, a half-page spread about a Korean shot-putter who used to be a Sumo wrestler who had fought in Japan.

"It is not as simple as that," the scrawny white-haired agent said, as he reached for the newspaper. Glancing at it with a look of boredom, he tossed it into the wastebasket. "We know you are a courier for Dr. Bern. Tell us where the package is, or you will never see Anna again."

"First of all, you must understand the total absurdity of your allegations. I had never even met Dr. Bern before the day you people picked us up and searched us. Did you not search me thoroughly?"

"Yes, we did."

"Did you not come to my home and search it with special detectors and search me before I came on the plane and after I got off?"

"Yes, we did."

"Have I not told you repeatedly that I have nothing to hide?"

"Yes, you have."

"Well, then, you know much better than I what Dr. Bern was carrying with him that day. He gave me some records which I insisted you keep, if you did not want me to take them. Surely, in this day and age, if he had wanted to transfer information, he could have used the web. I don't understand. Why would he need me? And why would you allow me to transport something that you gave me back, if you did not want me to deliver it? I will be sure to tell my editor in Moscow how you prod me to dispatch contraband files while I protest, and then complain when I do it! Threatening me and my wife cannot change this reality. This trip to Japan has been on my itinerary for months."

"True. We checked it. But, if you have lied to us, you will never return to Suchan alive. We are not playing games," the agent said.

"I'm going home. I'm not playing games either." Yon reached into the garbage, pulled out the newspaper and placed it back on the desk. "You can send one of your soldiers with me and another for my bags if you like." Yon boldly started for the door.

"Remove all your clothes. Your notes and equipment will be sent ahead. Put these on." The old pro gave Yon a plain brown shirt and pants. "And these," he handed him brown sneakers.

"You have no authority here!" Yon threw the clothes to the ground. "Excuse me," he said forcefully, as he nudged aside the agent at the door and walked to his flight. He feared that he could be shot right then, and that he might never see Anna again. But he also knew that he was a hero of the Russian people, and a man of his stature, particularly at this time before the Olympics, could not so easily disappear. He would play the bluff to the end.

The scrawny agent was unsure what to do. He knew there was every possibility that Imo never did have a chance to give Yon anything but the medical records. He also knew that Imo had ample opportunity in Vladivostok to transfer information over the internet as Yon had suggested, or that Yon himself had had ample opportunity to do the very same thing. He had checked the medical records thoroughly, and they appeared to be in order. Suspecting a microdot, copies had been made, and these were given Dubinoff, not the originals. But there was no microdot, and no secret meaning in the words could be detected. Since Imo had attempted to flee the county, it was reasonable to speculate that whatever the package was, if there even was a package, he may still have had it; and if that were the case, it would have perished during his plane flight.

When Dubinoff arrived back in Vladivostok, he was again searched thoroughly, and his visa was suspended for sixteen months. The veteran agent realized that indeed if Yon were innocent, he would look like a fool, and if the agents were incompetent enough not to find anything after such an exhaustive search, then they were better off allowing the well-known Olympic hero and sportswriter the benefit of the doubt. In other words, it was better to make him look innocent to save their own hides. In turn, they switched their interest to Heinreich, who was attending a luncheon where many journalists were also present.

* * *

Heinreich spotted Koswell interviewing Svenson Hjamerscht. "Hey, blondie," Heinreich said playfully to his competitor. "How many interviews you going to do?" He tousled Svenson's hair and looked Koswell in the eye.

"He thinks he can beat me," Hjamerscht cajoled.

"I already have," Heinreich spoke boldly. And then he turned to the American journalist. "Charles Koswell, right?"

"Yes, Mr. Bern. Good to see you again." Koswell turned back to Hjamerscht, to thank him for the interview, and then shifted his attention to Heinreich, who had already used his free hand to slip the film canister unawares into the journalist's jacket pocket.

"Charles," Heinreich said, as they walked over to the punch bar, "my friend Yon Dubinoff wanted to see you."

"Strange cat."

"I'm sure you already have the information he wanted to give you."

"Right," Koswell said searchingly.

"Did you know that my brother was a parapsychologist from Vladivostok?" Heinreich leaned over for some grapes and cheese from a tray, and whispered under his arm, "Please do not tell anybody yet, but I believe that Imo may have been the pilot that was just shot down off the coast of Japan." He brought the cheese to his lips and continued, his eyes betraying tears. "I know he was very unhappy, and he may have been planning to defect."

"Your brother!" Koswell exclaimed.

"Shush! Yes," Heinreich said under his breath. "You will, of course, leave Yon and me out of this. You already have the information."

"Of course!" Heinreich said more loudly, laughing as he sipped a glass of juice and bit into a cracker. "Perhaps, as you say, I will clear 7′10″ next month." Heinreich ignored Koswell for the duration of the luncheon. Their whole conversation had lasted 47 seconds.

To cover his tracks, Heinreich sought out four other journalists. Placing an affectionate arm around one French reporter, as was his custom, he walked the man to another section of the floor, and kept his attention for nearly an hour. As Heinreich moved away, Koswell became aware of two suspicious non-Japanese men eying the well-known high-jumper. He watched as they proceeded to follow Heinreich out.

"I already have the information?" Koswell repeated to himself as he sipped his drink, and listened to the drone of the cocktail party. Most everyone appeared to be boasting about either their voyage on the new supersonic ionospheric Orient Express, Tokyo to New York in 100 minutes, or their box seat tickets to the New World Series between the Tokyo Sandpipers and the Toronto Bluejays. Koswell noted two more suspicious Eurasians enter the room. He felt them scrutinizing him and some of the other journalists. They especially eyed the Frenchman. Koswell tried to engage conversation with a pretty javelin thrower from Greece, and was able to sustain the discussion until the party began to dissipate.

As Kos continued talking, he felt a strange jiggling in his pocket. Putting his hand inside, he nearly gagged. Slipping the round object out beneath his napkin he read: Rudolf Styne, *Modern Times*, NY. WORLD HUMANITY AT STAKE.

"Constantine, what a lovely name, and just like mine, it also begins with the letter C." Koswell found his heart racing as he placed the canister back into his pocket.

The javelin thrower didn't quite know what to make of Charles Koswell. She mistook his ardor for passion. She knew he was an old established American journalist, and that was enough for now.

Koswell looked over her magnificent young body. A small tattoo of a dolphin augmented her cleavage as it highlighted one breast. Ah, the new world, he thought, as his mind drifted back to where it always drifted to, his days in high school.

Charles Koswell had been a journalist for thirty years. Twice married and twice divorced, he hadn't had a steady mate in nearly ten years. And frankly, he liked it that way. He was his own man, master of his own ship. He smiled at the Greek girl at an appropriate pause in her sentence, her eyes agleam in his, as his mind kept drifting.

His oldest kid, Jason, had dropped out of college three years ago, almost to the day, and was writing screenplays in L.A., and his daughter, a senior in high school, was applying to Rutgers to study computers. A chubby nerd. He hated to think of her that way, as he reached out to touch the javelin thrower's bicep, to make a point, to keep her going. She was talking about her competition, the thrower from Kenya who had elbow strain.

Koswell thought about how much he loved his kids, and, he, like all parents, was hoping for the best. If the truth be known, he was happy that Gerty had gotten custody. Once a month, or once every other month, holidays, that was enough for him. Gerty had remarried. Ed was an accountant. Good for him. Good for them. And his second wife, What's-her-name, that's how he liked to refer to her, that marriage didn't really count, lasted only eight months.

Koswell was never too good with women. "Yes, injuries are always the problem. What kind of work-outs do you do?" He stroked her ego, she prattled on.

He never understood women. He understood men. The world of men. That was his game.

Koswell grew up with sports as the center of his existence. Actually played varsity basketball just north of New York City, in Westchester County for Riverside High. Second string, but what the heck, it was a top-notch team. A little overweight, Flabby Tits had been his nickname. Her breasts looked small, but man, they looked firm. "And, can you tell me once again why you dropped out of volleyball. Greece has a great team this year."

As, she went into it, he kept the drift. Flabby Tits, not a name he liked to remember. There it was. The crowd would go crazy when he got into a game, because it meant that either his team was way ahead or way behind, and so the tension was gone. His best shot, the three-point jumper from the corner. [Of course, then, it was only worth two points.] On a good day, he could hit four in row. If he wasn't guarded. His favorite memory, the Mount Vernon play-off game in May of 1978. Witaker and Wiley, two of the starters, had fouled out, and Sebastian, the 6′6″ center, had four. It meant real play, and it was against the best team in Westchester, one very tough league.

"If I hear that story one more time," Gerty used to say, "I'm going to commit hara-kiri." Well, he tried, told the story every damn chance he had, but she never made good on her word.

Two minutes to go, down by ten. He hit his corner jumper and was fouled in the process.

"My game used to be basketball," he told the Greek gal. And he went into it, caught her up to his drift. "Now, one minute-five, I make the free throw, down by seven." For that one and only time, the shouts of Flabby Tits didn't sound so bad, but he wouldn't tell the Greek girl that. "Gave the crowd the arm pump, and they let out a whoop."

He shows her the pump, she totally digs it. Kos and the javelin thrower have attracted attention by now, and a few other party-goers are listening to his story to the end. She smiles nervously to some of them.

"Sebastian steals the ball, thirty-seven seconds left. Fast break down the center, pass to me in the corner. *Swoosh!* Down by four. Go, Kos, go! The crowd went nuts." She was locked. His little entourage was locked. Go Flabby Tits, go! is what they really said.

"Down by four, twenty seconds left. Whitaker and Wiley, from the sidelines, cheering me on. Mount Vernon comes right at me. But I time the dribble and slap the ball. I think its going out, but Palmery makes a diving save, and slaps it back to me! I heave it the length of the court to Sebastian on the run, and he stuffs it backwards over his head, and is fouled to boot. *'Ah right!'* roars the crowd. Down by one. Eleven seconds left." Kos makes eye-contact swiftly, with everyone listening.

"Mount Vernon takes it out. Palmery lets the guy go!" Flabby Tits fouls him. "I yanked his arm. What was Palmery, *nuts??!* The guy takes two shots. Misses the first. The pressure is enormous."

Koswell pauses for dramatic effect, as he regulates the timing of the rest of the story with every other time he has ever told it. He thinks about the time he grabbed the mayor of New York City when Julia Roberts was there…

"Misses the second! Seven ticks left on the clock." Kos paces as if he really is playing the moment, and walks it off to catch his breath, before he continues. "Sebastian down with the ball, hits me on the run. I stop for a jumper, as the center for Mount Vernon, a 6'7" guy named Wandy, towers over me to block. A perfect bounce pass through his legs to Palmery, under the hoop. *Two* points!" The Kos shouts as he jumps up, makes the fist and gives another arm pump. "Buzzer sounds. Riverside wins."

The listeners break into applause. The story never fails.

"Yeah, it was thirty years ago, but it will always be like yesterday for me. It's what gives me the juice when I interview talent like yourself." He manufactures a smile.

"I come to New York some day. You take me on the sights?" She flashes a little more cleavage and catches his eye.

"Well, we are in Japan now. Let us do'em here. I'm taking a car to Mount Fuji while it's still daylight. Pack a few things. We can stay a night?"

"Well, I, er...."

"Separate rooms. Come on."

"But...."

"Hey, you're already my lead story on female javelin throwers from Greece. We'll have a great time." He flicks a fake cigar, Groucho fashion, and swaggers towards the door.

"All right, Mr. Koswell," she says laughing.

"Kos."

"Kos, I would love to join you."

They depart within the hour. Kos' car was in the hotel lot.

By the time they reached Mount Fuji, they had run out of things to say. But the site was so beautiful, the javelin thrower found herself giving Koswell a quick kiss before she ran out of the car.

"Will you take my picture with the mountain in the background?" she asked.

"Sure," he said, taking her camera. "I know a great hotel which overlooks it. We can eat there and stay over."

Koswell talked about a helicopter ride he had taken, a few years back, over an active volcano, Mount Kilauea, in Hawaii, as he made the drive to the Fuji Hakone International Hotel, just eight kilometers from the site. "I have some private business, so I'll meet you at 6 for dinner?"

"All right," she said turning away, eying the line of expensive shops that trailed off from the main lobby.

Kos made a go of it, trying to remember her name. He grabbed his car keys, went out to the lot, and checked the map for Shimizoe, a neighboring village where the *Trib's* local staff photographer Ando Kusamura resided. While driving over, he went through the list: Carol, Christine, Cindy, Celene, Cleo, Chalace, Chastity, Charlotte, Clara, Cody, Cady, Cathy...He turned onto Ando's block, went up to his door and rang the bell.

"Kos, how are you?" Ando welcomed his colleague into his neat-as-a-pin flat, ushering him past a number of journalism awards framed in the hall. One of them was a Pulitzer for his photo essay on nuclear mutations.

"So, how can I help you? Kos, you look nervous. Come, to the living room where we can sit down and talk."

Kos found himself sweating, as he filled Ando in on what little he knew. The more he talked, the more he felt a slight gurgling on the left side of his neck. He reached up with his hand to rub it.

"Can you believe they blew their own plane out of the sky? Must have been important stuff." Kusamura eyed the film canister as he talked. "Well, time to get to work." He ushered Koswell down a hallway and into a darkroom which he still frequently used. They continued their discussion as the film developed.

After printing a contact sheet and blowing up the thirty-six photographs, Ando led Koswell to the door, and gave him directions for the post office.

Ando was a pro. By printing the pictures and black-bagging each before he processed any of them, he could develop all thirty-six simultaneously. The saving in time was enormous.

As Ando processed and dried the prints, Koswell stopped at a tourist shop and bought four different Japanese dolls. Thrusting his hand underneath the dress of one of them, he ripped open the stomach and stuffed in the film. On this one he wrote on the collar: "From Russia with Love," and mailed it overnight to Rudy Styne in care of *Modern Times*. On a whim, he dispatched the other three dolls to Captain Whitmore, John Hirshon and Sally-Ann, also overnight, and then went back to Ando's house to review the booty.

The door was unlocked. Cautiously, Koswell entered. Walking on tip-toes past the living room, he edged his way down the hall to the darkroom. It was open. Ando lay slumped over a chair unconscious. The prints were gone!

Fending off a sense of panic, Koswell bent down to cradle Ando's head. "Are you all right?"

The photographer was groggy. He opened his eyes to focus. "I'll survive," he finally muttered as he began to come to.

"What if they return?" Koswell said, as the bubble in his neck grew tighter. He used his cell phone to call the hotel. Consantine! Her name just flashed into his mind. The desk clerk said she had checked out. "Just great," Koswell remarked.

"I thought it was you at the door," Ando gasped. "They grabbed and injected me with some kind of drug, and took every print they could find."

"Did they question you?"

"I think so. I'm still foggy. Kos, I know I told them your name, and I think I told them you were mailing off the negatives, but I didn't know where to."

"You said, every print they could find?"

"Yes." Ando smiled weakly. Reaching over with a shaky hand, he turned his print dryer back on. Two photographs rolled out. There were eight pages in all. Ando knew a Russian translator, and by 2 AM, Koswell was able to email the story to the states. The following day it appeared on the front page of the *York Tribune:*

MISSING UZBEK PARAPSYCHOLOGIST TELLS OF PSYCHIC RESEARCH FOR MILITARY USE
Charles Koswell

JAPAN. Eurasian parapsychologist Imo Bern, M.D. reported that at least five republics of the former Soviet Union have been involved in secret military and police work in parapsychology for over twenty years. Dr. Bern, who worked in a covert laboratory community for half a decade, was well known to the parapsychological community for his published writings on neurophysiology, telepathy and dream states.

The Siberian location, Yakutski Science City, a complex 400 miles north of the town of the same name, belonging to the Academy of Military and Medical Sciences, has five separate underground buildings which can be entered only via a coded digital lock, the numerical sequence which is changed every other week.

One such edifice, referred to as the Institute of Psionics and Neuroanatomy, was run by parapsychologist Alexi Patrenko, M.D., and former military pilot and suspected secret operative Georgi Boshtov, M.D. Bern estimated that 340 military personnel and scientists worked at the City. Bern also alleged that agents associated with political right-wing leader Petar Bonzovalivitch often made routine flights there. Funding for research was "unlimited," he said.

Bern's work in brain-waves and psychokinetic states was separated into two divisions. While one area of research was released for public consumption, another realm remained top secret. Experiments performed included:

1. Electric shocks to kittens to see if the mother cat responded in another room on another floor.

2. TV surveillance to see if people picked up telepathic signals and orders.

3. Studies involving monkeys' brains and electromagnetic fields.

4. Psychokinetic manifestations in humans with EEG brain-wave biofeedback, augmented by cybernetic engagement of depth electrodes and embedded computer chips, placed in higher cortical lobes and other organs in interior of the brain.

5. Remote control manipulation of such "wired" subjects (called cyborgs) for production of telepathic states.

6. Telekinetic disruption of communication systems, computer banks, web pipelines and targeted search engines.

7. Mass hypnosis, virtual telepathy and virtual reality, induction techniques to stimulate brain-wave entrainment procedures and mind control.

8. Experiments to see whether a fatal disease could be transmitted by means of short-range electronic beams or via ELF waves (extremely long frequencies) to different points on the globe.

Bern said that the lab used as subjects rats, dogs, cats, chimpanzees, orangutans, Bonobos and

```
also youths from the Republic of Tajikistan. He
also stated that fear of American interest in
military uses of psionic findings, and the
aggressive nature of the CIA, were instrumental in
the step-up of research in this area.
     Ando Kusamura, Pulitzer Prize-winning staff
photographer who helped bring to light these
reports, was drugged by operatives believed to be
linked to Bonzovalivitch. Many other documents
regarding more in-depth disclosures have been
stolen.
     In a related story, there has been speculation
that Dr. Bern may have perished this week during an
attempted defection, when a Siberian jet airplane
was blown from the sky by a Russian anti-aircraft
missile. The jet, believed to be an advanced
supersonic craft with a forward wing design, was
flying in international waters off the western
coast of Japan.
```

Koswell now began to calculate a way to beat that doll to New York. Unable to book the Orient Express, and scheduled for another two weeks at the pre-Olympic trials, he kept his room at the Prince, but drove, instead, to Narita Airport.

Careful so as to not be followed, he bought a ticket for Hong Kong and boarded the plane. Every passenger looked suspicious, even the stewardesses.

As the last travelers filed in, he grabbed his carry-on and slithered back out, letting the plane take off without him. Finding a spot in a far corner, he watched the crowd.

Unable to detect anything suspicious, Koswell decided to take a more direct route. He scampered to the gate scheduled for New York via San Francisco, and took that flight instead. Hoping this last minute change may have caused misdirection, he sweated the entire ride across the Pacific.

By the time Koswell arrived in San Francisco, he was a mental mess. Taking the scheduled flight to JFK seemed like suicide. He took a cab instead to Oakland Airport, just across the Bay, and booked a flight under the name Boswell for Newark instead.

"But your passport says Koswell."

"I know," Koswell lied. "This happens all the time. It's a typo, and I would appreciate it if you would correct this in the computer." Koswell stood there until she complied.

TWILIGHT ZONE

Rudy sat quietly by the window in a nameless hotel and stared out at the dingy skyline. Instinctively sensing Bash closing in, and rattled for the way he had been treated by Chessie, he realized how unprepared he was for this kind of battle. Frightened and hurt, he crawled under the plastic-coated bedspread and tried to sleep away the day. Hours dragged.

Finally, he forced the lead-weight of his body out of bed, and eased himself into a steaming tub. A strange chant began to emanate from deep within his chest. As it resonated off the bathroom tile, he began to relive the events that led to this moment, his telepathic dream, encounters with B.K. Pine, the Incredible Fandango, Shri Baba, and Ketchembach's death. Cautiously, he brought his mind back to Italy. He examined his own doubts about the wacky field of parapsychology, his fear of Bash's evil, the cruelty of Krantz's death. Once again, his mind raced for its life through the muck and slime of the subway. He could feel Bash gaining; he could touch the sorcerer's body once more, as mentally he again drove the steak knife deeper into sinewy loins. Primeval images poured forth, as the conscious realities of murder mentality and mechanical man pierced his nascent 21st century cosmopolitan defense structure.

Rising from the tub, as if reborn, he sat by a desk to sketch an article which endeavored to make sense of the nightmare that had become his uncertain life.

Rudy described his attempts to warn Dr. Kranz at the convention, and how Kranz was electrocuted; he discussed the suspected creation of Legionnaires' Disease by the Eurasians, and speculated about their conspiracy to kill all parapsychologists involved in neuro-biological research. He reviewed their work on brain-waves and telekinesis, and reflected upon the blood which dripped from his own hand.

Listing the number of other parapsychologists he thought vulnerable, Rudy speculated as to how PK could be used for psychic warfare. Just as he was completing the piece, a new thought dawned on him: Allan Churchway, the superpsychic who had vanished so many years ago. Manu was in danger, and now he knew why: they wanted his brain.

Getting dressed, Rudy ventured out of the protection of his room. It was one of those old hotels with the high ceilings and cold, weather beaten little white and black mosaic tile floors. The elevator creaked so badly, he decided to take the stairs instead. Pushing the heavy exit door open, he entered a clammy stairwell. The iron handrail had a twisted design. Like grapevines intertwining, built at a time when things were made to last, he grabbed it, and descended gingerly to the ground floor where the rail ended abruptly. There were five separate steps made of white marble that emptied into the lobby. Without a rail there, he stumbled, landing loudly, jamming his knee. The grubby desk clerk pretended to be busy. Rudy limped into the street.

At a second-hand clothing store, he purchased a mousey-brown wig, wire-rimmed sunglasses, a Humphrey Bogart hat and a mid-sized black coat long out of fashion. Bedizened in new attire, the reporter took a bus to his office as he tried to shake off the pain in his leg. He entered the building through a side entrance, ducked into the basement, and shed his disguise in one of the janitor's closets. He proceeded to the newsroom.

Self-absorbed in the notes he was carrying, Rudy merely nodded to Mort and Bill, both of whom displayed an odd and silent mood. Sally-Ann, however, was quite forward.

"Rudy, how are you?" she said, her boobs bobbing with each syllable.

"What's wrong with the boys? They hardly acknowledged my presence."

Mort vigorously banged away at his computer, and Bill seemed lost in virtual space. Something about the office felt surreal. Four funky Oriental dolls were lined up on the windowsill. The air was stiff. And Cal, who was usually so animated, sat like a zombie. There was no banter at all, and no real acknowledgement of him, except for Sally-Ann. She followed Rudy as if she were his shadow.

"How 'bout coming over for dinner, Rudy?" She reached over to grasp his hand, her breath quickening.

"I can't," he said, as he moved away.

Everyone stopped typing; the atmosphere became oppressive. In unison, the workers froze and stared at him. He felt as if naked in a dream. "I've got to see the captain," he muttered, and fled into the next room.

"Come on in, Rudy, come in." The captain spoke between pushups. "Glad to see you're back and through with that misconstrued parapsycho crap. Now, I don't want to hear anything more about that, except, of course, for the driving in Florence. Did you get a cab, like I said? How did it go?"

"Who needs a cab? It was just like driving in New York," Rudy kidded, hoping to get a laugh. But the captain seemed not to hear. It appeared as if he were talking on automatic pilot.

"Your piece on sex and TV was great, simply great. And I want you to continue with one on sex and radio, sex in the movies, sex in the pulp and paperback market, this new stuff with interactive video, do it all."

"But, captain...."

"No buts. Here is your assignment." Whitmore stood up without a pause in breath, and handed him a deadline schedule and another outline.

"Captain, there is a man, a Ukrainian agent, who is out to kill me." But Whitmore's mind was someplace else. Rudy could have said the office was on fire. He repeated himself trying to make eye contact. "Captain, there is a man, a Ukrainian agent out there, who is out to kill me."

"Rudolf, I think you should start with shock radio, especially women disk-jockeys. Then you can go over the dirty words in rock & roll songs, get some MTV clips for visuals, and late night interviews."

"Sir, my life is in danger. I'm not bullshitting."

"Then you can interview various authors such as Xavia Steinway, Gloria Redgrave, Erika Waters...." The captain didn't respond to anything he said.

"I'll start on it immediately, sir."

Styne thought it best to retreat. As if in slow motion, he made his way back to his desk. "Hey Bill," he tried. Bill continued mechanically to pound away at his terminal. Rudy searched the other colleagues for signs of life. There was none. The rhythms were off beat. "How you doing, Cal?" No response.

Rudy's eyes lit as Sally-Ann approached. "Sal," Rudy said, walking over to touch her. "I didn't mean to be so brusque with you," he said. Her face was smiling, but her body movements were forced, and her touch, spurious. "Sal, what's going on? The captain wouldn't even look at these notes."

Sally grabbed Rudy's papers and began ripping them to shreds. Her face became maniacal, and she began to shriek. Mort picked up his computer and heaved it in Rudy's direction. It landed with a resounding thud, as Bill lunged forward. Operating on instinct, Styne grabbed Sally under her armpits as if she were a rag doll, and swung her into the other attackers, as he wheeled for the door. Pushing Cal out of the way, he slammed it shut. The deafening bang echoed down the hallway, as he lit out for a stairway exit.

His first inclination was to run for the street, but that seemed too vulnerable a decision. Instead, he continued past the main floor on to the basement, and returned to the unlocked janitor's closet. Shaking in an animal-like stupor, Rudy hid behind a pile of serling rods, as he tried to figure out the twilight zone he had traversed. He knew Bash was powerful, but could he have really hypnotized the entire lot of them--including the captain? It was too unbelievable. He even waited to wake up from a dream before he finally allowed himself to realize the bizarre truth.

"Is that you, Mr. Styne? What are you doing in there?" It was the red-headed janitor. "And are these your things?" He held up the fedora and long gray coat. "How were those babes in Italy? As good as your last article on tits and TV?"

"Yeah, Homer, they are," Rudy faked joviality, the janitor's name suddenly surfacing into his mind. He ushered him in to speak quietly from the shadows.

"Hey, Mr. Styne, did you hear about Sally-Ann?"

"Rudy, Homer, Rudy." He wanted to repeat the janitor's name.

"Rudy."

"That's better, kiddo. No, so tell me."

As Homer began to speak, Rudy began to see him as more than simply part of the architecture of the building.

"Well, this hypnotist from Switzerland came into the office and had her suspended between two chairs. He took a half-dozen old typewriters and put them on her belly!"

"When did this happen?"

"Oh, maybe two, three hours ago. I came by and watched through the glass. It seemed best not to go in. The man scared me."

Rudy grabbed the janitor firmly. "What did he look like?"

"Tall, gawky, big moustache, gigantic eyebrows. Looked like a bird could nest in them."

"Homer, that man is a killer. He has hypnotized the entire office--every last one of them!" He tried to speak calmly and softly, but his pace kept quickening. "I think he is waiting for me on the street. Can you get me out of this building safely?"

Homer had always respected "Mr. Styne." He had read every article the reporter had written, had tracked his career for years, for Styne was the one man in the building who always said hello.

"No problem, Mr. Styne, er, Rudy. Here, put one of these on and when dusk comes, we'll take out the garbage. I'll get you down the block where you can catch a cab or a subway." He gave Rudy a janitor's suit which he proceeded to stuff with the recently purchased coat in order to add thirty pounds to his appearance. "There, that'll do it, Mr. Styne," he said, patting the stuffing so that the new stomach looked exactly right. He gave the reporter a baseball cap as well, turned the brim up for an after affect, and stood back admiring his handiwork. "Yep, you look worse than me," Homer quipped.

"Thanks." Rudy grabbed a seat after the janitor left. Searching the room, he spotted a stubby cigar, grabbed it along with the glasses he had purchased, stretched out his throbbing knee and waited for sunset.

Homer returned as expected, and together, they wheeled out the trash. Rudy changed his cadence by ambling with his legs apart and rocking from side to side. He tried hard to be a different person, (he truly wanted that), but all the while, beneath the upturned cap, he searched the landscape for the waiting assassin. They stomped down to the dumpster at the end of the alley, and Homer stayed with him until they were safely by a subway entrance.

Rudy reached out and thanked the man as he departed. "I owe ya," Rudy said.

"How 'bout those Yankees!" Homer gave the thumb's up sign, and Rudy reciprocated.

Rudy often found sanctuary in the subway, with its interconnected underground support system. True, it had recently saved his life. At least, that's how he looked at it. But he had always appreciated its sheer magical high-tech ant-colony aspect. The fact that one could duck down in one spot and pop up in another. Wall Street to Riverside, East Side to West. One of his favorite haunts was Grand Central Station. Its magnificent atrium, with its morphing mass of humanity that continually traversed its concourse, the zippy back-lit ever-changing posters and occasional concerts that were played for commuters in the grand hall, the constellations on the ceiling, the sunlight streaming down through regal palladium windows, the multiple byways leading to buildings, bakeries, sundry shops and overland railroads, the escalators leading up to the overlooks and the great building above it, called the Pan Am for so many years, then the Met Life, now TriStar Oracle. The fact that one could pop in at 46th Street and pop out at 42nd and do it all by foot, that one could descend to the main subway that ran along Lexington

Avenue up and downtown, or descend to the next level and go crosstown to Times Square which had its own similar array of multiple levels, which was one stop away from Grand Central's sister counterpart, Pennsylvania Station. Or one could descend even one more flight, below the Lexington Avenue line, more than five full stories beneath the heart of the city, and take a tunnel that was built in 1907, underneath the East River, to slip out of the Apple and go to Forest Hills, Jamaica or Queens.

Rudy took this journey, and lost himself in the crowd, keeping the hat on that Homer had given him, for the vague sense of security it seemed to offer, but dumping the jacket he had stuffed under his shirt at the first opportunity. When he got back to his hotel room two hours later, he called the one person he could think of that that might be of help, the journalist Irving Moth from the San Francisco Chronicle who he had met at Ketchembach's funeral.

"Bash is back in New York and he's been to my office."

"Were you there?" Moth gasped.

"Not when he was. If I had been, I don't think I would be calling you now. You're not going to believe this, but the sonofabitch actually hypnotized the entire staff. Every last one! They were like zombies. It was too bizarre. I don't know what to do. They almost *killed* me! My own colleagues. I'm telling you, they would have done me in if I didn't get out in time. I swear, I thought I was dreaming the whole thing, and even waited to wake up."

"Hang in there, Rudy. They're all probably home right now. They should be all right in the morning."

"I'm not so sure. It was terrible." Rudy filled Moth in on the psychotronics convention and the murder of Kranz.

"The media reported the death as an accident," Moth said, "and there was no mention of the conference being parapsychological in nature. I thought it was just another case of Legionnaires' Disease...Rudy, this all may be related to that Siberian plane that was shot down by their own missiles off the coast of Japan last week. My guess is that it was a defector that was worth more to them dead than the plane was worth in one piece."

"Do you think it was connected to Bash?"

"Could very well be. Read Koswell's lead story in the *Trib* this morning. Bash is mentioned along with a parapsychologist by the name of Dr. Imo Bern."

"Imo Bern!" Styne exclaimed, "I met him in Italy just the other day."

"He's the one who was probably shot down. See the whole story. Koswell's done quite a job."

"Everything is happening too quickly, Irv. I've lost control. What should I do about these people? They are all in a trance. It could be very dangerous for others as well as for myself."

"You mean, like your friend, Abdullah Manu."

"Exactly."

"I'll alert my contacts ASAP. Meanwhile, you shoot an email with the names and addresses of your associates to a Major Concord, 14-63 Murray Street, New York, New York, Department of Mental Hygiene, and I'll take care to the rest."

"Irv, I don't know how to thank you."

"Hey," Moth said. "Don't sweat it. Make sure you also call on the police with a description of Bash. Give one as detailed as possible...Oh, and one on those Oriental goons. Don't make it any easier for them."

Rudy dialed Rondo, a local cop he knew, and described the Ukrainian to him, adding that Bash had already murdered two people. He told the cop that Bash was an expert in the art of hypnotism and was not the usual criminal.

"We'll get on it," the Officer Rondo said, "And, if we get him, we can at least hold him for questioning until the big boys come down."

* * *

Thoughts came rapidly. Styne wanted to warn Abdul of the potential danger, but decided to go downtown first to obtain another disguise. Theatrical Un Ltd. looked the same to him as during his college days and brief stint Off Off Broadway. He threaded himself past rows of mannequin parts, stage props and period apparel, and stopped at the hair-piece department. A long-haired wig fit well. He purchased it along with fake Mark McGuire moustache and beard, and from the 60s department, flowered shirt, blue-jeans jacket, pants and rose-colored glasses.

"Are you the one who got that part in *The Man Who Went Yoko?*" the pretty cashier asked, as he purchased the items. "You can try them on in the dressing room if you like."

"Thanks," Rudy replied, leaving her to wonder. Following her advice, he left the store in his new disguise.

Using a throwaway cell phone, he dialed the *York Tribune* and got Koswell's secretary.

"I'm sorry," the secretary answered, "Mr. Koswell is not due back from the Orient for another week."

"If he should return, give him my cell number. We've got a fast-breaking news story, and I want to know where I can reach him." Rudy was fearful of leaving the number, but the possibility of Bash tapping it, that was really just too crazy.

After dialing Manu's apartment, the answering service informed him that Manu was performing at the University of Bridgeport that night. The reporter knew he had to get there to warn him. Although he derived some comfort from his disguise, in no way did he have the courage to approach his apartment or his car, so he obtained a rental, and drove north on Route 95 towards New England. "I wonder if Chess is in Vermont yet," he thought silently, cursing himself for not considering her earlier.

Just as he crossed the Connecticut border, his cell phone rang. Keeping one hand on the wheel, he looked quickly down to press the incoming button, and put the phone to his ear.

"Rudy, Kos here."

"Jeeze, am I glad to hear your voice."

"I can hardly hear you," Koswell said.

"I'm on a cell on the highway. If we get cut off, just wait and I'll call you back." Rudy moved into the middle lane and tried to stay in rhythm with the flow of the traffic as he continued the conversation.

"So, tell me more about your article in the *Trib*. I think I'm on the same story here. I know Imo Bern. Met him just last week in Italy."

"Yes, I know."

"You do?"

"He had a package for you which I mailed from Japan to your office. I stuffed it in a Japanese doll."

"Oh shit. I was just there. I saw that doll! But, there were three of them." Some schmuck in a Honda sliced in front of him. He checked the rear view, then the side view mirror, and shifted into the slower lane.

"Yeah, I bought two decoys as well."

"What was in it?"

"Negatives. Bern's personal notes, and top secret info from Bash's personal files. He gave his life to get that information. I'm pretty sure he's dead."

"Imo?"

"Yeah."

"My God."

"Did you read my article? We developed the negatives, but most of the data was stolen back by Siberian agents in Japan. I was lucky to salvage what I could. Christ, I think I'm being followed even now."

"You know I can't go back to my office now."

"I'll handle it," Koswell assured him.

"You'll go to *Modern Times*?"

"Sure."

"Where are you?"

"In a hotel. Thought it best. And don't worry. I'll get the package back tomorrow."

"OK, bring it to Vermont. It's safe. We can go over it there." Rudy filled Koswell in on the incident at the office, his talk with Irving Moth and contact with Major Concord, and gave him directions to Al's house. As he talked, he maneuvered over a series of overpasses and a number of Bridgeport exits. Moving into the exit lane, he slipped off the highway, and turned at the light for the university. Rolling onto campus, he proceeded to the main auditorium, and double-checked his wig in the rearview before stepping from the car.

The old college days and remoteness of campus life dashed through his mind. Manu's picture was on a poster on the outside wall of the building, his eyes painted in day-glow:

ABDUL MANU
WORLD FAMOUS PSYCHIC
To Levitate Objects Tonight!
$2.00 with ID -- $5.00 without

Rudy waited in line.

"He's a magician, pure and simple," said one student. "To me it's just a cheap date."

"Well, thanks a lot!"

"Jamie, you know what I mean, come on."

"Frankly, I don't," she said. "You have no imagination, Martin. Manu's been tested around the world. He's the real deal. Who do you think sparked all those parapsycho movies like *X-Files* and *X-Men*? This is the guy. It all started with him."

"You mean those freaks with blue skin and spikes coming out of their hands in *X-Men* are based on someone real?" another girl mocked.

"No," said the first girl. "They took it to the nth degree. Really, the level of absurdity. But it's all based on real people with real abilities, particularly this guy. I did some research. When Manu came on the scene in the 1970's, way before *X-Men*, he simply changed the landscape of psychic research around the world."

"Bullshit," another student chimed. "It's a pile of crap. I read it all in *American Scientist*. Manu's a fraud. He's not even a good magician."

"Then why are you here?"

"To prove he's full of shit. Any magician can duplicate these tricks. The Incredible Fandango did all of this last semester and swallowed balls of fire as well."

"Well hot balls to him!"

Rudy took a seat way back on the left. He was surprised to see the theater so empty. Tall drapes and old arch-shaped windows dwarfed the meager crowd. Although his off-beat appearance fitted in well, the phony beard began to itch. Slumping in his seat, there was no point in being conspicuous, he thought of a way to further mask his shape as he scanned the room for Eurasians. One head looked suspicious. The man displayed a stern demeanor, wore an unobtrusive blue woolen cap, flannel shirt and blue jeans. He appeared muscular and seemed not really to be part of the crowd. Styne tapped the shoulder of an Indian student. "Excuse me, is that Dr. Chin, from Mathematics?"

"What do I look like, an information booth?"

"Hey, lighten up."

"No, I don't know who that is."

"Do you know most of the foreign students here?" Rudy questioned.

"Enough of them. I don't think I've ever seen him before...or you for that matter."

"Thank you." Rudy searched the audience until the curtain opened.

A paper thin girl in a high-waisted mottled brown dress, Greek sandals with leather straps wrapped snakelike around her calves, an eyebrow ring and a diamond stud centered beneath her bottom lip, took center stage. She spoke into a wireless microphone.

"Ladies and gentleman," she belted, "I am thrilled to stand before you today." Shifting her weight to the other leg, she paused, self-satisfied. "Thrilled to bring you a man who has been tested for his psychic abilities at twenty-five science laboratories around the world, including the Sorbonne in Paris, the Royal Academy in England, Lawrence Livermore Laboratories in California, and at New York University, right here on the East coast. This is a man who has proven telepathic powers, and who also has the ability to counteract the force of gravity. I give you the most amazing human on the planet, the Egyptian born, and I might say, exceedingly handsome, Abdullah Manu!"

Abdul stepped out on stage to a smattering of applause and a few boos. He began:

"OK, I'm gonna tell you a little about myself and then we go into some relaxation techniques--I try to enter light trance. We see what happens...." Enthusiastically, Manu recounted his life story, a few hands in the audience were raised. "We forgo questions until end. OK? Now, everyone sit back and relax. Close eyes and allow waves of energy to soothe whole body from top of head to tip of toes. And make sure you relax all the exciting parts as well," he said to a few chuckles.

Styne took the time to go into quiet meditation. He felt extremely edgy. This brief period of silence and rest was welcomed.

CRASH! A bolt of lightning illuminated the room in a flash, and thunder shook the walls. Suddenly, the psychic began to radiate, causing some in the audience to gasp. As Manu began to chant, pulsating waves of energy emanated from his being, and rippled throughout the auditorium.

Although the reporter tried to maintain a sense of distance, he felt himself compelled, pulled by Manu's charisma. As he stared at the Egyptian, the psychic's appearance morphed, his form dissolving into that of a bald-headed monk in flowing lavender robes. There was no way for Rudy to view this except as a hallucination, but the change was so complete that this explanation seemed too simplistic.

The transfiguration continued to appear and disappear, again and again, as once more lightning flickered into the hall and thunder boomed. Manu dematerialized for a hushed instant leaving only the glimmer of his aura where he stood. And in a twinkling, he reappeared and began to speak in a deep mechanical voice.

"THERE IS A PRESENCE AMONG US WHO WALKS IN SHADOWS. MANU BEWARE!" The sound seemed to have a life of its own.

A hush overtook the room as Rudy watched a dark figure leave the audience. "Bash!" he gasped. The flannel-shirted Eurasian followed quickly, moving down the aisle towards the front row. Manu, still in trance, began levitating a chair and caused it to float around the platform, and even out over the onlookers. Bash slipped back stage through a door to the right, Rudy stalked after.

The Tajik rushed the stage. Automatically, Manu wheeled and pointed his right index finger. A green shaft of light streamed from the tip. Laserlike, it struck the man between the eyebrows, knocking him backwards. A muffled scream came from the crowd, as Manu began to hover in and out of the physical dimension, appearing and disappearing.

Rudy entered stage right, stumbling over the unconscious body of Ron Valequez, Manu's friend from the apartment. The curtain dropped.

Bash ran forward, grabbed Abdul, and injected him with a syringe gun that made him slip instantly into oblivion. Slinging the Egyptian over his shoulder, the agent ran towards the rear exit, punching out a stagehand who had come to protest. Rudy bolted forward, and tackled Bash around the knees. Manu was dropped, as Rudy drove Bash headlong, gaining momentum as he smashed the big ogre on his wounded arm and drove him into a wall.

The crowd delayed in their reaction before applauding to the closed curtain. "More, More," they shouted, stomping their feet in unison. Another of Bash's henchmen came in through the back exit, and barreled towards Rudy. Instinctively the reporter ducked, timing his return upright so as to throw the on-rusher, flipping him onto his spine. Rudy then hoisted Manu onto his own shoulder and lumbered for the door. His knee gave, and he stumbled, trying to regain his balance.

As Bash got back to his feet, Rudy struggled with his load. He felt Bash's pounding footsteps approaching, and so wheeled suddenly. Whipping Manu's feet like a ball and chain, he caught the Ukrainian on the side of the head with a stunning clout. Still weakened by the recent knife wound, Bash fell to the ground dazed.

As Rudy squeezed through the exit, he came upon the unattended getaway car, engine running and side door open. Limping over, and throwing Manu into the passenger side, the reporter rolled around him, put the vehicle in gear and sped off . The forward thrust caused the door to swing shut as Rudy headed out towards the open road. Through the rear-view, he watched his pursuers chase after in vain.

The look of horror on Bash's face brought a vengeful smile to Styne's lips. Elated, he weaved in and out of the flowing traffic. Lightning struck again and rain pelted down in torrents, but to the reporter, it seemed like a beautiful evening. Although shaking from the ordeal, his state of jubilation was overwhelming, and he burst into song. "I'm a Yankee Doodle Dandy, a Yan--kee Doodle, do or die. A real live nephew of my Uncle Sam...."

About two and one half hours into the drive, Abdul began to revive. "Where in hell are we? What's happening?" he demanded groggily. "Who in hell are you?"

"Bash, the sorcerer I warned you about, tried to kidnap you. He drugged you backstage." Rudy said smiling.

"Your voice sounds familiar."

"Oh, the disguise. I completely forgot." He ripped off the wig, beard and moustache.

"Rudy Styne, the reporter?"

"In the flesh."

"I was in trance. Have no memory." Abdul was shaking his head slowly and rubbing his arm where he had been injected. "How did you...?"

"Save you? I tackled and clobbered him with your feet, and then carried you to this car. I had to leave mine at the University."

"Where are we going? What do they want of me? What happened to Val?"

"One question at a time. Your friend is probably all right, although he was hit over the head, or drugged. It's not him they want. We are traveling to my friend's house in Vermont. There you can rest and decide what to do. I think they wanted to kidnap you. You're a powerful psychic. God only knows what their intentions were. Didn't they know the whole world would be watching?" Rudy almost asked himself.

"Press probably think publicity stunt. You know I don't do these presentations for money. Sure, like everyone else, I want bigger crowds. But now, I realize one serious student worth five hundred lemmings."

"Why not do more tests? Surely you could gain more credibility."

"You've seen the research. It would be easier to get a right-winger to vote for Hillary than get mainstream science to back me and print truth." Abdul paused and watched the road. "Rudy, I guess I have a lot to thank you for."

As they continued their talk, an owl swooped across the windshield, touching a feather along the glass. Carrying a mouse in its talons, its wings were spread in full display. The bird's eye seemed to catch Rudy's, as it banked back up and continued on its flight. "Abdul, if you are connected to higher entities wouldn't they step in to protect you?"

"Entities you speak of are millions of light years ahead of us. Our lives on Earth are but nanoseconds in their time. They help in little ways, but always maintain that the Earth must have maximum free will. Our life here is really so brief. At death, we simply pass to next dimension."

"Then what is the purpose of life on Earth?"

"God has plan. That is true, but he leaves much of the detail and even some big decisions to man. We create own future. With too much interference from above, we would never develop independence required to decide things for ourselves."

"What happens to the evil?"

"There no evil. Only ignorance--ignorance of law. What is evil on this dimension is balanced on next. For instance, World War II Germany, terrible for the living--and God did not step in, although he suffered greatly. But that is only one of many lives for the soul," Manu said.

"Then God did not step in so as to maintain man's free will?"

"Exactly. If he eradicate the Nazis, he could never kill the cause of disease. Even with Hitler's dark legacy hanging as a warning, man still fights to kill and rape his self. If God had stepped in, we would be sheep instead of men."

Their philosophical discussion continued for the duration of the drive, through Massachusetts, New Hampshire and the early winter forests of southern Vermont. Many homes and churches along the way were decorated with the colored lights of coming Christmas. "Rudy, I thank you for saving me. But I still feel uneasy about going to middle of nowhere and leave my partner behind. Suppose Eurasians know of this place?"

"Impossible."

"Suppose homing device in car?"

"Well, you're the psychic. Is there?"

"No, I not think so, but still I feel he waiting for us."

"But we left him hours ago in Bridgeport...and without a car."

"Yes," Manu said, "I know."

* * *

Agent Crankshaw had been with the CIA for seventeen years. Having erased six targets during that time, and having compiled a flawless track record in the field, he had worked his way up from errand boy to spymaster. But it was really the intrigue of the job that attracted him more than the actual encounters.

Agent Crankshaw was dressed in easy shoes, policeman style dark blue pants, light blue shirt with a tie, loosened as always, a shoulder holster with a Custom Glock packed inside, faux black leather pad & pen holder awkwardly stuffed into his shirt pocket, a cell phone holder on his hip, and a London Fog raincoat which he had actually purchased in London. As a rule, Crankshaw never buttoned the coat, no matter what the weather.

Crankshaw was a pragmatist, a backwater patriot with a college-educated mind. People, he said, were either bad or good. Mostly they were good, but the bad ones. Hell, that's why he entered the field. An MIT drop-out, Crank, as his friends called him, had graduated in the criminal justice program at American University in D.C. after a year-off stint working as a fisherman out of Mystic. But that was centuries ago. After only the first month on the job, he understood. No one knew anything, except there was a right and there was a wrong. America was founded on solid principles. That was his underpinning. Killing was not easy, but all he had to do was look around. There were times when that was the only sane course of action.

"Major Concord's on the line," his secretary said.

"Crankshaw here."

"It appears, Crank, that our friend Dr. Boshtov has succeeded in hypnotizing an entire New York news bureau in the space of half an hour."

"Why, we've been trying to do that for a quarter of a century."

"Your humor overwhelms me, but this is a serious matter. I want you to round up two of your best soldiers. Make sure they have FBI liaison papers, and get your ass over to *Modern Times* to guard the debriefing sessions."

"Yes, sir."

"We have information which leads us to believe that one of their reporters, Rudolf Styne, who was not present at the time, was Boshtov's target. I just got off the phone with him. It appears that the recent aborted defection off the coast of Japan is connected. Have you read Koswell's report in the *Trib*?"

"Of course, sir."

"What do you think?" the major asked.

"I can accept hypnosis as valid, even mass hypnosis, as I have been involved with this myself a few times in the field. But I draw the line way before parapsychic warfare. Frankly sir, I would prefer to watch the originals of the old Buck Rogers reruns."

"I agree with you, Crank. But if we can get the defection we are seeking, any smoke which blows our way will help screen our efforts. I want you to put a man on Koswell, and follow his every move. His article contains only the cream floating at the top. We still have to dig deep for the grit."

"Yes sir. But what about Boshtov?"

"Arrest him. It's vital we take him alive," the major said before he hung up the phone.

Charles Koswell hailed a cab for *Modern Times*. "45th and Fifth," he told the cabbie.

Kos did not like going to a place he knew would be hot, but he had to retrieve those negatives. The events in Japan had rattled him, even though it was not the first time he had been in a situation of danger. As he emerged from the cab by the MT building, two men in trench coats approached. "FBI," one said, flashing a badge and grabbing the reporter with an iron grip. "Let's see some ID."

"I'm Charles Koswell, you lunkheads. It was me who called Moth who in turn called you." He bent the truth, as it had actually been Styne who had made the call.

"You could be a Russian agent in disguise," Crankshaw said, stepping forward. He eyed Koswell suspiciously, but not for the reasons Koswell suspected.

"Or I could be a male impersonator from the Kit Kat Club, and you could be moles or rat finks." Koswell caused both agents to laugh. "You look more like CIA to me. Mind if I run my own check?" He gave them his wallet as he reached for his cell phone.

"OK, Koswell," Crankshaw said, not even glancing at the ID. "We can cross the street and go to that restaurant and talk. You can make a call from there, if you still want to after that, or maybe you could just fill us in on what you left out of your article."

"So you do know who I am."

As they crossed the street, Koswell noticed a Eurasian man pretending to window shop a few doors away. The man was dressed in black sneakers, bluejeans and a heavy tweed coat that resembled a suit jacket cut long. He wore a dark brown woolen scarf and matching toque. The attire reminded Koswell of a fisherman he had once seen. But he knew this was no fisherman.

The Eurasian pretended not to look at Koswell, but his abilities in deception were poor. Standing in an alcove of a jewelry shop two streets south of the main jewelry district, it was easy to see he had no interest in the place.

"I believe that man is a spy," Koswell said to Crankshaw.

"Mike," Crankshaw said to his partner. "Go check him out."

As Mike approached the suspect, Koswell shouted, "Look out!" and fell with Crankshaw to the ground.

Catching them off balance by the swiftness of the action, the man had pulled out a long-barreled pistol, with an apparent silencer attached. The bullet pinged off a cement wall by the restaurant, and ricocheted off a car.

Mike rolled behind a truck for protection and readied to fire, as the man zipped out towards Sixth Avenue, maintaining his safety by attaching his moves to the nearby pedestrians.

"I believe that chap is an agent of the Siberian Secret Police," Koswell said, as he and Crankshaw got back to their feet. "He has followed me from Japan...and that's not in my article."

Crankshaw whipped out a walkie-talkie and reported the incident. "That guy should keep Mike busy for a while," he said. "My name is Crankshaw. I'm a liaison officer working for the FBI," he said, which Koswell interpreted as code for a CIA operation. "We believe you have information regarding the Russian plane that was shot down over Japanese waters."

"Only the speculation, which I reported in the piece."

"And the source of that information?"

"A friend of Russo-Siberian high jumper Heinreich Bern, Dr. Imo Bern's brother. He contacted me in Japan. This man had met Imo before his ill-fated flight. It was his intuition."

"Who was this man?"

"I am not at liberty to say."

"Is there anything else you can tell us? How did you know about the parapsychological weaponry?"

"Dr. Bern smuggled out some documents which are lost at this time. I think you know that gun was intended for me." They each ordered a cup of coffee and some Danish, and continued their conversation. "If I get hold of something, I'll let you know," Koswell placated. He got up to leave but Crankshaw grabbed his arm and seated him again.

"Not so fast. We have reason to believe that national security is at stake." Crankshaw tried to impress Koswell with his best propaganda lines. "The release of those files could cause chaos and loss of confidence in America. I have been notified that you could be tried for espionage if the full documents are released."

"Cut the bullshit, Crankshaw. If you want some cooperation from me, you are going to have to meet me half way. Try me for espionage! Hah!" The reporter tried unsuccessfully to stare Crankshaw down, but at least his point had been made. Koswell felt angry and scared, but he went on. "Do you know about Boshtov being in this country?"

"Yes, we have a tail on him."

"Just like you had a tail on that goon of his? Boshtov is a psychic magician. Do you know that he hypnotized the entire office of *Modern Times* and that they almost killed one of their own reporters, Rudolf Styne?"

"How do you know this?" Crankshaw queried, and then relented a little. Separating American citizens from subversives was always a difficult task. "We have a psychotherapist up there right now with them. Part of our job today was to keep people from entering the office until deprogramming is complete. That is why I brought you here."

"How do you know the contents of the documents?" Koswell persisted.

"I can only tell you this off the record. There is a major defection in the works. That's all I can say. I shouldn't even have mentioned it, but I respect your writing."

"You're pulling my chain."

"No. I've read your column for years, politics and sports, yada, yada, yada."

"OK, I'm listening."

"If you get those papers, you contact me immediately. You may be very unhappy if you don't." Crankshaw gave Koswell a card and got up from the table. "You can reach me anytime at this number," he said.

Koswell wondered why Crankshaw had not mentioned anything about the disappearance of Rudolf Styne. He had to get inside the office and retrieve that package. "Hey," he ran up to Crankshaw, "can't you get me inside?"

"Yeah, maybe." Together they walked back to *Modern Times*. Having both been in the business so long, in a way they felt like old friends.

By the time they reached the elevator, Mike, the other agent, had returned. He was breathing heavily. "Lost the fucker," he said.

Inside the *Modern Times* office, all of the workers, including Captain Whitmore, were seated in a row. They were facing a bearded man who bore a striking resemblance to an overweight Abe Lincoln, the bow-tie, vest, suspenders and missing moustache heightening the effect. A tape recording of the morning's session was playing as the psychoanalyst stopped it periodically to reiterate certain points.

Mort, Bill, Cal, the captain and the rest of the crew looked like they had just witnessed a great tragedy. Sally was sobbing softly on the side.

It was the voice of the captain they were listening to: "I guess the man impressed me by his size and majestic yet primitive quality." The tape blurbed on. Koswell looked around the room and saw the four Japanese dolls he had sent standing by the window. His heart began to beat loudly. He feared Crankshaw would sense it, although the agent was some distance away, listening intently to the recording. "The man stretched Sally between two chairs, and Mort and Sam sat on her holding two old Selectric typewriters in their laps. And then the Swiss man, or so we thought, stood on top of them!...and that is about all I can remember."

"Didn't he later interview you, asking questions about Rudolf Styne?" the taped voice of the analyst questioned. "Relax, Mr. Whitmore, go deeper and let it all surface." As the tape continued, the psychoanalyst tugged at his beard, and smiled with half-shut eyes, as he proceeded to strip his patients to their naked psychic truths. "We must be eased into self-realization," he said over the sounds of the tape.

"Yes, he asked me about Rudy, wanting me to list his best articles," Whitmore continued on tape. "I told him about the ones on sex and TV. He said 'Good, good, have Rudy do more articles on this. He must not work on that pseudoscience, parapsychology, anymore.' I said, 'right,' and said 'yes, he must continue to follow up on his original studies.' Then I think he put his hand on my forehead or shoulders and...I can't remember...I can't remember...."

The analyst stopped the recording once again to continue the discussion. As he clawed his beard incessantly between insights, Koswell inched towards the dolls. Which one was it? This is dangerous, he thought. The agents will see me, and that will be that. The tape and conversation went on. Each person, in turn, heard themselves talking in trance, and each stopped and analyzed their previous actions.

Now Mort's voice was played, "I remember we were told that a man would come out of the captain's office who would look like Rudy, but would actually be Rudy's murderer, and that he must be captured and destroyed. When Rudy came out of the office we all knew in silent unison that he must die."

"My God," Mort blurted out over the tape, "I think if we had been able, we would have killed him." The tape was stopped again and the psychoanalyst spoke.

"What we have all witnessed here is a rather incredible example of the power of hypnosis." The analyst made eye contact with each and every listener as he continued. "The man who hypnotized you is Dr. Georgi Boshtov, alias Georgi Bash from the Ukraine. He is a powerful and villainous force. He has proven to you first hand something we analysts have been reluctant to disclose. Hypnosis can cause a man to go against his own moral code. Usually, however, and even with this case, the subject needs to be tricked into the act. I want you all to constantly *remember* yourselves and keep a clear dream diary. The government has asked me to come back daily for the next two weeks from 8-9:30 A.M., and at these times, we will continue these discussions and put the whole thing together in an orderly and concise fashion. It is imperative that the entire episode be made conscious to you all. There may be post-hypnotic suggestions which could endanger not only Mr. Styne and yourselves, but other people as well." The analyst packed up his briefcase and started for the door, talking to Crankshaw on the way out.

As the session ended, Sally-Ann and the captain approached Koswell. With Crankshaw so close, Kos had to improvise. He placed an affectionate arm around Sally and walked her and the captain out of earshot, over by the dolls. "It was so nice to send these, Charles," Sally-Ann said, reaching out for one affectionately.

"I'm glad you like them," Koswell responded, spotting Rudy's doll. There on the collar in his own handwriting was written: "From Russia With Love." Crankshaw shook the analyst's hand by the back door, as Koswell reached over to knock the other decoy onto the floor. "How clumsy," he said sticking his hand under the appropriate skirt, and pulling the film out, as Sally and the captain instinctively reached down to pick the fallen doll up. Deftly, Koswell placed the canister in his pocket as Crankshaw approached.

"May I see those dolls?" the agent said, weighing them in his hands, and holding one up to his ear.

"I know you're a respected Federal officer," Koswell jested. "I just didn't know you also played with dolls."

Koswell led both the captain and Sally to the elevator. "Let me take you both downstairs to lunch. My treat," he said loudly. Sally-Ann still bore tear tracks, and Whitmore's face looked as if he had suddenly aged many years.

As they rode the elevator, Koswell said, "I'm sorry to rush you people, but Crankshaw has been tailing me since I arrived in New York. Tell him when he figures all this out, that I'm on my way to the office, and needed to use the two of you for an excuse. I promise to keep the lunch offer standing, but at another time."

The two stood in the lobby dumbfounded as Crankshaw trotted over. He was holding Styne's present as if it were a tree limb, its skirt upturned, and guts of straw tufts protruding from the stomach. "Whitmore," he demanded furiously, "where did he go?"

"His office," they said in unison.

"La Guardia Airport," Koswell told the cabby.

DEFECTION

Shortly after Imo departed, Yakutski Science City became a madhouse. Grotchka's two subjects had broken loose and sliced her badly with scalpels. They had also destroyed thousands of dollars of equipment and killed two orderlies. Some of the military men had to be called in to control the problem, but this maneuver exposed the laboratory's secret human experiments to new recruits and members from lower echelons. The whole base, it seemed, had seen the two strange Tajiks with plastic and wires sticking out from their skulls. Now there was no telling how far the information would travel.

Patrenko immediately suspected Imo. He was the only viable possibility. His first step was to call in Raudow, but he was nowhere to be found. "Damn him!" Patrenko cursed. He took the elevator to the infirmary to check on Madam Grotchka. She lay semi-conscious, her chances for survival a real guess. There were deep slice marks etched across her neck, shoulders, face and hands. Three of the fingers on her right hand had already been amputated, and one was being sown back on the left hand.

"It was that prick, Imo," she rasped.

"Shush," Patrenko said quietly, trying to calm her. "The best thing for you to do is to get some rest."

She struggled to successfully lift her head. "It was that prick, I tell you, that prick, that prick."

"I know," Patrenko said, as he gently but firmly placed her head back down, and injected Madam Grotchka with a drug to make her go to sleep.

Alexi went back to his office to call Vladivostok. Dr. Bern was to be captured and sent back. When he returned, he would be interrogated thoroughly. Bash, unfortunately, was in America.

When Imo failed to return, and the story leaked about the jet they shot down, followed by the front page *York Tribune* article, Patrenko realized that his entire operation was shattered. A lifetime of toil in ruins, and all because of one underling. There was no telling what secrets Imo had divulged. Heads were going to roll, and Bash would be looking for a sacrificial lamb. Alexi had little choice. He took a plane to St. Petersburg to talk with Kopensky, but Vladimir was running scared. Having befriended members of the Academy of Pedagogical Sciences, Vladimir felt somewhat secure. He had already shifted emphasis away from parapsychology and back to neurophysiology, weeks before the final incident. "I'm sorry, Alexi, we have nothing to say to each other." He would only speak to him over the hospital intercom. "There is no need to see me."

After weighing alternatives, Patrenko took a train north to the docks on the Gulf. There, he slipped aboard a creaking fishing boat headed for Helsinki. Reeking of dead fish, the deck dangerously slippery from a recent catch, Patrenko moved cautiously, as he slid aboard, trying to find a decent hiding spot. A small hold filled with empty barrels caught his attention. He grabbed a nearby tarp from beneath a staircase, dragged it into the hold and positioned himself underneath it in the far corner, hiding among a stack of discarded crates. Pulling the tarp tightly over his shivering body, he prayed in the cold night air that he would not get caught.

As the ship plowed through choppy waters, Alexi reflected back to his childhood. At one point he actually realized that he was indeed praying to God! In spite of everything, he had to laugh silently at himself and shake his head. By the time the boat arrived on foreign shores, he was near panic. Unable to move, he remained quietly hidden until all sounds ceased. Then off he scampered into the cold thick night. Fortunately, he was familiar with the terrain. His destination was his first cousin's house, Jako's place, whose farm was only a few kilometers away. Alexi had visited Finland often as a child, having grown up with his cousin. As youths they had wrestled together and swapped dirty stories.

With brief hellos, Jako was quick to move Alexi into the cellar. He would keep him hidden, while feelers would be sent to the West asking for sanctuary for the Russian theoretical neuro-physicist Alexi Patrenko.

The following night, Alexi's paranoia reached such intense levels, that the sound of his teeth chattering morphed into the footfalls of the Russo-Siberian Secret Police. Trying desperately to stop the jitters, he only became more afraid. Picturing Bash storming down the cellar stairs, Alexi's fears amplified accordingly. He could only crouch in the shadows and rock himself back to some semblance of sanity. Already, he missed his land deeply.

Finally, six days later, Jako brought back a CIA agent. The man was taken into the cellar to speak to Patrenko. Cowering in the dark, the defector was afraid to say anything. "It's all right Alexi, he's here to help." Jako tried to soothe his distraught cousin, but then took Templar's advice and left the two of them alone downstairs.

Agent Templar was tall, dark and cool. Having attended the recent Psychotronic Conference, he had no love for this man who was responsible one way or another for the deaths of Kranz and the victims of Legionnaires' Disease. But also, he had his job to do. "You will tell us about all parapsychological and psychotronic warfare, how you transmitted the disease and electrocuted Kranz, where in the brain electrodes are placed, other technological advances, et cetera." Templar's monotone belied the hate he felt for the Eurasian.

"I did not kill Kranz....I can't," he began. "I can't. I'll be a traitor." Alexi said the last word as if it were leprosy.

"Then we cannot take you to America." Templar got up to leave.

Cowering back to the corner, Alexi listened to the muffled voices of Jako and Templar upstairs. And then he heard a door slam.

"Wait! All right!" The fugitive screamed up the stairs. Jako called Templar back, while Alexi sank his head in shame.

"Write everything you know. Everything. Every little detail. I will be back tomorrow afternoon to pick it up. If there are any lies, you will be on your own."

"Tomorrow afternoon, why so long?" Patrenko was pleading by now.

"Twenty-four hours. Get out your pen." The agent turned abruptly, and Jako took him to the front door. Alexi began to whimper. By the time Jako returned, his cousin was crying in uncontrollable waves, his dark plight echoing within the dank cement foundation.

WARP DETENTE

Al's house looked cold and stark against the Vermont night sky. Abdul had fallen back to sleep, Rudy had driven the last forty-five minutes in silent darkness. The endless stretches ahead seemed to envelop everything, as he propelled Boshtov's vehicle relentlessly northward. Chess should be waiting safely, he thought.

As he approached the driveway, he could see a thin trail of gray smoke spiraling upwards from the chimney. Rudy thought back to Auntie Velma, and felt her warning presence. Only one small light burned. He parked below the rise, leaving Abdul comfortably sacked out in the front seat. At least he would have a few private moments with his girl. As he sauntered up to the main entrance, an odd sensation overtook him. He knew Chessie was angry, but it was still unlike her not to run out, or at least come out, and greet him. Surely she had heard the car pull up. Maybe she was asleep.

He stepped onto the front porch and put his hand on the brass knob. As he turned it to go in, a snakelike limb wrapped itself tightly around his neck, and a metal protrusion stuck in his gut. "Move in quietly. Do not turn around." The voice warned in a peculiar accent. Rudy smelled dried blood.

Although the arm around his neck quivered, its grasp felt like tense steel. He wanted to wheel quickly, to catch his assailant with an elbow, to smash him through the wall, but that would be suicide. Captured, he relented, and entered the living room. Chessie lay tied up by the smoldering fireplace. Her mouth was stuffed with a dishrag and there was terror in her eyes. Rudy had never seen that look on any human before. The man pushed him into the room. He ran to her, ripping the mouth bandage off, and cradled her head into his arms.

"It's all right, it's all right," he lied. She was sobbing hysterically. "How many are there?" he whispered, after weighing the situation, and then he turned to face his attacker. With a shock of recognition, both men remembered their meeting at the New York Public Library, and later at Sam Weiser's bookstore. Rudy could see that the man's arm was injured, but the ferocity of his stare staggered the reporter.

"One," she sobbed.

With the cyber-human facing him from across the room, Rudy considered overturning the sofa that lay between them, and smashing the man with a poker from the fire. The car door opened and closed. As the Tajik turned to the noise, his body was smacked by the thrust of the heavy furniture. Rudy had grabbed the bottom of the chair, and overturned it with his forward momentum, pinning Chi Jhenghis squarely against the front wall.

chHNNGGG! The agent's trigger finger released a bullet. Haphazardly, it tore through the ceiling, his arm forced up by the chair's motion forward.

Calling out for Abdullah, Styne grabbed the outstretched gun hand with both his own and bit deeply. Crunching the wrist in his jaw, Jhenghis screamed and dropped the gun. Abdul came running through the front entrance.

Although still pinned, Chi Jhenghis smashed his steel-plated skull into Rudy's face, but the blows could not land cleanly. He wanted to destroy the American for all the sins that civilization had done to him. Squirming to get free with his other hand, he grabbed Rudy by the hair and tried to ram his head into the wooden arm of the chair. During the scuffle, Jhenghis' woolen cap came off, exposing the plastic plugs and naked wires. Once more he plunged his skull forward, tearing it across Rudy's forehead, etching bloody lines along its path.

With a swift kick to the left temporal lobe, Manu knocked the man unconscious, his wounded arm now oozing blood again. As he lay upon the floor, Rudy grabbed the gun and spoke, "Abdul, find some rope in the kitchen closet."

The agent began to awaken. "I'd like to blow your god-forsaken head off, or what's left of it," Rudy grumbled. "Don't move a fucking muscle."

Abdul returned with a rope and some cloth and tied the man's hands behind him tightly. He also tied his feet, put a cloth around his mouth and placed the fur cap back onto his strange crown. Rudy untied Chessie, as Abdul washed and dressed the assassin's wounded arm. The girl's body shuddered as she tried to describe her ordeal.

"It's OK. It's OK," her boyfriend said. "Shush, don't talk." Quietly he rocked and warmed her rattled being.

Abdul reached for the phone. "I call police."

RINGGG! RINGGG! "Hello," Abdullah said. "Rudy, it's for you."

"Rudy, Koswell. I'm at the Burlington Airport. I've got Imo Bern's negatives with me."

"I almost forgot," Rudy said. "I'll pick you up."

"Great," Koswell replied.

"You guys'll be all right?"

"We be fine," Manu said, as he moved over to console Chessie who nodded in agreement.

"Maybe we should hold off calling the police," Rudy suggested to Manu, "at least until we see what Koswell has given us."

"Sure," Abdullah said. "He going nowhere."

Rudy drove to the airport as quickly as he could to avoid a long period of separation. "Kos," he said as they met, "the guy who owns the place we're going to has a computer that can print negatives. You don't even need a darkroom. So, when we get to the house, we can get right to the processing."

"That'll be fine," Koswell replied. They drove through isolated country roads back to the house.

"You know, I know Manu."

"No, I didn't know."

"It was me who set him up with Hirshon and the Incredible Fandango."

"You mean, it is you who is personally responsible for practically destroying his credibility?"

"Guilty as charged."

"I'm sure he'll be glad to see you."

"That's some tree," Koswell said, when they arrived. The enormous elm looked more ominous in the moonlight, its branches reaching out over the house like the gnarled fingers of a giant witch.

"If you only knew," Rudy said.

Koswell was introduced to Chessie. She was still shaken by her ordeal, but managed a grim smile. When it came to meeting Manu, Koswell simply said, "Hi, Abdul."

"Hey, Kos," Abdullah said, "I never thanked you properly."

"You mean for practically ruining your life?"

"No, for giving me freedom. Couldn't take all those crowds. So, once you set me up with that little guy with white fur on face, what's his name?"

"The Incredible Fandango?"

"Yes, Fandango. What little turkey he is, huh?"

"I'm trying to apologize."

"No need. I mean it, Koswell. I only want believers. He part of the negative force. All ones that don't believe, they can have him."

"So, this is the guy." Koswell said, changing the subject, as he approached Chi Jhenghis. Jhenghis sat still in the corner. He had lost blood, and he was securely tied. Rudy removed his toque to give Koswell a look.

"Holy Mother of God." Koswell stared at the wires and dials. "They go right into his brain."

Jhenghis looked up at him with an expression that was hard to read. In some way, he seemed almost relieved to be shackled, but Koswell read it as a ruse.

"That's one dangerous cat," Koswell said, as he took out a camera and snapped a few photos.

"That's enough," Manu said, placing the toque back on the agent's head. He brought Jhenghis some orange juice which he held for the wounded man to drink.

"Come on. Let's get him down into the basement. We can tie him up to a post, and there's heat down there, too," Rudy said. "It's late, already, and we can decide about the police tomorrow."

Rudy and Abdullah carried Jhenghis to the basement, dressed his wound again with iodine and secured him to a main support beam, and then they returned to the living room. Koswell was sitting quietly with Chessie by the burning embers. He took the time to describe his meeting with Agent Crankshaw, and his successful attempt to retrieve the film at Rudy's office. "This is Crankshaw's phone number," Kos said, as he wrote it on a piece of paper and placed the card back into his pocket. "Maybe we should call him instead of the locals?"

"We probably should," Rudy concurred.

"That is one great story," Manu said.

"Yeah, I know," Koswell replied.

Koswell and Rudy climbed the stairs to set up the computer and print out the film, while Abdullah stayed with Chess by the fire to meditate and give her comfort.

"What the hell does it say? It's in Russian," Rudy said, after they brought up the first set onto the screen.

"What the heck is this?" Koswell said, as he looked at one of the photographs which did not have type on it.

"It looks like a fish or something," Rudy said.

Abdul entered and looked at the screen. "That squid," he said.

"Why would he take a picture of a squid?" Koswell said as he stared at the iridescent green eye in the photo.

"He must have been by the sea," Rudy said. "He's given us a clue."

The three men considered the odd picture, and then Rudy broke the silence. "What are we going to do now? This whole thing is in Russian."

"I had forgotten," Koswell said. "Ando knew a translator."

"I know Russian. Am fluent in nine languages." Abdul smiled broadly. "And, do not worry. Your lady is asleep. You have pen?" Abdul then sat down and scribbled out rapidly:

TOP SECRET:
HISTORY OF MILITARY AND COLD WAR USES OF
PARAPSYCHOLOGY FOR ESPIONAGE, OFFENSIVE
AND DEFENSIVE WEAPONRY, HARASSMENT,
ILLNESS AND ASSASSINATION

With Koswell on the computer, Abdullah writing the translation and Rudy extrapolating notes, they worked through the night. Occasionally, Rudy thought about his girl sleeping, but he knew she would be all right, and that there was little that could be done until morning.

Koswell finished printing, and downloaded the information onto an extra CD. Abdullah had translated a little over ten pages, but was too fatigued to continue. "There is quite a lot of shit here," Abdul said uncharacteristically. "My brain is exhausted. I'll just scan the remaining sheets and write them out tomorrow." The Egyptian spread out Imo's pages before him, stared at each for a few moments, and then turned in for the night.

Good work, Kos," Rudy said. "I'd better check on Chess before I hit the hay." Rudy took Imo's roll of film and the CD and placed them in a boot in the closet.

Peeking down the stairs, he found Chessie in quiet slumber cuddled up on the sofa, beside the fireplace. He slipped by her, and descended the stairs to the cellar, to get a few more logs for the fire, and check on the Tajik. The captured man lay tied and crumpled in a heap by the woodpile. Rudy wanted to kick him in the face, but instead, wrapped a blanket around the wounded man. Due to the soldier's size and fierce strength, Rudy had not stopped to calculate his age. Now that he was asleep, the reporter took a good look. I bet he's not over twenty-five, he thought.

Chi Jhenghis tossed uneasily as he slept. He had inadvertently nudged his cap off most of his head. Rudy lit a match and peered at the cybernetic skull. It was an awesome and shocking sight to see a man who's brain was half machine. Jhenghis awoke and looked up. Now, only a shadow of a total person, he was puzzled and scared. He recalled, for a fleeting instant, his father's yak herd in Tajikistan, the smell of the family's wooden barn, and the look of his mother's saw-toothed grin. When Eurasian storm troopers had abducted him at his prime, they also stole from him a family whose ancestors had built the Great Wall of China and had conquered most of the civilized world. Now he was also robbed of his higher cortical functions. He looked up at the American as Rudy reciprocated. With visions of wolf hides and mother's blood soup, Chi drifted to sleep again.

* * *

It was three in the morning by the time all in the household had fallen asleep. Dreams came thickly as daytime reality gave way to more primal realms.

Two hours later, each awoke to the sounds of guns cocked. Rudy opened one eye slowly. A towering black shadow crossed over him. The tall Ukrainian's winged eyebrows and sneering full-toothed cheshire grin reigned over him.

"Get up, Mr. Styne," Bash said, smashing Rudy in the jaw with the muzzle of his gun. One of the Tajik sentries stood by the staircase, machine gun in hand, as the other searched the rooms. Koswell panicked, jumped out of bed and tried to run down the steps, punching one of the guards out of the way.

Bash strafed the wall around him with machine gun fire, nicking Koswell's leg, causing him to tumble down the rest of the stairs. He trembled in a heap at the bottom.

"I'm bleeding. Someone help me." Koswell cried out as Chessie shrieked. The Ukrainian stared fiercely back, daring Styne to budge before he commanded. He kicked the reporter in the crotch, doubling him over, and then smashed him once again in the jaw. "Get downstairs," he said.

One of the soldiers led Rudy to the living room, as Bash approached Manu. The Egyptian was sitting in a lotus position, his eyes closed as he meditated in a moment of prayer. Respectful of Manu's abilities, the Ukrainian moved cautiously. "Get dressed and go downstairs," he ordered, not wanting to injure such a prize possession. Abdullah casually looked up at his conqueror, yet Georgi turned away.

Rudy descended the steps, having to climb past Koswell. "We're done for," Koswell mumbled, as he worked to bandage his badly bleeding leg. "Why doesn't he just kill us right off?"

"He probably wants to figure out how much we know, and who we have communicated with," Rudy replied under his breath.

Chessie was still wrapped in a blanket downstairs on the sofa. She was being watched by Chi Jhenghis, whose arm was blood-soaked with a new opening of the wound. His body vibrated perceptibly as he stood guard. Nevertheless, his face revealed pained determination. Chess had resumed the terror-stricken expression she had had from her first horrible encounter. Now Rudy also began to feel it. He approached her and tried to comfort her, although stunned himself from Bash's swift blows. "Let her go!" Bash snapped, as he motioned with his rifle. Rudy complied.

Bash wielded the instrument of death in a dramatic display of power. He placed his foot under a small end table, and booted it across the room, shattering the antique against the far wall. The low lighting from the fireplace magnified the shadows on his bony face. He approached the reporter once more. "We want your files," he announced. Two of his henchmen stood by the door in military attention, and the third guarded the living room. Each wore the same familiar fur toque.

Bash circled the room with his eyes. "Watch them. Shoot anyone who moves." He climbed the stairs returning shortly with Manu's transcript and the computer printed papers of the Russian sheets. "Where are the negatives?" he demanded. He walked over and pointed his automatic weapon at Chessie's skull. "She dies if you do not talk."

Koswell spoke quickly, as he limped over to a chair to apply pressure to his thigh to stave off the bleeding. "We mailed them yesterday to CIA headquarters."

"You're lying," Bash shouted, wheeling and shooting off a few rounds above and below him. The harsh staccato pierced the air as a half dozen large bullet holes splintered the old wooden structure.

Koswell began trembling again. His knees buckled, and he dropped to the floor in a faint. Yet, somehow, his body continued shaking in arrhythmic undulations. Blood began once more to gush from the thigh wound. Manu filed over to the spastic figure and placed both hands around Koswell's forehead. Having timed his movements against the grain of the situation, no one made an attempt to stop him. With his two thumbs, he closed the reporter's eyes and held tight. The body slowed to a minor tremble, and then stopped shaking.

Abdul looked at the makeshift bandage which Koswell had crudely fashioned. "I go to kitchen for water and hot compresses," he announced.

"Go ahead. I don't want him to die--just yet," Bash said, motioning to one of the cyborgs to follow him.

Manu returned with a bowl of steaming water and fresh towels. Clearing away the pants, he washed the bloody wound, and began to prepare a bandage.

"Get me a needle and some thread," Bash said, motioning to Chessie. "Watch them," he said to the guards. He approached Koswell to inspect the damage more closely.

Stiffly, Chessie walked to a cabinet, removed a sowing basket, and returned with a needle and thread.

The doctor deftly sterilized the thin instrument with a match and a bottle of liquor, and spoke as he worked it through the skin. "I'm going to ask you again Mr. Koswell. Where are those negatives?" Bash plunged the needle firmly into flesh and pulled it out ready for another stitch.

"Ow!" Koswell cried.

"Where are the negatives?" Bash repeated quietly, as he prodded the skin a bit too long, before he plunged for the next stitch.

"God, I don't know, I didn't hide them. I didn't." Koswell held his ground as best he could, but if the wound were reopened, the consequences could be fatal.

"I just want the negatives," Bash said.

Rudy had stood firm as long as possible, but now he knew he must react. "What guarantee do we have?"

Bash paused in his sewing and turned to him. "None, Mr. Styne. None, whatsoever."

He finished the stitch, tied a knot and broke the thread with his teeth. Grabbing Manu's bandage, he secured it to Koswell's leg. Surveying the scene and content he had center stage, he approached and grabbed Rudy by the throat. "You can tell me now, or you can tell me later." He slugged the journalist in the head, knocking him to the floor. "I'm in no rush."

In terrific pain, Rudy looked up with thoughts of rage.

"Frankly, Mr. Styne, I would like nothing better then to take your head back to Siberia with me, just to find out exactly how your reckless mind works. Speak." He grabbed Rudy by the hair, and threw his face against the leg of the sofa.

Rudy had battled Bash as a warrior in Italy, and had beaten him in Bridgeport, but now the odds were too much against him. Nevertheless, he thought, to release the negatives appeared to be suicide.

"Mr. Bash," he replied, his face still pressed to the side of the chair, "I have mailed the negatives to the CIA. Mr. Koswell was not lying."

Bash let out a roar that shook the windows. He picked Styne up like a piece of lumber and held him with both hands above his head. "Where are they!?"

Rudy saw his life pass before him as the Ukrainian brought him to the brink of annihilation.

"In boot in closet," Manu said quietly, turning to face his captor squarely. "Upstairs. Release him and leave with bounty."

Bash dropped Styne gruffly, as he continued to stare eye to eye with the Egyptian.

"Great going, Abdullah," Rudy spat at Manu. "You have managed in one moment to betray all that Imo worked for, and you have also left Bash with no reason to keep us alive."

"Do I look as heartless as all that, mister shoulder-stabber?" Bash kicked Rudy one more time for good measure. "Get it." He motioned to one of the Tajiks. The solider raced upstairs.

"You are a fool, Russian," Manu proclaimed in a deep voice, ignoring Rudy's rash comments. "This is only one of many dimensions. What will you do in next life?"

"I'll wait till I get there, Mr. Magician. I protect my country in this world-- from the evil war-monger capitalists. It is they who are responsible for the unrest and military aggression in the world. It is their lies, their senators, their operatives and their predator drones who curse our people and foster a civilization based on decadence, armed aggression, space wars, hate, selfishness and greed.

"Do you know who I AM?" Manu demanded, booming the last two words in a voice that seemed exterior to him.

The acoustics resounded deep within the Ukrainian's mystical psyche. Signs of self-doubt entered his eyebrows. "Enough!" Bash screamed. "Get back over there." He motioned towards the others. Styne's face was bleeding, and his body and head were sore. Bash collected the notes and photographs, and threw them into the fire. The soldier returned, and handed to his superior a canister of film and the CD.

Bash sighed, sat down at the sofa, placed his gun against his leg, and began to scan the negatives against the light. He was more calm now, a touch a sorrow in his eyes, as he thought of Imo, and wondered how he had found the material, and how long he had known about it. Relieved that this retrieval now prevented the possibility of irreversible embarrassment for Bonzovalivitch and Yakutski Science City, Bash was also aware that the recovery would help protect his own hide as well.

Chi Jhenghis took the negatives and placed them carefully in the flames. His bad arm appeared almost green in the eerie glow. Bash leaned back in his seat and began to grin, then turned suddenly back to Koswell and held up an imaginary gun. *"Ratt, tatt, tatt, tatt!!"* he shouted, as he grinned. Koswell succumbed once again into a seizure. "Stay right there!" Bash commanded Manu, preventing him from going to Koswell's aid. Like a cougar, Bash reached over and dragged the shaking prey to his corner. Taking Koswell by the ears and thrusting the head towards his own stomach, he got his victim to stop shaking, while at the same time, he also put Koswell into a deep trance. The spymaster sat the reporter erect in a chair and grinned back at Manu, then motioned for Rudy to come over.

Styne could not deny the magnetic pull of the Ukrainian. Standing by the sofa, Bash motioned with his forefinger. Reluctantly, Rudy edged closer.

Lifting his foot swiftly, Bash caught Styne on the chin and sent him reeling backwards toward the fire. Laughing heartily, he waited for Rudy to get back on his feet, and then motioned for him to approach once more. Suddenly, one of the Tajiks pivoted, lifted his tommy-gun and pointed it at his superior! As Jhenghis and the other cyborg stood still, the renegade aimed to fire. Chessie ducked and screamed, as Bash dove for his own weapon which lay against the wall, and with the same rolling movement, squeezed his finger. Machine gun bullets ripped through the cyborg's stomach, chest and arms. The Tajik seemed to smile as he expired, but then grimaced, as what was left of his essence was released from psionic bondage.

Incredulity swept over Bash's face as he stared back at Manu. He wheeled once more and pointed his gun at the other two sentries. "I'm all right," each nodded in turn. The dying man oozed red pools of rich blood, his face now contorting in perplexed horror.

During the next moment of stillness the psychic spoke. "Tarot reading, Dr. Boshtov?"

"You have quite a sense of humor," Bash responded. And then he looked back at the dead soldier.

"I'm sure he is in a better place," Manu said.

"Yes, I'm sure," Bash spat.

"So, the reading?"

"You're serious?" Bash was incredulous.

"Let us find out who you are, doctor...and who you will be." Abdul reached slowly and deliberately into his inside pocket and produced a Tarot deck. He moved very carefully so as not to arouse suspicion. Bash walked over, shoved Rudy once more with his foot, and proceeded to rest the muzzle of his gun on Manu's shoulder.

"There is no death," Manu said as he shuffled the deck. "Only transmigration."

"Get him out of here," Bash shouted in Russian, motioning to the other sentry to drag the body to the porch. "You stay here," he ordered Jhenghis, who nodded in compliance. And then he returned his attention to the cards. With unprogrammable mixed emotions, the other sentry returned and resumed his post at the door.

The sun rose.

Tiny flecks of light could be gleaned skipping back and forth between Egyptian and Slav. It seemed as if they were charged with opposite voltages. The staring and wondering continued for endless moments, Rudy taking the time to rub Chessie's back with his palm. Koswell still in trance, sat like a wooden Indian on the other side of the room.

The two mystics appeared to glow brighter, Manu's golden aura interpenetrating Bash's purplish red, then repelling it, and meshing again in alternating rhythmic pulsations. Light beamed from Abdullah's left eye towards Georgi's right, energy streaming back and forth.

An electrified zap ignited between them as a jagged crack split the ceiling, showering plaster onto the people below. Neither man relented.

"All right," Bash declared, "Deal." He sat back in his chair and smiled, affectionately patting his gun for reassurance. Now in a more quiet mood, he almost felt for one brief moment as if he were back at his Vladivostok hermitage, reflecting by the cool lapping Sea of Japan. He looked at the ashes in the fire and back at his captives. "I've already won," he said.

"Can I shuffle them?" Koswell spoke, as he started to get up. He was out of trance and Bash became disgusted. He had relaxed his concentration for only a moment and Abdullah had gained an edge. The Ukrainian grimaced. Picking up his gun, he aimed it at Abdullah's chest, motioned for Koswell to stay put, and then nodded for the reading to continue.

Rudy was hurting badly. His pride shaken, and his face swollen, he still was upset that Manu had given the film up so easily. Nevertheless he tried to figure out what the psychic was up to. He must have located those negatives telepathically, he reasoned.

"No," Abdul said, "you must shuffle." He reached out and handed the cards to Dr. Bash. The Ukrainian approached and stood over Koswell, who was sitting nervously on the sofa, gently soothing his leg. "I could put this idiot back in trance and have him blow your goddamn brains out." Bash responded using American slang quite freely, as if to show the captives how well he had infiltrated their country. Wanting to reestablish his authority, having lost two mental battles already, Georgi was nevertheless curious to see this so-called "superpsychic" in action. Further, he was curious to find out what the cards had in store. With the notes and negatives destroyed, he could allow Manu the luxury of this off-beat request. "Perhaps I may learn something, eh?" he said.

"Dr. Boshtov," Abdullah said, "you know bullets can not hurt me. Why, with your knowledge, are you so caught up in the Earth life?"

"Stick to the reading," Bash said impatiently. He placed the gun under his arm, and again told the soldiers to shoot anyone who moved.

Grabbing the Tarot deck skeptically, he eyed at it as a snooping gorilla might stare at a camera. Of course, he was familiar with the Tarot, but he had no direct experience with it. Its close connection with religion was enough of an anathema to steer him away.

"Shuffle deck thoroughly," Abdul said. "Today, I show you the Great Mystery." As Bash began to shuffle, Manu spoke, "Tarot is as old as civilization itself. It combination of two decks: one called Minor Arcana, which is almost identical to the regular Las Vegas deck of playing cards. This part of the Tarot was developed in Mesopotamia, the land between two rivers, as a way of keeping track of time. It shows our direct linkage to cosmos. It is just like a regular deck, except for four extra cards. There are 4 suits, 4 seasons, 52 cards, 52 weeks in year, 13 cards in each suit, 13 weeks in each season. The extra card, or joker for each suit, is seen as the Page card, like second jack. That is essentially the only difference. Thus, Minor Arcana is really a sophisticated calendar."

"Why is there an extra card in each suit?" Chessie interrupted.

Bash cocked his head to look at her. "Good question," he said. "You have answer?" He turned to Manu.

"Take season of Autumn," Manu said. "Every year, Autumn is the same. It is the transition from Summer to Winter. In the regular deck, there are 13 cards in season for Autumn. The suit for this season is Clubs in regular deck, or Wands in Tarot. Winter is spades or swords in Tarot, Spring, diamonds or pentacles, and Summer is hearts, renamed cups in Tarot. So, if cards are calendar, how would ancient man differentiate one Autumn from another? That is what the extra card is. It is a summary of that season for that year. And that card would change every year for that particular season. One year may be rainy Autumn, that would be summed up by one type joker or page card, depicting rain, another year may be sunny, different summary card used to tell that story. Each year, these cards kept as permanent record for each season. Scribes would be used to convert to stone carvings. Just as surely as Earth spin on axis, this deck contains a record of past, present and future."

"All right," Bash interrupted, feigning mild disgust. "And what about the rest of the deck?"

"Major Arcana, or Great Mystery, was added later by ancient Egyptians, my forefathers. The hieroglyphic symbology can explain man's metaphysical quest for initiation into the inner realm. There are 22 major cards, and each stands for the next step on journey of life. Each card, whether Major or Minor, stands for a different mystery describing man's link not only to outer reality, but to infinite and timeless inner realms as well. Cards that appear in your reading will tell something about synchronistic relationship to your occult spiritual heritage and destiny."

"What is the meaning of the Fool card?" Chessie found herself saying.

"Now, you get technical on me," Manu said with a smile. "There are really 21 Major cards plus one, which is the Fool card. This card really alter-ego of first card, of Magician. Fool also symbolize entire set of 21 other major cards. It is the card of the journeyman. No matter where one is on path, one always Fool."

Koswell sat puzzled, still shaken from his ordeal, unable to completely grasp what was transpiring. Rudy considered grabbing the tommy-gun by pushing the Ukrainian backwards, but Chessie held him tight. In the back of his mind he tried to figure Abdul's angle. The Egyptian was shrewd, he concluded, so there was no telling what his plan might be...if, indeed he had a plan. He glanced over to the sentries who stood immobile, pointing their weapons in their general direction.

Chessie had trust in Manu. She gave Rudy a reassuring squeeze as she leaned forward to get a better view.

"We do simple reading, Dr. Boshtov. I tell you about your past, present and future. You, in turn, will allow us a future." Abdullah gestured to the burning notes of Imo's.

"I'll keep it in mind," Bash bantered.

* * *

Abdul weighed the deck in his hand, able to maintain concentration over Bash's occasional rude outbursts of belching laughter. The psychic gently placed the cards down on the counter, and asked Bash to cut the deck three ways. The lug complied.

Placing the cards together in this new order, Manu carefully laid out five cards face down. He started from the right and worked leftward. After completing this simple maneuver, he said, "This end card on left will relate to your distant past, next, the second card, to immediate past, middle card to present, card to right, immediate future, and card at far right, your destiny."

Bash nodded assent, and Manu turned over the first card and then began. "This card is MAGICIAN, upside down. You come from a long line of sorcerers."

Your soul is part of group soul shared by Rasputin, Svengali, Jhenghis Kahn and Lucifer. MAGICIAN, upside down, reveal big misunderstanding in knowledge of powers. You had unloving childhood which helped cause stroke that killed mother." Bash nodded in agreement. Tensions seemed to relax as he became more human. "She unable to forgive even now until you forgive her. Work in magic foreordained, work in Black Magick by your own choice."

Bash absentmindedly placed his free hand to his chin, and gently plucked it, as he began to consider the reading.

Manu turned the next card over. "CHARIOT up-side down. Warrior pulled by two sphinx, one black, one white. White sphinx stand for goodness. You perform as healer and doctor. Topsy-turvy emphasize night side of nature." He pointed to the black sphinx. "You have knowledge of cosmic consciousness," Manu pointed to the stars, "but ruled too much by animal and Earth instincts. Ceiling of stars in card within realm of possibility for you, doctor, but must reverse dark path."

Thunder rumbled from distant mountains, as Manu turned over the card in the middle and pointed to it.

"ACE OF SWORDS stand for you at this moment. God's hand reaches out from cloud and holds up lance: Spear of Destiny. He gave you Life, doctor. This not a right, but a privilege which must be earned. He also gave you magnetic spirit. In order to connect with the source, you must see the realm of the invisible.

Yet Great Spirit can not be seen with naked eye. You *will* succumb to Natural Law just as any other humanoid. This card stands for might, power and ruthlessness, coupled with knowledge of metaphysics. You have succeeded in the past and today by ruling by sword, but Law of Karma dictates: Those who live by sword, die by sword. Next card will reveal the path you take."

The sleek Egyptian looked back up into his conqueror's eyes, and then he began to transform. The house gently trembled, and popping noises could be heard in the walls.

The atmosphere rippled like a mirage at the end of a long summer road, and then Abdullah faded, reappearing a timeless instant later as a pharaoh with black oval eyes, gold headdress and long flowing white robes. Everyone in the room lay witness to the transfiguration. Bash's face also transformed into one with incredibly short bushy eyebrows and a long beard parted at the center. The figure's cheeks sagged and deep bags could be seen underneath the eyes.

The pharaoh turned over the card of the immediate future.

As bizarre as the moment was, it somehow felt natural, as if a more fundamental reality had simply "stepped in." It was as if their oversouls collectively were preparing for this one moment.

It was the HERMIT standing in the dark holding up a lantern to light the way. "I AM THE HERMIT," Manu declared. Raising his hand to form the lantern, Abdullah began to glow beneath it, the sign of infinity appearing above his head.

Flowers sprouted from zapped ceiling cracks, and butterflies manifested, fluttering in spiral circles above Chessie's head. She levitated briefly, and plucked a pink tulip from above. As she slowly descended, Abdullah symbolically handed the etheric glow to the dark sorcerer who reached for it boldly, shining its beacon around the room. Chi Jhenghis' face broke out in boils, and frogs showered down upon the other sentry. Abdullah rose, held up two more lanterns, and spoke, "I AM THE WAY. I AM THE LIGHT." The Hebrew Ten Commandments came blazing from his heart in golden holographic tridimensionality.

Georgi shrieked as the nightmare crystallized. His submachine-gun transformed into a cobra which curled itself around his leg, and began swaying its capelike head in rhythm to Manu's pulsations of gold, violet and light green. "It not too late, Dr. Boshtov. You hold great power to do good or evil." Manu waved his hand and another snake appeared, wrapping itself around Georgi's other leg, completing the double caduceus of Kundalini. Bash was frozen in terror for the first time in his life. Protecting his genitals with one hand, he stretched his head far away from the seething serpents, and tried to ward them off with his other.

"God has given you will power to determine fate of millions." Abdul waved his hands rapidly in a small circle as he flexed his spindly fingers.... Ten miniature snake-like appendages slithered towards the agent's horror stricken eyes. Deftly, Manu snatched the coiled cobras that had embraced each leg and tossed them into the fire. *PUFF!* the image disappeared--but so had Bash's gun! The electricity went out, as both sentries froze, locked in a solid state of cybernetic shutdown. Chi Jhenghis' face contorted, his body began to tremble, as the front of his weapon drooped. And then a vestige of his old self seemed to reappear. He shook violently and broke for the door, disappearing through the morning mist. The gun of the other sentry also drooped, as all reality cues became skewed.

"Stop!" Bash cried out, but Jhenghis was gone. Bash stood stupefied. Having lost his control to the higher order, he permutated into a crazed animal. With teeth bared, like a cougar, he lunged forward, kicking Styne out of the way, as he grabbed Chessie by the throat.

Abdul levitated slightly. "Remember, Dr. Boshtov, Lucifer is not the devil, he is the tempter, the sly one, the fox. He has the power to heal or the power to destroy. You both. You chariot, you killer, yet also you are healer."

Bash held the girl as if she were a chess piece, not quite sure what to do next. Picking up the Magician card, Abdul resumed. "All occultists know Law of Osiris. We are one. No difference, no Russia, no America, no Egypt, no Israel, no separateness in higher octaves." Pointing to the canopy of stars above the chariot rider he said, "Secrets of heaven can be man's if he earn them. First, he must see through MAYA, realm of illusion," pointing to the two sphinxes, "duality."

"Why are you the Hermit and not me?" Bash demanded, gripping Chessie in a retreating display of lost power, trapped like the rest in the collective nightmare.

"You Hermit. You carry torch, but for the wrong reason. We are not your enemy. The United States is as misguided as your country. The enemy is own shadow, own dark side, own nature which you do not understand. There is only one enemy on Earth...man himself."

Abdullah pointed to the black sphinx. "You never kill other, only self." He pointed to Chessie. "You must do as alchemist." He nodded to the MAGICIAN. "Change your base nature into a golden one--white sphinx--and achieve unity--CHARIOT DRIVER."

"You say the United States is not my enemy." Bash continued his grip on Chessie, holding her as if she were a rag doll. "They fight against our cause in every country on the globe. Look at their history. They turn the world against us to prevent Olympics from being held in Moscow. They stop grain shipments in efforts to starve our people. They ignore test-ban treaty and detonate nuclear weapons while they talk our leaders into dismantling ours."

"They build up Star Wars defense shield while they invade our land with neon signs and capitalist propaganda. They place nuclear warheads in a dozen countries within 500 miles of our borders. They assassinate political opponents--in their own country as well as in others. They ridicule our people in books and films. Their senators give lip service to foreign aid, as secretly they fan the fuels to support our dismantlement. We were once a great empire and now look where we are. It was the Americans who turned Gorbachev's head which started our country on the path of dissolution."

"The earth is a small place, a teaching ground for humans," Abdul responded, as he began to glow more vividly. "Man is but a grain of sand. His atomic weapons not even hiccups in evolution of Solar System and Galaxy." He threw his hand out and produced a tiny holographic mushroom cloud. "But creator set up paradise here for us. Here is fruit and vegetable, here fish and river, rain, snow and sunshine. He has endowed you, Dr. Boshtov, with the mystical power and a worthy heritage, and you have squandered it. Already, you have murder many, even today you die by the sword. Now, leave us in peace and take light with you."

Manu twirled his hand once more. The lantern rematerialized. Bash pushed Manu's hand away and tucked Chessie under his arm, controlling his destiny in the only way he could. He reached over to the last card and turned it over. It was the TOWER. A tall building on fire was depicted.

"Believed to be Tower of Babel," Manu said. "These two people diving off top to their deaths represent Law of Karma...and power of Natural Law. There is rainstorm, yet Tower in flames, struck by lightning."

A zigzag flash struck the fireplace. Thunder rocked the house. **"DO NOT DESTROY THE GIFTS!"** Abdul boomed, his voice emanating from a whirlpool of light. Images of worlds past and future appeared as holographic thoughtforms surrounding each chakra of his body. Swirling from the solar plexus like a horn of plenty, the advanced primates witnessed the formation of galaxies, nebulae and solar systems, the creation of Jupiter and the Sun...and their spin-offs: Vulcan, Mercury, Earth and Moon, Venus, Mars, Titan, Saturn, Io, Neptune, Uranus, Pluto and Chiron

Manu played Akashic records in stereo, revealing to them the rise of the great civilizations: Lemuria, Atlantis, Toltec, Mayan, Greece and Rome, Easter Island, Tibet and Egypt, and all of their destructions. The rise of Western culture, French, American and Russian revolutions, the rise of Hitler, Stalin, Idi Amin and Saddam Hussein. Evil and poverty. The atom bomb and devastation of great cities: New York, Los Angeles, Paris and Moscow by earthquakes and deluge. The space age, lasers and dematerialization machines, séances, saucers and metal benders, life on terra firma and cerebration beyond.

Each person witnessed his own past and future existences. It became clear that the group soul which gave birth to Bash, had been a catalytic force in black and white magic throughout the centuries. He was not good and evil, but conscious and unconscious. Manu saw Bash as tragically misguided. He had been a Uzbek Shaman bringing babies into the world, and yet, he had sacrificed virgins. He was Rasputin who had healed the Czar's son and slept with his wife. He was doctor and assassin, knight and shadow.

Georgi began to cower by the foot of the sofa, having dropped Chessie long ago. All were in trance, their imaging pouring forth from a central source.

Manu's voice continued, "**JUDGEMENT IS UPON YOU. THERE IS NO ESCAPE.**" The sky grew dark. Black clouds hovered over. Thunder cracked.

Hail stones bombarded the roof with a massive shower of ***ratt-a-tat-tatts***. The wind howled through the front door, depositing little round ice packets which covered the floor in a melting marbled carpet, as Bash's voice could be heard above the din, "**SHOOT TO KILL!**" he belted out.

The remaining guard raised his weapon, warped by psi, and pulled the trigger. There had been no thought, only response to a commander's voice. The gun exploded in the sentry's hands, blowing off a forearm and part of the right side of his face. "Kill," Bash repeated as he reached for Chessie and pointed to Abdullah. Rudy yanked her back and fled out the rear door, as Koswell fainted behind the couch.

The sorcerer lunged for Manu and seized him by the throat, forcing the psychic towards the burning fireplace. Manu grasped the brick façade to try and keep himself from plunging in, as he did his best, with his other hand, to prevent Bash from getting a better hold. But Bash was persistent, and Manu was losing ground rapidly.

Unaware of Manu's imminent danger, Rudy and Chessie plunged deeper into the cold forest, running as if pursued by demons, fear forcing them farther and farther away from the house.

The badly injured Tajik dropped his head like a charging kamikaze and rammed himself furiously into the wrestling pair. With his remaining hand, the sentry clenched his superior by the groin, and squeezed, as he drove them farther into the seething coals. Rolling against red coals, Bash searched madly for the cyborg's neuroelectrodes, as Abdullah slithered free. Dazed, he leaned against the sofa to catch his breath, as Bash continued to fight, groping recklessly for his target. But the Tajik had pinned him against the hearth, and began to beat him with a fiery log. Blocking the onslaught with one hand, the spymaster finally reached the cyborg's control panel with the other. He clawed at the wires blindly, yanking connections from the midbrain and cerebellum. With flesh-burning thrusts, he wrenched himself free, leaving his victim smoldering unconsciously in the fireplace. Darting out the door, he sloshed through the hail, and made his way for an open road.

Manu watched the Ukrainian flee, as he stood up to take stock of the events that had transpired. Having been in trance through much of the reading, he had not had time to completely return to the Earth plane. He staggered over to the fireplace and dragged the dying roboman out of the coals, hauled him to the reception porch and piled him upon the corpse of the other sentry. Chanting a rhythmical ritual from the *Egyptian Book of the Dead*, Manu stared incomprehensively at Lucifer's work.

He turned to look for Koswell, only to find him sound asleep on the big sofa. A smile passed his lips as he searched Koswell's pocket for Chrankshaw's phone number, and gave him a call.

Unable to find his car keys, Bash continued towards the highway, clutching his scorched limb as an ostrich might tuck a wounded wing. He came upon a farmer's truck. It was a rickety contraption, but the keys were in it. Down the hill he rolled it, before turning the ignition. The vehicle backfired and rattled away.

Coming to an intersection, Bash turned the jalopy north towards Canada. Every bolt and spring strained to the pressure as he pushed the gas pedal to the floor. Fearing the possibility that his fuel gauge might be broken, he pulled into a nearby Sunoco station.

"Fill this automobile up, young man," he said as he fought off the burning pain. His shirt and coat protected him from irreparable damage, so he tried as best he could to separate his mind from the plight of his physical body. It was difficult, for the shoulder was still injured from the plunge of Rudy's steak knife, so he cursed the "son-of-a-bitch" as the attendant filled the tank.

"What'd ya say?"

"Son-of-a-bitch."

"Just what I thought."

"You have a rest room here?" Bash said, unable to contain the pain any longer without seeking some relief.

"Rest room. Sure. In the back."

The agent rushed out to wash his wound in the men's room sink. However, by the side of the building a rain barrel filled with icy water caught his eye. Removing the leather coat, he sunk the arm deep to the shoulder, gritting his teeth with the shock of the temperature change. The ice-cold fluids numbed the pain. He dried himself off, put his jacket back on and lumbered back to his car. "Lad," he attempted casually, "and what type of car are you driving?"

"1971 GTO, dual cams, 485 horse power."

"Is that it parked over there?"

"Sure is. What'd you do to your arm, mister?"

"How do I know a classic machine like that is not owned by your boss?" Bash said, leading him on. "I crunched it fixing the cherry-picking machine," as the boy pulled out his keys to proudly display them.

"Geeze, that looks a lot like a burn. Your jacket's all charred. What'd you really do?"

Bash contemplated murdering the kid where he stood, but pangs from the realm of Karma held him at bay. "Sleep!" he commanded, snapping his fingers in front of the youngster's eyes. As the boy folded, Bash grabbed the keys, walked over to the GTO and started the engine. *Vroooommm*. The Ukrainian grinned broadly as he sped away, leaving skid marks in place of the vehicle. Taking the hot-rod out onto the open highway, he continued north toward the border. Weaving in and out of the light traffic, he put on the radio, and contemplated strategies as to how best to cross into Canada.

Rounding a curve at 80 mph, his foot automatically hit the breaks, for there up ahead was a roadblock with three police cars strung across the highway. They were checking the motorists one by one. Bash swerved sideways. He considered turning 180 degrees, and then thought again and fishtailed forward, gunning it, swerving around the leftmost edge of the barricade, his car careening against the guardrail, but continuing on its way, zipping past the stunned patrolmen. Flooring it once again, he disappeared down the road before the chase cars even began to roll. Bash knew he would not be able to cross the border in the car he was in, so he exited at the first opportunity, tearing rapidly down a narrow single-lane trail. Trees flashed by in a whirr.

One police car took that exit to cover it, while the other continued north along the main highway. Bash sped forward pulling into the oncoming lane over double yellow lines when necessary, and passing vehicles on the right shoulder at other times. On straight-a-ways he hit speeds upwards of 145 mph, leaving the more conservative police driver far behind. Telephone poles passed like fence posts, the stroboscopic effect heightened by bright sunlight.

Going full throttle by now, feeling a bit more at ease, Bash continued to put more miles between himself and his pursuers. He took a left onto a larger road and dropped down to a modest speed of seventy-five mph, and then he changed roads a few more times, and changed roads again, continuing at the slower speed, but still heading north. He did not want to get caught for something stupid like drawing undo attention. Without a weapon, he had to be doubly careful. His decision was to cross the border after dark on foot, and get another vehicle on the other side. With secret contacts in Montreal, and a little luck, he planned to be in Moscow within 18 hours.

The car scooted up one hill and back down another. Picking up speed again, the fugitive loosened up. He looked down the road and spotted two moose grazing in low water off to the side about three-hundred yards ahead. There was a male and his lovely cow. He wondered if a calf might be somewhere nearby. Searching the surrounding swamp, he noticed some movement, and smiled as the little one stuck its nose out from behind low shrubs. But his smile changed to curses as the buck bolted across his path. Bent on an unavoidable collision course, Bash jammed his foot down hard on the brakes, but to no avail. He could see the knotted texture of the oversized antlers as he braced himself for impact. He only hoped the car would still be operational after the crash. Suddenly, and with grace, the animal leaped high. Out over the hood he jumped, crashing all four feet on the windshield, as he kicked off to limp into the woods.

With glass completely shattered, the view became impossible. Otherwise there was no damage! Somewhat relieved, Bash could only shake his head. He stepped out to look for something to knock out the crackled remains. As he battered the web-pattered windshield with a large club-shaped tree branch, searing pain returned to his flesh-burned arm. The squad car screeched to a halt as two policemen jumped out armed with shotguns cocked for use. Bash raised his hands in despair.

THE CELLAR

Alexi Patrenko cowered through the night in his cousin's basement, unable to write what he knew and unable to return himself back across the border. Even Jako's warm soup could not soothe his shattered soul. The CIA contact returned to find the doctor disheveled and frightened, a slight gray stubble blanketing his usually clean-shaven cranium.

Templar tried to ease Patrenko into revealing his secrets. This could mean an important promotion if he could bring forth a successful defection. But he also remembered Kranz's awful death, and was therefore allowing emotions to get in the way of professional responsibilities. "America will place you in a reputable university. You can continue your research for more respectable reasons and live like a VIP," he argued, not totally able to cover the contempt he had for the would-be defector.

"I know, I know, I know," Alexi kept repeating, as he backed off from the inquisitor to return to the shadows.

"Keep your voice down," the agent said. "Act like a man or hide down here till you rot." Templar got up to leave.

"Don't go," Alexi pleaded, grabbing Templar by the shirt sleeve.

The agent yanked his arm away in disgust, and marched up the stairs. "I'll be back tomorrow. You either shit or get off the pot."

Twenty minutes later, three Russo-Ukrainian soldiers stormed the house, shot Jako through the forehead with a silencer, and rushed the basement. Having tracked Patrenko through an intuitive lead about a cousin in Finland from a dying Madam Grotchka, they were delighted to find their prey still within reach.

Alexi heard Jako hit the floor with a thud, but was too fear-struck to seek cover. "Dr. Patrenko, you are under arrest for treason."

"NOOOOooooooooo," he wailed as they dragged him up the stairs, over his cousin's oozing corpse and into a waiting vehicle. Within three hours, Dr. Alexi Patrenko was chained to a wall in a Moscow jail cell.

ALL THE NEWS THAT FITS

Rudy and Chessie slowed to a walk, having dashed deep into the wintery forest. "How could Manu give that bastard the film? He didn't even try to..."

"For Heaven's sake, Rudy," Chessie retorted, "he saved our lives. Isn't that enough?"

"After Koswell risked his neck! After I saved his life. Imo Bern died for nothing."

That's not what you're really mad at, is it?"

"No," Rudy relented. "That Ukrainian fucker had us dead to rights. I guess Manu did what I couldn't." Rudy sat on a snow-covered rock and rubbed his swollen jaw. "Is this it for us, Chess?" He looked at her.

"You mean about the baby?"

He nodded assent. "I know you've been through hell. But, well, I just don't understand it. I thought all women...."

"Want kids?" She finished his sentence.

"Yes. I mean, I hadn't thought about having a child until that instant. We're not even engaged. Officially, that is," he added with a soulful look that made her reach over and give him a kiss.

Rudy winced as Chessie's lips gently caressed and then kissed his injured mouth. And then her lips continued its journey, traversing his entire face. Tiny kisses up to his cheeks and eyes and damaged forehead.

He sat there, eyes closed, as she took in his musty smell, and her breath quickened.

Rudy reached up with both hands, held her firmly, and gazed into her eyes. The love that flowed between them was overwhelming. Their lips touched, their tongues intertwined. Breathless, she pushed her head back and looked again deeply at him.

"That horrible," she searched for a word, "man, had me for eight hours. He never, well, you know what I mean, did anything, but he could have. He could have ripped me in two, if he had wanted. And all I could think of...." Chessie stopped in mid-sentence and walked away, unable to finish.

She put up a hand to keep him away, and Rudy let her go.

With her back to him, she grabbed onto a scraggily pine tree and whispered, "...was the baby."

Overwhelmed with deep sobs, Chessie collapsed and began to wail. Her cry was infectious, and the two of them sat and sobbed together on the soft wet snow until they were spent.

Neither Rudy nor Chessie could comprehend, or even accept, the fantastic events that had taken place between Manu and Bash. During their cautious walk back, they could only speak about subjects peripheral to that experience. As part of the mechanism of psi, the Bash/Manu encounter dissolved from consciousness as a dream disappears before dawning.

"I'm not even sure what I saw...." Rudy said, apropos of nothing, his voice trailing off in thought.

"Why didn't Manu run with us? And where's Koswell?" Chessie asked. Simultaneously, they broke into a run towards the house.

"Stay here," Rudy whispered behind a thicket, as he cautiously approached. Two Tajik bodies lay in a heap on the reception porch. Using a hedge as a blind, he crept forward and peeked through a side window. Two of the walls and part of the cracked ceiling were splattered with blood. The house, however, was silent. Rudy picked up a board and entered on cat's paws though the rear door. He listened and waited fully ten minutes, crouched behind a sofa, before he planned his next move.

"Ahh..."

What was that? he thought as he looked about. To his surprise he located Koswell sleeping peacefully on the sofa, his body having been hidden by three billowy pillows. Rudy could only smile and shake his head.

"Kos," he whispered, touching his colleague on the shoulder. "Kos, wake up."

"What, huh?" Charles shook himself awake and spoke. "What happened?"

"Where's Abdullah?"

"I don't know? Where am I?" Bewildered, Koswell had been unconscious during most of the events, and could hardly remember what happened. "Where's the Russian? Where are the notes?"

"Burnt! Manu told them. How's your leg?"

"OK, I guess; I was really out there."

"You certainly were!" Chessie broke in.

"You shouldn't be here." Rudy found himself reprimanding his girlfriend.

"I was afraid," she responded.

"Stay with Charles. I'm going upstairs to look around. You better check on his wound."

"Yes, you better, dear," Koswell said factitiously. "Go on, Rudy, I know I'll be in good hands."

Abdullah was stretched out comfortably asleep. A golden glow seemed to hang like a low fog about his pillow. "How could I have ever doubted him?" the reporter whispered to himself out loud. He tip-toed back downstairs and motioned to Koswell and Chessie.

"Abdul's asleep upstairs. He looks fine."

"Thank God," Chessie said.

Rudy walked out to the porch to study the heads of the two dead men. He stared in wonderment at the dials and wires. Chessie approached with a blanket and laid it quietly over their bodies.

"Nasty work," Kos said, as he lifted the cover. "Look at those dials and electrodes. They must go in about three inches!"

"My God, what's this world coming to?"

"Where's Boshtov, and the third soldier?" Koswell asked.

"They could be anywhere."

"I don't think they would hang around without a weapon." Chessie walked out onto the porch, holding up a submachine gun that was twisted and bent. Part of the front of the barrel was blown apart. "Manu's really connected!" she exclaimed.

"There's no doubt about it," Rudy said. "But who's going to believe it?"

"If we reported this story, we'd be the laughing stock of journalism," Koswell lamented. "We're trapped by illusion."

"The truth, I guess, is just too threatening," Chessie said.

"Tell me about it!" Rudy said. "You should have been there in Manu's apartment. It was amazing. Everything levitated. He even floated a girl across the room!"

"Baloney!" Koswell retorted.

"Kos, I know it sounds ridiculous, but I saw it with my own eyes. Ask Sally-Ann. She was there too."

"Sally-Ann?" Chessie shot Rudy an unmistakable look of jealousy. Turning back to the blanket she laid the gun underneath it as a shudder rippled up her spine.

"Some witness Sally-Ann makes! Boshtov hypnotized the lot of them," Koswell said, referring to Rudy's colleagues at *Modern Times*. "Hah!"

"Them!" Rudy and Chess responded in unison, staring at Koswell in astonishment.

"Did I really go under?"

"I'm afraid so," Chessie replied. "But don't feel too bad. He hypnotized me as well. It's a real blow to the ego to think we have so little real control over our actions."

Bewildered by the realization that he had seen so little of the fight, Koswell could only shake his head from side to side. "I'd better call Crankshaw," he said finally.

"Now, what did I do with that number. Ah, here it is." As he dialed, an unusual whopping sound was heard in the distance. "What the hell is that?"

A military chopper came into view and landed on the lawn. The familiar CIA agent jumped out with three other men.

"Bout time you men got here!" Abdullah said, sticking his head out of the upstairs window. "Boshtov has been picked up 85 miles north of here. His car hit a m..."

"Moose," Crankshaw completed the sentence shouting back. "How in hell do you know that?"

"How in heaven do I know? I'm coming down."

"Smells like burning flesh," Crankshaw said.

"It is." Koswell nodded to the hulks under the blanket.

"Thought you might be here," the agent remarked to Koswell as he lifted the blanket to take a look. "What the fuck. Look at the guns, and those crazy wires coming out of their heads! What the hell happened?"

"Lightning," Manu mused, pointing to the sky, as a small electrical spark jumped from his forefinger.

Crankshaw turned his gaze skyward. It was bright and clear. He looked about at the remnants of a few hail stones which lay unmelted in shady pockets around the yard. "Lightning?" he echoed contemplatively.

"Lightning," Rudy and Chessie repeated. Koswell stood uncommitted.

"Well, shit, this ain't lightning." Crankshaw reached down to touch the plastic and electrodes imbedded in the brain of one of the soldiers.

"Super-men," Rudy said. "Programmed to boost psychic energy, and to block out pain."

"Boshtov shot that one," Manu pointed to one of the dead soldiers. "We fight, but other drove us into fire. Boshtov pull plugs out of his brain, as I escape. He, however, badly burned. Skidaddle for highway. That way." He pointed west.

Chessie's eyes opened wide with the others as she considered the terrible life and death the young soldiers must have experienced.

"There's a third who escaped," Rudy added. "Just like these, only alive. His arm is wounded, but he is in pretty good shape."

"We'll find him," Crankshaw assured them. "He's probably down in the valley somewhere."

"Abdullah was unbelievable. He did it all." Rudy said.

"All?" Crankshaw questioned.

"Mind control," Koswell interjected. "Mind control."

Rudy continued, "We had top secret data on their complete parapsychological operations--how these," he kicked the corpses, "were created, what they can do, their plans to destroy computer banks, spread disease and create disorientation or blackouts. We had info on the quantum physics of consciousness, Bonzo's campaign of disinformation and more. But," he glanced over to the Egyptian, "Boshtov found the negatives and burned them." He motioned to the smoke of the chimney.

"Maybe we can salvage something," Crankshaw said. "Joe," he motioned to one of the other agents who had been roaming the house and grounds, "Collect those ashes carefully and send them to the lab." He turned to Rudy. "Is that all of it?"

"I'm afraid so."

The agents placed the dead in body bags and tossed them into the chopper. They completed their interviews and prepared to re-embark. "I want you to write out everything, everything you can remember," Crankshaw commanded. "We'll get you an ambulance for your leg."

"Thanks," Koswell said. "I'm sure a doctor from town will suffice."

"You know, of course, that you are not to release those findings to the press. This is top secret, high priority," Crankshaw said. "We already got Bonzovalivitch to reverse himself in public statements. And, if he becomes Premier," Crankshaw shouted as he stepped back on board the chopper, "a publication like this could simply destroy any chance of a total reconciliation."

"Fat chance," Kos shot back above the din. "Read it on page one tomorrow."

Crankshaw stopped the pilot and jumped back to the ground. He pushed his nose into Koswell's face. "I'm not fucking around. Don't mess with this. If you're a goddamn patriot, you'll understand what the words Top Secret mean. And don't give me that shit about first amendment rights. We're talking national security. I'm telling you now, don't force my hand. Worst case scenario, I get the two of you arrested for treason, and you guys are in and out of court for a minimum of three years. Monjo legal fees. You get my drift?"

Rudy started to interrupt, but Crankshaw went on. "Mr. Styne, let me make this perfectly clear. You look like an intelligent guy."

"Looks can be deceiving," Chessie chimed in.

Crankshaw ignored her, but Manu cracked a smile.

"You need to see that publication of their technological superiority could undermine the morale of the military, and even create a panic situation here at home."

"I doubt that," Rudy said.

"Well, I don't. We need lead time to develop counter weapons. So let me make it perfectly clear. I'm not asking you, I'm ordering you: Don't print this!....Look, if you have to print something," he said, relenting a little, "couch it, hide specifics, be obscure. Surely, you can do that. Help the government for a change. We're on the same side, you know."

"What the hell does that mean?" Styne asked.

"These are not my orders." Crankshaw said. "This comes straight from the top." And then in almost a whisper, he added, "The White House."

"The President!"

"No comment."

"Listen, we called *you,*" Koswell said. "I think that shows where our sentiments lie. Now give us something. What's up?"

"Maybe in forty-eight hours. Send your report straight to me." Crankshaw climbed aboard again as the helicopter lifted and disappeared as rapidly as it had arrived.

Rudy turned to Abdullah. "First of all, we must thank you for saving our lives. But damn it, why did you give Boshtov that roll of film so quickly? Maybe we could have hid the CD or something. Men *died* to get it to us. Now it's lost."

"I translated it, didn't I?" Abdullah smiled.

"Yes."

"So, let's get to work." Manu went inside and brought out an unused notebook. He began to write verbatim the translation he had written the night before. His hand moved so quickly that it became clear to the onlookers that he was in a trance.

"Photographic memory," Chessie whispered, watching intently. Manu looked up and nodded. His hand still continued to write as if by another force.

"Retrocognition," he said, as he returned to the task.

"Come on," Rudy said, "let's get this report going."

Koswell typed the headline:

EURASIAN COMMONWEALTH
OF INDEPENDENT REPUBLICS
INAUGURATES PSYCHOTRONIC INVASION ON WEST

> The Eurasians have developed parapsychological and psychotronic technology so far in advance of the West, that they have already planned and partially executed a covert guerilla attack here in the United States.
>
> This information was made available due to the defection of one Dr. Imo Bern, a parapsychologist from Uzbekistan who gave his life so that these diabolical paraphysical weapons, developed in secret laboratories in St. Petersburg and Siberia, would be revealed. Dr. Bern was stationed in an underground military and scientific complex a few hundred miles north of Yakutski, in central Siberia. Bern personally aided in the surgical procedures which led to the transformation of these humans into so-called "cyborg supermen" whose abilities rival that of the great natural psychics such as Abdullah Manu of Egypt and Nubea Lanilov from the Ukraine.

The article went on to describe all of the tactics spelled out in Imo's notes, including Bonzo the Pipe Dreamer's overt propaganda campaign to appeal to his constituency to rebuild the former Russian empire, and his covert plan to destroy the Western technological super highway with his platoon of telekinetic cyborgs.

Bonzo's link to Dr. Georgi Bash was revealed, as were the murders by Bash of various parapsychologists in London, New York, and most recently, in Italy at the psychotronics conference.

> If this information is accurate, it could mean great peril for the Western nations. No known defense system exists as far as we know. The Eurasians could, in effect, destroy or severely cripple not only the internet and telecommuni-

cations industry, but also any other electric
device, literally, any target on the globe or in
virtual space. And further, they would never have
to launch a missile to do it!

The next day, after having a doctor dress and care for Koswell's wound, the
four former captives drove triumphantly down to New York.

"Are you an avatar?" Chessie turned to Abdullah.

"Chessie! You're being too forward!" Rudy scolded.

"We are all messengers from God," Manu stated. "My soul trained before
birth to be conscious of vinculum in this present incarnation."

"Do you have any memories of Atlantis?" Chessie asked, ignoring Rudy's
scowl.

"Naturally. Atlantis was the second great civilization on Earth. Preceded by
Lemuria, sunken continent near where Tahiti stands today. I was son of prince
Eleazer, great oracle and healer. Many alive in America and Russia today live at
this time. Masters of Wisdom pray that we not make same mistake as then, and
destroy a world that took so long to recreate. God will let happen if man wills it."

"Do you still communicate with the Masters?" Rudy questioned.

"Now who's being pushy!" Chessie interjected.

"It's OK," Manu said.

"Who was Jesus?" Koswell asked.

"Who Moses? Who Abraham, Iknaton, Buddha, Mohammed, Washington,
Lincoln, Gandhi, Sedat, Gorbachev...Koswell. We are all same, All sons and
daughters of the One. Great Mystery for me is men like Georgi Boshtov. He is also
connected. He has eyes, but does not see. But is all God's plan. We are all made in
His image. Just must realize gift."

As the car rolled south, a family of fox crossed the road. "Did you see that?"
Chessie said excitedly, as just then a very large bird with a pointed beak swooped
from a big oak tree.

"That was an eagle!" Rudy cried out.

"Let's give the article to Hirshon," Koswell suggested. "It will make more of
an impact in the *Trib* than if it went to *Modern Times,* and they've already broken
ground with my earlier article."

"OK," Rudy agreed.

Rudy jumped out at Abdul's apartment. "I didn't mean to bark at you back in
Vermont," he said as he shook his hand vigorously.

"Thanks for saving our lives," Chessie cut in, running out to hug the great
psychic. She paused in awe of his gaze, and then leaned forward and kissed him
tenderly on the cheek.

"I guess we even," Abdul said to Rudy.

"I guess."

"I felt that I've seen the soul of the universe," Chessie reflected, as they got back into the car and dropped Koswell off at his apartment.

"I can't wait to sleep in my own bed," Koswell said as he departed.

"Me, too," Chessie sighed.

"I knew there was something between you!" Rudy kidded.

"Rudy!"

The following morning, Styne met Koswell at his office. They knocked on Hirshon's door. "It's got possibilities," Hirsh said. "But it's too long. We've got to cut out this Legionnaires crap and the psychic tape erasures. The murders are not provable, and these 'humanoid robots'--they've got to go. Clean it up. We'll call it: 'Eurasians Attempt Psychic Infiltration of the West.' OK?"

"Mr. Hirshon, the whole article is true. The public has a right to know," Koswell said.

"That's not the point. This is the most respected newspaper in the world. We printed your earlier story, and I'm willing to compromise, but I can't go this far. You know as well as I that there is a difference between so-called absolute truth and readership credibility. We create the reality, boys. The public's got to believe it."

"It's got to go as is, Mr. Hirshon," Rudy said.

"Well, not here it doesn't."

The journalists took a cab to *Modern Times*. Bill, Mort, Sally-Ann, Cal and the others bowed their heads in shame as Rudy entered. Rudy walked over to Mort and kissed him loudly on the cheek. "I love you all," Rudy announced. "Now that you've seen the sorcerer's apprentice, I won't have to show you the heavy stuff!"

This seemed to break the ice. Both Cal and Bill shook his hand, and Sally-Ann ran over and hugged him close. "I'm so ashamed, Rudy. I dreamt that that evil Boshtov killed you with a machine gun, and then he was impaled by an electric unicorn. My dreams are always so crazy." She stopped herself, and looked up quietly and whispered, "Forgive me."

"Styne, all I can say is that you better be here with that sex article." Captain Whitmore spoke from the doorway of his office, thumbs snugly clipped to his suspenders.

"But captain," Rudy protested.

"Just pulling your leg, Styne. Come on in men. Whataya got?" He read over the report as Koswell and Rudy waited impatiently.

"Well," they said.

"It's great, great...great. Did you take it to Hirshon?"

"Yes, he wanted to cut too much."

"Rudolf, you know this is too hot for us."

"Too hot! Are you kidding?!"

"Look son, I've got a stack of letters this high right here wailing about the 'irrational turn' we have taken because of your last article." He picked up a few and flipped them to Rudy. "Take some with you and read them over. We've never received so much negative input. Sixty-five people cancelled subscriptions, and we are being sued by the *Rationalist* and that whole skeptical crew for fraudulent claims on the paranormal. It's a real potboiler. They know they can't win, but they're making themselves a damn nuisance. I've got orders from above. Legal fees alone could top three mill.

"I'd fight it just on principle, but--Look at this letter I'm printing from the Incredible Fandango. He is prepared to offer this Manu fellow $800,000 to levitate an object paranormally in front of a group of concerned scientists." Whitmore pulled out a wrist exerciser which he began to squeeze as he continued talking. "Sure, in a daily newspaper I wouldn't hesitate to put it in, but we come out only once a week. We do theme issues, you know that. Let me sit on it for a few months...till the opposition cools down."

"But what about Boshtov? You know what he can do....What he did do!"

"I know he made a damn fool of me," Whitmore allowed. "He's caught, right?" The captain leaned against a wall to stretch his hamstrings. "Let sleeping dogs lie. Hell, Rudy, I gave you a free hand on parapsychology once. But, this shit is just too risky. And the Boshtov stuff, if that got out, we'd be the laughing stock of the publishing industry. *Modern Times* would be history!"

"Captain, if my life has any meaning, if what you have taught me these past years is sincere, then I simply must insist."

"Look, kid. I gave you carte blanche on the earlier piece. Where else have you seen coverage like that? Not in *Time,* the *Huffington Post* didn't do it, not on the major networks, not even *Vanity Fair.* We did it. And that's all we can do. Once is enough."

Koswell eased himself out of the room. The captain shifted his position to squat with his back against the wall to work his quadriceps, as he waited for Rudy's response.

"Am I fired?"

"Will you table the article?"

"Can I have a few days to find another offer?"

"Take six months."

Rudy walked out of the office in mental shambles. He felt as if his father had taken a switch to him wrongfully. Walking past Koswell and out of the office, he stood in silence in the empty hallway.

* * *

Heinreich had difficulty getting himself up from bed. He looked at the trophy which he had placed on the television set. Third place. Two inches off first. Could he beat Sven, or the Romanian giant? Could he get an extra bounce and go higher than he had ever gone before? He sat with his head in his hands, and he began to sob. He knew he had never really been a father to his children, his parents filled that role. He knew he was more like an uncle, but in a different category than his brother. But now, Imo was gone. Shot out of the sky by a Russian missile, and for what? A roll of film which Heinreich had dutifully given to Charles Koswell.

The Olympics were still two months away, but suddenly, it made no difference to him. He was surprised when Sven Hjamerscht approached him in the dorm.

"I heard you're dropping out?"

"It just doesn't seem to mean anything to me anymore," Heinreich said.

"I heard about your brother. Is it true?"

"I'm afraid so."

"Look," Sven said. "I'm not a political animal, and who knows what your brother was involved in. But I will bet you this. If he's up in heaven right now, he would want you to compete."

"Why would you care, especially when I have a real chance of beating you?"

"Look, Hein, I know I have an ego."

"You could say that again."

"And I've beaten you consistently."

"Oh. Barcelona doesn't count?"

"So, I had one too many girls the night before."

"Hah."

"The truth is, Heinreich, with all this publicity around me, I begin to lose sight of who my real friends are. There are so many, well, you know."

"Phonies?"

"Yeah. But you and I, well, I know we don't socialize off the field. I just don't want you to quit."

"I'm not sure I understand."

"If I win the gold, I want to know I earned it. You know as well as I, we are talking about two inches. If it wasn't for you and Sergi, well, if you guys weren't there, you know this would be a cakewalk, and it just won't mean the same thing."

Sven punched Heinreich in the arm in an affectionate way. "So go home. Grieve for your brother, and I will grieve as well. But you're a high jumper. Like me, that's what you are. You must come back."

"Thanks," Heinreich said.

An hour later, Heinreich found himself at the Honshai Temple near the flower district. He looked at the stained glass and the statues of the great gods, as he began to contemplate a life without his brother.

Heinreich had always taken his family for granted. Yes, he had lived a charmed life. Certainly he carried with him the pain of the loss of his wife, Kristina. She had been a light he could never replace. Tall and sinewy, long fine hair, sparkling blue eyes, that sense of adventure and love of unbridled fun. That was Kristina to him. But her death was different. Maybe it was because he was younger, or because it was so many lifetimes ago. He didn't know. But what he did know was that this loss was something else entirely. When she died, he felt a finality to it. With Imo gone, a more visceral part of him felt dead as well.

He walked back onto the main street. The masses a full head and shoulders beneath him seemed dwarflike. Heinreich had always felt tall, but here, in Japan, the alienation from the mainstream seemed more magnified. Maybe it was just this day. He knew he was out of sorts, and he knew that made him feel even more so out of place. But the way some of the people looked up and gawked at him. It was time to go.

He took a cab to the airport and booked a flight to Paris. He would be home soon enough, and there would be plenty of time for mourning. A lifetime. He needed his dose of Marcel.

Heinreich bit back tears, as he sat in his first class seat with a hand over his face to maximize privacy. An Asian boy recognized him. He forced a smile, and signed an autograph. But this just made him think even more of Imo. He went into the tiny bathroom and sobbed.

Returning to his seat, Heinreich stared out at the clouds, trying to make sense of the world. Should he compete at the Olympics? He'd been at it for over fifteen years. Surely he could retire. His heart wasn't into it, but his body was good for at least this next Olympic competition.

Sven had touched him. It made Heinreich think about who his friends really were. Marcel had always been there. An artist and free spirit, Marcel would show up at the most amazing places. That time in South Africa. He could have kissed him, he had been so depressed.

Heinreich took a cab from the airport straight to Montmartre. He got out by the Moulin Rouge, and paid the cabbie to bring his luggage to the hotel, which was near the Louvre. And then he turned to walk up Rue Lepic to weave his way to Place du Tertre, the highest point in Paris, the town square that Marcel called his sanctuary. He would surprise Marcel, and they would have lunch at the Russian Tea Room by the Sacré-Coeur, the magnificent white-on-white Byzantine Church that overlooked the entire city.

Heinreich strolled through the artists' stands to watch Marcel from afar. Marcel loved children, and made his livelihood by painting their portraits for the never-ending stream of tourists who frequented the hill.

Yes, he also had his serious canvases which he showed at a gallery on Boulevard Saint Germain, in between the old covered food market and Picasso's sculpture of the poet Apollinaire. Maybe they would go there later. Marcel would put this event in a light Heinreich could better comprehend.

It was a typical day on Place du Tertre, a patchwork plateau on the Mount filled with artists, open air markets and tchotchke stands. Families in their multicolors buying cheap crap to bring home as mementos, actors painted gold from head to toe, standing like statues, collecting coins, fooling children, more serious tourists purchasing oil paintings from the better artists or seeking out true professionals to sit for a portrait. Heinreich caught his eye.

Marcel raised a finger to imply that he needed a few minutes. He finished up a rendering of a set of twin girls, displaying in ever subtle ways their differences. Receiving payment from the happy parents, Marcel motioned Heinreich to meet him at the Tea Room as he took the time to close up his post.

The waiters knew both men and brought over their favorite treat, a cake made from rice and dates, and a hot beverage.

"Imo is dead," Heinreich said.

"Are you positive?"

"His plane was shot down over the Sea of Japan last week."

"So, that was him? My God. I knew he was frightened."

"I just want to thank you for being our liaison."

"Come." Marcel led the way to the big white church. From the stairs, they could see the Eiffel Tower in the distance, peeking above the skyline like the head of a giraffe above a herd of water buffalo. Entering the chapel, they sat and prayed, Marcel consoling the sobbing Olympic star.

Heinreich dreaded the trip to Tashkent.

"You know you must go home without delay. Your family needs you." Marcel saw Heinreich's hesitation and continued, "If you want, I will go with you."

"Thank you, Marcel. You have been a great friend. But I will be all right."

As was his custom, Heinreich landed in Tashkent unannounced. He paid a cab driver and walked up to his family's door. He hadn't seen his children in months although he spoke to them once, sometimes twice, a week. The fact was, his mother and father were raising them, and today he felt more like an older brother than an uncle, or, of course, a father. Truth be known, he liked it that way. He wanted to be patient with them, and be a dad, but he loved the travel, the independence, and that's how it had to be. He put the key in the lock and stepped inside. The place was too quiet.

"They're at the circus," Imo said from the shadows.

Heinreich stood there in shock. "I thought you were dead! The world thinks you are dead."

"I am, officially," Imo said. "And I know I can't stay because it is only a matter of time before Ma and Pa will be questioned."

"Have they seen you?"

"Of course. But your kids haven't, and they never will, and that's why I'm alone. I figured you'd be back, and I wanted to be here, to see you once, before I disappear."

"What happened? Were you in that plane?"

"Yes. It was a breakthrough design with an entire cockpit that could eject if a missile were seen in time. That's what saved us."

"There were two of you?"

"The pilot, Colonel Kandinsky. Unfortunately, he will not be able to return to Russia either. He's angry with me. Well, that's an understatement. But at least he's alive."

"You were in the middle of the ocean. What did you do, land on a boat?"

"I had drugged the pilot. We were headed back to Yakutski. That was a death sentence for sure. I had destroyed everything there before I had left, sent their secrets to the West. The human experiments. It was horrible, what they did. What I did." Imo paused to hold back the tears. Heinreich waited for him to continue.

"So, after he went out, I swung the plane around, with the full intention of landing in Tokyo. I thought once I got there, you would be able to help me find asylum."

"I'm not sure I would have been able to," Heinreich confessed.

"It doesn't matter now. Kandinsky was slumped over the controls, but I could take over from my seat. We were out over the ocean and I could already see Japan in the distance. That was when I saw it."

"The missile?"

"Yes. I guess I was half expecting it. I knew that the cockpit had flight capabilities. Retractable wings. So, I pushed the ejection button, and out we went. But I didn't know we had to manually jettison the parachute."

"You figured, with 40,000 fishing boats in the Sea of Japan...."

"Yeah. I thought someone would pick us up."

Heinreich smiled for the first time in a long while. "But that's not what happened?"

"No. Once, we were ejected, the force was terrific, the wings came out all right, but the canopy was still above us, and we just kept drifting and floating down. There was nothing but solid ocean below us, and I was helpless. I guess the shock of it all woke Kandinsky. He managed to show me how to jettison the canopy. And when we did that, the cockpit dropped like a stone, but then it swooped horizontal when the wings kicked in."

"And you got to shore?"

"We sailed in like a fuck'n heron!" Imo said. "But, it was really Kandinsky who flew us to shore."

"Where'd you land?"

"We found a small island off the coast of Hokkaido."

"You're talking about the cockpit?"

"Yeah, the cockpit. The design was brilliant. It is built for that very purpose, to become an ultralight."

"Glider?"

"Yes. There is no engine. I wouldn't have known how to fly it, but Kandinsky had been trained for exactly this possibility. We could have still crash-landed in the ocean, but he had us watch the gulls, we were pretty high up, and that's how we found the thermals. We would spiral up when we caught one, it was really amazing, and then we just kept going east. That's how we made it to shore. It was dark by the time we got there. We kind of landed in the low water. And then, well, he socked me right here." Imo rubbed his cheek which was still black and blue. "And that's when we parted company."

"Then, how did you get here?"

"I waited a day and then joined a fishing crew. It turned out they were going to Taiwan. The captain gave me a little money. I think he knew who I was. Anyway, I had enough to get a fake passport. You can get anything in Taiwan. Then, I took a mail plane to Bangkok, and did the same thing for Bukhara.

"I had figured all along, if I went to Tashkent, they could be waiting. I had a friend in Bukhara, and he gave me the money for the train for Tashkent. Of course, I slipped off a couple of stops before we got to town, and walked from there."

"Does anyone else know you're alive?"

"One other person."

"A girl?"

"Irina," Imo admitted. "How did you know?"

"It's all over your face, little brother."

"She's a nurse in Vladivostok. I emailed her from Bangkok, in code. She has hotmail, and we could converse in a chat room. She said she'll meet me as soon as I set myself up somewhere.

"And where would that be?"

"I don't know. I'm thinking a major city in a poor country. Maybe Africa or South America. Somewhere where I can practice medicine again, and atone for what I've done."

Heinreich looked at his brother and began to cry. "I thought I lost you. I was going to drop out of the Olympics."

"You can't do that. You want that blond idiot to beat you!"

"Sven."

"Yeah."

"He said that you would want me to compete against him."

"Damn straight I do. Beat his stupid pants off."

"The girls do that a lot better than I can."

The two brothers laughed. And then they hugged for what to them, seemed an eternity. Heinreich booked a room out of town where they spent two more days together, Ma and Pa Bern each taking turns to make clandestine visits.

"I thought I was a goner, Heinreich," Imo said during their last hour together.

"We'll use Marcel to communicate. And we'll use a code to keep in touch."

"You'll call me Moo Moo."

* * *

As the weeks flew by, Rudy's sense of outrage continued to grow. He had another unsuccessful encounter with Captain Whitmore, and Koswell fared just as poorly in his second try with Hirshon at the *Trib*.

"What are we going to do, die with this information?" Rudy ruminated with Koswell over the phone.

"I hate to say it," Koswell began, "but I have an idea."

"The *Public Enquirer*?" Rudy said, reading Koswell's mind. "You gotta be kidding."

"Who else is going to believe this shit?" Koswell countered, causing them to burst into laughter.

"If they change one word," Rudy retorted, "I'll sue them for every dime they're worth."

Rudy met Koswell in front of the 42nd Street Library. They walked over to the illustrious newspaper's branch office and met the head editor there, a man named Blake. Rudy figured him to be not more than 30.

"We've got to check your sources," the editor said, "but if you're clean, I think I can talk the big boy upstairs into putting this onto the front page."

"The big boy?" Rudy and Kos said in unison.

"Yeah, the guy who owns the paper."

"And just who is this big boy, Mr. Blake?" Koswell pushed.

"I'm sorry," the editor said coyly, "I'm not at...."

Rudy cut him off before he almost barfed from the cliché. "OK, OK," he acquiesced, "but you must print it verbatim."

"We want the terms in writing," Koswell added. "I'm from the *Trib*."

"The *Trib*, shit," Blake spat. "Our circulation is over fifteen mil. You're not even a close fourth."

The following week the article was featured on the front page of the *Public Enquirer*. The rag sat next to the cash register of every supermarket in the nation:

RUSSO/UKRAINIAN FACTION
PLANS PSYCHOTRONIC OFFENSIVE IN USA

Beneath the headline was a provocative full-color hologram of Monika Cloris in a wet tea-shirt. But pages 3, 4 and 5 contained the entire story as they had written it, even including a photo Koswell had taken of Chi Jhenghis' psychotronic head. On the bottom of page 5 came the following tag line:

NEXT WEEK: GIRL MARRIES BIGFOOT
INSISTS ON NUDE WEDDING

The phone rang. It was Crankshaw. "Hey you bastard," the agent said, "I told you not to print it." Rudy started to respond, but Crankshaw began to laugh. "No one's going to believe it though. You know, the *Public Enquirer* is the kiss of death."

"When does Boshtov go to trial?"

"Never."

"What do you mean, never? Is he dead?"

"Hardly," Crankshaw cracked. "He's back in Glasnost-ville"

"Russia? What, are you nuts??? You can't be serious!!? Rudy was incredulous.

"I'm dead serious. We traded him for a defector, a physicist by the name of Alexi Patrenko."

"You what!??!??!??!!!! YOU OUT OF YOUR MIND?!" Styne was screaming into the phone. "He's as guilty as Boshtov. Who do you think wired the device that killed Kranz? Who do you think killed Hereward! Who do you think spread Legionnaires' Disease in Italy!--Patrenko, you idiot....How could you? Boshtov is evil....He's a monster. The kingpin....You had him. How could you?"

"How could we!" Crankshaw interrupted. "Patrenko has given us more data than we know what to do with, and to save face, Bonzo's kissing our ass. That's how."

"Has he given you more than we supplied in the article?"

"Your information has been very accurate." Crankshaw said, as he hung up the phone.

REFERENCES

Rasputin's Nephew is a work of historical fiction based in an allegorical sense on contemporary events. The following articles were referred to.

Alaska Cool to Russian's Takeover Talk, *The Providence Journal*, 12/26/1993, p. 14.

An E.S.P. Gap: Exploring Psychic Weapons, *Time,* 1/23/1984, p. 17.

Bearden, Tom. A Technological Solution to a Problem Inherent in the Human Condition. *Journal of Occult Studies,* Winter/Spring 1997/78, Vol. 1, #3, pp. 273-282.

Brownell, Phillip. Rasputin, *MetaScience,* Vol. 2. [Rasputin quotes adapted from this article with permission.]

Elliott, Dorinda, & Barry, John. A Subliminal Dr. Strangelove: Using the power of hidden suggestions, this Russian scientist tries to rewire the brain. *Newsweek,* 8/22/1994, p. 57.

Freyer, Felice. The Power of Thought: Brain Center Attracts International Attention. *The Providence Journal*, 3/14/2002, 1: 3,4; 15: 2-6.

Fulop-Miller, R. *Rasputin, the Holy Devil.* Garden City, NY: Garden City Publishing Company, 1928.

Gardner, Martin. A Skeptic's View of Parapsychology. *The Humanist,* Nov/Dec 1977, 45-46.

Halarnkar, Samar. Brain Waves: New Technology Can Read Your Mind. *Newsweek*, 2/20/2012, pp. 14-15.

Harden, Blaine. Behind Steel Doors: Romania's Secret Police. *The Providence Journal,* 12/31/1989, A-1, A-7.

Herman, Victor. *Coming Out of the Ice: An Unexpected Life.* New York, NY: Freedom Press, 1979.

Ingalese, Richard. *History and Power of Mind,* NY: Occult Book Concern, 1901.

Kaplan, Bernard. Right-winger Zhirinovsky Seeks to Recover the "Lost" Soviet Empire. *The Providence Journal,* 12/26/1993, 1:1.

Kasturi, N. *The Life of Bhagavan Sri Sathya Shri Baba.* Bombay, India, 1969.

Krippner, Stanley. *Song of the Siren.* New York, NY: Harper & Row, 1975.

Livinenko, Alexander & Felshtinsky, Yuri. *Blowing Up Russia: The Secret Plot to Bring Back KGB Terror.* London: Gibson Square, 2007.

Luria, A. *Higher Cortical Functions in Man.* New York, NY: Basic Books, 1980.

Manning, Matthew. *The Link.* New York, NY: Holt, Rinehart & Winston, 1975.

Minney, R.J. *Rasputin,* New York: McKay Publishers, 1973.

Moss, Thelma. Psychic Research in the Soviet Union in Edgar Mitchell and John White, (Ed's), *Psychic Explorations.* New York, NY: Putnam, 1976.

Mishlove, Jeffrey. Ted Owen, PK man. *www.Mishlove.com.*

Neofascist Stuns Yeltsin Allies. *The Providence Journal,* 12/14/1993, p.1.

Brzezinski Phones Toth in London after Release, *The New York Times,* 6/19/1977, p. 16.

Ostrander, S., Schroeder, L. *Psychic Discoveries Behind the Iron Curtain.* New York, NY: Bantam, 1970.

Ouspensky, P.D. *In Search of the Miraculous.* New York, NY: Harcourt & Brace, 1960.

Panati, Charles. *The Geller Papers.* New York, NY: Houghton Mifflin Publishers, 1976.

Rensberger, Boyce. Émigré Tells of Research in Soviet Parapsychology for Military Use. *The New York Times,* June 19, 1977, p.1.

Rhine, J.B. *Reach of Mind.* New York, NY: Sloane Publishes, 1954.

Rogo, D. Scott. The Case For Parapsychology. *The Humanist,* Nov/Dec 1977, pp. 40-44. (Rogo was murdered in August of 1990.)

Seifer, Marc. Uri Geller. *ESP Magazine,* 9/1976, vol. 1, #3, pp. 14-18, 48-49.

-- The Physics of Consciousness. *Journal of Occult Studies,* Aug 1977, vol. 1 #2, pp. 148-157.

-- Second Annual International Kirlian Research Association Conference. *MetaScience Quarterly,* Spring 1979, vol. 1, #1, pp. 92-100.

-- Retrocognitive and Precognitive Displacements in Card Reading and Dream Telepathy Experiments. *MetaScience Quarterly,* Summer 1979, vol. 1, #2, pp. 41-52.

-- Evolution, Psychokinesis and the Group Mind. *Parapsychology Review,* Sept/Oct 1979, vol. 10, #5, pp. 24-27.

-- The Mind of the Skeptic and the Hierarchy of Doubt. *MetaScience Quarterly,* Autumn 1980, vol. 1, #3, pp. 285-295.

-- His Holiness: The Dalai Lama. *MetaScience Quarterly,* vol. 1, #3, Autumn 1980, pp. 313-317.

-- Gurdjieff. *MetaScience Quarterly,* Autumn 1980, vol. 1, #3, pp. 348-352.

-- An Interview with Uri Geller. *MetaScience Quarterly,* Autumn 1980, vol. 1, #3, pp. 335-344

-- Parapsychology and Esoteric Thought. *Parapsychology Review,* May/June 1981, vol. 12, #3, pp. 18-21.

-- Consciousness and the Anthropic Principle. *Journal of Conscientiology,* Jan 1999, pp. 203-220.

-- Uri Geller: Mystic or Magician? by Jonathan Margolis. Book Review. *Journal of Religion and Psychical Research,* Autumn, 1999.

-- Synchronicity & the Structure of the Psyche. *Journal of Conscientiology,* Jan 2001, pp. 193-216.

-- Speed of Mind. Unpublished, 1979.

-- *Transcending the Speed of Light: Consciousness & Quantum Physics.* Rochester, VT. Inner Traditions, 2008.

-- *Where Does Mind End?* Rochester, VT. Inner Traditions, 2011.

Seifer, Marc & Smukler, Howard. A Mass Public Experiment in Psychokinesis and Telepathy at a Distance with Uri Geller as Agent. *Journal of Occult Studies*, Spring 1977, vol. 1, #1, pp. 3-30.

-- The Puharich Interview. *Gnostica,* Sept. 1978, vol. 47, pp. 21-25.
Remote Viewing: Rhode Island to California. *MetaScience Quarterly*, Spring 1979, vol. 1, #1, pp. 3-8.

Smith, Andy. Paralyzed Pair Prove Power of Thought. Researchers at Providence VA, Brown University reveal advances in robotic controls via brain waves. *Providence Journal*, 5/17/2012, pp. A1, A8.

Steiner, Rudolf. *An Outline of Occult Science.* New York, NY: Anthroposophic Press, 1972.

Swann, Ingo. *To Kiss the Earth Good-Bye.* New York, NY: Hawthorne Books, 1975.

Toth, Robert. It Started, Ended on Ludicrous Note, But in Between It Wasn't Funny. *The Providence Journal,* 6/20/1977, pp. 17-18.

Ukraine Cultists Jailed to Avert Suicide. *The Providence Journal,* 11/13/1993, pp. A5.

Waite, A.E. *The Pictorial Key to the Tarot.* Blauvelt, NY: Steiner Books, 1971.

White, John. The Paranormal: Pseudoscience versus Future Science. *MetaScience Quarterly,* Spring 1979, vol. 1, #1, pp. 15-24.

Vasiliev, L.L. *Experiments in Distant Influence.* New York, NY: Dutton, 1976.

ACKNOWLEDGEMENTS

The impetus for this novel began in June of 1977, after the American newspaper reporter Robert Toth was arrested in Moscow by the KGB for obtaining a paper from a local scientist on telepathy and brain-wave biofeedback. The entire affair was covered in spectacular fashion on the front page of *The New York Times*. The piece not only discussed the full details of Toth's arrest, but also other parapsychological research that the USSR was conducting in a top-secret underground laboratory in Siberia. I was teaching courses on consciousness at Providence College School of Continuing Education. A young man in my late 20s, I was also co-editing a journal on metaphysics which had a loose affiliation with the University of Rhode Island. My goal at the time was to try to understand such things as depth psychology, the neurophysiology of memory, how a thought was converted into physical action and mental telepathy.

I was beyond the point of trying to prove the existence of ESP. Having conducted numerous successful class experiments in dream telepathy, PK dice throwing and remote viewing, I wanted to understand the underlying mechanisms involved. Why, for instance, was there so much telepathy between twins? Why did it occur at emotional times and so often during dreams?

I thought, after Toth's arrest, that universities would begin to seriously study extrasensory perception, not with the mundane thought of trying to prove that this ability existed--one need only do a meta-analysis of the thousands of successful ESP tests that have been conducted over the last hundred years--but to explain the underlying mechanisms involved. Toth spent a full week in the hands of the KGB, and during that time *not one* major media outlet, other than *The New York Times,* mentioned the subject of the science paper he received! I was shocked that the three TV media giants ABC, CBS and NBC, and the leading magazines *Time* and *Newsweek* had the audacity to cover the Toth affair, mention his arrest in major fashion and yet edit *out* any mention of the actual topic of the paper! At the same time, the paranormalist, Uri Geller, was being treated shabbily by the American press, so much so, that Uri soon moved to England where there was a more receptive environment.

Uri had been successfully tested for his paranormal abilities at such think tanks as Stanford Research Institute, Naval Surface Weapons Center at Oak Ridge and Lawrence Livermore Laboratories. Working with my partner at the time, Howard Smukler, who was editing *ESP Magazine* and also *Journal of Occult Studies* (the precursor to *MetaScience*) I was hired by him to write the lead cover-story on Uri. At that time we went to Geller's apartment in New York City, the year was 1976, and it was there that we saw him bend two keys in our presence by merely rubbing them. Soon after, I also interviewed Uri in depth for *MetaScience* and then saw him bend a large spoon at a New Age conference in New Jersey. In that instance, he vigorously rubbed the length of the spoon with his forefinger and it bent *upwards* against gravity! I was also touring a number of parapsychology labs including JB Rhine's place in North Carolina, and I had also spent time with the clairvoyant Matthew Manning, who was drawing pictures in the style of famous dead artists. During one of his demonstrations, I saw a distinct halo appear above his head. It was events such as these that sparked the novel.

Having taught parapsychology for over fifteen years, many of my experiences or knowledge of events related to the paranormal were alluded to herein. Meeting with JB Rhine's people at his laboratory the mid-1970s, with the Amazing Randi twice, once by chance on an airplane, we were sitting next to each other, working in graduate school in animal experiments and brain studies in a subterranean laboratory at the University of Chicago and performing dream telepathy studies and logging my own dreams all set the stage for aiding me in this treatise.

The first draft was completed before 1980. I fully expected the book would be published before Orwell's year, 1984. But, I was wrong. As time rolled on, and the world changed, and as I continued to look for a home for the book, I continued to update and hone the work. This treatise, although complete fiction, is based in large measure on facts. Those in the know, the many sincere parapsychologists who have persisted in their science throughout these thirty-five years of a hostile scientific environment, will recognize aspects of their story woven into the fictitious tale of a renegade group of Eurasian psychophysicists who are attempting to destroy the West by gruesomely tampering with the brains of unsuspecting operatives.

I would like to thank the following people whose personal correspondence contributed one way or another to the overall conception of the text: C.J. Atwood, Col. Tom Bearden, Philip Brownell, George DeLodzia, Dr. David Goode, Prof. Edwin Gora, Blue Horary, Meri Shardin Keithley, Dean Kraft, Jon Land, Matthew Manning, Dr. Herbert Meltzer, Sandy Neuschatz, Thelma Moss, Dr. Andrija Puharich, James Randi, J.B. Rhine, Sandy Neuschatz, Bruce Seifer, Betty Shapin, Shipi Shtrang, Ginny Stern, Ingo Swann, David and Virginia Thomas, J.T. Walsh, Wikipedia for their article on Russian journalists that have been killed and actor/friend Alan Wolf who apparently saw a ghost. I would also like to thank Jenny LaDean Baum who typed an early version of the manuscript and David Kraeuter who was kind enough to edit a draft in 2003; also DJM Films in New York, Billings Hospital at the University of Chicago, Providence College School of Continuing Education, University of Rhode Island Library, New York Public Library and the MetaScience Foundation. Special thanks are extended to Robert Adsit, Nelson DeMille, Prof. Stanley Krippner, Prof. Roger Pearson, Elliott Shriftman, Howard Smukler, John White, and in particular Adam Kay who edited the novel, and to Uri Geller, its inspiration; and to my parents, Stanley and Thelma Seifer, my many nieces and nephews and my understanding wife Lois Mary Pazienza, the inspiration for Chessie.

The Rudy Styne Quadrilogy should be read in the following order:

I. *Rasputin's Nephew*
II. *Doppelgänger*
III. *Crystal Night*
IV. *Fate Line*

Enclosed is an early chapter from *Doppelgänger*. Still working for Modern Times Magazine and now on the trail of NTroodr, a master computer hacker, Rudy proposes to Chessie. At the wedding, an ancient man known to Rudy as Uncle Abe shows up. Rudy really doesn't know how he is related, but he does know that Abe's last name is Maxwell.

For more information on any of Dr. Seifer's books, please visit his website:

MarcSeifer.com
mseifer@ verizon.net

AND NOW, A SNEAK PREVIEW FROM:

DOPPELGÄNGER
The Rudy Styne Quadrilogy
Book II

ELIAS & DEBORA MAXWELL

1906: Elias looked up at the sign posted above the entranceway of a long red-brick building: Maxwell-Bavarian Machineworks and beamed. His building. Steel supports, a flagstone base and lots and lots of windows half of which overlooked the rushing tributary which ran to the Iller River located there in southern Bavaria. With a labor force of over fifty, Elias prided himself in knowing nearly everyone by name.

As he walked into the factory a sensation overtook him that he had never experienced before. He felt larger, felt his being expand, felt his arms extend through the lathes, the presses and assembly line, felt his essence flow out through the windows through the spray of the cataract flowing through the waterwheel beside the massive generator, felt his shoulders rise to the ceiling and his head explode through the roof of the factory where it crested above the burgeoning hamlet.

From this position, Elias could look north towards Munich, east towards Salzburg, west to the Swiss Alps, or to the near south, to Kempten, perhaps the oldest town in the region, where his new automobile dealership had just opened up. In partnership with his wife's uncle, Adolf von Rosensweig, Elias had become an assimilated entrepreneur. He gazed behind him, upstream, past the series of cottages that housed his workers, past the stylish homes where his managers lived, past the long private lane lined with rhododendrons, to the hill, his hill where his mansion lay.

Elias Maxwell, son of Rabbi Hillel Maxwell and grandnephew of Judah Baruch Maxwell, most venerated cantor, was a capitalist. To the chagrin of his family, he was also a convert. A Protestant.

"We will have the doctor perform the circumcision," Elias proclaimed as his wife lay sweating in her bed, her newborn son, Abraham, already suckling.

"He will have a bris, and he will be Bar Mitzvahed, like his father before him, and like his father and grandfather before him. You may try to renounce your heritage, Mr. Elias Isaiah Maxwell, but you will not...." Debora broke down in tears.

A sense of pity and disgust swept through Elias. "I want a modern wife, Debora. We are no longer in the shetl. It is time for us to become Bavarians. As you know, Jews cannot own property, they cannot hold political office. They live as outsiders, inferiors!"

"Oh, so now my husband, wants to be mayor."

"I would be a good mayor. But with a Jewish son, impossible."

"And your father. You want the rebbi to convert as well?"

"My son will *not* have a bris. Why must you be so selfish? How can you take this great joy from me?" Elias demanded. "You want your new Abraham to grow up with a yoke on his life, a cloud over his head, a stain on his record, when all we have to do is give up pagan beliefs. It's nearly 1907, for Chrissakes! Why can't you wake up to the new world? Do you think I can run my operations and be successful as... as a Jew?!"

Debora felt her son begin to gasp. Aunt Ella, who was midwife, grabbed swiftly, and brought the boy firmly to her chest. Cupping her hand she swatted his back soundly. He hiccupped and burped. In spite of himself, Elias smiled.

Although her hair was messed, and there was sweat upon her brow, Ella still expressed elegant regalness and air of authority. She turned to face her nephew. "You vant a healthy son?" she said in Yiddish, her stare deflating the businessman as he shrank back twenty years to his life as an eight-year-old tearing through Tante Ella's kitchen, as she prepared Seder dinner. Swiping a pastry to her chagrin as she swatted his backside, he would scoot out the door, his mouth half filled with delicious treat.

"May I hold my son?"

Ella looked at Debora who turned away. Elias wheeled and rumbled down the stairs unable or unwilling to take on the two women, at least for now. There would be another day.

From the porch, he looked downstream beyond the factory to the blur of downtown Kempten seven miles in the distance. He felt he could almost read the bright new sign of his automobile dealership. He knew precisely where it was, across from the town square right in the center of the little metropolis.

He called Gunter, his manservant, on his new intercom, and had him bring the new Royce roadster up to the house and park it by the front door. Donning riding gloves and goggles, he pushed past and stepped into the driver's seat, commanded Gunter to "crank it up" and put the automobile in gear.

"I expect my shoes to be polished by the time I return."

"Yes, sir," Gunter said.

Steering the Royce around the semi-circular driveway, Elias put his arm out of the window the way he had been taught to make a signal, then he made a left turn and sputtered down the dirt lane. It was late spring. The first purple buds of crocus were beginning to peep throughout the lawn, the rhododendrons were also beginning to bud.

A brood of pheasants crossed in front of him, the driver instinctively braked to a slow crawl. Watching the strutting mother followed by a trail of six chicks, Elias felt a sense of pride since he considered them part of *his* estate, when suddenly, out from nowhere, the male swooped, fluttering dangerously close to his head, warning him off, causing him to duck, as the brood disappeared quickly into the brush. The vehicle lurched and rumbled over a moving object. Elias cut the wheel and slammed the auto into a maze of branches.

Picking rhododendron buds from his windshield, the driver shook his head to get his bearings. Removing his goggles, he loosened his collar as he watched the cock reappear to attack the animal he had just run over. A red fox lay smashed in the center of the driveway, it's neck broken, eyes still open, pecked at by the regal ring-necked bird. Elias would later swear that this bird had looked squarely at him in the eye to tell him that he too should protect his flock.

Debora sat up in bed and began to sob. "It's all right," Tante Ella said, handing her back the boy.

"Why is he so stubborn?"

"He vants to be a success. Is that really so hard to understand?"

"But is it worth the price of our heritage?"

"There is nothing new here, Debora," Tante Ella said. "Rabbi Sinschwartz has told us that intermarriage is as high as 40% in Hamburg, over 25% in Berlin."

"What will happen to our essence?"

"There are still many good Jews. We have survived for thousands of years."

"But what can I do, deny my son a bris to placate his pigheaded father?"

"Appeal to a higher authority, my dear."

Alone in the garden, Elias listened to the plaintiff melody of his great uncle's voice swirl out the sitting room and echo down the hill. Because of the fame of this renown cantor, Elias' father, Hillel, the cantor's nephew, was able to gain a post at Ben Zion Temple in Weissenbach, just over the border in Austria. It was the largest synagogue in the region.

Well aware that he was part of the educated aristocracy, Elias knew he had grown up with a silver spoon. But he also knew that it was not his father who "built a machine shop from scratch to turn it into a major industry," Elias mumbled as he paced outside. "Nor did my father erect a complex to house my workers. And he did not negotiate with goyem to obtain a lot in the town square to start an automobile dealership...."

"Are you coming in?" von Rosensweig nudged as he came out to fetch his reluctant business partner. "Or do you want your brother to hold the boy when the rebbi makes the cut."

"My brother! If Simon so much as touches...." Elias spouted. Throwing his cigar down, he joined his wife's uncle and marched inside. Von Rosensweig led him to the crib. There before them stood the whole clan. They numbered over forty. Although his mother was no longer alive, Elias' father appeared vigorous and self-assured. He stood arm and arm with his sister, Tante Ella, beside Debora, their eyes aglow with images of this new and "perfect child." And like a Goliath, also stood the cantor, his great uncle Judah.

"Eli, you been pissing in the woods?" the cantor cajoled, loud enough for the entire forty to hear.

Shrinking beneath the comment, the convert did his best to hide his revulsion as he watched the relatives break into laughter. He gained some comfort to see that his younger brother did not smile with the others, but rather, came forth to pat him reassuringly on the back.

"Congratulations," Simon said.

"Thank you, brother," Elias replied.

The mohel looked Elias in the eye. With a disdained air of resignation, the new father reached for a yarmulke and plunked it on his head.

Debora's eyes sparkled. Were those tears of joy or sorrow? Elias could not tell. A voice inside took over as he recited in Hebrew by rote the appropriate prayer. As he did so, he felt a large hand on his shoulder. Wheeling, he glimpsed clearly the ghost of his dead mother and the ghost of her father as well. "Wake up, schmuck," whispered the dead Grandpapa Izzie.

During this strange interlude, Elias looked over to the living, his father Hillel and granduncle Judah were dovening in his direction. Tante Ella's soothing voice and gentle hand smoothed Baby Abraham's shoulders. The little one lay on his back in the crib. A smile of contentment.

The mohel took center stage, stating that this tradition would not interfere with young Abe's ability to marry and reproduce when he reached proper age.

"May I say something," Elias found himself saying, the images of his dead relatives still powerfully hovering in his psyche, "that is, before the surgery begins?"

His father nodded assent, which halted the procedure for a moment.

Elias moved his gaze from his father and granduncle to his wife. "I know I have come from a blessed family, and I know I have not been a religious man. But I am a good man, and I respect my father and his uncle, my wife and her wishes. Abraham Maxwell has been born the religion of his mother, and he will be circumcised in a matter of moments in accord with a tradition that is thousands of years old. There is no easy answer for someone of Jewish ancestry in this world. The real world. I only wish the best for my son." He nodded to proceed.

The mohel chanted the sacred prayer as he brought out the cutting instruments. Capping the boy's penis with a little metal hood, he took out a small very sharp blade, held it next to the protected phallus, and sliced off a ring of foreskin.

Baby Abraham pierced the room with his shriek, as the family applauded and the feast began.

"Thank you," Debora said to her husband. She stood in deference by his side, her eyes still welled with tears.

"I know I'm an ass," he whispered as he gave her a kiss. "I'm only trying to survive in an unforgiving world."

"I know," she said. Their lips met. It was the first time they had kissed in nearly two weeks.

"There is a telephone call for you, Mr. Maxwell," Heidi, the maidservant said.

"Did you get the man's name?" Elias asked. He was sitting in the sunroom reading his newspaper. It was a Saturday morning.

"Count von Zeppelin, sir."

Elias flew from his seat, and picked up the phone.

Grabbing his gloves and riding goggles, the master of the house walked briskly to his roadster, pushed Gunter aside to crank the engine himself. Firing it up with a "humph!" he stepped into the driver's seat, put it in gear, barreled down the driveway and raced to his dealership. There, he waited with his partner, von Rosensweig for the great aeronaut to appear.

Elias had sold six automobiles in May, eight in June and now he was going to begin July with a sale to, of all people, Count von Zeppelin.

"This vehicle rides well, sir," von Zeppelin proclaimed, shouting from the passenger side.

Elias saw opportunity and took the great aeronaut on a ride to his industrial plant. Passing the Count's great airship which was docked in a nearby wheat field, Elias gazed on its gargantuan size and nodded humble approval.

"We also repair and build engines," the entrepreneur offered as he followed the river-road to the factory, Debora's uncle perched precariously in the rumble seat. "My kid brother is a master mechanic in charge of the machinists."

"Perhaps you could provide new engines for my airships?"

"I would be honored," Elias beamed, just as he pulled into the site of Maxwell-Bavarian Machineworks.

"What do you make of Orville and Wilbur Wright?" Simon hit the Count broadside as he emerged from the plant, his face stained with grease, ratchet in hand.

"I take it, you are Simon?" von Zeppelin said.

"I am honored to meet you, sir." Simon clicked his heels and nodded his head. "I let the workers out for a break just to watch your great airship float into our area earlier in the day."

"This is a beautiful part of the country," von Zeppelin said.

"Thank you," Simon replied, whirling to allow, with a gesture, the workers to stop their machines once again so that they could gaze out the windows at this amazing national hero. The Count reached for his captain's hat, gave them a wave and they broke out in smiles and applause.

"The Wright brothers have gone beyond Lilienthal's motorless gliders, that is for certain," von Zeppelin replied, "but for long distance travel and multiple passengers, I don't see how you can better my behemoths."

Marc J. Seifer

ABOUT THE AUTHOR

With a Masters degree from the University of Chicago, and a Doctorate from Saybrook University, Marc J. Seifer has taught courses on consciousness and parapsychology at Providence College Continuing Ed and psychology at Roger Williams University. Having conducted many successful dream telepathy experiments, in 1983, Dr. Seifer appeared as the "Psychic Sleuth" for TV's *PM Magazine.* He has lectured at West Point Military Academy, Brandeis University, the United Nations, CCNY, LucasFilms Industrial Light & Magic, at Oxford University and Cambridge University in England, before the Serbian Academy of Sciences in Belgrade, also in Croatia, Canada and Israel. His articles have appeared in *Wired, Civilization, Parapsychology Review, The Historian, Psychiatric Clinics of North America* and *Cerebrum.* Featured in *Brain/Mind Bulletin, The New York Times, The Washington Post, New Scientist, The Wall Street Journal* and on the back cover of Uri Geller's book *MindMedicine,* Dr. Seifer has also appeared on the BBC, NPR and Coast to Coast Radio and on TV on *The History Channel, American Experience* and *Associated Press International.* He is the author of *FRAMED! Murder, Corruption & a Death Sentence in Florida; Transcending the Speed of Light; Where Does Mind End?* The Rudy Styne Quadrilogy: *Rasputin's Nephew, Doppelgänger, Crystal Night* and *Fate Line* and the biography *WIZARD: The Life & Times of Nikola Tesla.* Called "A Serious Piece of Scholarship" by *Scientific American,* "Revelatory" by *Publisher's Weekly,* and a "Masterpiece" by best-selling author Nelson DeMille, *WIZARD,* is "Highly Recommended" by the American Association for the Advancement of Science.

CPSIA information can be obtained
at www.ICGtesting.com
Printed in the USA
LVHW080013170420
653534LV00017B/433